the KiLLING of the SAINTS

the KILLING OF the SAINTS

Alex Abella

crown publishers, inc.   new york

Published by Crown Publishers, Inc., 201 East 50th
Street, New York, New York, 10022. Member of
the Crown Publishing Group.

CROWN is a trademark of Crown Publishers, Inc.

Manufactured in the United States of America

Library of Congress Cataloging-in-Publication Data

Abella, Alex.
     The killing of the saints / by Alex Abella.
          p.   cm.
     I. Title.
PS3661.B3394K5   1991   91-4465
813'.54—dc20   CIP

ISBN 0-517-58509-X

10 9 8 7 6 5 4 3 2 1

First Edition

To Armeen,
sempre diritto!

the Killing of the Saints

prologue

Oyeme, chico, ven acá, *what's this, this big story I hear you're doing about the Cubans and the Marielitos in Los Angeles?* Coño, chico, *you know that the Cubans are always the top, brother, nobody smarter or sexier or better looking, you know? Look at what we did here in Miami, it was just a swamp for niggers and dying Jews before we moved in. We turned it into the capital of Latin American enterprise, the center of all the movement of business and peoples who want to be free and shop at Burdines and have a nice condo on the beach, or a house in Coral Gables and drive a late-model car.* Qué va, *brother, if not for us Miami would be nothing, just another sand barrier at the edge of a mangrove full of flying roaches and good for nothings. Everybody should do the same thing we did down here,* mi hermano. *But I'll tell you something, you know what? They don't have the brains or the balls to do what we did, to take a load of anger and resentment and turn it into concrete and gold, to let your desire point the way so that in the end the whole world is yours because you want it and that's it, you* *know? That's why we're better, that's why we're one of a kind,* únicos. *Lookit, if all the Mexicans in L.A. got together, brother, let me tell you, those Anglos would be fucked, man, that's what. Nothing can resist the will of a people whose time has come. It's a force of nature, like the wind, the tides, which are nothing, air and water, but if put together and driven by a will become a hurricane or a tidal wave that wreaks the vengeance long denied. But you know what? It's not gonna happen because there's nobody like the Cubans. Just look at the music, the jazz music, man, that's all Cuban and that's a fact. All these guys came down to Havana and drank our rum and fooled around with the ladies and got into the music and pretty soon, brother, they'd stolen all the good notes from us. Even rock 'n' roll,* mi hermano. *You don't believe me? Dig this, you know how important Bo Diddley was, right? You know, the dum-dee-dum-dee-dum, dum-dum beat of his, the one that spread through rock 'n' roll and made it so great? Hey, he himself admits he stole that from a Cuban song he heard. You see, you know, the beat,* el sabor, *that Cuban thing, like the pussy of a nice Cuban girl,* mi hermano, *incomparable. All these guys come and steal from us and then they claim it as their own. But that's OK, too, that's the past. No need to start worrying about that. You still don't believe we're the greatest? OK, look at sports—the greatest boxer, the smartest, the one that taught Sugar Ray Robinson all he knew, who was that? Why that was Kid Chocolate, my brother. And don't forget Kid Gavilan and Benny Kid Paret. And baseball—well, let's not even start with baseball, I can't begin to tell you the names of all the Cuban greats—Aparicio, Marichal, all the others. And José Canseco,* qué va, *there's nothing like a Cuban. You know, for such a little country, we're the greatest, that's why they call us the Jews of Latin America. We're the brains of everything south of the border. And north, too, it's just that we haven't been here all that long. Lookit, we're the fastest immigrant group to assimilate in the history of this country.* Coño, *man, more than the Jews even. We have professors, artists, engineers, reporters, dancers, musicians, fashion designers, businessmen—check out the biggest company in the world, Coca-Cola, who doesn't know Coke, right? I mean the drinking kind,* mi hermano, *although Cubans are also in the other stuff too. Who's the head of Coca-Cola?* Un cubano. *Who else? We know the stuff. Like I said, look at Miami. Our problem was that we always had this whole political thing behind us, you know, tying us down and keeping us really all blind to the realities of what we could be. That's why we've only flowered here, on this stupid, double-crossing, treacherous, perfidious American soil where everything is possible but where we see every day how we were betrayed when we tried to stomp out the bloody Nero with the cigar and the smile full of bullets and bones. But, hey, that's* historia antigua. *So then who cares about these Marielitos who came here expecting everything to be done for them, thinking this is socialism or something, that all they have to do is ask and it shall be given, knock and the door will open.* Coño, *man, these guys just don't want to break their backs, work their asses off like we did. They want everything just because they have a pretty face, you know? So all they do is complain about this and that and then pick up a* pistola *and think they can solve all their problems by pumping people full of bullets. I mean, most of them are just a bunch of niggers, brother, so don't go around bothering too much with them. They give us white Cubans a bad name, you know,* muy mala reputación. *It was that son of a bitch Fidel who fucked the Americans up the ass and us too. That scum, those human dregs he sent us, he got them out of Mazorra, out of the madhouse, and out of the prisons he got them. They're shit, man, they're not worth spit and you shouldn't worry about them. Just look at the great thing we've done, brother, look at Miami. And that's nothing, just you wait. Pretty soon we're gonna have Cuban congressmen and senators from all over the place, you wait and see. We already had a Cuban governor in Florida and what's her name, that congresswoman from Dade. Shit, man, they might even change the Constitution for us, brother. Make a Cuban born in Havana president of these U.S. of A., won't that be something! So forget about these Marielitos, brother, forget about them, they're scum, they're nothing. They're shit,* mierda. *Fidel should have killed them all anyhow. That's what they deserve, the firing wall,* el paredón.

1

In Los Angeles, cold weather is like death—it catches people by surprise, leaving them yearning for the warmth of the past. The day when two Cuban exiles carried out one of the bloodiest robberies in Southern California history was an even greater occasion for regret than most Southland winter spells. When the day broke, temperatures plummeted, forcing everyone in this coastal Gilead to pull the woollies out from under the pile of baggies, tank tops and folded sweats. Actual honest-to-goodness breaths of condensed air hung all day in front of people's mouths like word balloons in cartoons, and old aches and pains left behind after crossing the Tehachapis and the Arizona state line surfaced like old cracks in the foundation of the house. Home consumption of oatmeal and grits rose while restaurants and coffeehouses throughout the basin churned out hearty feasts of eggs, bacon, sausages, fries, double portions of cream and butter on everything, cholesterol and slim figure be damned. Those who had fireplaces lit them and kept them stoked for as long as they could, while the few foreseeing Angelenos ingested massive quantities of vitamin C to forestall the colds and flu that would come in the wake of the frigid snap as surely as the city sewers overflow into Santa Monica Bay after every storm.

The men who would carry out the carnage at Schnitzer Jewelers, José Pimienta and Ramón Valdez, however, were barely aware of the chill that descended on the city. They had spent the entire night praying to Oggún, the mighty warrior of the *santería* cult, asking for his help, his strength and his daring in the heroic deed they were about to carry out. Redolent of sweet basil, jasmine and frankincense, their three-rooms-and-a-bath apartment was a perfumed steam box of fatigue, fear and desire, hard by the building that once housed Aimee Semple McPherson's Universal Church of Faith in Echo Park. Even if they had opened the paint-encrusted windows to let in some air, the men would have been incapable of smelling the tortillas, burritos and menudo of their Mexican neighbors. Their sustenance throughout the night—coffee, cigars and a large mound of powder cocaine laced with methamphetamine—had rendered their senses useless. For twelve hours they knelt before the altar where they had arrayed the instruments of their devotion—.357 Magnum, .45 Colt automatic, sawed-off Browning shotgun with retractable butt, black Sten machine pistol, gray Uzi submachine gun, six sticks of dynamite, two grenades. Finally, at nine, the two men stripped, rubbed their bodies with oil, dressed all in white—underwear, shoes, socks, pants, shirt, coat and overcoat—hid their armory in the folds of their clothing and stepped out for the sacred mission at hand. In their absence, from the altar's lit candles, a tissue caught fire. The smoke alarm went off but no one paid attention until the entire apartment was engulfed in flames and the local fire fighters hacked down the front door with their axes. They found, amid the burnt offerings, several beheaded chickens, a quartered dog and charred bones that looked suspiciously like human remains.

The man who owned the site where José and Ramón conducted their hecatomb also said his morning prayers that winter's day. Barry Schnitzer had woken before dawn, draped his prayer shawl over his stooped shoulders, set the threadbare yarmulke on the crown of his head and intoned the Jewish prayer for the dead. Rising early was something that had always come easily for him, from the time he was a cobbler's apprentice in a small village in Galicia, when he was known as Levi Abronowitz. It was also what had saved him from the camps. Alone among the carload taking his people to Auschwitz, he was awake as the rotted floorboard in the freight train fell to the tracks, leaving a hole no wider than his shoulders. Without a moment's hesitation, before anyone else in the car realized what miracle of escape yawned before them, Levi dove for the opening. He squeezed through somehow, hanging from the underside of the car like a roach from a dining table. The board hit the track and, bouncing up, was caught in the gears, jamming the wheels. The train jolted to a halt. Levi was thrown to the ground, his head slamming against the dew-sprinkled crossbars in the roadway. He passed out briefly but his drive to live brought him to within seconds. He slipped through an opening next to the metal wheels, so hot that they raised blisters on his hands and knees. By the time the gates of the guards' car slammed open, Levi was already on the far side of the tracks, a small ragged man running for shelter in the grove of tall pines by the roadway. It would be hours before the rays of a slate gray sun would halfheartedly pierce the fog-enshrouded countryside. By then Levi would be hiding in a damp culvert, shivering from the cold but miles away from the railway of death, free to somehow find his way to his uncle in America.

Even after changing his name, marrying twice and making a fortune, the memory of that narrow escape seized him every morning like a stiff rheumatic joint to be warmed and flexed before using. No matter how high he rose he harbored that memory as a reminder that for some unknown reason God had picked him out, and not eight million others, to survive. Because of that, Schnitzer always felt an affinity for refugees, Jewish or not, feeling that from a wide perspective (and how could it not be wide, considering how narrow his escape had been?) everyone in the West is a displaced person, that somewhere in our persons we all wear the yellow Star of David. This affinity led him to hire, after he advertised for an assistant manager for the jewelry store he inherited at the Mart on Sixth and Hill, the dusky, sloe-eyed Armenian girl whose bright intelligence cut through her awkward English.

Hilda Sarkissian was twenty-five at the time, with a little girl and a shiftless husband who used to beat her, but she had worked out just fine for Schnitzer. Under his careful direction and using her Middle Eastern contacts—with her fluent Armenian, Iranian, Turkish and Arabic—Schnitzer's business grew until there were a dozen Schnitzer's Jewelers throughout the Southland, all geared to satisfying the little guy, the modest customer, the fry cook or office clerk who'd take home a pair of diamond studs and pay them off at ten dollars a week for years until at the end he'd actually paid enough to buy himself a whole necklace. Levi, who had gotten into the jewelry business without knowing anything about it after his wife's father had died, leaving the store and a name Levi informally adopted as his own, this son of a peddler without knowledge or skills, congratulated himself on his foresight at having hired his enterprising helper.

In the course of business both Hilda and Levi grew rich, moving away from Boyle Heights, the old East Los Angeles ghetto now filled with assorted Hispanics, to Northridge and Bel Air, respectively. Schnitzer had relinquished day-to-day control of the store to her a long time ago, but twice a week, almost ceremonially, he would drive down in his maroon Lincoln Continental to the flagship store at Sixth and Hill, to the shop that had made his fortune.

That morning in Northridge, Hilda Sarkissian's biggest problem was the same it had been for the last sixteen years, her daughter, Jeannie. Hilda had made an appointment at a local mental health clinic to treat her daughter's ever increasing weight problem, and now she had to convince Jeannie to let herself be interviewed, measured and analyzed in the pursuit of sleekness. As Hilda grabbed the keys to the Mercedes from the silver tray in the foyer, she heard the water running and imagined the clouds of steam filling her daughter's baby blue bathroom. She hesitated a moment, debating whether to knock at the door and demand that Jeannie come out, then decided to delay confronting Jeannie until dinner that night, when, after baklava and Turkish coffee, they could talk like ladies and maybe that stupid girl would get some sense in her at last.

Hilda walked out of the ample Spanish-style home with the red tile roof and the fancy windows looking out on a quarter acre of azaleas, roses and green, green lawn. She waved at Dolores, the Salvadoran housekeeper, whose battered Datsun pulled into the driveway as Hilda pointed the nose of her Mercedes down the steep sloping street to the on-ramp of the crowded 118 Freeway. She glanced at the dashboard clock and her businesswoman's impatience surged forth. Leaning on her horn, she zigzagged between lanes, trying to hurry downtown to the jewelry shop before old man Schnitzer arrived.

While Hilda was maneuvering her way, her shop manager, Carlos

Azevedo, was already removing the padlock and opening the con-
certina gate to Schnitzer's flagship store. He sniffed disdainfully at
the reek of urine left by a vagrant, intent, as blindly as a dog or a
cat, on marking off his territory. Born in East Los Angeles, among
the soot-covered casuarinas of Montebello, Azevedo had nothing
but contempt for the dozens of glassy-eyed, able-bodied men he
saw panhandling every day in and around Pershing Square. The
first time he heard TV commentators and newspapers referring to
them as homeless people, he bristled. *Pinche* homeless, he thought,
they're either crazy or bums. Homeless were my people. These
guys just don't want to work, they deal dope and drink Thunderbird
and steal ladies' purses, then go teary eyed and say society made
them what they are. *Chingaderas*. I tell you, if I was the mayor, I'd
put them all to work, digging ditches or cleaning the freeway, if
not to the *pinche cárcel*, I wouldn't care, just get them off the streets.
Azevedo turned off the alarm and let himself into the store.

Minutes later, over in Echo Park, José and Ramón left their
apartment, the fragrance of their body lotion lingering in the narrow
hallway of their building. The cold sun bit into their dilated pupils,
giving objects a hard cutting edge—the Spanish language signs for
doctors' offices, the tile roof of the Pioneer market, the low-riding
De Soto waiting for them at the corner. José turned to Ramón and
made the only comment to be heard until they entered the store.

"It looks like Havana in the winter."

"Yes, but it's colder. *Vamos*, it's late."

The De Soto that José and Ramón used to get to the jewelry
store was a lumbering behemoth from 1949, a loan from the owner
of a body shop, a fellow Cuban named Inocente González. When
police contacted him after the grisly events, the portly budding
capitalist rolled his baby blue eyes and said he had no idea José
and Ramón had such a thing in mind. Police were skeptical but
had no choice except to believe him when he said they told him
they wanted to go to Disneyland and didn't have a car, so González
lent them the De Soto, which he had seized on a mechanic's lien
after the owner skipped to Mexico fleeing arson charges. The De
Soto had been outfitted with special low-rider springs, said González, and Ramón had experienced some problems navigating it
through town.

The LAPD detectives, with their usual sagacity, surmised that unfamiliarity was the reason why the De Soto was scraping the pavement as it negotiated the entrance to the parking lot next to Schnitzer's. Eyewitnesses said the car made quite a sight, its sky blue aerodynamic hood and fenders and shiny chrome torpedo bumpers muscling through downtown rush hour traffic, as conspicuous as a Whittier Boulevard *cholo* strutting down Hill in flying colors with his *ruca* on his arm.

The parking attendant, Remigio Flores, a veteran of the rumbles in Frogtown and San Fernando, was shocked when the undercarriage of the car hit the slant of the driveway, throwing off sparks. Remigio meant to tell the driver to raise the suspension the next time, but he changed his mind when he saw the icy expression on the faces of José and Ramón after they got out and ordered him to keep the car running and up front by the exit, that they wouldn't take long. Remigio kept an eye on the pair and when he saw them entering the Schnitzer store, he knew without a doubt that soon he'd be hearing the whistling of bullets. So he did as he was told, parked the car up front and went inside his shack, his hand on the sawed-off shotgun he kept in a corner for protection.

The actual size of the flagship Schnitzer Jewelers store was relatively small, considering the volume of sales handled by Carlos and Hilda. On a 2,500-square-foot location, the establishment racked up sales of more than six million dollars a year, an astonishing amount, for practically all the items were under a thousand dollars in value.

In spite of the high volume of sales, especially around lunchtime, when the swelling crowds of typists, clerks and secretaries descended on Pershing Square, the store had never felt the need for more than one security guard. The man was named Gene Hawkins. Tall, rangy and black, he was also known as "Star" because he had the same name as a San Francisco 49ers football player. But where the gridiron ace was light and agile, Schnitzer's Hawkins tended toward reflection and deliberation. Chilled by the long drive from Compton in his Citation, with a heater that had broken down two months before, Gene had gone to the back of the store to fix himself a cup of instant oatmeal. There was only one customer in the store at the time, an elderly Asian woman with a small child, carefully surveying the filigree earrings on the velvet case.

Carlos was the first to see José and Ramón enter the store, walking abreast of each other like cheap hoods in a B movie. He was on the phone trying to reach Beverly Alvarado, a newly hired employee who was already an hour late and had not called in or given any reason for her delay. (Later, during the investigation, police would find that Beverly had gotten into a fender bender coming out of West Adams and was delayed by the other driver.)

The moment he saw the Cubans walk in, Carlos knew there was going to be trouble. He put the phone down, not bothering to let it ring ten times as he routinely did. The two Cubans had shown up three months before, buying pendants, earring, necklaces, all of gold. They wanted 18 karat but since the store sold only 14k they went along, especially after Carlos convinced them 14k was better because it lasted longer. They'd shown him a card for a discount signed by Mr. Schnitzer, so he'd cut the price by half, leaving an outstanding balance of eight hundred dollars, which they financed. While their job references were shaky—they'd only been working at the Meneses Body Shop for six months—Carlos figured he could always repossess if worse came to worst.

When it did, it was a messy affair, one of the messiest he'd ever been in. The men ignored his repeated phone calls to pay up. They claimed the jewelry was supposed to be a present from Schnitzer and they had no intention of paying for gifts. Carlos, refusing to believe Schnitzer would give away his merchandise to these low-lifes, called in the sheriff's department to do its duty by the merchants of Los Angeles and return the goods to their lawful owner. One of the sheriff's deputies who went into the apartment to rescue the jewelry told Carlos the items had been on an altar as an offering to some kind of voodoo god and that the men had sworn they'd get them back.

Carlos turned to Hawkins, nudged him with his elbow.

"Hey, Star, check out those guys."

Hawkins turned and saw the two black Cubans swagger in. He put down his instant oatmeal and unclipped the safety strap of the holster of his .387 Magnum.

"Be careful," said Carlos.

It was Hawkins' shuffling gait, the kind of lopy, off-balance walk that made him such a comforting figure even when packing a gun, which sealed his fate. José saw him approaching and before the guard had cleared his throat to ask, "Could I help you, gentlemen?" he had already tapped Ramón on the arm. They had no prearranged signal but Ramón, seeing the large figure in blue with his hand on his gun, in a split second whipped out his Sten and to the amazement of everyone in the store, including himself, fired two shots at Hawkins' knees, which buckled as the bullets tore through the bone and cartilage, exiting in a perfect oval shape above the upper end of the calf.

Absolute silence descended for an instant, a moment in which all the people that time and circumstance had brought to the store paused to contemplate the bloody disaster before them and to ponder briefly if the same fate awaited them. Then the silence died.

The Asian customer, Nam Do Pang, burst into a stream of obscenities in a high keening pitch while the little girl, her granddaughter, broke out in sobs and cries and quickly wet her pants. Hilda and Schnitzer, who were in the back office examining a shipment of aquas brought by their Romanian friend, Vlad Lobera, rushed out. Carlos pressed the silent alarm button by the side of his desk to alert police of a robbery in progress and stood up, his hands up, a quivering smile on his lips.

While José pointed the gun at them, Ramón went to Hawkins' side to take his gun. But Hawkins, through some inner reserve of courage that even he was unaware of, refused to be disarmed and swatted at José's hands, as if he were a child grabbing a brownie from the cookie sheet.

"You're not gonna take it, let it be!" hollered Hawkins.

When José finally got hold of the gun, Hawkins struggled briefly. The gun went off and the round slammed into Hawkins' thorax, collapsing his left lung and snipping the main artery to his heart. He gave a quick shudder, then went limp into death, blood dripping from his mouth and nose.

Nam Do Pang attempted to get through and out to the street but Ramón kicked her back into the store.

"Don't move or I'll kill you!" The woman cowered by the emerald earring display case and embraced her granddaughter.

José unraveled two Hefty plastic bags he'd been carrying in his pocket and opened them, puncturing a hole in one in his haste. Then, with the butt of his gun, he smashed the glass cases, shards flying out in showers, setting off another silent alarm. He swept the cases clean, tossing the velvet-lined boxes over his shoulder, moving rapidly from case to case while Ramón kept his gun trained on the group.

Perhaps even then a greater tragedy could have been averted but Carlos chose that moment to show off his *cojones*. He spoke to José and Ramón in the broken, halting Spanish of the barrio: "You know this will cost you the life."

José glanced up at Carlos briefly, then at Ramón, who waved the gun, ordering him to go on plundering. Whether out of humiliation or out of some unavowed death wish, or simply because all his life he'd been able to get by through bullying, taunting and hectoring people of color, a foreman with the field hands, Carlos needled the Cubans, not realizing the cultural chasm that divides Castro's children from the sons of Montezuma:

"*Pendejos*, assholes, don't you know the white man is waiting for you? You kill a man, you forget about it. Put down your arms. You don't think that voodoo shit of yours is going to do something, no?"

José looked aghast at Carlos, who did not know he had just uttered the worst insult he could have ever cast at a *santero*. Ramón stood trembling, hesitating whether to shoot Carlos for his impertinence. The little girl's cries broke through the haze of drugs and the singleness of mind with which Ramón had come into the store, her yelping like bells going off in his head, signaling crisis, alarm, imminent death, setting off panicky memories of fire drills when everyone in the Combinado del Este prison would leave their cells running the minute they heard the bells to race down to the yard, and the curses and the taunting and whippings and blows with rifle butts, ax handles, two by fours and chains of the jeering guards rang in Ramón's mind as he turned and stuck his gun in the face of the little girl.

"*Callate, callate*, shut up or I'll kill you, shitty chink!" Ramón was about to press the trigger to blow her brains out because it didn't matter anymore, it was just another life and now he, Oggún, would be able to add her slanty-eyed little head to the mound of skulls his followers laid before him when the old Asian woman covered the girl's mouth with her hand, and pulled the child toward her, telling Ramón in Vietnamese how stupid her little grand-daughter was and that she would never bother his lordship again.

Ramón struck Carlos in the jaw with his rifle butt, throwing him to the ground on the carpet of shattered glass.

Carlos got on his knees, rubbing his mouth, his broken upper lip filling his mouth with blood. He spat out a tooth.

"Oh, my God!" whispered Hilda, as though that blow was in some measure harder to explain than what had happened to Hawkins or the threat to the little girl. It was vicious, uncalled-for violence, the whirling cyclone of pain she had seen one time too many growing up in Iran. She moved behind Schnitzer for protection while the old man looked on and pondered if he had enough time to make it to his desk and take out the gun he kept taped to its underside.

"What the fuck's wrong with you niggers," said Carlos, still defiant. "What are you, crazy? What are you going to do, kill us all?"

José had stopped plundering and set his bag, half full, by the display counter. Ramón had told him there was an outside chance this might happen, that some fool would put up continued resistance even after the guard was out. He shuddered now as he looked at Ramón, in full embrace of Oggún, as he pranced around in the arrogant posture of the god, belly forward, arms akimbo, legs spread wide. The god had descended from heaven and José feared for what the *orisha* would demand. To refuse him would be worse than death but to obey him was just as tragic.

Meanwhile, in the back, Vlad Lobera, the adipose Romanian who had brought in the aquas for Schnitzer, scanned the old man's office, searching for a way out. It was a windowless cubicle with two doors, one leading to a small bathroom and the other to a hallway which connected the office to the shop in one direction and to the emergency escape in the other. Lobera had heard the gunshots blaring Hawkins' death and now he didn't dare step out. He felt his bowels moving out of fear and ran to the bathroom, locking it behind him. There he would smoke cigarette after cigarette, sitting on the commode, his pants around his ankles, listening but not knowing who spoke, feeling the terror as the bullets rang time and again.

"*Oggún, ña ña nile, Oggún kembo ti le,*" implored José, throwing himself on the ground and kissing Ramón's feet. "Please return to your house, oh mighty God, do not honor us with your presence for you are a mighty being and these are petty dogs."

"Dogs are my favorite meal," replied Ramón, laughing. "My anger has been aroused. I will not rest until I am appeased." He stomped his right foot just like the god, shaking his head and moving the rifle in his hand like a spear.

But Carlos, with that same reckless impulse of the matador kissing the rump of the bull as it gallops past him inches away, with the same daring of the Acapulco high diver who plunges down ten stories off the cliffs at the precise moment when the incoming waves will mattress his fall—which is to say, with stupid thoughtlessness—Carlos rushed to grab Ramón's gun.

Oggún, the proud god who inhabited Ramón, looked on with contempt at this measly attempt to disarm him. With his free hand, Oggún seized the two-hundred-fifty-pound warrior, lifted him above his head like a squirming iguana and slammed him against the wall.

"No, no, Oggún," cried José, but Ramón pointed the gun at the unconscious body and riddled Carlos with forty-seven bullets in two seconds of deafening fire. Ramón walked up to the lifeless body, knelt on one knee and scooped up a handful of the warm blood of the victim, smearing the life source on his face.

"*Oggún niká! Oggún kabu kabu, Oggún arere alawo ode mao kokoro yigüe yigüe alobilona, Oggún iya fayo fayo!*" cried Ramón, raising his arms in victory, his feet stomping the ground, a tall black man in white clothes in the guise of a god.

Hilda and Schnitzer had crouched down behind the display counter when Ramón and Carlos had gone into their mano a mano. Now, seeing the gunman in full delirium, the two of them started crawling away, moving to the back door. But before they could turn the door handle that would have opened to salvation, Ramón spotted them. At that instant, his task completed, bowl full of the warm human blood he loves, Oggún departed for his tribal home- land. In his place, left shaking, sweating and confused, stood Ra- món, who woefully looked around at the destruction his divine alter ego had caused. He felt lifeless, exhausted, his mind a blinding torrent of suds swirling down a drain. He saw, far away, like figures moving down a football field in the slow motion of TV replays, Hilda and Schnitzer clawing at the door. A voice that he recognized as his own but that seemed to emanate from elsewhere shouted out, "Stop! Stop or I'll shoot you!"

He felt like asking José who was it that had managed to imitate his voice so convincingly and then he saw himself casting down the empty Sten and taking out his pistol from his waistband and he felt like asking if that was the wisest thing to do. He saw the bullet come out of the gun and pierce through Hilda's bobbing brown hair and blast into the base of her skull, which exploded into three pieces. The bullet then entered the old man's right shoul- der piercing the layers of padding in the jacket and the shirt fabric and the undershirt and burrowed into the flesh and cartilage and gristle of the shoulder coming out on the opposite side and lodging itself in the acoustic tile by the door. A second bullet spewed out of the gun and traveled with the speed of death toward Schnitzer's jaw.

Ramón stood in the middle of the store, his gun still in his hand, and overcome by the uselessness of it all, collapsed and sat on the ground.

"*Coño, chico*, what the fuck have you done?" shouted José in Spanish, knowing the god was gone. Ramón looked blindly around him, then shrugged his shoulders.

"That's life," he muttered, remembering the song his wife, Mar- itza, played time and again at their apartment near El Prado in Havana when their little girl died of typhoid.

(In the back office, on his seat at the commode, Lobera felt another spasm as his bowels moved again.)

Ramón staggered to his feet, bracing himself on the counter, his knees still wobbly from too much divinity, too much anger and blood. He looked down and saw the old Asian woman and the little girl, staring wide-eyed back at him. Then he looked out the door for the first time and saw the police barricading themselves down the street. A bullhorn blared, "We have you surrounded. Come out with your hands up!"

Ramón had not counted on the police blocking his escape; in his plans he had always given himself enough time to make a clear getaway. He glanced quickly at his gold and diamond Piaget which showed the time and the phases of the moon—10:35 A.M., rising crescent. He could not understand where the time had gone. By his plans at this moment they should have been on their way out of town, down to the apartment he'd rented in Encinitas to hide in before heading down to Baja. What happened? He noticed the bodies strewn on the glass- and blood-covered floor and smelled the sweetness of the blood on his face, saw the crimson stains on his white suit. His eyes landed on the old woman and the girl, still cowering by the emeralds.

"Grab that old bitch for cover and tell the man we've got hostages."

As José disentangled the woman from the child, Ramón grabbed the girl by one arm and pulled her away.

"Tell them we've rigged up a bomb and we intend to blow it up if they try to storm their way in."

The next two hours passed in a confusing welter of voices, threats, telephone calls and whirring of helicopters overhead. Police turned off the ventilation system and the electricity and the sweetish smell of blood mixed with that of the excrement the bodies had voided. Negotiators for the police tried uneventfully to convince José and Ramón to give up the hostages and surrender, but Ramón refused to speak to them after the second phone call, asking for an intermediary, Juan "Cookie" Bongos, a morning DJ at KQOK, the number-one Spanish-language radio station in Los Angeles.

Bongos was a short, slim, terrier-haired man in his late forties. His dark mestizo face was plastered on billboards all over Hollywood and Echo Park, reminding Hispanics that Cookie was the next best thing to a prize-winning Lotto ticket in town. But Bongos found nothing funny when he entered the jewelry store at around eleven that morning. He saw the same carnage he had covered as a reporter back in Central America, in places like Huichinalgo and

El Playón, monuments to death, rooms full of slaughter commandeered by madmen.

The smell was so overpowering that Bongos gagged, almost retching into his handkerchief. He carried a tape recorder with him and turned it on. The sweaty, sour-smelling, blood-streaked captors poured out their message.

"We want a helicopter, with a safe-pass to the airport and a flight to Algeria or we're all going to die here!" hollered José, nervously.

"*Igualdad*, equality, that's what we wanted," said Ramón in a raspy voice. "Equality of treatment and consideration. Respect. Nobody had respect for us. They thought they could do what they wanted with us. Well, they were wrong. We demand the respect owed a human being."

"And tell these sons of bitches they have an hour to give in or we'll blow up the place. We don't mind dying. We're dead already," insisted José.

"This is the inevitable process of the fight for equality and dignity," continued Ramón, ignoring the desperation in José's comments. "If the Anglo won't listen to us and our situation, this is what he'll find. The streets will run crimson with blood and the weeping of the widows and the cries of the children will be heard throughout the land.

"As blacks and as Cubans we have been doubly discriminated against. This is the bitter harvest—raise crows and they will eat out your eyes.

"We are here to recover our honor, our dignity, which had been stolen by these men and their cohorts. What happened here, we are not responsible for, it was beyond our control."

"OK, you've heard enough," broke in José. "Now go tell the sons of bitches they've got an hour or we'll all go up in smoke."

Cookie left and in the half hour that followed no words were spoken in the stuffy jewelry store except for the quiet crooning of the old lady calming down her frightened granddaughter. José and Ramón sank into their own reveries, heads low, fingers on the triggers of their weapons. Finally, the whirring of a helicopter broke the stillness, as the aircraft slowly sank through the canyon of concrete and glass and touched down in the street in front of the store.

A bullhorn blared, "Gentlemen, we have acceded to your demands. This helicopter is ready to take you to the airport if you'll come out now."

Ramón and José looked at each other jubilantly—their gamble had paid off! They got up, took their arms and walked over to the old woman and the child.

"You take the old lady," said Ramón, "I'll take the kid."

But the moment he laid hands on the little girl, she started to scream and holler, kicking and biting, resistance born of fear. José slapped her but the old lady jumped in to defend the child. He threw the old lady to the ground. As she got up, a sharp pain pierced her left side, then she slapped down to the ground again, striking her head against a display case, dying from the blow. The little girl broke loose from Ramón and hugged the lifeless body. Ramón took the old woman's pulse.

"*Coño*, this shitty old woman just died, would you believe that?"

"What do we do now?"

Ramón thought quickly. Like Pizarro, like the conquistadores, the road went in only one direction—forward. That's it, like El Cid!

"Pick her up and hold her like she's still alive, as a shield till we get to the helicopter."

José tried the front door to the store.

"Coño, it's locked!"

"Look around, there must be another exit."

With the screaming little girl in his arms, Ramón kicked open the back door leading to the hallway. At the end he saw the emergency door. José followed, carrying the body of the old woman. Ramón put his weapon on the floor.

"What are you doing?" asked José.

"I don't want them to think I'm going to kill her because then they will shoot me. She's too small for protection. You hold the gun, OK?"

"OK."

Ramón walked out holding the little girl aloft, his arms around her waist. The moment they stepped out of the shop the girl stopped kicking and fighting, staring in surprise all around her.

On rooftops and street corners, from behind dozens of black and whites parked around the store, bristled dozens of guns in the hands of police. The helicopter waited a few dozen yards away, its blades whirring, ready for takeoff.

José came out next, his machine gun pointed at Ramón and the little girl, as he struggled with the body of the old woman.

They walked cautiously toward the helicopter, dozens of officers observing them quietly, guns pointed at them. From inside the helicopter a man waved.

"Come on, *apúrense*," shouted the man in Spanish.

Ramón walked on to the chopper as a sharpshooter on a rooftop took a bead on Ramón's head and pulled the trigger. Ramón shifted his head at the last second and the bullet missed; it struck the pavement, then bounced up into the little girl, who gave a muffled scream before going limp. Ramón put her down and looked up at the chopper—three shotgun barrels appeared from inside the cabin, trained on him and José.

Ramón put his hands up, as did José, who let the body of the old woman drop with a thud to the ground.

"I wanna lawyer," said Ramón. "*No hablo inglés.*"

"Me too," said José.

2

their case was a dog. They knew it and the D.A. knew it. The judges knew it, the clerk knew it, even the court reporters knew it. Me, I wasn't so sure.

When I first heard of the bloodbath at the Jewelry Mart, I gave José and Ramón the benefit of the doubt, the same kindness I extended to child molesters, auto burglars, coke peddlers and sundry rapists and malfeasants. In Los Angeles crime is a growth industry, fueled by greed, poverty and illegal migration. As one of its ancillaries, sanctioned, nay, blessed by the judicial system, I couldn't afford to take sides against them. I might be working for the accused at any time.

See, when guys like that used to ask for me that meant they were completely and inescapably against the wall. They had lost their faith in the entire process, from cops to priests to family, friends and lawyers. Even public defenders had, in some way or other, subtly or grossly, with pointed fingers or whispered counsel, robbed these people of their hope and dignity.

Take this deal, they always urged, the jury is never going to believe you, a convicted felon with arrests and time served, take the deal, the jury always goes for the cop, take the deal, you won't get a better offer than this, take it, take it. What reason does a cop have to lie? So, when these guys were finally up against the wall, when they thought no one would stand up for them, when they were staring at twenty years in the hole and they knew they had to find another way out, they would get in touch with me. I knew

I was their last resort, the ugly girl who becomes the belle of the dive at a quarter to two. I was their last card, but I could also be their trump card. Sure, they would have liked to hire their own private attorney, one of those fancy lawyers with Ferragamo shoes, ostrich skin attaché case, silver hair at the temples and gold in the cufflinks, the guys with all the right schools, titles, degrees, clubs, cars and watches. But just a look at their Filofaxes would have cost these guys three hundred dollars and all too often that was exactly the same kind of money for which they were facing a sentence of four, six or eight years in the joint, not counting enhancements for use of a gun or for parole or probation violations.

Instead someone at Biscayluz, Wayside, HOJJ or County Jail would slip them my name, literally on a piece of paper torn from last week's *La Opinión* or from last year's *Time* "Man of the Year" issue. They would call, I would listen, and if I felt it was worth it, I would show up in court. The judge invariably would question my qualifications and shake his head at my fees. I, also invariably, would argue that the defendant had requested my services and that if Your Honor were to look around, Your Honor would find that my fees were by no means out of the ordinary even if they were off the schedule approved by the Judicial Council. I lied, of course, but then I remembered my law school years only too well.

I, in other words, was their court-appointed investigator, the sorry substitute for the counsel they couldn't, for some whim or reason, afford to have. I was the guy who would go out and try to interview the witness they always claimed was there and who they were sure would testify if only I could reach him and tell him the kind of trouble his playmate was in. The address? "Down on Forty-fourth and Central, home, check out Ruby's Ribs, ask for Raymond. He be always there." Whenever I would try to point out that an address and phone number would be much more useful, the clients would always rise up in fury, indignant that I, of all people, would question their honor and integrity and the wisdom of their decision. "Yo, home, understand, you're working for me, check this mother-fucker out or what you be doin' for your money?" Sometimes, faithful to the blood in my veins, I would try to reason with them, knowing all too well that it was a losing proposition. So off I would go, the obedient servant, to look for their wondrous witness. If I located his whereabouts, the witness by then was dead or missing, out of the state or the country or totally indifferent to the fate of his fellow Crip, Blood or compadre. Most times the witness had vanished as completely as the constitutional rights that get left behind on the sidewalk once the suspect enters the squad car.

The moment I would inform my clients of this state of affairs, I would wait calmly for the ensuing explosion of surprise, recrimination and slander, claims of such misconduct on my part that they wanted a new investigator. That's when I would twist the knife and tell them I'd gone through the hours granted by the court and that if they wanted me to investigate further or get me relieved, they'd have to ask the judge personally and did they remember how I had to plead to be appointed in the first place. That usually would calm them down. From that point on, I would take the lead. If I didn't tell them that the court approved more hours as a matter of course, as long as it was not on the record, it was only because I needed my clients under my thumb. I told myself I knew what was best for them. Besides, I'm sorry to say, I liked to see them squirm. It was the psychic price I thought they should pay for the help I gave them. After all, they were usually guilty as sin.

Having learned Spanish at an early age, I would often get cases assigned to me by the courts and the Public Defender's office when, for some reason, their clients refused to thankfully accept the prosecution's generous offers. On a winter's morning, weeks after the massacre at the Mart, I trundled down Temple Street to the Criminal Courts Building bearing bad news for one of my clients. The childhood friend he had sworn would substantiate his presence at the Las Cortinas bar at the time a supposed dope transaction went down was long gone from the country. Not only that, the bar had been shut down shortly afterward by the Alcohol Beverage Control people for being a place known to be used to harbor bookmaking, in the mellifluous words of the complaint filed against the erstwhile owner, one Tiburcio Perez from Los Cochis, near the city of Culiacán, in the province of Sinaloa, in, of course, Mexico.

I felt sorry for my client but took some solace in the wonderful view of the snow-capped San Gabriel mountains overlooking downtown Los Angeles. It was a clear morning following two days of rain, which had turned to the white stuff of skiers' dreams above the three-thousand-foot level. I recalled my first visit to Los Angeles before I moved here, when, in the middle of an 85-degree hot spell in February, I glanced east from the glittering intersection of Dayton and Rodeo Drive in Beverly Hills and saw the massive snow-draped head and shoulders of Mount Baldy sixty miles away. I swore then that one day I too would live in this magic land where snow and warm sunshine, fire and ice, cohabitate in flagrant embrace. Well, I kept that pledge, although the results weren't quite what I prayed for.

At the corner of Broadway and Temple, the hundreds of supplicants of justice were already hurrying for their appointment with the custodians of legal wisdom. Black people, brown people, yellow, beige, white people; tall, thin, obese, short, graceless people; the homely and the proud, the gorgeous and the shy; old men wrapped in Salvation Army castoffs and Valley girls in soft Italian leather; Chicano gang members in their chinos, Pendletons and Hush Puppies; their old ladies, their *rucas* with their manes of hair teased out to the max framing drippingly mascaraed eyes; black South Central preachers clothed in cheap suits and dignity, accompanying their brethren, faith and Bible in hand; shiftless, incestuous white parents, chain-smoking cigarettes, herding their runny-nosed towheaded runts forward; bewildered jurors from the suburbs of Pasadena and Palos Verdes; the alcoholic defense counsel; the corruptible district attorney; the fair, the dark, the keen, the dull-witted, the happy, the dumb, the ones in pain, all streamed into the dark mausoleum with marble floors called the Criminal Courts Building. I took a last look at Mount Baldy, knowing that by noon, when I left the building, the sublime, pristine shoulders and peaks would be a sootish yellow brown from the smoggy filth of life in this basin and that neither I nor anyone on this earth would be able to halt the besmirching tide that floats in the air and falls, with gravity's solemn pull, on us all, the virgin and the soiled, the hopeful and the lost, the searchers and the dead. I took a deep breath and joined the streaming flow.

"Charlie, Charlie Morell!" said a man's voice somewhere in the lobby as I waited for the elevator.

A mass of gray-and-brown curls bobbed far above the heads of the crowd, broad nose and thin lips flared in a smile that lit up a sallow complexion from days in court and lockup and nights in libraries and the Second Street Bar. Jim Trachenberg's briefcase flapped away from his body, as it hung from a shoulder strap. He approached quickly, covering the length of the lobby in just a few strides. As always, he seemed slightly befuddled, not quite believing he was six foot seven and by gum and by golly a real bona fide counselor at law. He waved a copy of *El Diario* in my face.

"How you been, Jim?"

"Seen this?" He thumped the newspaper with his free hand, self-esteem exuding vigorously.

"They struck gold in La Mirada?"

"I'm in the paper, man. I'm on the Schnitzer case."

Shining on page one of the Moonie rag stood Jim in all his awkward glory, an angel of righteousness and justice hired at four hundred dollars a day, to save and protect the immanent constitutional rights of two mass murderers. The photo was murky and all I could make out, besides Jim, were two men in county garb, one a tall, light-skinned black, the other bigger, broader and black as only the children of pure Africans can be. The caption, written in the florid style of Latin American newspapers, blared, "The accused perpetrators of the heinous homicide at a luxurious downtown jewelry emporium face justice for the first time."

"Still feeding off the public trough, I see."

"Yeah, sure, I was appointed 987 but it's a good case. You want in on it?"

"Good for what, Jimmy? They have no defense. They were there, they robbed the store, they killed the hostages. That's special circs. No matter how you slice it, they're going to get gas in Quentin. What you gonna do, plea them insane?"

"Charlie, Charlie, you've been around here too long. You sound just like a D.A."

"I sound like a reasonable man."

"There are always mitigating circumstances."

"Yeah, right, let's see, it was a sunny day, right? And one of the guys was out of town and the other one, hell, he just didn't know what he was doing, right? No, wait, better, he was drunk and he doesn't remember."

The thin tinkle of the elevator bell rang and dozens of bodies smelling of fear, alcohol and tobacco, mixed with hairspray and cheap cologne, rushed to the door. Jim, happily unaware of his size and bulk, pressed through the crowd, which parted like ice floes before a breaker. I followed in his wake.

"I don't get it," I said as we pressed in tight, a fat lady in front of him spilling out of her red satin dress, "how come you were appointed? Isn't the PD's office supposed to handle cases like this?"

"Judge Chambers disqualified the PD because of the circumstances. I got one, the ADC got the other."

"Why she do that?"

"Hey, Charlie, what's the matter, you don't read the newspapers?" said a voice from the back of the elevator. I turned to see Ron Lucas, the Santa Monica lawyer who'd grown wealthy from his Colombian clientele, shake his perfectly coiffed head.

"The mail from Medellín is slow nowadays, Ron."

"Just read the *Times*, Charlie. Our boy here did a quick song and dance. He claimed the personal relationship between the PD and the accused constituted a conflict."

"I guess I better start reading the papers after all. What relationship?"

The doors opened on the ninth floor. Lucas stepped out, lizard skin briefcase in Rolex-adorned hand. He shouted, "Those guys killed Dick Forestmann's uncle. You know Dick, don't you?" He headed to Division 55 to defend yet another native of Bolivar's homeland.

"I know one when I see one," I muttered. The other Dick was *the* Public Defender, a small, unprepossessing man with a thick mustache, which he grew to compensate for the almost totally bald pate that shone under the yellow lights of the courts. A nicer man you could not meet until you crossed him, at which point he'd turn into a banshee from hell. With his temper tantrums, it was no wonder the judge had disqualified the entire office—Dick would have been only too glad to pull the plug on the defendants himself.

Jim got off at the judges' lounge on the tenth floor. "Meet me for lunch at Untermann's? I really got to talk to you."

"Sure thing."

My client that day took the news rather well, all things considered.

I commiserated with him when he bewailed his injust fate, how he really wasn't the guy who had dropped the six plastic Ziploc baggies containing a white substance that resembled cocaine in a cache behind the elm tree in MacArthur Park and then raced away in a blue Ford Thunderbird model 1979 with California plate 3 Adam Roger Nancy 746 when undercover officers tried to apprehend him. Yes, of course it was a terrible thing that the *pinche* fucked cops traced the license plate to you and that it was a real *fregada*, a real fuckup, that after you sold the car to Manuel (yes I remember that was the name of the buyer and I know too bad he never told you his last name) like you said it was just *muy triste*, very sad, that you forgot to reregister the car with the DMV, shit, I mean, I haven't reregistered mine either even though the finance company signed it off almost a year ago. After all, when there's a business deal between men, just a handshake is sufficient, *no*?

What evidence do they have, he wailed, his words all running together in a jumble, they didn't even get a good look at me, they have no fingerprints on the bag and I have my witnesses!

Painfully I reminded him that his witnesses were gone and that he did have a small history of prior sales—an arrest record dating back to 1979, just ten days after he'd crossed the border in the hollowed-out wheelwell of a Dodge van driven by a coyote who'd dropped him off at the corner of Broadway and First, right in front of the State Building and the *Los Angeles Times*.

So he got the public defender assigned back to him and the D.A. offered him a four-year sentence, high term, for that case and two other probation violations, meaning he would serve two years, minus the five months he'd been in plus two and a half months for good time/work time they'd apply against the sentence, which meant in all likelihood he'd be kicked out just after doing around one year in Chino because of the overcrowding. In the end he seemed almost happy and he waved at his four kids and his wife, a short rotund woman with a gold-toothed smile who'd brought in the entire clan to watch their papa go off to the white man's jail.

I skipped out on lunch with Jim that day. The thought of facing another greasy lamb sandwich while confronting his latest expression of befuddled eagerness, watching the pieces of dripping food spackle his long-suffering tie, was more than I could bear. We all have our limits.

I didn't set foot again in the CCB for another two weeks. I was busy moving to a second-story flat in Los Feliz, the old Italian neighborhood by Griffith Park, as well as conducting an extraordinarily complicated investigation of a check kiting scheme run by a family of scar-faced Nigerians on an insurance company.

I was at my desk in the den, having finally figured out the complicated paper trail of deposits, withdrawals, letters of credit and warrants when the phone rang.

"Charlie, it's Jim Trachenberg."

"Hey, what's up? Thought you were busy defending those Cubans with your brilliant oratory."

"That's why I called. The son of a bitch kicked me after a Morrisey hearing."

"No shit. What an idiot. Doesn't he know you're the best that money can't buy?

"That's not all."

"What?"

"He wants you instead."

"Say what?"

"He's going pro per. And he wants you as his court-appointed investigator."

3

the massive red-haired deputy was reading an "Archie" comic when I walked up to the security window. The second deputy in the booth, a wiry black watching a football game on a portable TV, saw me out of the corner of the eye. He nudged the redhead, who glanced up annoyed at having his intellectual stimulation interrupted. I slipped him my card, license number 56774 LQ, issued by the Bureau of Consumer Affairs. He glanced down at the picture, then at me. In the photo I have a pained expression, caused by a curettage done by my chipper Beverly Hills dentist the morning the snapshot was taken.

"You packing? If you are, please secure the gun in the locker," said Lurch, his reedy voice magnified by the intercom.

"I'm clean."

"Let me see your briefcase."

I flashed its contents at the peering giant. He grunted, satisfied it contained only files and records, useless papers that would never stop the likes of him from delivering justice the American way.

"Walk through the metal detector."

I stepped around the machine as a test. By that time he'd already pushed the button that opens the gate. It would be so easy, I thought.

The sally port, bars and crossbars painted forest green, clanked as it slowly slid open. I stepped into the passageway between the two gates. The deputy should have waited until the first sally port was closed before opening the second, but I suppose he was afraid he'd forget Archie's story so he flicked the switch that opened the second gate right away. Way too easy.

Walking inside the interview room I was assaulted by the sweet and sour smell of fear and Pine-Sol common to all lockups in California. A slow afternoon in County Jail. Only a handful of attorneys and probation officers were in there, sitting down at the two long benches, reviewing their cases, waiting for their manacled clients to poke through the door at the end of the room. I signaled to the deputy at the desk by the door, waving at one of the empty booths on the left. I closed the door, sat on the metal chair and spread out my file, awaiting the arrival of Ramón de la Concepción Armas Valdez, the so-called brains behind the Jewelry Mart massacre.

Ramón's record up to that outburst of garish violence was fairly representative of those of the Marielito criminals who have graced our shores since 1980. The five to ten thousand jailbirds and lunatics that Castro folded into the mass of his fleeing political enemies made an already suspect bunch of uneducated blacks, mulattoes and recalcitrant whites hard to digest. Among law enforcement agents, the term Marielito had come to mean the roughest, most heartless type of criminal, who would use force way beyond what was necessary, who took sadistic pleasure in creaming the opposition, any opposition—shooting someone full of bullets out of suspicion he might throw a punch, cutting off someone's tongue for talking to the police, spraying acid in his girlfriend's face for giving someone else the eye—small, loving details like that. Ramón had been different only in degree, not in spirit.

His official entry to this country was registered in Key West aboard the *Jason*, a fishing scow so overwhelmed with refugees that its decks were only inches above the waterline. The inspecting INS agent had written down, "Possible criminal element—recommend internment." Ramón admitted doing time in Cuban prisons, yes, but only for political crimes, a wide category of illegal conduct that in Cuba encompassed everything from speaking badly of your boss to being caught in an act of sabotage. According to the INS records, Ramón never volunteered many details about his life or why he felt it necessary to voice his opposition to Castro. A veteran of Angola, he had a cushy job at a munitions factory, with a wife and a daughter and a modest but comfortable apartment near El Prado in Havana. But after his unspecified defiance of the regime, he lost his job, house, wife and the kid, until all he had left was either outright banditry or suicide—then the port of Mariel opened. The INS had its doubts about him, but ultimately waved him on, reasoning he couldn't be any worse than the thousands of others who were rushing in.

"Señor Morell?" asked a heavy voice with the thick, pasty accent of Cuban blacks. I looked up from my files. A large black man, about two hundred fifty pounds in a six-foot-two frame, stood like a Nubian statue, his shadow falling expectantly over me.

"Yes?"

There was something respectful about this giant. His expression was at peace, brown eyes seeming to shine with a request for forgiveness. He had such quiet strength that I thought either I'd been sent the wrong man or he'd found Jesus in jail (and I don't mean Jesus Lopez). I looked for the telltale jailhouse string cross hanging from his neck or the New Testament clutched in sweaty hand but failed to see them.

"*Habla español?*" he asked, almost tremulously, as though the question itself were a sort of imposition that might land him in trouble with a trusty. It was hard to believe this was one of the men accused of murdering six people.

"*Sí, cómo no, siéntate.*" I motioned at him to take a seat. His hands were broad, calloused, his fingernails still harboring the ingrained engine oil and lube grease of the manual worker. A mechanic? Double-check his file.

"My name is José Pimienta. They call me Bobo," he said, with a benevolent smile. "Ramón sent me. He says he wants you to talk to me first."

"What, what? Wait a minute. You guys are getting this whole thing wrong. You're not calling the shots. You need me, I don't need you. And if I want to talk to one of you, that's who I want to talk to. You're not running the show, I am. Deputy!"

"No, listen to me. He can't talk to you."

"Why not?

He hesitated, his ebony face tremulous from contained emotion, the pain stored inside bursting from every black crease. The deputy rushed over, the clinking of his handcuffs like the bell on a billy goat. José talked fast.

"He's sick."

"What do you mean he's sick? What does he have?"

"I mean he's praying."

"What? Come on, make up your mind, what's with him?

"He's sick, he's sick from praying. He's a man of God."

"Great, that's all we need. A killer priest."

"No, don't you understand?

The deputy stood behind José, his brown shirtsleeve taut from contained muscle. He gripped a blackjack in his right hand.

"Something wrong?" asked the deputy with the nervous quaking of Dobermans before they leap.

"He's a *santero*," added José, "he's praying and he can't talk, he's sick."

I waved the deputy away.

"That's all right, he's going to behave."

"You sure?"

"No problem, Ray. We're OK."

Yemayá. Ecué. Shangó. Oggún. Yamba-O. The polyphonous names of the African deities of *santería*, the mystery cult that claims millions of followers and powers beyond description.

"Is that why he sent you first?"

"Yes. He wants me to tell you his story first."

"Do I have a choice?"

"I can go."

"I don't believe this. All right, go ahead. But make it short."

José said he and Ramón had met at an initiation rite in Regla, a suburb across the bay from Havana peopled almost exclusively by blacks, the center of *santería* activity in the province. The Cuban government had outlawed the cult as counterrevolutionary superstition, so Ramón and José's meeting was held late at night in a secret place, far from the prying eyes of the *comités de vigilancia*, the neighborhood committees who keep a detailed ledger of the comings and goings of all the residents of each block in each city. The initiate, a ten-year-old blind black albino boy draped in a coat of many colors, met with his god in the basement of an abandoned bakery near the wharf, in the presence of two hundred men and women who risked their jobs and freedom for the privilege of watching the divinity possess its disciples. After the drumming and the dancing and the possession, when fear and suspicion had given way to the giddiness of communion and exaltation, José and Ramón were introduced by an old woman, Macucha, who had known the families of both men. She predicted that the two would become inseparable, like the twin gods the Ibeyi, messengers of the Yoruba pantheon.

José had just registered for the military service, while Ramón was already a veteran of Angola, where he'd fought against the Unita-led forces of Jonah Savimbi. Both were marginally employed, as cook and shoemaker, when the gates of the Peruvian Embassy were rammed open and thousands flooded in. Ramón had been among the first few hundred to scale the spikes and land on the precious patch of Peruvian soil. José, on the other hand, had been quietly walking to work at the kitchen of La Estrella Restaurant when the neighborhood committeemen, knowing of his counter-revolutionary feelings, picked him up in an old U.S. Jeep, told him, "You're going!" and drove him straight to Mariel, where he was dumped with the restless crowd awaiting embarkation.

Without family, friends or sponsors to spring them from the refugee camps, José and Ramón languished as guests of the Immigration and Naturalization Service for a full year after their arrival. They were finally released when the Catholic Relief agency located a distant relative, a maternal aunt of José's living in Caguas, Puerto Rico, who reluctantly agreed to be responsible for their welfare. They never made it to the island. Once freed, they stayed among other boat-lift refugees in the decaying waterfront art deco hotels of Miami Beach. In the Cuban affinity for diminutives, they were now Marielitos, the little people of Mariel, instant pariahs of two nations. The self-fulfilling prophecy of a crime wave came all too true.

"Yeah, sure, but that's no excuse, José. Plenty of people are down and out and don't turn to crime."

"You Americans don't understand. Let me explain."

Ramón and José's first contact with U.S. law was over a minor transgression, an unauthorized knife hidden in their tent in the settlement quarter for the refugees put up under downtown Miami's freeway overpasses. An unidentified assailant had stabbed several people in the camp, taking their money and food. The INS suspected Ramón and José, but since no witnesses dared step forward, no formal charges were filed.

In their second contact, the two were detained as suspects in the fatal robbery of a convenience store near the Tamiami Trail. An informant told the cops José had been crying into his beer, remorseful over what he and Ramón had done to the owner of the El Cebollón. It turned out the proprietor had been hogtied one night while alone in the store, then murdered execution-style in the storeroom, next to boxes of rotting plantains. Although clumsy detectives questioned José and Ramón separately—clumsy in that the suspects somehow endured an awful fall at the station house that broke José's ribs and smashed Ramón's nose—neither of the men confessed. They were released and the case was closed shortly thereafter when the informant was found floating facedown by the piers near the Miami River bridge. His mouth had been sewn shut, apparently while he was still alive.

After that, José and Ramón faced charges with regularity. Aggravated assault, robbery, possession of stolen merchandise, bookmaking, possession of a controlled substance, sale of a controlled substance, sexual battery, fondling a minor, a litany of charges José blamed on prejudice, resentment and mistaken identity. But at no time was there ever a conviction—no one would press charges or come forward to testify. Law enforcement finally got its break when the DEA nabbed both of them as they were riding in the backseat of a car driven by Aníbal Gutiérrez, a well-known art connoisseur and holder of the local Pizza Man franchise. During their search, agents found that Ramón and José were carrying concealed Sten submachine guns; in the trunk, stuffed inside supermarket brown paper bags, officials stumbled on fifty kilos of cocaine packed in neat, plastic-wrapped bricks with the legend "Bolivar's Best." Gutiérrez's lawyers were able to suppress the evidence of the drugs, arguing there was no probable cause to stop the car and thus the agents had no right to search the vehicle. Gutiérrez returned to his

Degas, dough and drugs with hardly a worry. But Ramón and José were sentenced to sixteen months each and after doing their time were sent to the federal penitentiary in Atlanta, pending deportation to Cuba.

Their fate took yet another turn when the Reagan administration botched the deportation agreement and informed the prisoners they would soon be returning to the land of their nightmares. The prisoners rioted and after taking dozens of hostages, set the facilities on fire. In the negotiations following, the Justice Department agreed to review all the cases and somehow, in the pell-mell rush to comply, José and Ramón slipped between the bars.

They returned to Miami but things were different by then. Gutiérrez had been killed in an accident, after his speedboat flipped outside Lauderdale and exploded. The Marielitos had moved out of Miami Beach, the old art deco hotels and apartment buildings having been taken over by yuppies, who waxed orgasmically over the etched glass windows and sinuous modernist lines. Even the authorities had changed. A Cuban mayor had taken office in Miami and he was determined to root out the undesirables of his own kind. Police, who before only showed up on emergencies, patrolled the area constantly. That's when Ramón and José, still together after all their travails, decided to head out west, to the city of dreams by the Pacific.

I looked up at the clock. Three hours had gone by and I still hadn't started questioning José on their new life or the crime on hand.

"Look, that's all fine and dandy, but let's talk about what happened that day, José."

"OK, sure, but I got to tell you something."

"What's that?"

"I don't remember anything that happened."

■

"That's his defense, you understand," said José's attorney, splaying his manicured fingers on the edge of the Biedermeier desk, varnished nails glistening in the sunbeam piercing the picture window. Outside, a lonely hawk circled the canyons of Bunker Hill, hunting for a field mouse amid the rubble of construction sites.

Clayton Finch Whitmore Smith III seemed at ease in his legal aerie, surrounded by Hockneys, Rushas and Diebenkorns, his California hipness only heightened by the tiny Fragonard by the door. The fine wool crepe fabric of his Clacton Fricton custom-made suit draped as elegantly as the arguments he propounded in court when defending his usual array of wealthy businessmen and Hollywood stars.

"We're going to hold a competency hearing as soon as the two shrinks pick him over. I think the guy's flipped, all that voodoo stuff."

"*Santería*," I said. "Voodoo is from Haiti."

"No matter, the effect is the same, to temporarily derange the participant into believing a divinity has manifested itself."

"Sounds like Mass."

That stopped his argument in midbreath. He stroked his cropped reddish beard and smiled.

"It does, doesn't it?" He chuckled. The glint of his smile and the pleasant folding of the wrinkles around his gray eyes gave Clay an appealing boyish look. I could see why jurors, especially women, were swayed by his oratory. Now he turned stern, his hand wagging the Mont Blanc pen at me to press his point.

"What we have in *santería* is a prehistoric, anti-Western cult that possesses its participants, deprives them of the use of reason and makes them commit offenses that in their ordinary state of mind they would never dream of carrying out. To me, that is one of the best definitions of insanity ever propounded and that's why we're using it."

He leaned back in his leather chair, expecting my insincere praise.

"Are you saying I should tell Valdez to cop to the same thing?"

"Charlie, I wouldn't presume to tell you what to do, that's between you and him. By the way, when's the arraignment?"

"Next Tuesday. Judge Chambers."

"Good." He scribbled quickly in his calendar, then looked up. "I hear there's no way she's going to allow him to go pro per in trial. I suppose you told your guy he's not exactly doing himself the greatest service."

"If I ever get to talk to him. I've been to see him twice at Old County. The first time he claims he's sick but it turns out he's in chapel, praying. Second time, they can't find him. They lock down the place, search the whole joint. He'd been laying in bed the whole time but somehow the guards didn't see him."

"Quite a guy. I just thought of something. Your guy cannot use the same defense we're using. He is the priest, the one who brings people into a trance, so he did it knowingly, casting aside his rationality to invoke the dark forces. Evil, not just malice, aforethought."

"So dramatic. Is that why you're doing this pro bono, Clay? You're gonna sell it to the movies?"

Clay slammed the desk so hard the clasp of his Rolex came undone.

"Dammit, Charlie, can't you take anything seriously?" he said as he reclasped his watch. "I know all about you. I know why you came out here, running from Dade County with your tail between your legs. You were great and you fucked up."

"Mind your manners," I said. "You're swearing."

Clay's expression darkened and I saw the flinty streak that got him out of the shadow of the sugar refinery in Vallejo where he was born and that impelled him through Stanford, Harvard and the State Department, making him partner by age thirty in Manuel, Caesar, Brewer and Smith and multimillionaire by age forty.

"Don't play fucking games with me," he said. "You know perfectly well why we took this case. This office has a pro bono policy and everyone here, from Caesar to the rawest recruit from USC, has got to do it. It's my turn, that's all. And no, I'm not selling it to the movies. Are you?"

"If I can, I will. I got bills to pay."

4

It was the kind of Sunday when everyone in L.A. wishes for a beach house in Malibu. Except for those who have one—they wish for a beach house in southern France. Although those happy few might detest having to put up with the town's cinderblock surf shops, neon-lit fast-food stores and miles of traffic on weekends when the entire San Fernando Valley is on its way to Zuma Beach, at least the beachsiders know they have what everyone desires, their own private ocean. The azure windswept waters lapping at the yellow dunes, the surfers bobbing in the swells, the occasional spinnaker raking the horizon, the smell of salt spray and jasmine, these are the precious reasons why they paid a million dollars for a thirty-foot stretch of beachfront, these are the treasures for which they lied, cheated, hustled and swindled.

Up in my neck of Los Angeles, the landscaped hills and terraces of Los Feliz, we have a similar situation with Griffith Park. The difference is that instead of a beach we have dales with picnic benches, in place of the ocean there's a narrow polluted creek wending around littered roads and crowded parking lots, and the lucky few are the thousands of Central Americans who flock to the park in their Datsuns and Toyotas. These refugees from war and poverty cram six and eight at a time into their Japanese jalopies, patched up with spit and bondo, rolling on bald tires, tinny radio turned to Radio Amor, K-Love, tremulous love ballads by Julio Iglesias, José José, Emanuel, floating out of the car window as a pink pompom flies from the antenna and the pair of Styrofoam dice dangle from the rearview mirror. Lines of cars miles long head into the park, where the families—it is always families, no matter if the group is made up of six men thrown together by poverty and circumstance, they are all *familia*—park their cars, take out the ice chest with meats and chicken to be grilled at the barbecues by the benches, pop open a few *cervezas* and toss out the soccer ball. Within minutes the pickup games start, Salvadorans, Guatemalans, Mexicans and Hondurans, mixed groups of brown flesh and desire recreating in the park the old game of bola their Indian forefathers played in the jungles of Petén, Tikal and Tazumal.

These are the lucky ones. They are not the ones who crossed battlefields, trekked across deserts, dodged border guards, outsmiled coyotes and escaped landlords to make it to El Lay for a job paying the minimum wage. There are plenty of those, hundreds of thousands if not millions of menials who keep the Southland engines humming. These here in the park are the ones who have already tasted a measure of success, think of families and outings and roots, who look to a future in this country when they will have their own *mercado* and their own *casita* in Pacoima. And now on weekends, they pack little Juan, Enrique, Josefina, Fernando, Miguel, Eleazar, Aurora and the old lady into the Datsun to go out to the park.

I always envied them their dreams, small and constricted as they might seem to an outsider. Even if flawed, their compass had a setting. I, on the other hand, felt adrift, with not much going for me other than an Ivy League education and a thankless job that kept me twirling, spinning without reason, in a peeling golden cage.

That Sunday I knocked downstairs at my landlord's apartment door, framed by bushes of cool, fragrant lilies and honeysuckle. But Enzo Baldocchi's Ligurian face peered out the door and shook his head no at my invitation, pasty breath still reeking of vodka and amaretto, while a woman's voice in the background queried in Sicilian the identity of the son of a bitch who didn't know what time it was. So I set off on my own, starting at an easy loping pace up the hill. For a week the temperature had been slowly rising, a few degrees per day, so that now on that Sunday at eight the air was as warm and treacherous as a Latin embrace. Mild Santa Ana winds sweeping down from the high desert had wiped the sky clean, to the baby blue of an O'Keeffe painting. Sprinklers on the deep front lawns of the Mediterranean mansions up the hill raised clouds of vapor, wafting occasional hints of juniper and citrus.

Two blocks up from my apartment, the road takes a sharp hairpin turn left, rising a quarter-mile in a matter of a few hundred feet. I leaned forward and swung alternately with my arms, my upper body at an angle to the ground, feeling the strains on my quads and buttocks, my wobbly knees, the pinpoints of perspiration on my T-shirt coalescing into wide swaths of sweat. Breathing hard, I reached the corner and glanced down at the skyline of downtown ten miles away, the office towers standing like upended shoeboxes against the girthing Baldwin Hills. I couldn't see them but I knew that behind those hills the endlessly bobbing oil derricks, greedy maniacal jays, kept pumping out the oil that first made the city wealthy, before Hollywood, aerospace and sweatshop labor.

I tried to catch a glimpse of County Jail, where Ramón and José were being housed, but even with fifty-mile visibility from my vantage point I was unable to pinpoint the squat gray bunker at the foot of Chinatown. They were due in court on Tuesday for their arraignment and motions and I still had not been able to interview Ramón. Two weeks had passed since he had petitioned the court for my appointment. During that time I'd been unable to do anything other than review the paperwork, hampered by his refusal to give me leads to support an investigation. I had no idea how he intended to proceed or what part I would play in his defense. Maybe on Tuesday he'd change his mind and ask for a public defender after all. Maybe I would simply pass on the case.

This last thought cheered my day. I came out on Longfellow, then ducked and slithered under the rusty barbed wire fence with the NO TRESPASSING sign covered with the blue graffiti of the neighborhood white punks, Stoners, and ran clear into the brush. The yellowish dust swirled around me as I beat a painful climb up the well-worn path to the top. I bumped against an oak tree but felt no pain, seeing with curious detachment how the broken branch gashed the skin off my forearm and the dark red blood oozed out. Finally, panting and cursing under the little breath I had left, with a last back kick, I surged to the top of the hill, to the dusty clearing looking out on the entire basin.

A smell of orange blossoms and eucalyptus drifted my way as I stood panting, drinking in the view of the city at my feet. I kicked a couple of old beer cans and grinned at a bluebird pecking on a used condom. Los Angeles, city of love.

The phone was ringing by the time I got back to my desk. I picked it up before the fourth ring to shortcut the answering machine.

"Hello," I said, breathless.

"Out for a run, I bet," said Livie, and the room turned dark.

I must have held my breath a few seconds for she asked querulously, "You still there?"

"Of course." I glanced around my desk, trying to stop the sinking feeling, anchoring myself in the dull safety of the everyday. Papers and files, a creased calendar book, a clock whose batteries had run out, pencil holder, staplers, a rarely used thesaurus. I looked at my runner's watch. Half hour to lunchtime in Miami. A drop of blood from my scrape fell on the white phone. "Good morning. How are you? How's Julian?"

As always, the rapierlike answer struck deep.

"I didn't call to trade amenities, Charlie. I'm still like the last time you saw me, angry and abandoned."

"Let's not get into that again."

"No, let's not. Drifters are like drunks, all the moralizing in the world won't do them or you any good. They'll still break your heart."

"Please. You sound like a country-western song. What do you want? Didn't you get my check?"

"I got it, all right. But don't you think you've forgotten something?"

A loaded question, that. I try very hard to put a thousand and one things out of my mind. More often than not, the very things I try to exorcise come back to haunt me and taunt me, parking themselves at my mind's door so they can spring on me like a collections man saying, We got stuff to talk about. "No, what?"

"It's April seventh. Someone wants to talk to you."

She passed the phone and before the party got on the line I knew already who it would be and my heart leaped in pain and joy.

"Hi, Daddy."

"Hello, Julian. Happy Birthday. Did you get my present yet?"

Julian squealed with delight. "You didn't forget! Mom said maybe you were too busy."

"How could I forget you, guy. I'm sure you'll get it in a day or two. The mail is late sometimes."

"Yeah, Dad, that's it, the mail's late."

Julian. Golden curls, hazel eyes, dewy skin smelling of Pears soap and baby powder. Noisy, hyperactive Julian, who today turns seven.

"So what you doing, champ? Going to any parties?"

"Well, Mom made me a cake and I'm having all my friends over. Philie, Bobby, Carlos, Rene and Donna. Then we're going to Lucaya. It's rad!"

"I'm sure it is."

"What did you send me, Daddy? I wanna know 'cause I already got all these presents but nobody gave me what I wanted, what I really wanted."

A true son of Livie, I thought, comparison shopping already.

"And what do you want? Maybe that's what I sent you."

"A Robocop! A Teenage Mutant Ninja Turtles Video Game!"

"Well, maybe you'll like my presents then."

Julian made a whooping noise.

"All right! You're the greatest dad! When you coming to Miami?"

"I don't know, sport. But I'll tell you what, maybe you'd like to come out to Los Angeles soon. We can go to Disneyland—"

"I don't know, Daddy. Everybody says Disney World is better and Mom's taken me there three times already."

"OK, then we'll go to Universal Studios and you can watch *King Kong* and *Jaws*."

"That sounds cool!"

Julian turned to Livie, who must have been standing next to him, ready to protect her child from his feckless, heartless father.

"Can we go to L.A. and go to Universal, Mom? Can we?"

I overheard her say something I could not make out. Julian came back on the line, disappointed.

"Mom says she doesn't know." Then a whisper, "She still doesn't like you."

"That's all right. Things change."

"Mom wants to talk to you so I'm gonna go now."

"OK, champ. Happy Birthday."

A rattle, then Livie's stern and well-modulated voice, which resonates so beautifully when she anchors the evening news.

"Don't even think about taking him away."

"Just for a vacation."

"No way. You want to see him, you come here. I don't trust you and we both know why. By the way, I'm getting married. I'll write to you. Goodbye."

"Who is it? When?" I didn't ask the why since it was so obvious. But Livie hung up before I could ask more, the ringing of the line a blank to be filled by the failures of my past.

The widow Chambers was in a bad mood. A San Diego attorney who had the misfortune of arriving twenty minutes late to her court for a continued 1538.5 hearing had been found in contempt and fined a hundred dollars. When he had protested at the unusual and stern punishment, knowing that although the court officially opened at 8:30 the doors weren't even unlocked until 9:00, the widow ordered the bailiff to drag the screaming and shocked counsel to lockup to ponder his alternatives until a full contempt hearing later that day. His puzzled client looked dumbfoundedly around, saying, "I'll get you out, Counsel, I'll get you out!"

Deputy Bill Smith came out of the lockup grinning, his dun-colored features animated by the sweet thought of revenge against the kind who will get shot first come the revolution.

"He should have known better," he confided. "Now *he's* hollering for a lawyer."

"I wonder how he feels being in such close quarters with the people he defends."

"The custodies aren't in yet, bus got delayed coming from Wayside, so he's there all alone. You here to see who?"

"Hey, to see you, talk about old times, shoot the breeze."

"Fuck, yeah. Your boys, the Cuban twins, are not in either."

"Thanks. So, how's business?"

Bill had a small video company on the side, taping weddings and anniversaries for the citizens of Moreno Valley, a new development two hours away in the rattlesnake center of Southern California, Riverside County.

"Doing OK. Did the local Lion's Club Ball the other day."

The clerk, a dark-haired man with the impressive name of Curtis Franklin Burr—a direct descendant of the saturnine little man who killed Alex Hamilton—waved at me.

"Judge would like to see you in chambers."

"Right away."

The judge's name, Connie, was spelled out in needlepoint and framed between two fuchsia hearts behind her high-back leather chair. On her desk was another picture frame, with snapshots of her three daughters. Up on the shelf of the Swedish teak bookcase all judges get with their office, more pictures of the daughters— one in cap and gown, another in dress whites at Annapolis, the third with a pink baby and a fat husband. Hanging from the paneled walls were diplomas from law school, plaques from when Chambers was a D.A., a picture of her hugging the former street cop who rose to become L.A.'s first black mayor. Nowhere did I see a trace of the man to whom she owed her name and position, John Chambers, the former Pasadena jurist so popular among the good white citizens of that smogbucket that upon his death the governor felt compelled to name the widow to the post. But that had been six years ago, practically a generation by California standards.

The judge looked up from her opened *Cal Jurist* tome. Blond, heavyset and apple cheeked, she was the little Dutch boy grown up, with a hundred extra pounds and a sex change operation. She let out a short hacking laugh to hide her discomfort at having a stranger in her sanctum.

"Hello, Charlie. Sit down, sit down."

I did as I was told. I wasn't about to contradict her.

"Yes, ma'am?"

"I want to talk to you about this case of yours, Valdez and Pimienta."

"Well, Judge, actually I'm just here for Valdez. Pimienta is represented by Clay Smith."

"I know that," she snapped, the faint semblance of bonhomie wiped from her voice. "But you and I both know that Pimienta won't shit unless Valdez tells him to, if you'll pardon my French."

"I can't really vouch for that, but that's the way it seems, yes."

"Well, let me tell you, I'm not going to have any scenes in my court during this trial, you understand?"

"I'm not really sure I know what you mean."

"I don't want any dramatics, posturing or pouting by anyone. I've already told Clay what I'm telling you, whatever my decision is, it sticks. I don't want grandstanding for the jury or restatements of positions I've already ruled on or any questions that might *accidentally*, underline that, disclose unwarranted information to the jury, understand? I want a clean record, no hung jury, no mistrials, no reversals. We start at the beginning and end at the end, like a nice train ride. Get on board, you understand?"

Chambers hacked again. I leaned back in my chair.

"Perfectly, Judge. But I'm not counsel for Valdez, he's going pro per. I'm only a P.I."

The judge didn't respond directly to that. She swung around in her chair and walked over to the Mr. Coffee atop the filing cabinet by the wall.

"Want some?" she asked.

"Black, please."

She handed me a mug decorated with more fuchsia hearts. I briefly considered whether the profusion of hearts was from regret or a bad conscience but couldn't decide. The judge brushed against the black robe hanging from a rack as she wobbled back to her desk, then dropped into her chair. Blowing at the steaming mug, she barreled her eyebrows at me with a mischievous smile.

"What's this I hear about Florida?"

"It's a big state, Judge. What was it you heard?"

Chambers took a sip of her coffee, her smile broadening her already wide cheeks.

"Something about you and a case in Dade County, when you were still practicing. You were censured, weren't you?"

"If the truth be known, I was suspended for a year by the bar. That's when I decided it would be best for me to start anew out here in California. But I was never found guilty of anything. Even if I had been, you know that convicted felons can take the bar and practice in California. However, I'm not practicing, so excuse me for saying this, but I don't see what you're getting at or what business it is of yours."

"Well, the way I hear it, and this is just hearsay, mind you, not admissible in court, I hear you were indicted but you had good friends in the State House. Good friends who got the indictment dropped."

"Funny, that's not the way I remember it."

"Well, be that as it may." She put down her mug, her suspicions confirmed. "I'm telling you all this because I feel your client needs the benefit of counsel."

Saved at last. But why was I starting to think of this case in terms of salvation and burning perdition?

"Does that mean you're denying his pro per status?"

Chambers leaned forward, her full weight on the elbow planted on the green blotter.

"Not for now. I may later. It depends on how effective his defense is. I don't want this trial to be a travesty, to have him screaming his head off for things that are not germane. That's why I want to make sure you advise him thoroughly on the case. I know this is unorthodox but I don't believe in standby counsel, waste of tax-payers' money. If the man wants to hang himself, well, let him. But I want him to do it the right way. The legal way. I think this is the only way to assure he has decent representation. He didn't want a public defender, he didn't want a private attorney and under our system of law, he has every right to be his own counsel. *If* he knows what he's doing. I'll be the judge of that." She caught herself at her unintended pun and chuckled. "Naturally, that's what they pay me for."

This was it.

"Sorry, Judge, I'm bowing out."

She jerked herself upright. "What do you mean?"

"I don't want to take this appointment."

"For what reason?"

"I can't even talk to the man, he's not been cooperative. Besides, it's a loser case."

"Since when does an investigator take on a case betting on its outcome? That is the most cavalier reply I've heard in my entire legal career. You will do it!"

"Judge, I don't have to."

"Yes, you do. I'm up for presiding judge in three months. If you don't take this case, I will personally make sure your name is off our list. And I'll talk to Orange and Ventura as well. You'll have to go back to hustling for every two-bit idiot that knocks at your door, a cheap dick, that's all you're going to be. I'll make sure everyone knows why. I'm also certain that the *Times* will be interested in talking to you about your background."

A brief silence, as I looked out the window, gray smog creeping in on little car chokes.

"Is this a threat?"

She took a deep breath, then let her smile peek through again. "No, Charlie. Call it judicial persuasion. Look, I like you. Matter of fact, I think you should take the bar and join the club again. I'm just requesting, as a personal favor, that you handle this case. Won't you?" She was grinning.

"Well, since you put it that way. I've always had a fondness for lost causes."

"All rise!"

The handful of attorneys, the shifty relatives of the prisoners and the wisecracking court personnel, ever present Styrofoam cups with oversweetened, creamed coffee in hand, rose under the funereal yellow light pushing through the dirty grid lighting panels overhead. Judge Chambers, at the far right of the court, exited from her chambers and stood next to the clerk, hands folded across her ample girth. Deputy Smith, with more seriousness than I had otherwise observed in him, intoned, the legal acolyte:

"Facing the flag of our nation and the principles for which it stands, Department 179 of the Los Angeles Superior Court is now in session, the Honorable Judge Constance Chambers presiding. Please have a seat and put away all your reading material."

With a murmur, the audience sat again on the wooden pews, as the attorneys and court staff sank into the upholstered green leather chairs and the judge climbed up the three padded steps to her bench.

She plunked herself down and looked warily at the stack of case files rising to eye level.

"Good morning," she said.

"Good morning," chimed back the court staff.

"Bodies are in, Your Honor," said Deputy Smith.

"Good! Let's do—" The judge was cut short by a small, carrot-haired attorney who leapt to his feet as though stung by a bee.

"Your Honor, I request priority. I'm due at a trial in Division 37 in five minutes."

Chambers looked the dapper little man up and down, his celery-colored silk suit, orange shirt and tie, a gold bracelet on each wrist, and a ruby pinkie ring that for all its garishness might have spelled out HOMO in caps.

"Mr. Veal, you will please wait until the court has handled certain other matters of the highest importance."

"But Your Honor, my trial!"

"What is it? A marijuana possession case, Counsel, or is it something bigger, a speeding ticket perhaps?"

But Veal, although bent, was no sissy.

"I am certain, Your Honor, that were you in my client's shoes, you would not think so lightly of the charges he faces now. I was ordered by Judge Reinholdt to be at Division 37 to start promptly in"—Veal glanced at his watch—"three minutes. Given, as you know, that it takes at least five minutes for the elevator to make its way down from the fifteenth floor . . ."

Chambers had taken all she could. She hammered her gavel. "Enough! Sit down, Mr. Veal. The court clerk will inform Judge Reinholdt of your delay. John, bring out Valdez and Pimienta."

"Yes, Judge."

Veal took a seat next to me. "Wait till the bar panel finds out about this," he muttered.

I heard Smith calling out the names inside lockup, then a brief moment of silence during which the bodies stepped out of the cell, the clanking of the sally port, the rattle of the keys, cuffs and chains. A second deputy came into the courtroom through the hallway doors and stationed himself in the last pew, arms crossed, staring at the wooden door by Deputy Smith's desk. The door swung open.

Pimienta shuffled out first, dressed in blue county overalls, his wrists bound by cuffs linked to a yellow plastic-covered chain wrapped around his midsection, so that his hands were permanently fixed to his sides, elbows akimbo. His legs were shackled with the same yellow chain, allowing him to take only a half step at a time, like a slave shuffling off to the auction block. His powerful arms rippled as he stood next to counsel table, unconsciously opening and closing his hands, as though to grab at the freedom that now was so out of reach. Looking around the court, he noticed me in the front row and smiled, nodding gently. I nodded back at him.

We heard a racket from inside the lockup; a tenor voice hollered in a Cuban accent, "Don't push me, man!"

Presently Ramón stumbled out, chains ajangle, almost falling on his face. He straightened up and turned back to stare behind him at a brawny deputy, who moved to grab hold of Ramón but stopped when he noticed the judge frowning at him. Deputy Smith sauntered in after his muscular backup and stood to the side of Ramón. Now Ramón, panting, took in the courtroom with suspicious eyes. It was the first time I'd seen him in person. He was taller and more filled out than the pictures I'd seen in his file, as though he'd spent the last few months working on his pecs instead of his defense. Whereas José was onyx black, Ramón was a light nutmeg color, a mulatto, really, in any other country except the United States.

Ramón let his hazel eyes rest on me, his gaze of cold analysis broken up by the buoyant Cuban smile of recognition. It was then I noticed the rivulet of blood dripping down his chin from his broken lip.

"What happened to this man, Deputy Smith?" asked Chambers.

Smith almost controlled a smirk. "Your Honor, Mr. Valdez was accidentally struck by the sally port as he stepped out of lockup."

Ramón looked at Smith with contempt.

"Is that true, Mr. Valdez?"

No reply.

"Is that true?"

Still no answer. Chambers turned to Burr.

"Does he need an interpreter?"

Burr shrugged, and checked the case file.

"*Necesita intérprete?*" asked the judge.

Ramón glanced up at Chambers, shook his head. "No, thank you, Madam Judge. I will be all right."

He may have had an accent, the glottal stops of American speech replaced by a liquid unemphasized flow that lilted at the end of the phrases, but he knew the stuff.

Drops of blood splattered on the table.

"What happened to you?"

Silence. Ramón took a deep breath then sighed, knowing that whatever minor victory he might obtain in court would be canceled a thousand times once back in jail.

"I tripped and hit myself."

"Somebody get this man a Kleenex. Are you badly hurt?"

This was an opening he could use and, as I was later to learn, Ramón never let a chance go unused.

"Just a little bit, Your Honor," he said through bloody teeth and lips. "But I request that the chains be taken out, Your Honor, so the accident won't happen again. It's hard to walk like this and prepare for one's defense when one is in chains like a wild animal."

Chambers shook her head in agreement. "You're probably right. Deputy Smith, please remove the shackles."

"Your Honor," said Smith, "these are safety precautions for the security of the court. The sheriff has determined these men are highly dangerous."

"Deputy, don't tell me what my job is. Remove those chains!"

"Yes, Judge."

Smith took out his key and with a few quick motions, freed Ramón, who stretched his arms with relief. The brawny deputy finally handed him a Kleenex.

"Thank you, Deputy," said Valdez.

"According to the file, he doesn't need an interpreter, Your Honor," said Burr, who'd finally found the right spot in his papers.

"That's very useful, Curtis. Might as well proceed to the arraignment. Are the People ready?"

Dick Williams, the deputy D.A. assigned to the court, stood, propping up his case files with the stump of his left hand. Tall, thin and black, the elegant Mr. Williams refused to speak about his deformity, leading people to wonder if his fingerless appendage was the result of a birth defect or if for once the long arm of the law had got caught in the wringer.

"Your Honor, I am substituting for the deputy who will be handling this case. This is just for arraignment purposes for today only. As you know, I'm being transferred to Santa Monica and my office still hasn't settled on the trial deputy."

"Very well. And the defense? Ready for your arraignment, Mr. Valdez?"

Now that he could move his his arms freely, Ramón slipped into his legal role with confidence.

"Ready."

"Well, then, let us proceed. No, hold it, where is counsel for Mr. Pimienta?"

"Here, Your Honor!"

Clay Smith rushed into court at that moment, briefcase flying, pinstripe Brioni suit creased by his extralegal exertions. A short Asian man dressed all in black followed, video camera on his shoulder. Behind him came a paunching, middle-aged soundman and last, almost as an afterthought, entered the reporter, a young man with curly hair.

"I brought some friends," said Clay, as he set his briefcase on the counsel table. The news crew moved to the side of the room and dutifully entered the vacant jury box.

"Not so fast," said Chambers. "Did you fellows file a request with the court?"

The reporter looked at the soundman, who shrugged and looked at the little Asian cameraman. The roly-poly shooter flashed an appeasing smile as he searched his pockets, then produced a much folded piece of paper.

"Yes, Your Honor, here it is." He proffered the paper to the judge.

"That's all right. Sometimes Department 100 doesn't forward them, that's all. You may record the arraignment but do not interrupt the proceedings."

"Of course not, Your Honor."

The cameraman snatched his tripod, unfolded the metal legs and set up his Sony, placing the document on a chair. From my vantage point I saw that the paper he'd waved was the takeout menu of the Hong Kong Seafood Restaurant in Monterey Park.

The courtroom doors swung open again and this time a battery of cameras and reporters stormed in, ready to take their battle stations.

"Ladies and gentlemen," said Chambers, "I'm only allowing one news crew in here, and that's these people from . . . what channel are you from?"

"Thirteen, Your Honor, KCOP," said the reporter in a high-pitched voice.

"Good. I like Hal Fishman. Well, you folks out there are going to have to ask these gentlemen for a copy of the tape, once the proceedings are done."

"Aw, but Your Honor . . ."

"Nothing doing. You folks leave the court right now with your cameras. Thank you very much. The People may arraign the defendants."

The KCOP news crew sat in the jury box, pleased to watch their competition smashed, even if the judge had pegged them with the wrong anchor.

The arraignment took less time than one would have expected, considering Ramón and José were each facing six counts of murder, six counts of kidnapping, two counts of robbery and twelve allegations on the use of a weapon. José took in the proceedings calmly, with the bland detachment of a child who sees grown-ups signing the closing papers on a house. Ramón, on the other hand, was all studious concentration, pulling out a small pair of round wire-rimmed glasses to read the closely typed pages of the information. He corrected the spelling of both his and José's name, then sonorously proclaimed, "Not guilty!"

At the end of the reading, almost as an afterthought, Williams said his office would be seeking capital punishment for the defendants, as the crimes occurred during special circumstances, murder during the commission of a robbery. Clay countered by saying his office would file moving papers opposing such action. When Chambers asked Valdez if he had intentions of joining the motion, Ramón said, "We concur with the District Attorney's office that if such a crime was to have been committed, it would be special circumstances. But since to oppose would reveal the defense, we do not object to such classification."

Clay looked at Valdez closely, puzzled by what he'd heard, then glanced at the judge and raised his hands in mock exasperation. Chambers also chose to ignore the comment, setting the pretrial conference for three weeks from that date. Ramón spoke again: "Your Honor, before departing for to date, I would like to give oral notice I will file"—here he checked a handwritten legal notepad page—"motions to quash and traverse, discovery, compliance, 1538.5 and others on the date of the pretrial conference and date setting."

"Any idea how many others?" asked Williams sardonically, "or will you just be picking them off the book as you turn the pages?"

"Mr. Williams, do not speak to counsel, excuse me, the pro per, please address the court," said Chambers. "Mr. Valdez will hand you proper written notice ten days before, no doubt. Right, Mr. Valdez?"

"Of course, Madam Judge."

"That will be all, then."

This time there was no waiting around while Ramón decided if he wanted to see me or not. He was already expecting me in a glass booth by the time I reached the interview room at County Jail.

He greeted me with a warm smile but with some diffidence in his manner, his body bent forward, arms on the table, a business associate discussing the finer points of policy with a marketing expert. Business as usual, nothing personal.

"How could you do it?" I asked him in a businesslike way.

His smile vanished but instead of the angry reply I expected, Ramón looked stunned, as though my question posed an intellectual challenge he could only barely discern.

"How did I do what?" he replied, in English.

"How could you kill these people?"

"*Oye*, man, I didn't do it."

"Then who did?"

He leaned back in the metal chair, tilting his head to get a better look at me.

"Pimienta did it. I was just there for the ride."

———

Clay did not take too kindly to the news. He raised his groomed red eyebrows and banged his phone, jarring the crystal vase with the black tulips. He had been about to dial reservations for us at a restaurant on Flower. Judging by his reaction, I assumed I no longer rated a free meal.

"That's his strategy now, isn't it. Well, you can tell him it's not going to fly. Jesus, the guy *is* flipped. Maybe you should have *him* analyzed. Do you realize I was about to cut a deal with the D.A. on this?"

I tried to keep up a disinterested appearance. Just because I couldn't even get the D.A.'s office to tell me who was going to be the deputy assigned to prosecute the case was no reason to get upset. Availability, after all, was one of the reasons why clients hired Manuel, Caesar, Brewer and Smith.

"What's the deal?"

"If they cop to the murder, they'll drop the robbery."

"That means no special circs."

"That's right. No gas. With any luck, they'll be out in, oh, about thirty years."

"That's one hell of a deal, Clay. I'm impressed."

For all his negotiating skills, Clay would have made a better prosecutor than a defense attorney—he believed a sense of humor was a sign of weakness. He took my comment seriously.

"I think it's a great deal. I figured the insanity plea wouldn't cut it so I jumped when they offered this. My guy's ready to take it if your guy will."

I shook my head no.

"So what would you do, wise guy? Keep fighting a case you know will buy them a one-way ticket to hell?"

"What makes you so sure?"

"Oh, come off it. They couldn't be in a worse jam if the cops had videotaped the whole thing. By the way, I see in the discovery papers that they do have a tape of the party."

"Negative," I said. "That is, they have it but it's no good."

"What do you mean? All jewelry stores are supposed to have a running tape of everything that happens inside."

"I checked it out. Our boys were either very lucky or very smart."

"How's that?"

"For one thing, the hidden camera all shops have, it wasn't working at Schnitzer's. They'd been meaning to fix it but never got around to dicking with it on time. Then something funny happened to the two you can see."

"I can't wait to find out."

"Cops aren't sure how but they suspect that during the standoff, when the electric was out, one of our boys got into the back room where the VCRs are kept. He apparently punched in the rewind button. So, when the power was turned back on, the cameras rewound then automatically kicked back on in record."

"That means everything was lost, recorded over?"

"Exactly. Irretrievable."

"Well, no matter. We still have six bodies, a witness that sees them going in, an arsenal of weapons, a bag full of jewels and stuff, another witness that heard everything from the back room, their fingerprints all over the place, I mean, it's incredible!"

"Hold it. We know they went in armed, that's true. But, and this is the all important but, we don't know who did the shooting. The police—well, the LAPD, in its infinite wisdom, neglected to get powder marks from our boys or prints from the weapons."

"Get off it."

"Moreover, the witness in the back just heard stuff, but as he himself says in the report, he couldn't make out who was speaking or what was said."

"Right. And the bag with the goodies? I suppose we can just toss that aside—who cares about a little thing like that."

"Hey, we don't know why those jewels were put in there or, for that matter, how the cases were broken. All we know is what these two guys tell us. Everybody else is dead. So, if Valdez says Pimienta did it and Pimienta says Valdez did it, then, who's to know?"

"Somebody did it, you got six fucking bodies, for Christ's sake."

"Maybe nobody did it."

"Right, so who killed these people then, God? Was it the wrath of God?"

"Maybe."

"Pleeeze! Get back to P.I. work, my man, you've been out of touch too long."

"You know, you could be right."

5

I had seen the house hundreds of times before, every time I would drive up the Sunset Crest from Beverly Hills to Brentwood. In a leafy neighborhood of mansions meant to soothe the insecurities of their owners, this one property was as unnerving as the spread owned by the Arabian prince who had painted in the pubic hairs of the statues on his grounds. But while that Muslim fantasy shocked by its prurience, this one offended by its perverted realism. Dozens of bronze, life-size statues of people from different walks of life were set all over the property, depicted in such breathless realism that if not for their metallic flesh, you would have thought them real. A policeman made of dirty copper stood amid the azaleas, writing a ticket to a bronzed cyclist; two stiff out-of-towners in bermudas pointed their cameras for a snapshot; a yellow Japanese gardener hoed the clematis and two brazen kids clambered the wall to peer into the grounds. I felt like one of those runts as the gate opened and I drove my dusty 944 onto the graveled driveway.

The original house had probably been one of those neo-Tudor Gothic homes that midwesterners by the thousands built when they came out West and made their first real money. Most of it had been torn down, by the looks of it. A low, long Modernist building, all angles and glass, had been superimposed on the remaining foundation, a child of Neutra riding astride Stanford White.

Massive strands of exotic flora surrounded the flagstone path down which the Guatemalan butler led me. Peeking out beneath bowers, in scattered clearings, stood more bronzes of people engaged in typically sylvan occupations—bird-watching, landscape painting, lovemaking.

The wife, wearing just a smidgen of a bikini bottom, was lying on a chaise longue on the sunny side of a free-form black-bottom pool. She was tall and angular, with the trapezoid back and firm deltoids of the woman who makes her gym her temple of beauty. Her long blond curls fell compliantly on her shoulders, afraid to disrupt the perfect symmetry she had planned. In repose, she had the gathered look of the hunter contemplating the next kill. A broad-shouldered, dark-haired man dived off the board at the far end of the pool in a perfectly acceptable swan dive for such a warm steamy day.

"Mr. Morell, *señora*," said the houseboy in a falsetto. Mrs. Schnitzer opened her eyes, looked in my direction, nodded.

"*Gracias*, Alberto." She stood up, slipped into a white terry bathrobe, shook my hand firmly and efficiently. "Thank you for coming," she said in the clipped tones of somewhere back East.

"Don't mention it, Mrs. Schnitzer. I'd like to offer my condolences."

We sat at an antique white wrought-iron round table set with four mesh chairs, the kind usually advertised in *Architectural Digest* against a backdrop of massive waves breaking on black boulders. Alberto set, discreetly and unheeded, a Villeroy and Boch teapot on the table. The broad-backed swimmer rhythmically cut his way through the water to the pool's edge, turned underwater and swam away doing a backstroke.

"Thank you. I miss Barry very much. He gave me everything I have." She focused her blue-gray eyes on me to reinforce her words. I couldn't help but glance momentarily at the swimmer. She smiled. "Tea? It's an old Indian trick. Hot tea will cool you off faster than cold liquids on a warm day. I can't stand air conditioning, plugs up my sinuses."

I shook my head no. As she poured herself a cup, her bathrobe opened, her right breast with its dark brown nipple peeking out. She put down her cup, readjusted her robe. Leaning back in her chair, she gazed at the swimmer. When she spoke, it was with a cold mixture of contempt and disdain.

"Delmer is just a fuck, Mr. Morell. He's a friend of the family who was always interested. It's hard being alone. At least I know exactly what Delmer wants. That's something I appreciate. You should always know what you want and never attempt to hide it. Even if you do, people will know."

Delmer now reached the far end of the pool, stopped and waved at Mrs. Schnitzer. She waved back, with a tepid smile. Delmer rose out of the pool in one swift motion, sauntered to a chaise where he picked up a towel and strolled away, drying his ample, hairy back.

"I understand, Mrs. Schnitzer. Frankness has its charm, although sometimes people wear it just a little too thin. So, tell me, why exactly did you want to see me?"

She turned, deliberately elusive. "I'm a friend of Clay Smith's former wife, Darlene. I understand you're going to be representing one of the men who killed my husband."

"I'm not his attorney, just his investigator."

"Yes, I heard that too. Well, Mr. Morell, I'll go straight to the point. I'm ready to give you a hundred thousand dollars if you drop the case. With that you should be able to start a new business for yourself. Or maybe you'd want to go back to Miami."

In the distance I heard the humming of an overhead plane, the only alien sound to breach this bower of hate.

"You realize what you're doing is totally illegal."

"Mr. Morell, please, let's don't play games. It's very simple. I want these men to die. I'd rather do it legally but I will resort to other means if I have to. If you're off the case, I know they will hang themselves."

"What makes you so confident of my ability to prevent that from happening?"

"I know what you're capable of doing if the mood strikes you. That's why I'm making you this offer, to put you in the mood."

She made a dramatic pause then gave me Tenuous Smile Number Five right out of the Strasberg method. Sunlight filtered through the four-carat diamond in her engagement ring. "I could be induced to add some fringe benefits."

I shook my head, flattered and amused. For all my success at covering my past, I might as well have taken out a commercial on the "Cosby" show.

"Thank you, Mrs. Schnitzer, but I don't shit where I eat."

Unperturbed, she took a sip of her tea. "Good. What about the body of the offer, then?"

"I'm curious. Why are you willing to offer so much money to get the man who set you free?"

She put down her cup, ran her fingers through her hair, took a breath. "You don't seem to believe me. I loved Barry very, very much. This is going to sound corny but he rescued me from myself. These are the facts. I'm a stockbroker who gets laid off in the crash of 'eighty-seven from the slump and a coke habit. I have a five hundred dollar a day habit. After I lose my job I become an escort, you know the type. A high-class hooker, to support my habit. Barry's wife had just died and one night he needs an escort to the opera. He is naive about these things and calls up our outfit from the listing in the phone book. I'm lucky enough to be sent out. He takes a liking to me, learns about my problem, gets me into the Betty Ford clinic. Finally he asks me to marry him. He doesn't lay a finger on me until our wedding night. Treats me like a lady throughout, as though I were some kind of divine creature. Then he gets killed like a dog. End of facts. There's no way I can repay Barry. I've tried by taking care of our investments and making sure the foundation he set up lasts long after I'm gone. But that's not enough. I want revenge, Mr. Morell. It's that simple. I want to make sure the bastards who got my Barry get what's due them, full amount, with penalties."

I stand up, regretfully. "You're going to have to hire another agent, Mrs. Schnitzer. I don't know if I'm going to stay with this case but even if I don't, it wouldn't be because of your money, even though it's very tempting. Believe it or not, I always try to do what I think is right. I won't be a whore, no matter what the price."

She was not at all upset by my refusal. She poured more tea into her cup, then lit a cigarette with a solid gold Cartier lighter.

"Some of us have no choice, Mr. Morell. I hope it never happens to you. Thank you for hearing me out."

"Thank you for the show. I'll be sure to give Clay a rave review. Four stars, steamy summer attraction. Nudity and moral ambiguity. Rated F for fool."

She finally snapped. "Get the fuck out of here."
"And foul language, too. I'm on my way."

I should have spotted them right away but my attention was still lagging behind at the Schnitzer mansion, flitting from subject to subject in the meditative trance Angelenos learn to develop to cope with driving long distances. I was tooling up Benedict Canyon Road, the winding two lanes that rise from behind the pink folly of the Beverly Hills Hotel, climbing a thousand feet over the range to wind up in the San Fernando Valley. I won't say that I was calling myself stupid for having turned down the hundred thousand but I certainly wasn't congratulating myself either. It's rough being honest in a place where everyone is pimping to get bought. After all, Los Angeles is the town of the deal. Do me a favor and I won't forget you, scratch my back and yours will get scratched in time too. Clay was ready to cut a deal, the D.A.'s office was willing to deal, hell, Ramón himself probably would make a deal if he only could. But I was tired of deals, of offers and shares and tenders, of this constant view of the world as a never ending board of futures. I wanted something solid, with value beyond the monetary, beyond the senses, eternal. That's when the front bumper of the Continental nudged, ever so deadly, my 944 almost down the cliffside.

My front wheels spun on the gravelly curb; the rear of the car skidded on the cracked blacktop. I braked, jerked the wheel away from the edge. I could see a thousand feet below in the fold of the ravine the shake roof of a rustic million-dollar home. The black behemoth in the rearview mirror was bearing down on me again, coming full tilt in my direction, aiming to tip me over and down. Through the Lincoln's tinted windshield I thought I saw two black men dressed in the white T-shirts and blue bandannas of the Crips gang. One of them held his hand out in front, his index and little finger extended with the others folded underneath, the horn of hexes. Why the hell do they want to kill me? I thought. I downshifted into second and accelerated out of the curve, thanking good Dr. Porsche for his brainchild. The Lincoln managed to bump into me right as I was whipping out into the straightaway. The force of the impact sent me careening down the middle of the road, almost making me lose control of the wheel. I managed to swerve back to my lane seconds before a Pioneer Bread delivery truck would have plowed into me. I wanted to blast out of there but the hairpin curves forced me to slow down. The Lincoln bore down on me again.

It seemed like a bad TV series. I was struck by the sudden absurd realization that in L.A., even killers watch too much television. But now there was no easy getaway. I saw my chance up ahead at the lookout point facing west, a three-car-wide strip of blacktop ringed by a low metal railing.

I barreled into the point, the Lincoln still on my tail. I slowed down as I entered, then stopped. Thinking I was about to run off, the Lincoln accelerated to hit me and tip me over once and for all. I watched them in my rearview mirror, the black tank hurtling down on me; then, at the last moment, when a nanosecond of hesitation would have given me a set of unwanted wings, I stepped on the accelerator and twisted the wheels left as far as I could, my 944 snapping to like a well-trained stallion, surging out of the tight corner. The clumsier Lincoln, seeing its prey fly away, attempted to stop and maneuver out, wheels spitting clouds of gravel and dust. Unfortunately for my pursuers, the momentum of the acceleration made their vehicle skid, whipping it around so that the tail struck the railing and broke through. The car teetered on the edge of the cliff, rear wheels spinning frantically in the air. Suddenly the driver's door was thrown open, but that only made the Lincoln lose its precarious balance and before the occupants could exit, the car tipped over and fell, slamming the side of the cliff as it tore through space. I could hear cries and shouts above the din of the impact as the car kissed an oak tree, then plunged into the ground, crushed into a ball of plastic, steel and bad design, exploding in a fiery blast. I stopped at the curb, got out of the car and retched my breakfast.

The investigating officer, a balding, jowly sergeant named Porras, said it might be a few days before they could sift through the wreckage and determine whose mangled, charred bodies lay inside. He sent me on my way after I told him I had no idea who or why. The worst part was that I wasn't lying. I really didn't have the slightest notion. None of the cases I'd worked with had turned out so badly that my client would want me dead and in the Valdez case, things were just too uncertain for anyone to want to do me in, at least not yet. I should have investigated more, I should have looked deeper into it, but I turned away. Random violence, life in the little city.

The week after the "accident" I went to visit Ramón. For some reason he felt like playing the *tártaro*, the Cuban high-life, the party animal who shucks and jives through storms, curses and death.

"*Qué pasa*, brother?" were his first words the moment I sat on the aluminum folding chair in the glass booth. "I heard you had a little car trouble a few days ago."

"Good news travels fast. How did you know?"

He seemed tempted to withhold his sources, but feeling tropically expansive, he waved his hands as though they had roller bearings at the wrist.

"A little bird. Jail bird, get it?"

"Bad joke."

"Pimienta, my man. His lawyer told him."

"You two are still talking?"

He smiled so wide his teeth were fangs. "Sure thing, man. We're like brothers."

"If that's the case, why do you want to pin it on him?"

"Hey, I love him, but that don't mean I'm going to die for him. He understands."

I shook my head at his display of fraternal affection and pulled out a notepad.

"As you wish. Let me tell you, your brother's attorney is not so hot about the idea of your claiming your *hermano* did it. Frankly, I don't know how you'll be able to swing it but then since I'm not your lawyer, I don't give a shit. You asked for me, guy, I will be your P.I. But that's it, *no más, entiendes?* I'm not going to tell you how to run your case and I'm not going to answer any legal questions. If you don't know what you're doing, that's fine by me too. Get yourself a lawyer, then. But I don't know anything about the law and even if I did once, believe me, I've forgotten it. So now, suppose you tell me who your witnesses are and what you want me to look into."

Thinking back on it I realize I probably laid it on a little too thick. But the outburst didn't seem to bother Ramón. He leaned back in the chair, so far back he balanced it on its hind legs, then he crossed his arms behind his head, staring at the oil-painted green ceiling.

"Groovy, brother. I understand where you're coming from. You need your space to get ahold of yourself and realize the consequences so that's fucking A. Let me tell you, there's a couple of people I want you to contact, for credibility purposes."

"Are you filing a discovery motion?"

He glanced down sardonically, eyebrow raised. "You said no legal questions."

"I have to know, to see if I have all the info I need."

The store Ramón sent me to was located in one of the trashier stretches of Temple Street, two miles west of the Hall of Justice. BOTÁNICA DEL SABIO INDIO read the sign out front with a picture of a high-cheekboned Cherokee in full headdress. A block away slovenly undercover cops slunk out of the Rampart police station, a piece of fifties flatcake architecture that was the only building in the neighborhood not graced with graffiti. Across the street, the All-American Dance Hall, a salsa music club where on any given night half the customers are narcs and half are nickel-and-dime dealers, had not yet opened its doors. That would be at sunset, at the same time that the fancy disco the next street over started its dinner run. Owned by a former bit actress in B movies, Baby Boîte had been set in the neighborhood for its automatic cachet, born out of the *nostalgie de la boue* of jaded Westsiders who think all life in Los Angeles ends east of Crenshaw Boulevard. At night three armed security guards patrolled the small parking lot around the white barred club, protecting the Ferraris, Mercedeses and Rollses from the inquisitive residents of the barrio, for whom a single hubcap from one of those luxury conveyances would be enough to support their family for a month. The area, like an old whore, was much more acceptable under the cover of darkness. Then the sodium streetlamps would leave pockets of gloom that hid the overflowing trash cans on the sidewalks, the empty bottles of Thunderbird in the gutter, the used cans of Castrol Oil and the occasional bloody syringe scattered among the dried-out weed of driveways and park-ways. But in the daytime the burned-out cottages, the racks of dollar fifty-nine T-shirts offered by anxious Salvadoran women outside discount stores, the soot-stained windows of the Guate-malan bakery in the pocket shopping mall, the poor struggling suppurating life of the neighborhood around the shop was impos-sible to ignore, a desperado grabbing you by the shoulders and shaking you, saying "Do something, do something!" I turned my back on it all and entered the shop.

Inside statuettes were everywhere, crowding the shelves, surging off counters, grouped on the floor and in racks by the door, pressing together like so many pilgrims on the way to Santiago. Ostensibly the images of saints—Saint Barbara, Saint Lazarus, Saint Peter—they stood in for spiritual powers far stronger than the followers of the Nazarene. The figurines were the Christian countenances of the old African deities—Shangó, Yemayá, Ochá—the hewers of lightning and carvers of the sun, who like so many immigrants took on a new name and identity upon reaching American shores. Stacked on the floor were prayer books for contacting these pow-erful beings, the orations to the Seven Powers, to Our Lady of the Waters, to the Great Saint Peter, who holds the keys to heaven. There were also potions in spray cans guaranteed to bring blessings, money, love, success, the constant desires of humanity, when sprayed in the moment of need. Displayed behind glass doors and piled up to the cobwebbed ceiling lay balms and ointments to draw back the straying lover, to ward off the evil eye, to make the cards sing and show aces and kings and queens upon command, to bring the almighty blessings of the Holy Trinity upon the suffering head. Finally, for those few who truly knew, glass jars of ingredients for the preparation of secret remedies and incantations, sarsaparilla root, dried and fresh green basil, camomile, raicilla, cascarilla, man-drake, musty roots and grainy powers, all promising an exit from the crowded slum where the Botanical Shop of the Wise Indian opened its doors for business every day from twelve to eight, Sun-days excepted.

The bearded young man behind the counter slurped a cup of ramen noodles as he watched the "$100,000 Pyramid" on a 27-inch Panasonic TV. At first, he ignored me but glared in my direction when I started sticking my fingers in the pile of pennies sprinkled with cigars in front of the figure of the beggar on crutches whose wounds are licked by dogs.

"How can I help you?" he said in the flat Cuban Spanish.

"I'm looking for Juan Alfonso."

He didn't reply but turned around to watch the program as Dick Clark nudged a failed contestant into remembering the word that could have earned him ten thousand dollars or a vacation in Acapulco, all expenses paid.

"Do you know where to find him?"

He didn't take his eyes off the screen. "He's out building a better life."

"Aren't we all."

"No, he's doing it, *chico*."

"Good. I hope he profits from it. Can I interrupt his prayers and see him anyhow?"

The young man turned and spoke through a mouthful of noodles.

"That's where he is. The community center. It's called A Better Life. It's on Mariposa and Rayo."

"He does construction too?"

"This store is just for the saints, not for lucre. We have our own construction company." He looked around, took out a card from a drawer, handed it over. "Indio Construction Company."

"We?"

"He's my father."

The tall, fair-skinned, blue-eyed man leading the construction crew did not look like any Indian I'd ever heard of. The only real Native Americans at the site were the wiry brown Salvadorans and Guatemalans who hustled around carrying buckets of paint, ladders, trowels and bags of plaster. But Juan Alfonso, the man Ramón had sent me to talk to as a possible character witness for the trial, was every inch the Spaniard's son.

"The Indian is my head," he said.

"Excuse me?"

He hollered at a worker for not mixing the right shade of yellow on a door frame, then turned to me again.

"My head, you know, my spiritual guide. I become his conduit during the session."

He walked away to scream at another worker for carrying an empty nail gun. I stood on the site, looking at the sky, the door frames, the slanted slab foundation and wondered why anyone would think being an investigator is glamorous work. I was contemplating the downside of being a lifeguard when Juan Alfonso returned.

"Did my son send you here? That son of a bitch should rot in jail. Tell him I'm not getting him out of any more tight spots. He can throw away his life for all I care."

"Your son?"

"C'mon, are we playing charades or you can't hear me? Didn't Roberto send you here so I'll bail him out? I told him he should stop using those rocks, they're going to kill him. Let him stay in the can awhile. Does he think we came to this country so he can be a wastrel, a drug addict and skirt chaser? I'm not helping him out, you tell him that, and that's that!"

"Sorry, I'm here about Ramón Valdez."

Juan Alfonso shifted gears, but barely.

"*Coño*, another son of a bitch. You know, for such a smiling man you sure bring a lot of bad memories. What does he want?"

"He wants to know if you'll testify for him at his trial."

"Are you crazy? You know what he did?"

"No, I don't."

"Look, it would take all day to tell you and I'm really busy here." He wrote down an address on his business card. "Come tonight to my house and we'll talk. I'll tell you all about that son of a bitch, may a bad stroke of lightning break him into little pieces."

He handed over the card. "You're his lawyer?"

"His investigator."

"That's good because you got a lot of investigating to do."

He paused, squinted at me. "So tell me, is it true women really go for detectives?"

"Only when they think you got something on them. Then you don't want to, it's too messy."

"Don't talk to me about messes. How do you think I got to have ten kids? Let me tell you, it's one headache after another. It's dad give me that, *papá* I need money for a new car, *papi* a new house, *viejo* get me of jail. Then they never thank you for anything. It's like pissing in the wind."

The second party that Ramón wanted me to find proved as elusive as a smogless day in August. Lucinda Luz, a relative with whom he'd stayed when coming to Los Angeles, no longer worked at the dressmaker's on Alvarado. The store manager, a square-faced old woman with a hairy wart on her forehead, said she'd pass on the message but she wasn't too hopeful she'd see her soon. As I understood it, Luz had sponsored Ramón and Pimienta when they'd been released from Atlanta, but judging from the address where she lived, a crowded noisy tenement with a large courtyard overrun with half-naked children and lines of laundry, their living quarters must have been as oppressively confining as their cells. Luz wasn't at the apartment, so I slipped my card under the door then went up to Enzo's for lunch.

My landlord was the owner of Baldocchi's, a landmark Italian restaurant in Los Feliz, the kind with singing waiters, oregano-reeking pastas and yes, straw-covered bottles dangling from an overhead trellis draped with dusty plastic ivy. Enzo was ecstatic to see me.

"Hi, Charlie, take a seat. Be with you shortly."

So I did, in front of a mural of a typical Italian port village with multicolored boats, umber buildings and harmoniously cresting hillsides in the background. Enzo sat at the table with a glass of Frascati.

"Problems, Charlie?" he said in the Tuscan dialect he learned on his nonna's knee.

"What else is new. How you doing?" My question opened the door to the Italian's favorite subject, himself. Enzo marched in with gusto.

"Business is great, I can't complain, but this help, *Dio Santo*, they're going to give me a heart attack! You know these people . . ." He jerked his head at the Mexican busboy collecting dishes. "They have no sense of pride in their work, they don't want to do something good. They just want to get it over with *e via*, let's go home. Like right now, look at Sergio."

We watched the maître d', a lantern-jawed fellow with a pencil-thin mustache and a golden earring in his left ear, flitting around a table with two blond, permed USC coeds.

"He should be keeping an eye on the house, not the girls. He mixes up reservations, forgets seating arrangements, it's murder. I don't know what to do."

"Why don't you get some Italians to come help you?"

Enzo looked indignantly at me. "Are you kidding? They wouldn't last a week here before some fancy West Side place would snatch them up."

"You mean only Mexicans will take the job?"

"Listen, I'm not prejudiced. Salvadorans, Guatemalans, Hondurans, I don't care where they're from, as long as they do the job. Maybe you know somebody?"

"If I hear of someone, I'll holler."

Juan Alfonso's house, in the hills around Silverlake, was a Craftsman from the early 1900s, two river-stone pillars in the porch propping up a sagging roofline. He'd planted a sea of flowers in his gated front yard, lilies, clematis, calendulas, poppies, bluebells, gladiolus, which grew in careful abandon around the cottage. I parked a half block away under a lemony-scented magnolia tree, its white blossoms littering the pavement. The water in the reservoir glowed a reddish orange from the dying rays of the dying sun as I walked up. An old woman with long gray locks glared out the window of the ramshackle house next door the moment I opened the gate to Juan Alfonso's, then she slammed her shutters closed. An owl hooted from a nearby rafter. The door was open. I walked through.

In the living room, two couples sat on a flowered print plastic-slipcovered sofa, watching "Jeopardy" on the rear-projection 40-inch TV set. Juan Alfonso's son sprawled in the middle of the couch, still munching, this time from a bowl of smoked almonds he held tightly in his lap. One of the couples, with the yellow complexion and low forehead of Nicaraguans, was dressed all in white, she in a form-fitting dress that emphasized her heavy breasts, he in a sheer guayabera, smoking a cigar. The other couple was mulatto, with the broad nose, narrow forehead and small eyes of Caribbean blacks. Dressed in nondescript clothes, the woman slowly massaged the man's shoulders. They all looked up as I walked in, eyeing me curiously but not unkindly.

I heard laughter just then and Juan Alfonso came out of the kitchen at the rear of the room, a can of Sprite in his hand. Next to him was a young woman, not much older than a girl, with cinnamon skin, high cheekbones and large hazel eyes, waves of dark hair with sun-bleached accents falling on her shoulders. She wore a mottled green and yellow dress, the colors of a fallen leaf. Tall and slender, she smiled as though she knew me, her eyes shining with equal portions of malice and innocence. Juan Alfonso shook my hand.

"*Chico, coño*, it was about time you got here. We were going to start without you."

"What are you doing?"

"I thought I told you. We're going to have a little conversation with the gods."

"Not a *bembé*?"

"That's what you white folks call it. We, the initiated people of color—for I may have a white skin but my soul is black as a runaway slave—we call it a conversation, a visit, if you like. You got questions, they got answers. Let me introduce you to someone I'm sure you want to know."

He turned with a satisfied grin to the girl.

"Lucinda, this is the man who came to see you, Charlie Morell."

She proffered her hand. It felt smooth and scented of jasmine. For the first time in years, my heart skipped a beat. Watch it, I thought.

"Did you get my card?"

No sooner had I said that than I realized the silliness of the question but she played along, a schoolgirl teasing the class dummy.

"What card?"

"You should have called me. I want to ask you some questions. When's a good time to talk?"

"We can talk right now." She looked at Juan Alfonso as though seeking guidance. He, perhaps thinking of his ten children, shrugged his shoulders and walked away.

"Remember Albertico is about to arrive," he said indifferently. He headed for the living room table, picked up a flower arrangement and walked down a creaky stairwell to the basement.

Lucinda grabbed my hand and steered me to a loveseat at the far corner of the room, where the blare of the TV was not as painful. She snuggled next to me in the chair, fine skin and solid bones, a dark doll smelling of perfume, playful and conspiratorial.

"Who's Albertico?" I said, as I pressed her slender hand in mine. I felt the compulsion of the gambler set loose at the green-felt heaven of the gaming table—one lucky roll is all I need and everything will be fine, Lord.

"Oh, he's the drum. Juan Alfonso doesn't like to start without the roll to Our Lady, Yemayá. He's always late."

Up close I realized that the impression of youth was due to demeanor and slimness, that the small net of fine lines around her eyes put her closer to thirty than twenty, as I had first thought. Her perfume struck me like a cresting wave, a lover's tug.

"What did you want to ask me? Ask me anything."

"Not so fast, maybe you won't like it. It's about Ramón Valdez and José Pimienta."

She wrinkled her nose as though detecting a foul smell. "Those two? Let me tell you, they've done nothing but give me trouble since I sponsored them. Maybe I should have let them stay in Atlanta."

"What kind of trouble?"

She paused, claimed back her hand. "What is it that you'll be doing for them exactly? You're not a cop, are you?"

"I'm their court-appointed investigator. Ramón was the one who said I should contact you. He thought you and Juan Alfonso could testify for him at the trial. About his character."

I had allayed her suspicions somewhat, but then her slender face flew into a welter of emotions. "And what character!" She paused. "That was incredible, what happened at the store. Those poor people. And that little girl. It's so sad. You know, it's all because of the rocks."

"What do you mean?"

"They were both OK, until they started doing rocks and then, forget it, you couldn't deal with them anymore."

"Rock cocaine?"

"Is there anything else? Listen, when they came out here I was working as a domestic for this Cuban lady in Pasadena. She had a big house, up there in the hills. It was beautiful, like something out of a sugar plantation. White walls, red tiles, *muy linda*. Well, she said she had space to put them out back in the guest house. She felt she had to do her part to help Cubans who fled, you know? So I guaranteed that Ramón was OK, that he learned his lesson. Well, it was all right for a while. You know how Ramón completely dominates José, it's something incredible, so whatever Ramón said, that was the law. Now this lady was impressed with Ramón. Did you know he has two university degrees from Cuba?"

"No, I didn't."

"Psychology and civil engineering. He speaks Russian and French, too. Well, so the old lady was really impressed and got him a job in a construction site. She and her husband—she's a widow, he got cancer—they made their money in construction in the fifties when they left the island and came here so she knew people. That's how Ramón met Juan Alfonso. They started making good money fixing up houses and bought a couple in Altadena. But then he took to smoking that stuff and went crazy. He lost the job and the houses he'd bought and then one of them, I don't know which one, broke into the main house and stole some jewelry and silver. The gardener saw them as they were running away. So the old lady had enough and threw them out and then fired me too, thinking I was in on it. That's when they really started going crazy."

"Did she ever report it to the police?"

"No. She figured it wouldn't be worth the trouble of going to court and testifying and all that. She said she'd learned her lesson."

"What was that?"

"Never trust a fellow Cuban again, especially a Marielito."

The rhythmic clapping of a tribal drum broke through the din of the TV and our conversation. I turned to the door and saw a small, heavyset black man with a small carved *batá* drum hanging from a golden string around his neck, grinning. Everybody in the room turned to him and a hubbub of voices rose in greeting.

"Albertico! About time you showed up!"

"Where have you been? You think the saints don't have better things to do?"

The drummer walked lightly into the house but lost his winning smile when he saw me sitting so close to Lucinda.

"Who is this one?" he asked her. She stood up, took his hand.

"Don't be jealous. This is Charlie, he's here about Ramón and José."

"Those two? Bad children of Oggún, they got what they deserved. What are you going to do for them?"

"I don't know that there's anything I can do."

"He's their detective," added Lucinda.

"Investigator," I said.

"He wants to talk to people who know them," she continued.

"I already talked to the police," said Albertico, his lips turning downward.

"Well, this is different, this is for them, not the police, *chico*," said Lucinda.

"We'll see," he said and turned his back to us. "Everybody ready?"

Juan Alfonso stuck his head out the stairwell.

"*Vamos, vamos!*" So Albertico led the way down the creaky steps, a drum major leading the spiritual parade.

The altar was set up at the northeast end of the basement, a converted rumpus room lined with fiberboard panels pretending to be fine wood, its floor covered with a shaggy orange carpet. A plastic bucket full of water freshened bunches of verbena, sweet basil and nightshade, the offerings to the image of Saint Lazarus. Next to the spurious saint disowned by the Catholic church stood a framed print of Saint Barbara, the crowned amazon with the sword who signifies the Dionysian god Shangó. At her feet, baskets of offerings—bananas, ears of corn, pine cones, bay leaves, a vase of red geraniums. Other figures crowded the altar—a large black doll dressed in calico, Saint George on his steed, the Holy Child of Atocha, a profusion of objects dedicated to the cult all illuminated by twelve votive candles, the only source of light in the cool damp room.

We sat in a semicircle of metal folding chairs facing the altar. Juan Alfonso produced a bottle of rum, which we passed from mouth to mouth, then he handed out cigars for all to smoke. Mine was an Old Dutch, brittle and dried out in its plastic wrapping. I contemplated walking out at that moment, leaving these benighted people the blessings of their rituals and returning some other time, when the light of day would allow for clear questions and forward answers—that is, as forward as any of these people were ever likely to be. But then I committed the gravest sin possible for an investigator, I became curious beyond the demands of the job.

It's a risky proposition to let your curiosity lead you into opening bundles that should be left tied, into wiping clean the glass and prying open the paint-encrusted doors just so you can take in the view. Still, I couldn't help it. I fooled myself into believing participating in the ritual would draw me closer to these people, that this way I would gain their trust and get the answers I was seeking. Never mind that essentially I had no questions worth asking and that any answer they could give me could only partially solve the puzzle of the two murderers who now sat deservedly in jail. It was more than that. I wanted to know about these people and by so doing to come to know myself as well, the pieces of myself that were scattered among these Caribbean exiles like the arms of a starfish, which, torn from the body, will grow a new center to replace the missing heart. I wanted to hear my own story, I suppose, and it was soon delivered to me, in drunken tones, amid banging of drums and clouds of rank smoke.

The little nondescript woman was the first to speak. Almost as if she wanted to be delivered of a particularly heavy load, just minutes after we sat and shared the rum and smoke, as the pounding of the drum by Albertico wove a tapestry of ancient sounds, her face began to contort itself into the strange faces children make when trying to scare their playmates. Eyebrows would fly, then swoop down, her mouth would open into the O of a fishmouth and close with lips bent inward, nostrils would flare and wiggle, facial muscles would twitch, then her whole body would sweat and shake as in a bout of malaria.

She put her hands forward, pushing some weight off and pumped her arms in the air. The others were expectant, looking on as Albertico pounded his drum to the echoing beats of the Yorubas. Lucinda was particularly ecstatic, her smile wide and her eyes flashing, high cheekbones sculpted by a dew of perspiration and the flush of excitement. The woman stood up and jerked spasmodically in the semicircle in front of the altar as the others clapped and shouted words of encouragement in an unknown language. Then the woman became rigid, stiff as a pole, and spun around like a top, whirling at higher and higher speeds until it seemed she floated off the ground, propelled into the air by the centrifugal force. She came down and hit the floor facedown with such noise I was certain she'd broken a bone, but then she turned and smiled and leaped up and shimmied, waving her arms.

"*Shangó, Shangó, aché, awó, aché,*" shouted Juan Alfonso.

"What is it?" I whispered to Lucinda.

"It's the god Shangó, that's his dance. He's come down tonight and he's going to speak."

The woman danced around the room, taking swigs from the bottle and spraying us with rum. She came up next to me and I was preparing myself for the spritzing when she swallowed, fixed round possessed eyes on me, then rolled them upward, so that only the white showed. She cackled with enormous untapped malice.

"Here you are, Carlitos," she said, in a voice ten times as masculine as I would have expected from her.

I didn't know what to say, whether by speaking I'd be addressing the woman or the so-called god in whose power she seemed to be. I kept quiet.

"Tell the people here why you've come, Carlitos, why you really came. Tell them who you are."

Albertico stopped pounding his drum. I could feel all their eyes on me.

"What do you mean? I am me, who else could I be?"

She cackled again. "Spoken just like the dissembler you are. I am Shangó and I know your artifice. You have come here for the key to spring *el negro* Ramón and that *marica* vermin, José, from the dungeon. Hah!"

She danced around a little, flailing her arms in the air, shouted, "The music, the music!"

Albertico pounded his drum again. I felt oppressively hot and cold at the same time, my breath coming out in sharp gasps, as though I were running up a very steep and dangerous hill.

She planted herself in front of me, her hands on her waist.

"Don't you know they are the followers of my enemy, Oggún? That lame blacksmith, hah, I fucked his wife up the ass. But you, you want to help those two. How can you help them, Carlitos, when you can't help yourself?"

Words would not come out, they stuck to the ceiling of my mouth.

"Don't be shy, Carlitos. Tell these people where you're from!"

I snapped, stood up. "You're full of shit, you little tramp, you stupid people with your stupid dancing, thinking you can fool everybody. You can't fool me! You're just little monkeys dreaming of big things, wishing you were somebody else instead of who you are."

The woman smiled knowingly. "Then why are you ashamed, Carlitos?"

"Ashamed of what? Oh, what's the use, I refuse to argue with a madwoman."

I took one step; then her words stopped me. She pressed her face against mine. "Tell them how you were born in Havana. Tell them how ashamed you are of being Cuban. Tell them how you killed your father."

I looked with disgust at the dark, drooling, contorted face in front of me, a mocking, leering chimp. I heaved her to the floor and raced out of the room, the woman's cackling following me up the creaky stairs, into the now moonlit night outside the house. I ran to my car, collapsed on the hood. I cried.

6

"**C**ome quick! She's having a heart attack!"

Doreen, the substitute clerk, stomped her feet like a child whose toy has been snatched away. Deputy Smith, a baby D.A. and I rushed to the back.

Judge Chambers was laid out flat on the floor, barely moving. Her usually flushed face was sheer white, her breath shallow and spasmodic. A green suede pump, shaken loose, lay upturned on the Tabriz Persian rug. For some reason I told myself to remind the judge her shoe's heel cap needed replacing.

Bill knelt down by the judge and took her pulse, right underneath her ear. He shook his head.

"She said she thought she had heartburn, then she just keeled over!" shrieked Doreen, hovering over us. I looked up and saw the baby D.A., just two months out of law school, playing nervously with a lock of her curly black hair.

"Hey, Charlie, I need you!" said Bill.

Don't let it happen again, Charlie, pay attention, Don't slip. One life gone is enough.

"Call an ambulance, don't just stand there!" I hollered. On my knees, I put my ear to her nose and tried to detect her breath. None. I looked at Bill, shook my head.

"OK, together," he said.

I nodded. I'd been through this routine before. He put both hands on the judge's chest and pumped while I opened her mouth, moved her tongue out of the windpipe, pinched her nose and started to breathe air into her lungs. Her thin lips felt cold and squishy, like a plastic doll's.

The minutes dragged on without response. Other people came into the room, but none was the white-coated attendant who could relieve me of my painful duty. For a moment I was back in Miami and the figure into whose lips I was breathing life, too little too late, was my father Adriano, rigid and cold.

The judge jerked, gave a short moan and vomited into my mouth. I spit out the green and white swill, my stomach turning.

"That's good, she's alive!" said Bill.

With my tie I wiped her mouth and continued blowing, my tongue tasting the acid bile of life.

Bill took her pulse again.

"It's pumping." he said. "Don't stop now!"

I breathed in and out rhythmically. She felt warmer, little pinheads of blood returning to her alabaster skin. She opened her washed-out blue eyes once, looked bluntly at me, then closed them again. Suddenly:

"Move it, move it!"

A black man in white shirt and black pants shoved me out of the way, placed an oxygen mask on her face. The second paramedic jostled Bill away, ripped the judge's silk blouse, unhooked her small cloth bra and placed two fibrillators over her tiny left breast. The noise rang out like a gunshot in the room. The paramedic looked at his colleague, who nodded. The fibrillator jolted the judge back to life, her body arching on the beige carpeted floor.

"She OK now, she's back," said the man with the oxygen mask, who was taking her pulse with an instrument attached to his wrist.

"Let's go!"

The two young men put her on a gurney and broke their way through the crowd of bailiffs, attorneys and clerks who had witnessed the unexpected brush with death.

"Good job, Charlie," said Bill, pumping my hand.

I went to the bathroom to rinse my mouth. I looked out the window at the swirling smog of Civic Center garlanding poisonous wreaths on the clock tower of the *Times* building across Mirror Square. I heard my sister calling out for me that day in Kendall, by the canal where the alligator had once crawled up. *"Carlitos, Carlitos, come, come!"*

■

I was sixteen then, with the cruelty that teenagers possess in equal measure to their altruism. My sister Celia was crying, her thirteen-year-old's garish makeup streaked by the frightened tears running down her chubby cheeks.

"What's wrong?" I asked, kicking on my motorbike, the little Peugeot I had to buy with my own money because my father would not get it for me.

"Papá is dying, he was talking on the phone and he had a fit! Mamá is out visiting Aunt Julia and I don't know what to do!"

I got on my bike, revved the engine under the heartless Dade County sun. The air smelled of weeds and brine. I looked up. Two lofty clouds held up a turreted castle in the sky.

"I'll go get some help," I said and drove away.

"What should I do?" screamed Celia.

"Think of something! Use your brain, for a change."

To this day I don't remember the reason why I was upset at my father, what minor argument or quarrel we'd had in the continuing warfare we'd engaged in since I was thirteen. From the time we'd come from Havana when I was ten, our life had been a constant butting of heads, my mother and my sister acting as soothing and unavailing intermediaries. Perhaps it was all due to our opposite reactions to coming to the United States, the predictable clash between old exiles who never forget the glory of the life stolen from them, and young immigrants who must urgently attend to the fleeting pleasures of the moment before they become shadows in someone else's dream.

Bobby Darin, Sandra Dee, the Beatles, John F. Kennedy, long hair, all were abominations to someone who longed day and night for his triumphant return to the land of dominoes, cigars and *guarachas*. I was not the son he'd expected, the fearless freedom fighter who with youthful vigor would carry aloft the banner of democracy and bring liberty to the tyrannized land. He was not the father I wanted, a calm provider who would take us to Little League games, teach us to swim and drive and give me pointers on how to pick up girls. Sadly, we were distanced from each other by our failure to live up to the vacuities expected of us. He didn't see I was a confused, driftless kid with too much intelligence and too little cunning. I didn't realize he was a burdened man, working at a gas station and speaking Spanish in a land where being a spic was only a shade better than being a nigger, no matter how white your skin or blue your eyes. We were "Our Cuban brothers with their vivacious personality, sparkling eyes and love of song and dance who yearn for the day when their homeland will again be free from Communist oppression." We were a cause, not a people. He adopted that cause as his own and lived it. I turned my back on it, knowing that way lay sterility and death. I had no past to speak of, my life a vista of ever expanding horizons. My father felt he had no future to claim, that the very signs and markers where he lived were mocking reminders of his foreignness, of his self-willed but no less terrible alienation.

I wasn't gone long, maybe three or four minutes, enough to realize that I had to face the situation and not just run away, that even if I made it to the hospital a couple of miles down the road, that Papá could be dead by the time the ambulance finally arrived. I turned around in midtraffic and headed back.

When I came in Celia was weeping over his still body. I look back now and I cannot understand the cold rage that possessed me then, my total disregard for other people's feelings. I saw them as weaknesses and, wrathful Savonarola, took their plight to be the result of their own incapacity to measure up to the demanding standards of life.

"Quit bawling," I said. "Have you called anyone?"

"I tried to reach Aunt Julia but the line is busy. What do we do?"

Her face was contorted by a grieving love I'd never known she felt. I grabbed the phone and called the operator. The woman who answered had been a nurse's assistant in the Second World War and after telling another worker to send an ambulance, she gave me detailed instructions on how to breathe life into my father. As I put my lips against his, I felt like the Iscariot taking leave of the Master and trembled, finally, at the monstrosity of my departure.

His prickly beard felt like a wire brush on my chin. He had come to when the ambulance arrived. His bloodshot blue eyes were fixed on me as they lifted him onto the stretcher. He knew.

"He'll be OK, right, Charlie?" asked Celia.

"Sure. Of course. Everybody has heart attacks. He's OK, you'll see."

Wires sprouted from my father's body, tentacles of pressing life, when I saw him in his hospital room. Celia, uncertain whether to cheer or cry, babbled away the story with a smile through a cascade of tears.

"*Dale un beso a tu padre*," said Mamá, stern faced and accusatory, a small woman with white streaks in her hair steeling herself for the years ahead. Her sheltered life as the daughter of a cattle rancher in Camagüey province must have seemed as remote to her at that moment as the silent "Gunsmoke" episode playing on the overhead TV.

I kissed my father as my mother told me.

"Hi, Dad," I said, blankly. He blinked hard several times, the muscles in his jaw knotting from the effort to speak. I turned to Mamá.

"What's wrong with him?"

"*Lo que has hecho, mi hijo*," she said, sighing. As always, we spoke in two languages, two worlds, neither of us admitting the existence of the other although understanding its every element. Words as barriers, words as weapons.

"I didn't do anything," I replied. My denial fell flat in the room, my mother sinking her cold gaze into my frightened face, thinking where did this strange creature who calls himself my son come from.

"You have done nothing," she repeated in Spanish.

At least the doctors were more charitable than my mother. If not for my belated efforts, Papá would have definitely died. But the lack of oxygen in the early stages—those few minutes when I capered in my motorscooter in the sun-baked streets in search of a way out—had taken their toll. The stroke left Dad paralyzed on the left side and spastic on the right, his mental faculties apparently as acute as before but now encased in a carcass that drooled uncontrollably and only occasionally controlled its sphincter.

For the next two years the smell of human waste permeated my life. If at first Celia and I were heartbroken, disturbed by the tragedy, comforting Mamá and even taking turns helping her change the bedsheets, empty the pan, wheel the foul body out to the sunshine, after a while we turned against this servitude, this devotion to a wasting memory. Papá's insurance refused to cover anything but the hospital bills, so Mamá hired a lawyer to sue for the rest of the benefits. With little to live on, first Mamá sold the gas station, then the house and we moved back to the Cuban ghetto around S.W. Eighth Street, stucco boxes teeming with refugees lagging in the race for prosperity in the alien land.

I had never been much of a student before but now I became a prize pupil, making the honor roll and ultimately winning a scholarship to Brown University. In due time I went to law school and found my way out of the barrio for good. It would be good and heroic to say I turned to my books in an attempt to right the injustices perpetrated, that I became a lawyer so as to someday champion the cause of my family and wreak havoc on those who had assailed us and brought us to a lesser state. But these are the words that a son of my father would use. Not I. I am no hero or avenging angel. In my hands, the sword of righteousness would dwindle to a pallid sparkler. Books and learning were simply avenues to the main chance I knew would come by and by. If I picked law it was because I felt at a preconscious level that it would be easier to hide behind the pillars of justice than in any other profession. I wouldn't have to reveal myself, tear open my shirt to bare the gaping wound. I knew I was cold, repressed, dominating, calculating, manipulative, unprincipled, with no clear concept of right or wrong save what I could get away with. Yet I also, like all people, wanted the acclaim of my contemporaries, and what better way than to bask in the prestige attached to the foremost profession of our legalistic society? At one point I even toyed with the prospect of elevating my incompetence—personal, not professional, for I rarely lost a case—to the state and national level, to run for office and join the cabal of repressed, approval-seeking attorneys who have been running the country since its foundation, the first Cuban to blazon the American political firmament.

Celia, though, did not have a major fiend to whom to surrender. Instead she gave herself to a succession of minor Lucifers named Tony, Joey and Chulo, who only succeeded in getting Celia pregnant and in trouble in school (in this, as in all other things, it pays to go all the way). First she started cutting classes to go to glue-sniffing parties where sessions of spin the bottle would wind up in hurried fucking in closets, bathrooms and rooftops. Then she started not going to school altogether, spending her time with her gang, her *pandilla* of misfits at Madison Junior High who pined for the freedom that turning sixteen and leaving school would mean. Three times I had to take her to the abortionist in Sweetwater, the old Cuban Jew who had known Emma Goldman when she was exiled from the U.S. and lectured in South America on women's rights. Abortion was still illegal and each time Celia would swear, with clenched fist and drawn face, that she would never get knocked up again, only to fall for yet another pair of pouty lips and slim hips a few months down the line.

Celia's absences from school made the rubicund face of the truant officer, Mr. Upham, a familiar sight in our family, always dropping by and counseling with Mamá for the never-to-be-reached solution. Mamá would speak to her and I would speak to her but nothing short of a chastity belt would have worked. Me she ignored, ordering me to mind my own business. But with Mamá Celia would burst forth in a tirade of accusations, all centering on the sordidness of our lives, our hand-to-mouth existence, the oppressive heat and confining futures of Little Havana, the shit-smeared monster who sat in his wheelchair and wouldn't just die so we could finally collect the rest of the insurance. Mamá would call Celia a whore, a lost soul, a daughter of the devil, while Celia would call her a harridan and cold-hearted bitch, who wouldn't even let her have her *quince-añera* party because we had no money.

"How am I supposed to tell the world I've become a woman if I can't have my *quinceañera*?"

"Don't play the virgin with me! With all the cocks that get into you, everyone knows you're a woman—you're everybody's woman, nothing but a streetwalker, spreading your legs for a nickel!"

"At least I enjoy it, which is more than you ever did with that pile of refuse in that wheelchair!"

"I forbid you to talk about your father that way!"

"So stop me if you can, then! If it was up to me I'd wheel him out on Sunday so the garbage man would take him away! But with our luck, he'd probably leave him on the sidewalk!"

(Throughout all this Papá would follow the argument from his wheelchair with terrified blue eyes, which for years had been progressively drained of their color to the faint blue of spoiled milk, trying gallantly to move his mouth to articulate a sound but succeeding only in drooling and moving his bowels in agitation.)

These tirades would end up with Celia and Mamá crying in each other's arms, asking themselves why God had seen fit to punish them and forgiving each other for their respective insults. They would seal their pledge by washing my father, mother and daughter sponging off the waste they had caused, Papá happy to be in his bubble bath, then powdered and changed, a fifty-year-old baby with a gray beard. Mamá would wheel Papá back to their bedroom, Papá to sleep and Mamá to pray her rosary, while Celia would wait until late in the evening, once the only light in the house was the votive candle to the Virgin of Covadonga, to sneak out and meet with her latest boyfriend and the cycle would start its fetid turn again.

Once I went away to college, I didn't return for two years. When I finally came back, I found Papá had suffered another stroke and all he could do now was to roll his eyes and chew his food. Mamá hugged me when I dropped my bag in the living room, which seemed smaller and more stifling than I recalled.

"You've grown," she said in Spanish. "I'll bet you grow up to be as tall as my father. You know we are the descendants of the Huanches, the original inhabitants of the Canaries. They were all like you, tall and blond. *Que bonito, mi hijo.*"

"Thanks, mom," I said, embarrassed by her unusual outburst. "And Celia?"

Her mouth turned awry, as though she'd bit into a green guava. *"Por ahí anda, puteando."*

"What do you mean, she's whoring?"

"I mean to say that's what she does now, the little slut," answered my mother in Spanish that sounded straight out of the Castilian plain. "She left school and is working as a waitress in a nightclub. She makes more money in one night than your father made in one week and she spends it all. See, come here."

She took me by the hand and led me to Celia's closet, full of gossamer gowns and silk blouses, with dozens of pairs of shoes and boots, and even mink and sable furs, shedding their expensive hairs on the warm tiled floor.

"Look at this! Tell me, how can an honest working girl earn enough for this? She's a *puta*, that's what she's become, God help her soul."

I sometimes wish Mamá had been right and Celia had been a streetwalker. Instead she had fallen for the biggest pimp of the Cuban people, after politics—drugs. She made no effort to hide it from me, thinking as a member of her generation I would under-stand and approve. The first thing she did once we were together was close the door and whip out the little hand-tooled leather case with the small mirror, straw, two full vials and silver-plated razor blade. She spread the coke and chopped it into lines with the same concentration she'd once shown when baking lemon meringue pies.

"What do you think you're doing with that?" I asked.

"What does it look like, stupid?" She snorted up the lines greed-ily, then dipped her finger in the glass of water and let the drops fall into her nostrils. "I'm trying to forget all about this. God, I hate this place."

She sat on the edge of the bed, rocking back and forth, in con-templation. "Do you remember our garden back in Havana, Char-lie? I've been thinking about it a lot lately. I don't know why. Remember how Ignacio grew anemones and tulips? Everybody said tulips couldn't grow in Cuba, but he did it. I asked him once and he told me the secret—he put the bulbs in the refrigerator. We had the best garden in the island, didn't we? Sometimes at night I start remembering how I used to run and hide under the bushes, by the trellis or near the well. It's the best way to fall asleep. I have such wonderful dreams. Then I wake up, and everything is worse off. It would be better if we forgot, if we could just wipe that whole fucking stupid island off our fucking minds." She paused, inhaled from her cigarette, flicked the ashes away. "God, I hate this place."

It was an August afternoon. Dad slept a siesta, Mamá was in church. A truck thundered down the street, rattling the windows. The hot humid haze hung in the air like words never said, like regret and infinity.

"Why don't you go back to school?"

"Not everyone can be smart like you, Charlie. Some of us have to suffer with our limited minds. I'm doing what's best for me, just like you did what's best for you."

"Working in a nightclub is the answer?"

She laughed, the drug now plucking the string of happiness.

"That's what she thinks. What am I going to tell her, that I sell lady for a living?"

"Pardon?"

She snorted contemptuously. Her round brown eyes had become deep and fulgent. She fluffed the streaked tips of her hair.

"Don't be so naive. Anyhow, I'm not intending to stay here long. I'm going to Colombia for a while. Tony wants me to meet his family."

"You're going to get married, then."

She laughed again. "You *are* young, even if you're older than me. This is strictly business, you know. I mean, OK, so we've been doing some serenading too but that's only because he's so cute. You know, you should talk to him. He says his people would pick up the cost of your schooling, if you were to work for them later."

I got up abruptly, disgusted. "I don't want to know about this."

"Go ahead, leave," she hollered suddenly. "Run away, just like you always do, that's your specialty. Carlos Morell, Ph.D. in escape! You and Houdini!"

"I don't have to take this either."

I walked out of the bedroom, through the living room, down the stairs and into the street. She ran after me.

"Yes, you do have to take this, because it's your fault, Charlie, you brought us here. It was you who didn't know what to do, it was you who made our life a piece of shit, it was all your fault, your fault!"

I ran away down the street, people turning from their shopping, the old men in the domino tables looking up from their hands, the couples at the coffee stand at the corner sipping their *cafecito*, staring at me.

"Come back here, *maricón*! Don't be such a coward! Take it like a man! You don't like it when I sing you the truths, do you? Well, I won't stop, come back!"

I crossed the street, dodging traffic, across the parking lot of the welfare office and into the schoolyard, losing myself in the crowd. What was the use of arguing? She had the freedom of resentment, blame laid elsewhere, the soul burning with indignation. I carried the weight of responsibility, the hurting knowledge of sin. I would have traded places with her in a second. But still, I didn't want to know about it, I didn't want to hear about it, I didn't want to think about it. I'd dug a hole and buried the child. I didn't want it back.

Celia and I avoided each other after that, and never mentioned the incident again. A few weeks later I left for Jacksonville, to make some money picking oranges before school started. Celia moved to Colombia that year, just a few months shy of her eighteenth birthday. Technically she was a minor and Mamá made noises about having her deported back but her threats were useless. The next time I visited Miami, Mamá had turned over the living room to the many saints of the Catholic church and like the priestess of a forgotten Punic cult, wore only black among her images. She went to Mass twice a day and said the rosary after each meal sitting at the window watching the traffic go by, fingering the holy beads as she rocked herself in her cane and mahogany rocking chair, mechanically reciting the paeans of praise to the Virgin: "*Santa María, Madre de Dios, ruega por nosotros, pecadores, ahora y en la hora de nuestra muerte.*"

I, bored by the torpor of the room, drowsy from the heat and the rice and beans of the meal, would close my eyes and imagine her as she once was, when we were still in Havana and Papá ran the largest oil refinery in the country and we lived in our own gray-walled mansion in the Vedado and Mamá headed a dozen charitable ladies' associations and we had two maids, a butler, a gardener, a cook and a nanny in a paradise that I was certain to inherit as surely as the sun rises, the sugarcane grows and Uncle Sam lives. But it was all right. In fact, this longing for lives never lived led me to a kind of peace, knowing that our finely crafted plans for the future had been dashed by an indifferent maelstrom of politics and violence. (Was there ever much difference between the two in Cuba?) Back in Havana I would have become what the Communists call a social parasite, that is to say, a reduced tropical version of a Mellon or a Du Pont, wasting my days on women, Mercedes-Benzes and teak-planked sailboats, grasping the wheels of power as effortlessly as a lesser man spins the face of a combination lock. On those nights when the swampy mustiness of Miami would plug my sinuses and the din of passing cars and Spanish curses would reach my ears in my family's tenement in Little Havana, I would imagine myself in the real Havana, the soaring old white and gray city ninety miles away. I, dressed in a white linen suit, would lie in a gutter with my back riddled by a dozen bullets from a revolutionary gunman, my blood draining and mixing with the street debris, the dead leaves, the cigarette wrappers, the spit and black gunk floating on my mortal crimson rivulet spiraling down a drain and somehow I would be happy.

The final chime of fate in this story sounded when I was in my last year of law school and had returned home for one of those brief periods of torture called vacation. Celia had moved back from Medellín, her brief marriage to Tony having collapsed when she decided Colombians, her husband most prominent among them, had to be the filthiest people on earth, no matter what social class they came from. Never one to suffer from the absence of male companionship, Celia had taken up with Adolfo, also known as Pipo, the Nissan dealer who had sold her the Silver Z Tony bought her as a wedding present.

I tried living at home but I no longer had the patience (or the stamina) to put up with my mother's constant praying and the decomposing smell of my father. With money I had saved from clerking at a law firm in Newport the previous year, I rented a tiny studio in Fort Lauderdale. A schoolmate got me a job at Rickey's Bar, which featured wet T-shirt contests every weekend for the price of a warm stein of pisswater beer. I visited home as little as possible and dreamed about my family every night. I don't know what dreams Celia had, if any, about the wicked joke luck had played on us.

Yet the situation, sordid as it might have appeared, had actually improved. The insurance company had settled the case and Mamá had enough money to hire an occasional nurse to relieve her of her duties. Papá's condition had stabilized, so that he only fouled himself involuntarily once a day and his drooling no longer came in torrents. He could even mutter words, words that were not essential to his life but that must have had some other meaning besides the obvious, words like bread, milk, water and liberty.

It was a Saturday afternoon. I was on stage at Rickey's, emceeing one of the wet T-shirt contests, my eye set on a little redhead named Donna with perfect pear-shaped breasts when I got the call. As the contestants paraded in their bikini bottoms, drenched tops clinging without mercy to their torsos, I grabbed the phone at the bar.

"What the fuck is it?" I barked over the persistent beat of the latest single of the Doobie Brothers.

"Charlie, Charlie, it's happening again!" said a woman's voice.

"Celia? What the hell's going on? I'm at work!" I shouted over the din. Donna, waiting for me to introduce her onstage, doused herself with a pitcher of water, then gave me the eye.

"It's Papá, Charlie. He's dying."

The same web of wires streaming out of my father, the same aggrieved faces, the smell of disinfectant, a cloudy view of the bay from a hospital window. Only the floor is different from the one years before.

"I didn't know, how was I supposed to know he was allergic to shrimp?" protests my aunt Julia in the waiting room, her authority hanging from her words like the wattles from her neck.

"I made him some *frituras*, the fritters everybody likes. I never heard of such a thing. He eats them fine, no problem."

She stops, looks at all of us in the room, Celia, my cousin Alvaro and his wife Magdalena, my uncle Rafael, my father's compadre

Virgilio, a succession of faces that keep popping in and out, grieving choruses of the day. I feel the grit of the sand in my loafers from driving straight from the beach to the hospital. I force my attention to her words.

"Then, five minutes later, he starts making these noises, uggh, uggh, aggh, aggh, like he's choking, his face turns red, he can't breathe. I don't know what to do. I try to call everybody and I can't get in touch with anyone. So I called the ambulance."

All day and all night Julia repeats the story to the new arrivals, the old mariner reciting the tale of familial woe, a public confession for absolution from the gathered, who all nod and say yes the poor thing what could she do they would have done likewise and there is no blame, that is just destiny, God's way for which man has no name.

Celia and I step down the hall for a cigarette, watching the islands in Biscayne Bay shimmer in the late afternoon heat.

"Do you hate her?" asks Celia.

"How could I? It's all for the best."

She takes a drag from her Marlboro. She looks thinner yet harder, as though the pounds shed have revealed the thin reed of steel at the core. Her brown eyes, now a shade of hazel from fatigue, seem enormous in her hollow face.

"The doctor says he won't recover. I don't know. Mamá's been praying at the chapel all day. She's convinced there's going to be a miracle. I don't believe in miracles anymore."

Celia laughs nervously. "I stopped believing when I caught Papá putting the gifts from the Three Kings in the box full of straw we hid under the bed. Remember?"

"It was shredded newspaper."

"That's another problem with you. No imagination."

We both smile.

It's four in the morning and all the guests are gone. Celia is asleep in the waiting room outside the emergency ward, Mamá is still, like the nun she once dreamed of being, on her knees in prayer at the hospital chapel. No one is stirring, the entire hospital seems shut down, off duty, on vacation. The faded red carpet lies before me like a well-trod path to a ravine of spent hopes. The double doors of the ward open automatically. I enter, pass the nurses' station. Empty. The patients, wrapped like blood-stained mummies, lie silently in their beds, drugged into sleep.

My father is hooked to a respirator. Awake. His blue eyes flutter in recognition when I approach. We are the only two souls awake at that moment, staring at each other across the divide of life and culture. For a brief, vertiginous moment I become him and I see myself standing at the foot of the bed, sun-bleached blond hair, stained shorts, youth plucked from the shores. I see myself and I know what he wants. Father moves his lips, attempting speech. I come near, to decipher his meaning. His eyes dart to the side, frantically alert, more alive than any time since we left Havana, his eagerness to speak painful to behold. I shake my head. He moves his lips and somehow a breath comes out, a breath that wants to be a word. I shake my head again. Straining, he tries once more, the breath this time flowing through the vocal cords, ringing the word so beloved of our people, of the Spanish race, the eternal partner of sin.

" '*uerte*," he utters, then the lips finally obey after all these years and in confluence with the larynx and the soul the beautiful, splendid word flowers.

"*Muerte*."

Again he darts his eyes to the side. I look at him hard, he nods slowly. There is no doubt. I kiss him once then I move to the respirator. I don't know what switch to pull. He glares at one by the bed, a foot away from his hand. I turn it off. Father automatically shudders as the air is cut.

I sit in the chair at the foot of the bed and watch Papá as his skin turns red, then blue, as the lungs fill with liquid. Our eyes are locked. I think of nothing, can think of nothing, time is a fluid that congeals around me as his face twitches from asphyxia. He stops breathing.

A minute goes by. What am I doing? I ask myself. What do I feel? I am closing the door, I reply, I am cutting the cord, releasing the spirit, letting the man fly free to the green-eyed island of his soul he should have never left. I feel nothing, then a hollow in my chest, then a pain I know I'll always carry. I'm oddly detached, I'm not there, someone else is occupying my body, I am nowhere.

Two minutes. Three, four, five. I get up, take a last look at my father. I kiss him on the cheek.

"Bless me, Papá. I love you."

I turn the respirator back on and I slip out of the room. I walk down the hall, then race down the stairs, out to the back and to the bay and I jump in the water, the cold dark water of night. I swim and I swim and forget, forget, forget.

7

the banged-up Dodge Colt barely kept its wheels on the ground as it rounded the corner a block away, out of Fifth onto Broadway. The crowd of late-night shoppers on the street—fat old ladies in tattered shifts lugging shopping bags, girls in bright flowered rayon dresses, young studs in leather and jeans, all speaking the soft Spanish of Central America—parted like the waves before Moses' staff. The car zigzagged around the traffic waiting for the light, the driver, young, brown and desperate, gripping the steering wheel in terror as his three passengers urged him on. Then, darting out of an alley, an equally battered Ford Monarch came onto Broadway in pursuit of the Dodge. A young black man with a wispy mustache was steering with one hand and speaking into the walkie-talkie he held with the other. The Monarch whizzed past me when yet a third car, a maroon Chrysler Le Baron, surged out of another corner, a makeshift Kojak light on its roof beaming its red eye at the crowd, the siren of the undercover police wailing like Joshua's trumpet. Suddenly the car stopped in front of me, its passenger door flew open.

"Hop in, Charlie! Come on!"

I peeked in. Sitting in the front, next to a very bothered Asian agent at the wheel, was Anthony Stuart Reynolds, the judge who had inherited Ramón's case after Chambers' stroke. Reynolds wore jeans and was in bad need of a shave, a sharp contrast to the natty figure I always saw him cut in court with his Italian suits, Missoni ties, Charvet shirts and hand-tooled English shoes.

"Let's go, man, we're gonna lose 'em!" he said in his broad Charleston accent.

What the hell. I hopped in. The car catapulted down Broadway before I even closed the door. All three of us were crowded into the front seat, which smelled of cigarettes and pizza, watching the faces of the pedestrians gaze worriedly at us as they stepped out of the path of the vehicle.

Judge Reynolds excitedly pushed his tortoiseshell glasses up to the bridge of his nose, an old dog with a new bone.

"Goddamn, this is just like 'Nam. I was a helicopter pilot there, you know that? I understand now why some of these here fellows just don't want to leave Vice. Were you in 'Nam, Charlie?"

"Sorry, sir. By the time I was out of college the draft had ended."

"You missed something there, Charlie."

"So I understand, sir."

He flared the wings of his bulbous nose, one single vein swollen with blood, and ran his hand through his thinning blond hair. I had a vision of him in twenty years, all pink and fat and bald, nose cratered with burst capillaries, plumped on the bench in a capital case, his enthusiasm vanished, his gut barely hidden by the black robes, looking forward to four-thirty and the first Scotch of the day as counsel argue for justice.

"This is Officer Nakamoto, from Rampart."

"How you doin', " he said, then looked back at the road, swerving around an RTD bus on Seventh. The walkie-talkie crackled; the lead officers in the chase relayed information to the cars pursuing.

"I just thought, given how often I deal with these cases," said the judge, "that I ought to see how these things are conducted. Well, mark my words, it's been—did you know close to eighty percent of all our cases are drug related? I thought, hell, with that and all, superb, if I may say so, just superb. We sure have a fine outfit here."

I thought most likely he wouldn't be saying that if he knew how imaginative narcs could be in obtaining confessions from dealers— pouring ashes in their eyes, tossing them down stairways headfirst, applying live wires to open wounds, using cattle prods on the temples and the ears—but it was doubtful we'd see much of that during this dog-and-pony show.

The chase had now come out of downtown, heading down Sixth, east toward the closest refuge of the dispossessed, the barrio at Boyle Heights. The words spitting out of the walkie-talkie became more frantic, the officers desperate to cut the suspects off before they reached their haven.

"Car twenty-six. We see the Dodge bearing east, crossing the SP overpass at Fourth. Do we have another unit in that direction? Over."

The answer faded in and out as we hurled down the desolate side streets on whose sidewalks homeless, crazies and winos bunked for the night.

"Unit forty-seven nearby. Heading to location. Over."

"Ah, yes, the thrill of the chase," said the judge, flushing, as happy as the shooter in a field of quail. "Well, since I got you here, Charlie—Whoops!"

The car flew in the air for a few feet as we hurled over a bump and landed on the overpass spanning the Southern Pacific railroad yards. The lines were cobwebs of steel, extending for miles, spreading the blight of commerce throughout the basin.

"I was saying, since I got you here, I want to talk to you about this Valdez fellow. I've been assigned the case by Judge Obera, our new presiding judge?"

Like so many southerners, his statements often ended in questions, rhetorical devices leaving no time for the listener to respond, only to assent with an obedient nod.

"It looks like Judge Chambers will be out for a while still. It takes a while to recover from those things, I hear. Now, I've been reviewing the case and I think there's some procedural matters that need to be addressed. Since you are performing an ex parte sub rosa advisory counsel role for Valdez, I think you should point out those matters to him because I want a clean record—"

"That's what Chambers said."

"Well, hell, me too, you think I like to have a bunch of ninnies in Appeals overturn my—Hot shit, there they are!"

The Colt skidded to a halt at the end of the long overpass, its path blocked by a black and white patrol car, light bar casting yellow, white and blue patterns on the ground. Two uniformed officers looked up from a bleeding, crumpled body on the pavement. The Colt doors opened and all four occupants ran off in different directions. The original narc chase unit swept down the road, swinging ahead of us, and stopped, tires squealing. Two undercover officers came out, one of them holding his badge high.

"Police! Narc unit!" he shouted and ran up a hill after the driver, who scurried down an alleyway. One of the uniformed officers turned and with surprising speed pursued and captured the oldest and fattest of the group, who doubled up and vomited on the cop's shoes, saying in between heaves, "*Perdón, perdón!*"

"There's our man!" shouted Judge Reynolds, pointing at a swiftly moving figure running down a flight of stairs to the Los Angeles River. "Let's get him!"

Nakamoto jammed the brakes and in what seemed like one swift motion opened the door, took out his gun and hurled himself down the stairs. Judge Reynolds went for the handle on our side but the door was stuck. He slid over and exited through the driver's door, screaming, "Hey, wait for me!"

I hesitated briefly, shrugged and plunged ahead. I didn't even stop to think why I should be joining such a suspect chase. For Judge Reynolds, running after the drug dealer was a natural extension of his devotion to law and order—not to mention a fine opportunity to play cowboys and Indians. But for me? I had no reason. I just followed blindly. The answer would come in the doing by and by. Nakamoto and Reynolds raced down the steep narrow flight of wooden stairs that dead-ended on the paved river embankment. The river, a squalid stream only four feet wide at that point, chugged on through a slot in the pavement to its deathbed in Long Beach Harbor. Ahead of us the suspect, wiry and short, with flowing black hair, leapt from the last landing to the roadway on the embankment, landing catlike on all fours. He stood for a second, then hurled himself down the twenty-foot slope, down to the flat of the river. Nakamoto tripped as he made the last few rungs and dropped his gun, which landed in the gravel behind the steps. Judge Reynolds collided with the officer and they rolled down in a heap. I came down the steps behind them, just in time to see

Nakamoto disentangle himself, reach for the gun and point it at the fugitive.

"Put that away!" ordered the judge, who got up and let himself down the embankment with a war cry. Nakamoto, embarrassed, holstered his weapon and followed.

The dealer, arms and feet pumping, ran straight down the river aiming for a darkened railroad trestle over the waterway a half mile away. Knowing they'd probably lose him if he managed to reach the span, Judge Reynolds and Nakamoto pressed on even harder, two hounds after the frightened hare. I followed about fifty yards behind, my legs just warming up, my lungs expanding, breathing in the sulfurous, metallic air.

Reynolds was the first to fold. He doubled over and fell on his knees, face flushed from hyperventilation. Nakamoto stopped to help, figuring one live judge was worth many loose drug dealers. As I ran past them I heard the judge holler at me, "Go, get 'im, boy!"

The absurdity of his words was matched by the ludicrousness of my actions. I had no stake in the pursuit, it was just me and some poor idiot running for his life under the cloud-covered moon. But I wasn't thinking then, I was caught up in the pounding imperative to triumph, to come home with the trophy.

The man ran up the embankment, his sneakers easily scaling the steep surface. I had almost caught up with him when I slipped, my leather-soled loafers unable to provide the purchase I needed. He ran to the stairs leading out of the roadway and into the trestle. I got up, kicked off my shoes and raced up the embankment, determined no matter what to win the race, grabbing hold of him just as he was about to grip the rail leading him to the stairs.

We rolled around on the ground. I held him tight in my arms. Suddenly, like a captured animal, he became still, his frightened brown face staring at me like a bedridden patient facing death. I could feel his heart beating through the sweat-soaked shirt. Panting, I took in his wide black eyes, his stained teeth, his pockmarked complexion.

"*Cómo te llamas?*" I asked.

"*Jesús*," he answered. A moment of breathless silence, worlds in the balance. The clouds moved, the moon shone bright, a train shunted somewhere in the yard. I heard the whirring of an LAPD helicopter nearing us. I opened my arms.

"*Vete, corre.*"

He looked at me sharply for the briefest moment, then smiled widely, a gold tooth shining in the dark.

"*Gracias,*" he said and fled into the darkness.

I took a deep breath, sat for a moment, then stood and waved my arms so the LAPD helicopter would shine its spotlight on me and Jesús could fly back to his world.

"You're a learned man, Charlie. Tell me, who was it that said the law is good? Was it Christ?"

The lime green walls seemed to vibrate from the hot lights of the interview room. Through the glass, prisoners, dressed in orange and blue jumpsuits, LOS ANGELES COUNTY JAIL PROPERTY stenciled neatly on their backs, sat shackled to their seats in rows across from their official visitors—the probation officers, the attorneys, the investigators. The inmates were models of urbanity, smiles and good manners on display as they discussed murders, rapes, drugs, arson and theft. Only occasionally did the glint of well-hidden evil peep through in a cold smile or a quick killer glance.

"No, it was Saint Paul."

"What is good?" asked Ramón.

"Well, there are those who say good is what makes you feel right and complete," I said, treading carefully through the landmines, "that it is that condition of which there can be no other. Then there are those who say good can never be attained, that good is a state to which we aspire but cannot achieve in its totality, whether it is heaven or the Platonic ideal. That's because they believe good is the contemplation of the eternal, even if just for the briefest moment, of the thing that hides behind all things."

Ramón smiled, noticing how almost against my will I was being embraced by the serpent of his question. "Look, I don't think Judge Reynolds is going to let you get away with philosophical asides. He's going to want you to stick to the business at hand, did you commit those murders or not."

Ramón sat forward, eyebrows raised for emphasis, kinky hair a brush of wonder.

"But my argument, my argument is a philosophical argument."

"The law won't allow it. And the judge will make sure you follow the law. He already told you yesterday, when he advised you of your right to counsel."

Ramón sat back defiantly.

"What kind of law is it that won't allow me to question its standing? This is no better than in Cuba, where Fidel and the party say this is the law and that's it, end of argument."

"You can bitch all you want but those are the laws and you can't change them."

"We will see about that."

Then, sitting upright, he slipped on his glasses, scanned his yellow notepad, putting a checkmark after some of the items listed.

"Did you contact Juan Alfonso?"

"Yes, but he won't be a favorable witness. He hates your guts."

"Good. That's what I need. He's a hostile witness so I can subpoena him."

"It doesn't make any sense."

He shook his head patronizingly. "His hatred will only confirm my involvement in the religion. It will legitimize my status."

He put another checkmark on his list.

"The police report?"

"I forgot. Here it is." I took a copy of the murder book out of my case and placed it on the table. It was six inches thick and heavy. The sense of wasted life clung to it like a dire perfume. Ramón removed the rubber band holding the hundreds of pages of reports, interviews, analysis, diagrams.

"Any pictures?" he asked.

"At the end. I made copies of the best. Or maybe I should say the worst. I don't know which they're going to show the jury."

He extracted the ten pages of photographs of death and desolation and examined them carefully, analytically, weighing in his mind the pros and cons of each piece when presented to a susceptible jury of his presumed peers. I felt a wave of hatred toward him, a loathing so intense I had to dig my fingernails into the palm of my hand and press until blood broke through. Who am I, God, to aid this monster, this hideous creature that with a wave of his hands dismisses so airily the torture and suffering he's caused? *Why am I here? Why?*

Ramón put the pictures down. "Who's the prosecutor? Have they decided yet?"

I took out a handkerchief, wrapped it around the palm of my hand to stanch the bleeding. Ramón watched, made no comment.

"Yeah, they decided. Her name is Phyllis Chin. I haven't met her yet."

"*Una china*. They really want to make this a circus. Who is she?"

"She's new to the department. Just transferred in from Alameda County. She was chief deputy D.A. over there, but her boss lost the last election and she was kicked downstairs, prosecuting speeding tickets in Pleasanton. She was going to run for office, but a drunk driver on the wrong side of the freeway plowed into the family station wagon. She was the only one to survive. Amazingly strong woman. They allowed her to prosecute the driver."

"That's unheard of."

"Exactly. Don't know how she managed it. But she did and put the guy away for life. Then right after that she sold her house and everything and transferred down here."

"Tough cookie."

"So it seems. That's not all."

"What else?"

"It seems she insisted, practically begged, to take on this case."

"Isn't it unusual for a new person to handle a case this big?"

Ramón said this without the slightest self-consciousness, convinced that the import of his actions was an uncontrovertible fact.

"It is. But Pellegrini wants to leave himself an out."

"What do you mean?"

This was going to be fun after all, I thought.

"He figures they've got you dead in the water. There's no way they can lose this case. But, just in the event he gets beat—remember McMartin and the Twilight Zone, those were sure winners too—just in case, then he can turn around and pin it on Phyllis. She'll be the sacrificial lamb. She'll spend the rest of her career in Pomona and Pellegrini will be safe come the next election. I mean, everyone knows he's been gunning for governor since he took the bar exam."

Ramón was briefly silent. "She shouldn't have taken this." Then, "I look forward to meeting her."

"She wants to meet you too. In court, come trial time."

■■■

The sheriff's deputy, a large woman with rolls of fat hanging over her gun belt, showed me a clenched fist of a smile as she led me into Judge Reynolds' office. Swiss travel posters showed the snowy peaks of Zermatt on the wall. On the judge's desk, a picture of a smiling little girl with a gap-toothed smile in a Halloween witch's costume.

The judge waved me to a chair when I entered. Across from his desk sat a short, handsome Asian woman with fine bones, jet black hair and eyes, dressed in a tailored pink linen outfit.

"Well, I'm glad I finally got y'all in here. Charlie, I want you to meet Phyllis Chin."

She shook hands firmly, with more strength than one would expect from such a petite woman. There was no warmth but no coldness either in her smile, just measured politeness.

"Nice to meet you," she said.

"I just want to go over some of the details here before we start the main order of business, the selection of the jury?" said the judge. "Now, I have to know, Charlie, if your client is going to demand some of the pissant motions w'all know are just a waste of time or whether we're going to do business as we should."

"Judge, you know I can't make those representations."

"You're not his attorney?" asked Chin, truly surprised.

"I thought I'd mentioned that to you, Phyllis. Charlie here is de facto legal adviser for the defendant, who's pro per."

Phyllis's pale ivory skin flushed. "Judge, I'm going to have to insist counsel be appointed. This case is too important to leave it in the hands of an ignorant criminal. The people of this state demand justice be done, that we don't spend our energies in a travesty that the Appeals Court will overturn down the line."

Reynolds, amused by Phyllis's assertions, cupped his hands in an inverted V, a Richelieu in the court of the Sun King.

"Well, Mrs. Chin," he drawled, "I commend you for your concern over the appearance of justice in this here matter and your sincere and heartfelt preoccupation over the intrinsic rights of the People for a fair trial. In fact, I'm so impressed I'm truly debating with myself the advisability of allowing Mr. Valdez the right to self-representation."

"Exactly my point," said Phyllis, leaning urgently forward.

"But there's just one little thing y'all forgot," said Reynolds, calm and cold. "*I'm* the judge. I determine the ground rules. I say whether he's fit to be his own counsel or not, not you, not your office, not District Attorney Pellegrini, not even the governor or the Supreme Court or even, God help him, the president of these United States. I'm the judge in this courtroom and I say he can be pro per. You may not like it, there's no rule saying you have to like what the magistrate does. But you are going to follow what I say. Do you understand me?"

Phyllis sat ramrod straight, curling her hands in her lap with the poise of a prize pupil at a finishing school.

"Yes, Judge, I understand," she said, eyes blinking rapidly.

"I'm glad to hear that. Charlie, has discovery been satisfactory?"

"As far as I know, sir, there has been no problem with any of the evidence requested."

"What about the sheriff's department? I know how they operate. Are they causing any problems with Valdez going to the legal library in county jail? I don't want to hear no bullshit from him."

"No, sir, the sheriff's department has gone out of its way to grant Mr. Valdez unlimited access to the library. We've retained a runner for minor copying and office work that needs to be done."

"That's just fine. That's what I want to hear. Now, is he going to file any motions or not?"

I looked out the window at the smog-draped San Gabriel mountains standing guard over Los Angeles, Mount Baldy a yellow joker's cap fifty miles away.

"Let me put it this way, Judge. If I were him, I would, just to make the record for the future."

"Good enough for me," said Reynolds, getting up from his chair. "You tell him he's got until the end of this week to file his written motions because I want to start on this right away. Too many months have already gone by. Anybody want some Blue Mountain decaffeinated?"

Reynolds moved to a coffee machine atop the credenza next to the window. Phyllis shook her head no, so did I. Reynolds poured himself half a mug.

"Now let's move on the jury selection. Assuming Mr. Valdez files for a change of venue claiming prejudicial pretrial publicity and assuming—now, I'm not saying this here is what I'm going to do because we all know that's not kosher, like they say in Harvard—but assuming that I deny that motion, I would want to impanel about six hundred jurors."

He raised the mug to his lips, took a sip.

"That's because I think, and I hope y'all agree, that the same jury should be in for both the guilt phase and the penalty phase. Faster that way. As it is, I figure this here thing is going to take at least six months altogether. Do you share my opinion, Mrs. Chin?"

"That sounds about right, Judge."

"Good. So we are all agreed then. Mrs. Chin, I suppose you will be bifurcating the case against Mr. Pimienta, since he will be giving state's evidence?"

Phyllis allowed herself the pleasure of a smile.

"No, sir. We will be filing charges against both defendants. The case will not be bifurcated."

The judge put his mug down.

"Goddammit, why in hell didn't you say so before? Now I'm going to have to call the other attorney in and go through this whole thing again."

"Sorry, Judge. You never asked."

Reynolds' forehead vein popped, but then he grinned.

"You li'l rascal. Fine. We'll meet again, then. We'll call Mr. Smith's office and have him here tomorrow. Now, good day to you both."

Once out in the hallway I followed Phyllis, who stepped briskly to the elevator.

"Sorry about the judge in there," I said.

"He's an incompetent asshole," said Phyllis. "We're going to paper him and get the case to another court."

"You're going to disqualify him?"

"We'll take anyone else. He's obviously biased."

The elevator door opened.

"Going up?" asked Phyllis. The fifteen bodies crowded inside nodded resignedly. Phyllis strode in. I followed her to the door of the D.A.'s office.

"When did you decide to press charges against Pimienta? I thought he had turned."

Phyllis pressed the numbers in the combination lock and the door clicked open.

"This morning. He refused to name Valdez as the killer. Says he can't remember who did the shooting. He's of no use to us now."

She stepped into the corridor, deputy D.A.'s in shirtsleeves walking past us, dozens of case files in their hands.

"See you under the big top," she said.

■

A melody from an opera sailed out the open windows of Enzo's apartment, a teasingly familiar aria, its name hiding in that corner of memory where song and sentiment share the same bed. I opened the French windows of my office and sat at my desk, idly contemplating the patchy hills of Griffith Park.

There really wasn't more I could do as an investigator. Since I wasn't in control of the case, I couldn't decide on any more witnesses or gather any more evidence other than what Ramón told me. I ran down the list in my mind. I had visited the jewelry store, now locked up and sold to a developer. I had talked to the different hostile witnesses who were supposed to testify, except for the parking lot attendant who saw them going in and the reporter who interviewed him. They were both out of town. Then there were the so-called friendly witnesses, Juan Alfonso, Lucinda. Lucinda. What had happened to her? I picked up the phone and rang her apartment. No answer. I put down the receiver, shifted in my seat. A peregrine falcon swooped down a thermal and plunged to earth. When it came up, it carried in its talons a still-writhing pigeon. The phone rang.

"Hello. Morell Investigations."

"Did you just call me? It's Lucinda."

On hearing her high, childlike voice, all the feelings of lust and affection she provoked danced before my eyes. I could smell her perfume, feel the pliable, smooth skin of her hands.

"How did you know?"

"I was in the shower. All of a sudden I thought of you, it was like you were standing there beside me."

I contemplated her nakedness in my mind's eye, her long neck, her small rounded breasts, the gathered-in waist, the slender, smooth legs ending in the dark triangle of desire.

"Did you like it?"

She giggled. "It felt so familiar," she said, "like I should tell you to soap my back or something."

"I could do that."

"But I just stepped out of the shower!"

"Then we'll have to find something more stationary. Would you like to come see me? I want to talk to you."

"As long as you promise that's not all we're going to do."

"That's an easy promise. Anything harder in mind?"

"We'll see when I get there. What's your address?"

I gave her directions. She said it would take her about a half hour for she had to stop for gas. When I hung up I realized I hadn't spoken to her since the day I'd run out of Juan Alfonso's house, yet I still felt linked to her as though we had been together for a long time.

I straightened out the mess in the apartment, opened a few windows, hurriedly changed the sheets and towels. In what seemed like a flash, the bell rang. I opened the door. Lucinda, high cheekbones, hazel eyes, cinnamon skin, gleaming smile, in a white dress and straw chapeau, a polka-dot scarf around her neck.

"Hi," she said.

"Hi," I said.

She stepped inside. I closed the door. Biting her lower lip she turned to me. Trembling like a puppy, I walked up to her, took off her hat. I kissed her. Her tongue slid into my mouth like a long-lost friend, her arms wrapped around me, little fists beating softly on my back, her slender body pressed against mine. I ran my hand up and down her body, feeling her shoulders, her breasts, her ass. I lifted up the back of her skirt and pried away the soft silky panties, stuck my finger down her crack. She eagerly unbuttoned my shirt, kissing my neck, my shoulders, my chest. I was in heaven, I was in hell, I was everywhere, I didn't care, I was in her.

8

the phone by my bed rang sharply the next morning, crashing the wall of warmth and light flooding the room. A breeze from the Pacific softly stirred the window shades. Lucinda, asleep, slender back ending in a waist two palms wide, moved her arm as though shooing away a fly. I had been awake for some time, thinking about her and Ramón and my life, etching her body in my mind for lack of canvas or a painter's hand, but now the reverie was at an end.

"Hello."

"Mr. Morell? This is Sergeant Porras of the County Sheriff's. We'd like you to come to headquarters, we have a few questions to ask you."

Porras threw a little rag doll on the desk. Brightly colored, dressed in a tattersall skirt, the doll had no features, just a round bulb for a head, a small string of cowrie shells where the neck would have been.

"We found this in the wreck of the car that tried to kill you the other day," said Porras, in a matter-of-fact, almost disgusted tone of voice. He looked at me neutrally, a man used to reading faces like truck drivers read maps.

"Do you know what this is?"

I picked up the doll. Coarse cloth, filled with sand. Magnet of prayers and maledictions, prehuman figure of supernatural powers that cavort among us.

"Have no idea. A girl's doll. Is this what you brought me here for?"

Porras extracted a True cigarette from a soft pack, then inserted the already tasteless stick into a water filter. He flicked on his Zippo, threw up a cloud of expensive cardboard smoke.

"That's the symbol of one of the gods of the *santería* religion. One of my buddies tells me it's someone called Yemayá."

"So what?"

"You said you didn't know who these guys were, who tried to ram you."

"Correction. They did ram me. They tried to kill me."

"Whatever. Do you have any connection to this *santería* horse-shit?"

I almost fell into the trap but not quite. "Not personally. Some people I know are into it. But hey, I know some Jews too. And some of my best friends are Christians. You know, the kind that carry the Virgin of Guadalupe dangling from the rearview mirror?"

Porras frowned. He stuck a hand in his desk drawer and tossed out a number of objects on the blotter—beads, coconut shells, crucifixes, bangles, a statuette of Saint Lazarus.

"Found these too."

"What can I say? Maybe they were going to open their own *botánica* and decided to stage a little sacrifice to appease the gods. What the fuck am I supposed to know, Sergeant?"

I refused to take them seriously in his presence, to grant these avatars the respect they craved, acknowledgment of the many faces of God peeking through their soiled wrapping.

"You know, you have a problem with your attitude."

"I don't have a problem. I like my attitude just fine. It's your insinuations I don't particularly like."

"Jesus Christ, Morell, here we are, trying to help you out and you treat this whole thing like it's a joke."

"What, am I supposed to cry because you show me some dolls? Who are you, the cookie monster?"

"You don't appreciate anything you don't do yourself, do you? Well, this is no joke, amigo. These two punks knew exactly who you were, where you were going. Look."

Porras extracted a plastic sandwich bag from under a mound of files and reports. He took out two Polaroids charred around the edges.

"That's you entering the Criminal Courts Building across the street. That's you with your car, its license nice and clear, on Lot Seventeen. By the way, I didn't you know you had a sticker for that lot."

"I have high friends in low places."

"Funny. They had you pegged, buddy. Your ass was supposed to be flying down that canyon, kissing L.A. adios. So now you want to tell me what's all this about or do you want to keep on acting like a *pendejo*?"

"Excuse me?"

"That's asshole."

"Mr. Asshole to you."

"Fine, Señor Asshole."

I raised my hand in fake fluster. "I have no idea what it's all about. Why don't you tell me who were these guys."

"Shit, guys in the department told me about you. They were right."

"What they say?"

"That you deserve to die. That you've messed up a lot of clean busts by sticking your two bits in the holes."

"You're mixing your metaphors. Who were these guys?"

Porras let out a breath of frustration, put out his cigarette.

"We haven't run a make on them yet. You're a low-priority item. But we'll get to it. We'll let you know."

I got up, stretched. "Well, thanks. I always wanted to see the sixth floor of the Hall of Justice at noon."

If I hurried, I had enough time to drop by KQOK and pick up the dubs of the tapes that Cookie Bongos, the reporter, had made of his interview with Ramón and Pimienta at the Jewelry Mart. As I got into my car, I reflected once again on how quickly everything ages in Southern California, how buildings and structures seemingly built to last for centuries are quickly outgrown and rendered useless by the never ending population boom, the ever increasing magnetic attraction of bodies to a land that was never meant to hold more than a few thousand souls in dusty squares and lonely pueblos.

In a place like this, I thought, only dreams are real, the artificial is the norm, all that counts is your belief that you will be able to impose your vision on everyone else. This has always been fertile ground for visionaries—Upton Sinclair, Louis B. Mayer, Michael Milken—so it was only fitting that Ramón had brought his brand of *santería* to this land. A cult that now apparently was threatening my life. Only it didn't quite make sense.

That my two would-be killers had been *santería* followers didn't bother me much; anyone could be a follower of the cult, from the white-templed, black-robed judge to the sleazy real estate developer to the burly cop on the beat—like Jewish or Spanish blood, the least likely person could have it. But their having had pictures of me and my car was infinitely more serious. That meant someone who knew me well had pinned me, giving specific instructions on how to find me and what to do. And if that person had tried once, in all likelihood he or she would soon try again.

I tried to think who would want to kill me. I'd had many cases since coming to L.A., but I truly could not remember a single one in which I'd been threatened with death. This meant that the 664/ 187, as the cops called it—the attempted murder of my person by two unknown suspects utilizing a vehicular weapon—was tied in to Ramón's case. Whoever it was obviously did not want me helping Ramón or finding out something about the case. Or was it some*one*? Could it be that whoever tried to murder me did not want me to contact a witness who could radically influence the outcome of the trial?

I didn't know and there was little likelihood I would find out why until the sheriff's office finally traced the identity of the would-be killers. Until then it was all speculation, idlings as futile and disturbing as wondering about the next earthquake; it would happen when it was time, not a moment before or after, and worrying about it would not stop the ground from shaking.

The radio station was set in the midst of Hollywood, just a few blocks south of the old RKO transmitter, its miniature Eiffel Tower still slicing the air atop the peeling tenement. I parked in a lot littered with smashed beer bottles and slid three folded dollar bills into a meter slot. At the corner of Hollywood Boulevard, stringy-haired boys and girls with shiny faces and needle tracks in their arms shared plates of french fries the Indonesian fry cook dispensed at Symie's Burrito Factory. A black and white zoomed by, weaving through the midday traffic, which refused to halt for a mere police emergency.

The wailing of an ambulance followed me as I entered the building. I detected the scent of caraway and pickles in the air. The aging doorman opened up his paper-wrapped sandwich, bit tremulously into the pastrami. He looked at me once, decided I passed muster, then returned to his racing form. I scanned the directory, found that the station was next door to Rothman's Tax Service and climbed the wide marble steps to the third floor.

For a station with such a wide following, the headquarters of KQOK were surprisingly small—four fake wood-paneled rooms, including the crammed reception area where a *chola* from Guadalajara sat doing her nails and reading *Cosmopolitan en español*. She waved a delicate brown hand down the hall at the broadcast booth.

Bongos was inserting a cassette with some of his trademark sound effects—the blaring of sheep followed by the ringing of a cowbell, then a gross fart and an old woman crying *"Aee, aee, aee!"*—when he noticed me through the glass partition. He waved me inside, flashing the same gap-toothed grin plastered in billboards all over Echo Park, Pico Union and downtown. A small man, his head was out of proportion to his body, far too large and imposing for such a thin, frail frame.

"I'll be right with you," he said, his English carrying traces of his native Salvador and the lilting, open-ended phrasing of East L.A. speech. He pulled from the rack by his chair a commercial for Colombian coffee, then cued up two records on the turntables, and in a whirl of motion, eased on over to the sponge-covered mike.

"Híjole, what coffee. I'm so wired I could fly. You sure it's only brew? It's from Colombia, the land of . . ." He played another sound track of someone sniffing, then a siren and a machine gun firing and a gruff voice saying in English, "You're under arrest!"

"Aee, aee, aee, aee, aee," cried the old lady again.

"But don't worry," said Bongos, "it's only coffee, señor. So here's some music to dance away that . . . *cafeína*."

He flicked on the turntable, playing a fast paced *cumbia* from Medillín, then he wheeled around and faced me.

"What can I do for you?"

I told him what I was there for. He frowned, fingering his fat mustache.

"Ah, yes, Officer McCloskey told me you'd be dropping by."

He wheeled around once more, opened a drawer, took out two cassettes. He tossed them at me, then rose from his chair as a smaller, darker man with bottle bottom glasses slid into the seat, placed a record on the turntable and put his lips to the mike, ready to swallow it whole.

"Good day, lovers of love," he said in a low, throaty, rumbling voice, "the moment of angelical, divine, amorous transport that will take you to the stars of emotion is here once again in this, your 'Program of Love.'"

Limping slightly, Bongos led me to his office, a service closet in which he'd stuck two filing cabinets, a board across them and a chair.

"How'd you get hurt?" I asked.

"A memento from D'Aubuisson's people in El Salvador. They didn't like some of my coverage of the Arena party so they broke my legs into four pieces."

"You were lucky to get out alive."

"I'll say. Especially after they put a bullet through my head. That healed but the left leg never mended right."

He plopped down in the chair and opened up a file drawer, and planted two other cassettes on the desk.

"Here, let me have the ones I gave you. These have better-quality sound. You understand Cubans? Some people say they're incomprehensible."

"I'm Cuban too."

"Are you? I thought you were a *gabacho*, an Argentinian. Well, there you have it."

"Thank you."

"You can keep those. But let me tell you something about those guys. They're not all there, you know that. Something happened in that store that had nothing to do with a robbery or anything like that. It's like they saw something, they peeked into an abyss, then retreated out of fear for their souls. But by the time they got back, it was too late, they had already been dragged down into the pit. I don't know if that makes sense. Do you understand what I'm telling you?"

"I think so."

When I returned to my apartment, I found the front door un- locked, the windows flung open and the bed still warm. On the dresser, in a childlike hand, with the kind of spelling and gram- matical errors a third grader makes, Lucinda had laboriously scrawled me a note. It read, in Spanish,

"I'm going. Looking for work. A man says he finds me some today. By your indulgence. Lucinda."

She had started to write 'I love you' but had left it incomplete, putting down only the *te q* of "*te quiero*," then quickly scratching it out, not daring to presume any lasting links from just one night of passion.

I took a shower and barely bothered to towel, the Santa Ana winds wiping the moisture off like an invisible sponge. I made myself some coffee, opened the balcony doors and sat staring at the observatory.

I'm fourteen, living in Opalocka. A mulatto family, rare among Cubans of the day, has moved next door down from New York. The girl, slender and cheerful, is my age; she waits for me every day when I come from school. We sit under the orange tree in her yard, blossoms drawing bees buzzing for nectar. I shoo away a bee, feel her small breast. We kiss, my first kiss.

"Carlos, come here," bellows my father, unexpectedly home from the garage. I scurry away, caught in the act of love.

I open the door to our house, he slaps me so hard I hit the wall.

"I don't want you fucking around with little colored girls!"

Stunned, all I can say is, "Why, Dad?"

"Because all they want to do is get pregnant so they can sink their hooks into you, because you're too young to throw your life away, because I forbid you!"

I slither down the wall to the floor, where I sit, still reeling. I lick the blood from the broken lip. I realize he's right, that behind that love is the specter of unwanted commitment, of marriage and duties and obligations far beyond what I can envisage or desire. I go to the kitchen and put an ice cube on my lip. After the explosion, papa slips quietly away. I never see her again. I never explain, I never talk to her. A month later we move to Kendall, a hurried relocation that I now realize was directly linked to that one moment of discovery. Is that why I am drawn to Lucinda? Is she just another round in our unending conflict? Will I ever escape?

A book fell to the ground in my office. I sat up, startled. I visualized the espalier in Enzo's garden, an inviting stepladder for anyone wanting to break in. I put down my coffee mug, stood up quietly and moved to the kitchen. I took out my .38 from the pasta jar.

Another book fell with a thundering thud. Then I heard a filing cabinet drawer sliding out, its rusty hinges squeaking. I raised my gun and advanced quickly to the far wall, waiting to see if the intruder would come out. The noises continued in the office. My heart was a runaway train plunging down a steep hill. Yet another noise. I scooped across to the bedroom and glanced inside. No one there. I scurried to the partition dividing it from the office and pressed my damp hand against the wall. A bird trilled a sunny melody from the eucalyptus tree outside. A gasp, then a moan, as though the intruder had somehow injured himself.

I whipped around in a dance of fear and twirled into the doorway, holding my gun with both hands, pointing it inside the room. A thick-set man with a broad back and gray wavy hair was hunched over my files, lifting papers, his breathing tortured, raspy.

"Freeze or I'll fucking blow your brains out!" The man put his hands up. There was something familiar about his profile. What was it, who was it?

"Turn around, slowly." The man turned, papers cascading in delayed time to the floor. I gasped, my breath rushing out of me, as though I'd fallen into an icy lake.

The clear plastic breathing apparatus of a hospital patient dangled from his nose, his face contorted into a frozen spasm, skin with the pallor of the dead, eyes hooded, barely open. My father looked gravely at me from beyond the grave, silently, neither loving nor hating, affirming nor denying, just being at that moment, existing in a frozen instant. Then the features began to dissolve, melting, as though wiped by an invisible eraser, until at the end only two mournful eyes gazed back at me and then they too were gone and all that was left in the room was a cold mist and the smell of burnt matches in the air.

9

ecember seven, the day that will live in infamy, was the day our trial finally began. It had been over two years since the carnage at the jewelry store, yet Ramón's case had never been far from my mind, no matter what other investigation I might have been conducting. Twenty-four months of delays, appointments, substitutions—a speedy trial by the standards of Los Angeles justice, abetted by the certainty on the part of the prosecution that all they had to do to win was show up in court for, after all, what defense could there be? Even at this point I couldn't see any and Ramón had not volunteered any. Is this really the purpose, I asked myself, for Ramón to become some perverse sacrificial lamb, some guilty creature slain for—But that's silly, I told myself. Totally senseless.

Hurricane-force Santa Ana winds had scoured the basin the night before, reaching speeds of a hundred miles an hour, suggesting, with alarming clarity, the terror of Nature set loose. Trucks jackknifed in the San Bernardino freeway, electric lines plunged from Palos Verdes to Glendale, brush fires that at any other time would have quickly been spent instead blackened thousands of acres in the Santa Susana and San Gabriel mountains, threatening homes in Malibu, Monrovia and Pacific Palisades. The shutters in my bedroom window hummed all night, sighing from the repressed force that wanted to set them free, while in the distance the wailing of ambulances and fire trucks lifted into the air in a chorus of emergency. The hours stepped fitfully forward as I lay in bed, my heart pounding, thinking the building would topple, waiting for the end. Instead, otherworldly in its stillness, a lilac dawn arose like a maniac who murdered his family and in the morning goes down to fix his coffee, unheeding of the bodies strewn by the stove.

In the Criminal Courts Building, jurors waiting to be impaneled jammed the hallways, hundreds of people standing around, like so many schoolchildren waiting for the bell to ring to go into class.

The day has come, I thought as I swung open the doors to Judge Reynolds' courtroom, the skirmishes are over, once more into the breach.

Perhaps I should have walked out of the courtroom at that point, renouncing this charade of a lawyer sans brief, a counsel without a cause, but the centripetal force of the event drew me further and further in. Besides, I felt I had a role to play, an obscure but all important part that would reveal itself in the doing, a duty that went beyond giving aid to the needy, regardless of personal op-probrium, one that had been preordained, somehow somewhere by a greater being outside the confines of the legal system. My last chance to flee evaporated as the bailiff brought out Ramón and José to the tinkling of jail chains.

Both men were dressed in civilian clothes. José wore a baggy light beige suit with a wrinkled shirt and a six-inch-wide flowered tie, looking as though he'd merely traded one uniform for another. Ramón had on an old gray double-breasted suit of mine which fit him perfectly; with a chill I saw for the first time that we were indeed the same size.

The bailiff unlocked the cuffs. José ambled over to Clay Smith's side and sat in the defendant's wooden chair, a blond female in-terpreter speaking into his ear.

Ramón slid into his seat and nodded at me.

"Nice day for a hanging," he said in Spanish, barely smiling.

"They gas them in California."

"Details, details. You have to learn to rise above your circum-stances. Go for the big picture. That's the secret."

"That's why you're here, right?"

"Not for long."

Ramón scanned the courtroom, nodding to himself with satisfaction as he spied the expectant crowd, the lines of reporters at
the far end of the courtroom, the extra bailiffs conspicuously posted
every six feet around the perimeter of the hall. Jim Ollin, the latest
glamour boy of the local TV news wars, was standing by his
cameraman behind the bar, pointing his notebook at us like a lance,
ordering a zoom-in. Ramón gave him a wide smile, then turned to
me.

"Tell Ollin I'll talk to him in jail this afternoon, if he's interested."

"All rise!" intoned the head bailiff, announcing the judge's entrance.

"You're crazy," I whispered to Ramón, "he could blow your
whole case."

"We'll see," he said, putting his hand to his heart when the bailiff
mentioned the flag of our country.

In her corner, like a prizefighter surrounded by her coach and
second, Phyllis was ringed by the head investigator, Detective Ron
Samuels, and her co-counsel, Deputy D.A. Phil Hammond. She
looked calmly at Reynolds in spite of the resentment she must have
harbored for having to put up with him, instead of another judge.
Pellegrini had turned down her proposal to change judges, un-
willing to trade in a known quantity, no matter how deficient, for
an unknown magistrate who might spoil their solid chances of winning with some arcane legal requirement.

Reynolds sat in his upholstered blue leather chair, cleared his
throat, looked quickly at the file in front of him as though he'd
momentarily forgotten what case he was hearing. He glanced up.

"The People versus Valdez and Pimienta. Are the parties ready?"

"Ready for the People, Your Honor," answered Phyllis, standing.

"Ready for defendant Pimienta," said Clay, also rising.

"We are ready," said Ramón, folding his hands on the table.

"Get up!" I whispered. He shook his head. Reynolds frowned,
his eyes shining through his horn-rimmed glasses.

"Mr. Valdez, you will rise when you address the court."

Ramón smiled apologetically, almost making one think that he
truly regretted what he was about to do.

"Your Honor, there is no legal requirement that counsel be stand-ing up when talking to the judge. Since I am acting as my own counsel—"

"Yes, there is!"

"If I may inquire, Judge, where is there that I can find this legal requirement? It is not in any book that I am aware of."

"It doesn't matter if it's not, it's the tradition of our system."

"Who says one must follow tradition blindly, with all re-spect?"

Judge Reynolds banged his gavel in frustration. "I say it! This is my court and in my court, sir, you will follow my standards!"

Ramón shook his head, obdurate. "Judge, to rise before you is to stand before a man and to pay homage to a man, not a principle. I can only honor the law and the flag, sacred symbols of our country. If you rise when you address me, I will rise when I address you. You are just a man, you are not the law."

"Sir, I am the l—" Reynolds hesitated for a brief moment, for the first time aware that camera lenses were pointing his way and that reporters were scribbling every word of their confrontation. But pride won out.

"Bailiff, remove this man from the court until further notice. Counsel, approach the bench!"

Now Ramón finally stood up.

"Judge, I am counsel and cannot be removed from the court without good reason!"

"I have good reason. You're in contempt, sir. Bailiff, put him in the holding cell until we decide what to do with him!"

Ramón struggled briefly, enough to make the "Six o'Clock News" viewers get their money's worth.

"This is an abuse of power, Your Honor," he shouted, as three bailiffs hauled him away. "You are not the law, no man is the law. You cannot act like the King George in this country, like the Com-munist commissar, we are a country of laws!"

The door to the cell slammed closed behind them. I could hear Ramón being slammed against the wall and the dull thumping of blackjacks on his body.

"Don't hit me!" he shouted.

"You too should approach, Mr. Morell," said the judge. I snapped to.

"Yes, sir!"

"You ever seen a cockier son of a bitch!" said the judge as Phyllis, Clay and I drew near the high bench.

"Totally uncalled for, Your Honor," said Clay, looking to score sympathy points.

"That little coon, calling me King George! Why, when my people were chasing the redcoats out of Carolina his folks were running for zebras in the jungle!"

Phyllis sounded a note of quiet caution. "Judge, perhaps we ought to confer in chambers. Someone is likely to overhear us."

"Good idea." The judge banged his gavel. "This court is in recess!" Then, to us, "I guess we better see if the jungle bunny's right. Let's hit the books."

That afternoon, lips swollen, cheeks puffy and slashed, eyes narrowed into slits, Ramón greeted me like the winner of the prize match.

"I gave it to them, didn't I?"

"I'd say you got as good as you gave."

Our interview had been moved to a booth in the high-security wing of the jail, away from the general prisoner population. The isolation suited Ramón, who proudly stretched stiff arms as much as the double length of chains and padlocks would let him.

"What do you hope to gain?"

He grinned. One of his front teeth had been knocked out, leaving him with a seven-year-old's touching gap-toothed smile.

"This trial is not going to be won in the courtroom, Carlitos. I have to bring the outside world in as the jury. They're the ones who will decide my destiny."

"You really think the judge is going to let you control the trial?"

"What choice does he have? I already set the ground rules. He came off as a tyrant and everybody in the whole world knows it by now."

"That's your opinion. Some people may say what they saw is a killer who has no respect for our legal system. You could actually be antagonizing people."

Ramón waved his hands. "I already lost those people a long time ago. They're the ones who automatically think you stole the mango the moment they see you walk in front of the bodega. I'm talking about laws here. I want to make sure that everyone follows the strict meaning of the law and justice, because if they don't, I'm sunk."

This last statement was accompanied by the same emphatic up-and-down hand motion I'd seen used by Castro on TV, my father in a political argument, all Cubans on occasions when noise and bluster count for more than logic and reasoned argument—tip of thumb to tip of index finger, the other three fingers held straight out, as though the speaker were calibrating a ring or measuring the neck of a milk bottle or just jerking you off.

Law and justice. Ramón didn't see any irony in his words, for now he looked at me expecting confirmation, assurance that his plea had reached a responsive listener. I felt sick, ashamed of myself and what I was doing, like a boy unable to stop lighting matches to the furry tail of the neighbor's cat.

"We'll see what happens. I told Ollin he could talk to you. He practically came in his pants."

He grinned, his remaining teeth shining bright.

"I know. I called him at the station."

I was surprised. As a high-security prisoner, Ramón was to be watched all the time, and above all, was not to have access to communications, either with other prisoners or the outside world. He was housed alone, in a twelve by twelve cell. His only link to life beyond the pale green walls of his cell and the crowded court-room were his visits to the library, when he'd be flanked by two bailiffs.

"How did you manage that?"

He shook his head evasively, not willing to be drawn out. "Friends. Brothers in the faith."

"*Santeros?* Here?"

He scowled, the speed of his kaleidoscopic changes matched only by the weight of his insincerity—each attitude a pose, a mask to be tried on according to the effect desired.

"We're everywhere, *mi hermano*. Where you least expect it, there's a *santero*, or someone who doesn't practice but believes, or thinks, Well, I better go along with it just in case. That's how we survive."

I couldn't resist asking, "But Ramón, if there are so many of you and *santería* is so powerful, what are you doing in that chair?"

He smiled, put his hand on mine.

"Here's a lesson to be learned. One day Ochosí, the king of heaven, gathered around all the lesser gods and told them there was a field that needed planting, so that the fruits of the earth would spring forth. He asked who would break the field. So cocky Shangó, of the lightning bolt, threw down his bolts, but all they did was burn the field and nothing grew. Then Yemayá, the goddess of water, came and covered the field with water. But all the plants drowned and nothing grew. So finally Oggún, the blacksmith, went to his forge, shaped iron on his anvil and fashioned a plow. And with that plow he broke the field so Ochosí could scatter the seed, and a beautiful field of yams grew. You know what the plow is made out of? Swords and shields. Look at how Christianity spread, look at how the Muslims won—on horseback, with a cutting sword."

"And you're the Christ of this new religion?"

"I am not the new savior because we don't have to be saved. There is no original sin. There are many saints and many avenues to heaven. But I am bringing the message of the saints down to earth."

I was exasperated. "Look, let's not fuck around anymore. You killed all these people for no fucking reason and now you're trying to come off as a messiah of some sort to save your ass. OK, now, tell that to the papers, tell that to the media, the judge, the jury, but don't give me this shit. I don't want to hear it."

I got up, the chair falling backward to the floor. I was storming out of the booth when Ramón called out mockingly, "But what if I'm right, Charlie, what if I'm telling the truth?"

I stopped at the door and turned. "What is the truth?"

Ramón flashed his gap-toothed smile. On my way out, I saw Jim Ollin with his camera crew in the antechamber.

"He's ready to roll," I said and left.

■

When I got home, Lucinda was in bed, wearing my pajama top as she perused an old family picture album of mine. She had set a half-consumed glass of guava juice on the marble-topped nightstand, the edge of the glass smeared with her ruby red lipstick. The room was laden with moisture from the open bathroom door; I could see the tub still brimming with bubble bath. A scent of jasmine and verbena wafted in the air, Miles Davis's "Sketches of Spain" issued from the CD player.

"You should have been a geisha," I said to her, putting my briefcase on the dresser.

She smiled. "What's that?"

"It's one of those Japanese ladies who always take care of their man."

I crawled into bed with her and put my head on her lap. She rubbed my forehead with cool hands.

"You don't have to be Japanese to be like that. But really, *mi amor*, I hardly do anything for you. All I do is hang around the house. I don't work, I don't do anything."

She unknotted my tie, eased me out of my jacket.

"That's not true. Just your being here is enough, just having you around."

I opened the pajama top, sought out a breast, suckled on the brown nipple.

"Oh, honey," she said, in English. "My life, my heart," she said, in Spanish.

Afterward, when Lucinda was washing up in the bathroom, I leaned over the edge of the bed and craned my head down, leafing through the picture album. There was my grandfather, thin and dour, eschewing the white linen suit of the prosperous businessman of 1920s Cuba for the austere black of his Catalan forebears. My father, a little blond boy in a white sailor suit, stood in front of him, staring at the camera in the group shot of all the top tobacco merchants of Havana. Next to that picture, another of my father as a cadet in a military school, his adolescent hair darker, his odd heart-shaped birthmark clearly showing on his cheek. My mother, in a Schiaparelli ball gown during her debut at the Biltmore when she turned fifteen. Then there I was, naked and jubilant at the beach in Varadero, a stream of pee arching from my groin, like a putto in a Roman fountain. My sister, in her favorite lilac dress, blowing out the candles on her tenth birthday, surrounded by dozens of children and my mother wearing a party hat. Then the last two pictures of our family in the island, both taken at our cattle ranch in Camagüey—my father, a map on the hood of the Jeep, his trusted .45 in his side holster, posing as if he were some African explorer. In the last picture in the book I am riding my favorite horse, Pinto, an Appaloosa pony my father had bought in Kentucky. My straw hat sits high on the crown of my head and I smile peacefully at the photographer. It was January 1959, and the whole world was smiling at Cuba.

I looked up from the picture, startled. An LAPD helicopter was cutting through the night, practically buzzing the apartment. The whirring of the blades sliced the air into ribbons of throbbing sound, filling the room with the urgency of the needs of history. A glimmering band of white, like a klieg light on a stage, swept outside my window. Down on the sidewalk, a small dark-skinned man ran thorough the bushes of our backyard, knocking over the pots of cyclamens and begonias, trying to hide from the light.

"Don't move! You're under arrest!" boomed the helicopter a hundred feet above the building. The man ignored the warning and like a cat in a fenced-in yard, scrambled for a way out.

"*Cazzo di Dio, cosa fa questo stronzo!*" shouted Enzo, slamming his shutters open.

The man looked up in my direction at that moment. Our eyes locked. I did not recognize him, although he could have been any of the thousands I had worked with; in his lean, sharp features there was a glimmer of recognition, a half measure of acknowledgment, but he didn't make a sound. Then, with a leap, he vaulted over the far wall of the yard and vanished into the dark. The helicopter pursued him, still booming, and still the man ran, obviously with no intention of surrendering just because he'd been sighted. I moved back inside the room.

"What was all that noise outside?" asked Lucinda, her face still shiny from the water she'd splashed on. It was then I realized the entire scene could only have lasted a few seconds, just moments when I realized that he and I were one and the same. But who was

the enemy and what was the crime—and would there really be a
way out? Stop it, I told myself, stop this nonsense right now. You
can't let go, you must hold on.

"Nothing," I told Lucinda, "just the cops chasing somebody. He
was probably trying to break into somebody's house."

This seemed to reassure her; she sauntered back to the bathroom.

"It's really gotten terrible lately," she said from inside the bath,
"there's so much crime everywhere nowadays. You can never be
sure that the little you have isn't going to be taken away from you.
It's really not fair, you work so hard and then someone comes and
just because he likes it, takes it like that. What kind of world is
this? They should get a job, is what they should do. These *vaquetas*,
these good for nothings."

She peeked out the door to see me sitting on the edge of the
bed.

"It's the fault of the Socialist government, you know. They're
all used to getting something for nothing."

"Most thieves are not Cuban, or even Marielitos."

"No, but they set a bad example and that's why the others do
it. Anyway, no decent Cuban should be involved in crime, don't
you think?"

"I thought all decent Cubans were dead or in prison for political
crimes."

"Oh, you!"

The happy eyes of the boy in the picture stared back at me from
across decades of oblivion. Was that really me, did I ever have so
much trust in things, in the world, in God?

Lucinda came out and pulled her things out from drawers, her
lace panties, her silk undershirt, a thick blue sweater.

"Where are you going?"

"To see my girlfriend Martha. Remember I told you the other
day. She's visiting with her mom from Miami."

"I don't remember."

Lucinda put her hands on her hips. "Now, Carlos, don't start
with me. I told you if you wanted to come and you said no, you
were busy. You can still come if you want."

"I must have forgotten. You won't be long, will you?"

She came up to me, kissed me. "No, baby, you know I can't stand to be away from you for long. We're having dinner at Candilejas. You can still come if you want."

"No, that's OK. I'm tired. I think I may be catching a cold. You go ahead. I'll go to bed."

She kissed me on the forehead. "You take care of yourself. You know that I couldn't live without you."

"Liar."

"It's true. It's written in the stars, you see. Lucinda and Carlos will love forever, until death, for all eternity. Amen."

I woke up panting, an oppressive feeling on my chest, a knowledge that somehow I had committed a grievous fault, that my being alive was an abomination which cried out for correction. The pillow was drenched with sweat, and through the humming in my ears I could still hear the last few words of my dream, "Beware the red tide." I shivered from a sudden chill. Getting up, I washed up, changed into fresh pajamas and returned to bed, flicking on the TV.

Eleven o'clock. I was switching channels when a familiar face flickered on the set. I returned to the channel—Ollin was interviewing Ramón. It was a well-prepared shot, backlit with the uniform flat illumination of Spielberg movies.

Ramón's features took up the entire screen, the camera picking out the gap of his missing tooth, his flaring nostrils, the sparkling hazel eyes, which acted as semaphores for the relative importance of each point he made. For the first time, through the filter of the camera, he was convincing; for the first time he became something other than a loudmouth braggart or a cold-hearted killer—someone informed, lucid, who saw his place in the context of American history.

Ollin did not ask him directly about the charges and Ramón certainly did not offer to discuss them, focusing instead on what might have driven a man with Ramón's background and situation into a life of crime.

"Oh, it's very easy, sir," purred Ramón. "The temptation is all round us and it is very easy to fall. Look at my own case. I am an educated man but after coming here, I was reduced to doing things I would have never dreamed of doing just to keep myself alive."

"What kind of things, Ramón?"

Ramón shook his head, the shame almost more than he could bear. "Bad things, things I'd rather not talk about."

"Were they against the law?"

"How could they not be against the law, when everything is stacked up against people like me?" Ramón stared directly at the camera. "We come here, trying to work hard, and all we find is people who cheat us and abuse us, who steal our money and seduce us, then throw us in jail for living up to the image they made of us. You know, you made us out to be the dark mirrors of yourselves and then you punish us for being like that. This country has got to realize that this continent was taken from people like us, and that projecting their fears and anxieties at us is not going to make this land any safer. We're a rising tide, mister, a rising tide that carries all boats to sea and we will not be denied."

But here Ollin did something totally unexpected; he showed some intelligence. "Ramón, that's not true. This society is the most open society in the world. People of all colors and origins get to rise and prosper here. Besides, not everybody is discriminated against—and there are laws against that, too—and not everyone who's the victim of discrimination turns around and gets into a life of crime. You're just making excuses."

"That's because you're white, educated, from the middle class. You have no idea what it's like to be brown or black and be treated like an idiot just because you are not fluent in the language. You don't know what it is like to know that this country was yours and that it was taken away from you. You don't know how it feels to be afraid of Immigration all the time, to be lost in a place where all you can hope is forty dollars a day if you can find the work. You don't know how it feels to know that you're not even second class, you're third class, that even American blacks are better than you are, that there's a Beverly Hills out there and that you're living here, in Echo Park and South Central, while others get rich."

"But what about the judges, the police, the many businessmen and government officials who are Latinos?"

"They're the puppets of the Anglo masters."

Ollin shook his head, exasperated. "OK, let's assume what you say is true—and you sound just like the black radicals of the 1960s—"

"The Panthers were good people."

"That has nothing to do with the law and with the killings at the Jewelry Mart. Two wrongs do not make a right."

"It has everything to do with it. I'm beyond your right and wrong."

10

Judge Reynolds never wasted time getting to the basics. As a legacy of his military background, he believed in straight arguments and plain interpretations of law. With him you knew exactly where you stood, or sat.

Ramón had prepared a brief requesting that the judge recuse himself for bias. As I turned it in to Curtis, the clerk, I knew that from that point on the trial would ring with legal fusillades, one unprincipled tactic after another in an unceasing attempt to win the longest shot in the judicial records of Los Angeles County. Curtis took a look at the motion, block printed on lined yellow legal paper, and chuckled.

"Is he for real?"

"Ask him yourself."

"I'll take your word."

Curtis strolled out of his cubicle by the side of the judge's bench and entered chambers. I heard a muffled curse, the thumping of a book, a glass broken. The clerk returned ashen faced, took his seat, lit a cigarette with trembling hands.

"I hate this job," he said. "If it wasn't for my kids . . ."

"I know, Curtis."

The courtroom was packed to capacity again, with more than a sprinkling of off-duty clerks, public defenders and D.A.'s taking in the show. The court fleas, a quartet of red-faced, shabbily dressed retirees who haunted the courthouse for entertainment, had secured a corner of the middle front row, right next to the dozens of reporters from newspapers, wire services and television stations. In the back a group of *santeros*, with bracelets and necklaces of cowrie shells, nervously fingered colored rosaries. I heard the whirring of cameras as I returned to the counsel table and sat next to Ramón. He had acquired a pair of round tortoiseshell glasses like the judge's, which, with my suit and tie, gave him the look of a black academic out of Howard University.

He gave me a full-toothed smile.

"It was a cap, the jail dentist put it back on," he said in Spanish. "I've had fake teeth since I was a kid, *chico*. From living on sugarcane after the Bay of Pigs invasion."

"I don't get it."

"The G-2 arrested my folks," he whispered unemotionally. "They shot my old man for counterrevolutionary activities and sent my mom to a prison camp for five years. I ran away and lived in the countryside for a year. Lost most of my teeth from malnutrition. Eventually some militia people found me and sent me to the political orphanage. But that's another story. How did the old shithead take it?"

"You're playing with fire."

"Why the fuck not. They've already prepared the stake. Might as well have some fun. You don't deserve to live if you can't laugh at death's beard."

"Spare me the florid Spanish."

He reverted to English. "Charlie, Charlie, this is a stage and we're all going through motions, get it?"

The spectators broke into a mild hubbub behind us. We turned and saw Claudia Weil, the chief correspondent for one of the TV networks, dressed in a blue silk shantung Chanel, her crew in back of her. She smiled at Ramón. He waved.

"Hey," growled the bailiff.

"OK, man, OK," answered Ramón promptly. He leaned over to me.

"Tell her I'll talk to her this weekend. I want to see how the trial goes."

"You intend to try your case in the media?"

"Something like that."

Just at that moment Lucinda walked into the courtroom, looking lost and searching. She spotted me, smiled, and took the seat one of the court fleas offered her.

"This is really drawing them out," said Ramón. "I haven't seen her since—"

"All rise!"

The entire courtroom rose as the bailiff intoned the customary announcement of the judge's arrival. I stole a glance at Lucinda. Then I felt as though someone had stabbed me in the heart. In the last row, standing among the curious audience, stood a man with my father's face, staring at me as though saying *No, it is not a dream.* Then he walked out of the courtroom. I wanted to run after him, embrace him, beseech him to stop, to talk, to bless me, to tell me plainly I was forgiven.

It's not true, I thought as I sat down. It's not real, it's not him, it can't be him, no, not him. Pay attention, pay attention, pay attention.

"Good morning," said the judge flatly.

"Good morning," came the chorus of players and spectators, except for Ramón.

"Before proceeding with the case of the People versus Valdez and Pimienta, there're some housekeeping matters I want to take care of. Mr. Valdez, yesterday you refused to rise when addressing the court, citing some lack of legal precedent—"

"Your Honor, if you allow me—"

Reynolds banged his gavel. "No, sir, hear me out or I will have you placed in the lockup again."

"Yes, sir," replied Ramón gleefully. Didn't Reynolds see how Ramón was playing him?

"If you think that your misbehaving and lack of ordinary courtroom courtesy will cause this court to commit reversible error, you are very much mistaken, sir. I was not born yesterday or in another country. I recognize what you're doing. Allow me to remind you, Mr. Valdez, that I am the judge and you are the defendant and I know the legal pitfalls of such manipulation. You will not rule the court, I will. So, since you insist on not rising when addressing the court, then you will remain seated throughout the proceedings.

Should you rise, that will be open contempt of court and will be dealt with accordingly at the conclusion of the trial, whenever that occasion might be."

He gripped Ramón's block-printed petition with thumb and index finger as though it were a dirty diaper.

"As regards this motion for the court to recuse itself, it's denied." He tossed the sheet into the basket by the clerk. "Bring in the jury."

The clerk pressed the buzzer, alerting the twelve jurors in the adjoining room. The wooden door presently opened. Mrs. Inez Gardner, a black, obese woman, entered, surprised to see the cameras.

"Showtime, people!" she said to the other jurors, who trooped in Indian file behind her. The whole courtroom burst into laughter, even Judge Reynolds allowing himself a little smirk. Only Phyllis, her chin cradled in her hands, did not smile.

The joviality vanished by the time the rest of the mostly middle-aged, white, female jury wriggled into the blue polyester covered swivel seats. Ramón and I had argued over the composition of the jury during the selection process. It was true I had every intention of not getting involved, but there was something antithetical in the way he chose the jury which practically forced me to take an active role. All those years of weighing people's backgrounds, likes and dislikes, hidden prejudices and obvious biases, their religion, ethnicity and the thousand and one details that make a successful jury—which is to say, a jury that votes your way—had made it impossible for me to sit passively as Ramón selected, almost perversely, precisely those people who were likely to send him to San Quentin.

In his monstrous pride Ramón systematically kicked out all the minorities he could from the panel. Phyllis found herself in the unusual position of having to file a Hitch's motion against the defense, alleging prejudice on the part of Ramón for showing a bias toward white Anglos! The last three jurors of color had been quickly selected as a compromise after Reynolds threatened to throw out the entire panel and start the selection process once again.

Clay, who had let Ramón take the lead in the jury selection—as though he too had become like Pimienta, a docile follower of the *santero* priest—had urged Ramón to let Reynolds carry out his threat. I agreed. With murders, the longer it takes to get the case to trial, the better it is for the defendant. Evidence may be altered or misplaced, witnesses may die or become unavailable, and those people who come to testify may find that their memory of events is not as sharp or convincing as it once was. But Ramón wouldn't hear of it, he became enamored of his nine white Anglo God-fearing Christians, believing they alone would save him. So now, as I reviewed their faces, staring anxiously at the court and ourselves, I shook my head in professional exasperation—but also personal satisfaction. He had as good as put the noose around his own neck. His prerogative, all right.

Now Judge Reynolds scanned the faces of the jurors, to ascertain they were indeed the people who had been chosen. He looked down, cleared his throat and read the title of the complaint and the case number.

"Good morning, ladies and gentlemen. Well, this is the day we worked for all these months. You are the triers of fact who will determine whether the defendants, Ramón Valdez and José Pimienta, are guilty or not of the crimes charged. It's a mighty responsibility but I'm certain it is one you will faithfully discharge. In order to find the defendants guilty, you must be convinced beyond a reasonable doubt of the truth of these charges. Now, y'all know just what reasonable doubt means?"

It was a rhetorical question, but the judge erred in letting an interval of a second lapse before his next sentence.

"I know!" exclaimed Mrs. Gardner, raising her hand.

"Thank you, ma'am, I'm sure you do. But just to make sure everybody does, I will read you the definition that the highest court in the land, in its wisdom, has determined is the working principle to be applied here. Now, reasonable doubt is not mere doubt, because anything relating to human affairs is open to some imaginary doubt, but rather it is that state . . ."

I shifted uncomfortably in my seat, tuning out the farrago of half-baked notions about doubt that all judges in California are compelled to issue at the start of trial, when they know fully well that the jury is as apt to be convinced by a defendant's smiling face as it is by the reasoned argument of the impassioned counsel. If the jury likes your client, it will find a reason to set him free—but if they don't, all the logic and persuasiveness of Daniel Webster will not get him off the hook.

"Both parties in this case may wish to give opening statements," said Reynolds. "Now, remember that anything the attorneys say is not evidence. Evidence, the truth, is what comes out of that witness stand, or what is presented to you, the jurors, for your direct examination. The arguments of the attorneys and their questions can only be considered insofar as they tend to shine the light of truth on the evidence. Now, the People give the first opening statement. The defense may later also give its own, if it so chooses, although"—here he threw a warning look at Ramón, who was busy reading his handwritten notes—"in most cases the defense reserves that right until after the prosecution has presented its case. Now, one of the defendants, Mr. Valdez, as you have seen, has chosen to act as his own counsel, which is his constitutional right. I remind you that you should not infer anything negative or positive about the fact that Mr. Valdez is acting as his own counsel. However, for security reasons, Mr. Valdez will be conducting his case from the counsel table. Does the prosecution have an opening argument?"

"We do, Your Honor."

Phyllis stood up, all five feet and one half inches of her in fiery red. Her investigator, Detective Samuels, looked admiringly at her, expecting great things. She pulled away from the table and without a word of warning, walked behind us and planted herself behind Ramón and José.

"These are the accused. These are the men charged with one of the most horrible crimes in the history of Los Angeles County, crimes that showed a wanton disregard for life, property and human suffering. I want you to remember this, ladies and gentlemen, every time you look at them. I also want you to remember this."

She stepped briskly to an easel which she had set up by the jury box, and peeled away a wrapper from a display card, showing the blown-up photos of six corpses.

"These are the victims of that crime. Three men, two women and a little girl, age seven, a refugee from Vietnam, killed as a direct result of the actions of the defendants, killed before she knew what life was all about. Every time you see the defendants I want you to think about these victims and remember, they are responsible for these deaths."

Clay came to life, stood and slapped his papers on the table.

"Objection, Your Honor! This is prejudicial and assumes facts not in evidence!"

"Counsel will refrain from interrupting," warned Reynolds. "This is only argument, after all. The prosecution has the right to say anything it wants to at this stage."

"But Your Honor, there is no foundation, no evidence has been shown linking the people in these photographs to my client. It's a gross abuse of my client's right to an impartial jury."

Ramón watched the exchange indifferently. Pimienta, as he had done throughout the proceedings, stared down at the tabletop, ashamed to lift his eyes to the world. The jurors and the public followed with their eyes the arcane language, their raised eyebrows and worried expressions evidence they knew something important was going on but they couldn't quite figure out what.

"Counsel, your objection is noted for the record. Mrs. Chin, please proceed."

Clay waved his arms in frustration and more than a touch of theatrical helplessness. "Your Honor, I must beseech the court . . ."

Reynolds swung his chair toward Clay, barely controlling his irritation.

"Mr. Smith, if I hear another word out of you about—"

A low rumble, like a freight train coming through the courtroom, abruptly cut the judge's wrath. He stopped, glanced around anxiously. Others in the court, more experienced with the ways of California, ran for the exits. Dozens followed, and the doors quickly jammed with screaming spectators who had not imagined they'd come to their own burial. The floor started vibrating, as though the building had been mounted on a stirrer; the walls moaned.

"*Qué coño es esto, chico?*" asked Ramón, What the fuck is this?

The moan became a loud roar, as of herds of lions and bulls and elephants squealing from fear, a ghastly chorus of destruction. The walls cracked, the overhead light grids swayed, then fell at the corners of the room. Mrs. Gardner stood up in front of her jury seat, hands together, eyes raised heavenward,

"I'm sorry, Lord, please forgive me, Lord!" she cried, then was jolted to the floor, landing next to where other jurors already lay, covering their heads with their notebooks. Judge Reynolds, immobilized by surprise, remained in his chair, watching with awe. Lucinda broke through the crowd surging out of the court, jumped over the bar and came to me. I took hold of her arm and yanked her under the table with me. Ramón scurried in after us.

"*Terremoto!*" I cried.

The noise kept ascending in an unbearable crescendo, the thunder and wailing an irresistible force that would not be spent. I felt the entire floor sway from side to side, as the building gyrated on the flexible beams installed between the fifth and sixth floors, still shouting out a screech of agony from the unaccustomed wrenching and twisting.

Another light grid fell, this time directly on top of where we'd been sitting just a moment before. I looked to my right and saw Pimienta, Clay and Detective Samuels also crouching under the table. Behind us, all the reporters and cameramen had fled except for a lanky cameraman from CNN, who with incredible aplomb kept videotaping as though he were shooting the Rose Bowl from the press deck. A wall collapsed, billowing clouds of plaster dust rising in the air. The drinking fountain at the far end of the court was wrenched off the wall, the pipe shooting out a spray of water that turned into a grimy stream spreading down the gray carpeted floor. The noise of unspecified destruction rang all around, things being shattered, damaged beyond repair, in the maddening confusion all around us.

Then, just when it seemed as though the clamor could be no louder and the walls would stand no more, the shaking stopped. A great void and calm floated down from above, as though a great judge somewhere had ruled, This far you shall go and no farther. I heard the clanging of hundreds, thousands of alarms throughout the city, a warning late and futile. I peeked out from below, then stood up, still wary, ready to dash down should the tremors continue. But they didn't—all their fury was spent. Then I noticed D.A. Chin still standing where she had been when the objection had been raised, her hand still up in the air, as though the heaving and shaking had activated an automatic Off button. The jurors sat back in their seats, brushing the dust off themselves, and Clay, Pimienta, Samuels and all the others crawled out from their hiding places. Phyllis turned to Judge Reynolds and calmly asked, "May I proceed with my opening statement?"

For the next two days, all anyone talked about was the quake— where were you when it hit, how strong did you feel it and was this the big one that's been predicted for the last fifty years. It wasn't until the trial resumed, weeks later, that the Caltech seismologists were able to pinpoint the center exactly—a spot bordered on the west by Broadway, east by Spring, north by the freeway and south by First Street—in other words, within one hundred yards, give or take a few feet, of the Criminal Courts Building.

Everyone's nerves were rattled afterward. At night I would wake up from the slightest unfamiliar noise, dreading to hear that low rumble again. Although Lucinda never let anything get in the way of a good night's sleep, during her waking hours she too was jittery and ill humored. For the first time since she'd moved in, we fought over things that even at the moment in which we exchanged angry words we both knew were insignificant and served only as an excuse to rid ourselves of the vile premonition of disaster waiting to strike at any moment.

The earthquake worked to Ramón's advantage in one respect— it closed down the entire CCB for a week. That allowed me to go and investigate the witnesses Phyllis had planned to put on. Her intention had been to hand us the list of witnesses the day before testimony started, jamming them on us, before I could locate the skeletons in the closet for which they hoped to obtain leniency from the prosecution. But with the unexpected respite, I had plenty of time to dig up the bodies.

The first name on Phyllis's list was Remigio Flores, the parking attendant who'd spotted Ramón and José rushing into Schnitzer's Jewelers. His address was listed as El Sereno, an East Los Angeles neighborhood whose name translates, appropriately enough, as the watchman. But neighbors said the man I wanted had moved under police protection a month before. His landlady, a honey-skinned woman with dry curls daubed yellow and a smile full of crooked teeth said two uniformed officers had come in the middle of the night and helped Flores get all his possessions out of the nine-by-twelve room he'd been renting from her. The cops had even paid his last two months rent—$345.50.

"He hasn't done anything bad, has he?" she asked.

"Not that I know of."

"Is he still alive? In my country, when the police comes and gets you in the middle of the night like that, you never return."

"What country are you from?"

"I'm from Guatemala, from a little town called Huaquexchipotl, up in the mountains."

She stood in the doorway to her apartment, a fat shoulder jammed against the door frame. Behind her two roly-poly black-haired tots, faces smeared with chocolate, fought on a tattered couch over a toy truck. The smell of boiling beans escaped out the front door. On the wall hung a crushed velvet tapestry of the Last Supper, where Judas spills the salt and John asks, Is it me?

"Well, let me tell you, in this country, it's the opposite. If the police come for you, you never disappear, they're always taking you from one place to another. You're like a grieving soul that's never laid to rest."

"Aee, *Dios mío*, what a terrible fate. It's better to be dead then and find your peace."

"Yes, it's terrible, I agree. Do you know how I could find him?"

The stands at the soccer field in Griffith Park were full by the time I got there, a sea of brown faces waving banners of the respective teams—blue and white for the Colonials of Antigua, black and yellow for the Senators from Guatemala City. Mothers handed out sodas and tacos to their brood from large tin pots, giggling maids and housekeepers on their day off pointed out their favorites in the teams. Old men with callused hands argued about the strategy of the reigning world champions; an occasional vendor moved up and down the benches, selling coconut candy balls and packets of spicy hot corn nuts that stained your fingers yellow. In the field, young men who the rest of the week were car wash attendants, pump jockeys, busboys, gardeners and assorted day workers, warmed up in their sparkling clean satin uniforms, basking in the sun of admiration shining down on them from the stands.

The Colonials' team captain called over a boy of about twenty, with curly black hair, fair skin, deep-set brown eyes.

"Remigio Flores?" I asked.

He looked suspiciously at me, a nervous feline eyeing the open window.

"And if I were, what's it to you?" he snapped back in Spanish.

"I'm a court-appointed investigator on the Valdez and Pimienta case."

"Who? What?"

"The Jewelry Mart murders," I said.

"*Ah, no,* no way, I'm not saying anything," he replied, walking away. I followed.

"Why? Because of the police?"

He whipped around, spat on the ground before me, close enough so that a few stray droplets fell on my shoe.

"I'm not afraid of anything. But you guys are crazy, the devil's got into you. I saw what they did when they went in there."

"What did you see?"

"I saw them go in with their weapons, all spaced out, looking like they were from another planet, *mano.* And their car, it smelled of coke and PCP. They even left their glass pipe on the front seat. They were *locos.* I saw them go in and just chop 'em down, just like you cut down a banana tree with one stroke of the machete, *whack!* That's it!"

"Did you look at them through the front window when they went in?"

"Sure I did. They planned the whole thing. First thing they did was start smashing the glass counters, then they started shooting."

"Did the guard pull his gun out first?"

"I don't want to talk about it any more, OK?"

"Did he or did he not?"

A heavy hand fell on my shoulder.

"Dude doesn't want to talk to you, bub." I turned and looked into the well-developed pecs of a Manhattan Beach surfer type, six four, blond, tanned, back the size of an African shield.

"Who the hell are *you,* bub?" I brushed his hand off my shoulder. Surf Boy showed me a regulation LAPD badge.

"Detective Moat, LAPD. He's under protection, let him be."

Not to be outranked I pulled out my ID. Moat looked at my pained expression in the photo, handed it back smiling.

"Cool, dude. Fucking P.I. So what."

"I've got a right to talk to him."

"If he wants to talk to you. He just said he didn't."

"No, he didn't. How would you know?"

"*Andale, pues, ¿me tomas por otro gabacho pendejo?*" said Moat with a ringingly clear Mexican accent.

"Hey, maybe you think you're a whitey asshole. I just said I want to talk to him and you're stopping me. I'll have to report this to the court."

"Dude, you can take your report and stick it up your butthole."

"Am I going to talk to him or not?"

Moat hesitated, then called Remigio over. "*Tú quieres hablar con este gringo?*"

"I'm no fucking gringo," I said.

"No, man, I no talk."

Moat turned, opened his arms expansively. "Tough tamales."

Remigio looked at me hatefully, then spit again. This time it landed on my shoe.

"*Excusa,*" he snarled. Just then I caught the tattoo of the snake and the stars on his left forearm, the symbol of the Abakuá cult, follower of Shangó.

"Remigio," I shouted as he walked away, "*Shangó kuramá, ya kurumamá, ya kurumá.*"

He turned and looked at me in sheer terror, then set off running. Moat shook his head in despair. "What the fuck did you do?"

He sprinted after Remigio, catching him somewhere near the Mulholland Fountain on Los Feliz. By that time I was in my car, driving home. I saw the two of them arguing violently, Remigio obdurately shaking his head. Moat slapped him and Remigio finally calmed down. I turned left on Los Feliz and tooled up the hill.

I'd meant to scare Remigio, repeating the ritual words the god Shangó mouths whenever he possesses one of his followers: *You know me not to speak of me.* I knew that would frighten him. But I should have known he'd be even more scared of the LAPD.

11

the house was in flames, the walls issuing long red fingers of fire that wanted to grab me and hold me in pain forever. I heard the moans and yells of the others trapped before me in burning rooms down the corridor, the din of their suffering an unbearable howl of pain. The exits were closed behind me and the windows were gone; tall, smooth flanks of fires danced all around me. A foul smoke, of sulfur and burning hair, in masses gray and blue, floated in the room, choking me, revolting me. I had no idea where the exit was, all I knew was I had to go forward, a firewall twenty feet high crackling and hissing with the sputtering of consumed existence twirling behind me, a siva of destruction. Only the ground, covered with a viscous, porphyritic liquid, was not aflame, cooled by the torrent that issued from somewhere ahead. I couldn't remember how I had entered the all-consuming room or why, I knew only—deeply and darkly—that I had to perform some deed, convey some message, leave my mark somehow. I struggled onward down the corridor, flames reaching out, wanting to grasp me, the cries becoming louder and heavier. The corridor started narrowing in on me, so that now the flames were only inches away, their heat singeing my clothes, the smoke peeling my lungs. I dropped to the ground, crawling, and realized the liquid was blood. I looked ahead. Another wall blocked my exit. Out of the raging holocaust I saw my father, strapped to a cross, medical tubes dangling from his body, doomed—I knew—to burn for eternity. I screamed in pain for him, in suffering, in revulsion and fear, I screamed until I thought I could scream no longer but no sound would come out, my words were all muffled, taken from me by the mocking red and yellow flames that smothered me . . .

—

"Charlie, Charlie!"

Lucinda straddled me, her knees on my shoulders, worry lines creased on her brow, eyes wide open and startled. She moved aside, I sat up. The pillowcase was wet with perspiration, my T-shirt soaked through. My heart raced desperately, lunging ahead of life's rhythms, still crawling for a way out. A pinkish gray dawn peeked over the hills of Griffith Park.

"You were shouting like a madman," she said. "I had to hold you down, you were moving so much."

"It's nothing, just a dream," I said, looking for my lost composure. My head still buzzed and I could still feel the burning flames licking my body.

"What was it?"

"Nothing. I, I just dreamed I was in hell, that's all."

"Hell," she said gravely. Then, "Did you see your father again?"

"He was in the flames. On a cross."

She lay down beside me, silent for a while, both of us feeling the slow ticking of madness dissipate.

"You have to go see Juan Alfonso," she said. "I'm telling you, someone cast a spell on you, somebody wishes you evil."

"Don't be silly, that's mumbo jumbo." I got up, washed up, came back towel in hand. "Besides, who'd want to do that?"

I'm fifteen, trying to sell enough magazine subscriptions to buy me the moped my father refuses to pay for. The manager has taken a group of us out to Homestead to go door to door to make our pitch. The sun burns down in the middle of the afternoon, tall grasses at the end of a paved road that stops abruptly on an abutting field. I knock at the last house on the street. A woman in her thirties with plain eyes and dark hair opens. I recite my pitch. She smiles at my fumbling and says she'll buy Vanidades. *She invites me inside. A large white concrete block house with terrazzo flooring and painted grates. I enter the living room as she goes to her bedroom for her checkbook and I am astonished at the sight. A floor-to-ceiling altar, as wide as the room, decked with flowers, fruits, pictures of saints, implements of magic, all shiny and new, like a thousand small creatures looking at me with curiosity from the stacked altar. The woman comes out, check in hand, sees me staring in fascination at the offerings. She smiles, then frowns and puts her hand to her head.*

"Come," she says, giving me her hand, "someone has cast a spell on you, you must be cleansed. Come, don't be afraid, good-looking, women will never harm you. Come."

She leads me to a side room, sits me on a rush chair, sprinkles holy water on me, takes golden scissors and snips the air around me, reciting unknown words, her eyes closed. She takes a lit cigar—lit when? by whom?—then sprays the smoke on me. At the end she says, "Someone dark wishes you evil. I tried my best. It will not harm you. Your mother will lose her fertility. Your father—"

"What about my father?"

"Your father will always be with you. You will be wealthy and you will be poor and you will be wealthy again and your name will not be forgotten." She sighs, blinks her eyes, then hands me the check.

"Now remember, two years for the price of one, right?"

I go home and over the next few months I haunt the botánicas of Little Havana, I collect stamps, books and prayers, learn about the divining coconuts and the sacred stones and figurines until the day I come home and see my caldron in the garbage, the stones scattered, a Catholic priest blessing the house.

"Never again," says my mother, "never again." Two months later cancer is diagnosed, she undergoes a hysterectomy. Never again.

■

The chef was pudgy and pockmarked, dressed in white, his apron stained with the butter and herbs he brushed on the focaccia. He tossed the pizza dough and then wrestled it into shape on the marble cutting board. Knowing he was being watched, he gave a little extra polish to his movements, a seemingly careless flourish here, a just-so motion there for the benefit of his audience, so we would all know that although dark and Mexican he could be as great an artist as all those other milk-white *gabachos* who worked alongside him preparing the hundreds of loaves consumed at the Crocker Restaurant every day. Someone dropped a glass on the floor and the chef looked up from his labors. He saw me, smiled.

"Hola, Pancho, cómo estás?"

"Very good, Señor Morell. How you been?" he replied in English, determined to show off his newly acquired knowledge of the language. The last time I'd seen Pancho he'd been picked up for selling coke just two days after serving a three-year stretch in Chino for armed robbery. I was the only one who believed his story that the police had the wrong man, that he was just having a beer at the pool hall when the narcs busted in. I rounded up three witnesses to testify that Pancho had just walked in off the street that day and that the real dealer was another man, also named Francisco, who had run out the back. The judge dismissed the case and reprimanded the cops for their "excessive zeal," code words for ramming the ignorant to make their bust.

"Carmen, she is well?"

"Yes, thank you. About to relieve herself."

"Congratulations! How many does that make?"

"Four girls and three boys. Already picked out his name. Adolfo Fidel."

"May he grow big and strong."

"Thank you, Mr. Morell."

I gave my name to the captain. He checked his list, picked up a menu and led me through the sea of tables occupied by the mid-rank executives who descended in packs from their lairs in the granite and glass towers of the complex.

"Are you a friend of Francisco's?" he asked.

"He was a client of mine. How is he doing?"

"Well, I don't want to say this, but it's something terrible. He thinks he's making tortillas instead of focaccia, it all comes out real dry and overcooked. They've told him many times but he just won't listen. I'm afraid they're going to let him go soon. Here's your party."

Clay was sitting in the upholstered booth, martini in an extra-large glass on the marble-topped table, reading a report. He waved at me to sit down.

"Get a load of this," he said, passing the file. "It's from the coroner's. It says the little girl showed signs of sexual abuse when she died. Chin just picked that up this week. They're going to amend the complaint to reflect that. You figure what kind of chance these guys have, not only killers but child molesters as well."

"How do they know it happened at the store?"

"C'mon, Charlie, you know they don't care if the charge doesn't stick. They just want to prejudice the jury even further. Even supposing they were willing to find them not guilty of the murders in the first degree, there's no way they're going to let child fuckers walk the streets again."

"What did Reynolds say?"

"He has to allow it, what can he do? They can amend the complaint down to the wire. For what it's worth, I know our guys didn't do it. It seems the little girl had a vaginal infection ever since she got out of the refugee camps in Malaysia. Wouldn't be at all surprised if grandma was turning her out."

"How's that?"

"For money, what else? A whole bunch of them old geezers really get off on diddling little girls. You hungry? I'm starving."

Clay raised his hand. A tall slender waiter dressed all in white with a pink bow tie approached, announced his name was Chuck, that he would be our waiter and recited a litany of overpriced specials. Clay's speculations on the little girl had spoiled my appetite so I asked for a bowl of minestrone.

A busboy came up.

"*Señor Morell?*"

"*Sí.*"

"Don Francisco, he send you this." He set down a basket of freshly baked focaccia. The fragrance of rosemary and garlic tickled my nose. Pancho was smiling from the other end of the room.

"Tell him it's the best *bolillo* I've ever had." The busboy shook his head gladly. I waved at Pancho, who waved back and resumed his pounding, kneading and brushing.

"Lemme have some," said Clay. "Hey, this is good! Well," he continued, between bites of bread and sips of his martini, "the case looks bleaker than ever for our boys."

"Nobody ever said it'd be easy."

"Yeah, but now it's impossible. So my guy's turned."

"Again?"

"You know the old Chinese saying, the wise man always changes his mind. I just cut a deal with Chin. They'll recommend second-degree manslaughter."

"But that's just seven years, max."

"Yeah, that's right. He might walk after he testifies at the trial, what with credits and all. Course he is going to have to say Valdez was the only one shooting, that he was the one who planned it, that it was a robbery originally and that's what Pimienta was in for but that Valdez freaked out and got a little trigger-happy."

"Jesus."

"None of that either. He'll testify this had nothing to do with religion, that they weren't really involved in *santería* or anything, it was all a scam to rip people off. That's how they made their money after coming to L.A., that and some petty coke dealing."

Clay seemed happy he was telling me this, relieved that now he could join the winner's circle once more. Chuck brought a floury minestrone, green peas floating on a goldenrod mess.

"Well, that certainly changes the game," I said, stirring the soup.

"Ah, don't take it too hard. You know, if your guy pleads, he's still got straight life, no parole. That's better than the gas chamber."

"If that were the case he would have pled a long time ago."

"Listen, Charlie, I've known you for a while and I think you should bail out now. Declare a conflict, make something up. What's the use? What are you getting out of this?"

For a moment the prospect of release flapped before me like a bright yellow flag, snapping in the wind of freedom.

"I can't do that. Look, seriously, I know this is going to sound ridiculous, but no matter what the guy did, he's going to need somebody to help him."

"You forget he's defending himself. You're not his lawyer. I figure there's somebody else maybe can convince you better than I can. There she is."

Cutting through the crowd, Mrs. Barry Schnitzer, born Barbara Taylor, dressed in an all-white Ferre linen outfit with white gloves and wide-brim hat, swept into the restaurant like a Russian grand duchess. From her demeanor you would have expected little girls scattering rose petals before her, serfs lifting the hem of her train so it wouldn't touch the ground. Clay stood, pecked her on both cheeks.

She eased into the booth, tossing her blond curls out from under her hat, so they would fall in a shiny cascade on her shoulders.

She extracted a filigreed case and took out a cigarette, which Clay promptly lit with a greedy smile. Theatrically, meter measuring every beat, she exhaled then deigned to look at me.

"We meet again, Mr. Morell."

"Certainly not my idea. I wasn't expecting *poule sur le divan* for lunch."

"Beg your pardon?"

"Bad joke. Since when are you two working together? Oh, silly me, I forgot, you two run in the same crowd, the buyers and the users. That's how we met originally. So tell me, was my life decided over dinner at L'Orangerie or after drinks at the Riviera Country Club?"

"Give her a chance, Charlie."

"What's the use, I know the message. It goes something like, Mr. Morell, I loved my husband so much I won't rest until I have given you all my money so you will beg off the case. You know, this really shows a lack of imagination on your part. You haven't given me a single reason why I should quit, except for money. I think of dozens every day. But to you, anything that isn't status or money doesn't exist. Terra incognita—remember your Latin, Clay? Outer space. There are other things in life besides big fat bank accounts or"—I fingered the lapel of Clay's suit—"custom English tailoring. But you guys wouldn't understand that. You know, I feel sorry for you, I really do. You're prisoners of your own desires, you're blinded to anything other than dollar signs."

"There is nothing else, Mr. Morell," said Mrs. Schnitzer, flicking the ash from her cigarette. "I believe someone named Marx once wrote something about materialism and the market economy. Money is the Western world."

"Must have been Groucho's missing brother. Look how well it turned out for Russia. In any case, Mrs. Schnitzer, this is no longer the West of old. In fact, sometimes I look around and wonder if we're still the U.S. or whether by some twist of fate we've slipped into a big Johannesburg. But I'm sure you wouldn't know about that."

Mrs. Schnitzer patiently heard me out. "Frankly, I don't know which is more remarkable, Mr. Morell, your contempt for our system or your inflated sense of self-worth. Your kind of posturing went out, I think, with Diogenes and the Romans. Or are you the honest man the philosopher was searching for in Rome?"

"Better, Mrs. Schnitzer, much closer to the mark. Only it was Athens, not Rome. But apparently I'm still not getting through. As I'm sure you'll recall from your stock trading days, sometimes people do the most ornery things for no reason at all, just because someone got their dander up. So let me level with you and give you the first free piece of advice you've gotten in years. There is no way on God's earth that Ramón can win this case. Clay here will tell you that his boy is going to sing until the cows come home, and seeing that he was the only witness to the event, Valdez better start saying his mumbo jumbo because he's going to meet that big mamba snake in the sky pretty soon. So do me a favor, leave me alone, will you? You are a very beautiful woman, but somehow you manage to insult me every time I see you."

"I'm sure you've heard the old Spanish saying, There is no worse blind man than the one who doesn't want to see. It's obvious you don't know Valdez."

I shook my head, unbelieving. "How do you know him so well, if I may ask?"

She inhaled calmly, in perfect proportion, a funnel tipping into her pink lips.

"I had some dealings with him."

"In what capacity?"

"Barbara, I advise you not to say anything else," warned Clay.

"What's this?" I asked.

"That's all right, Clay. I was once interested in some of these tribal religions."

"What? Wait a minute. Now you're telling me that you were personally involved with Ramón?"

She readjusted her hat, like someone readying to leave in a few moments. Her reserve slipped just a fraction.

"I didn't say that. I was interested in all that voodoo stuff. After all, I'm sure you know so many of our help are devoted to this kind of nonsense that I thought it might be amusing to attend one of their ceremonies."

"Let me guess. The deceased went with you, didn't he?"

"Barry did go once or twice. We were...I know it sounds funny but at the time we were worried about a hostile takeover and he thought it wouldn't hurt to have all bases covered, so to speak."

"Barbara, I urge you, don't say another word," said Clay, his face flushing a beet red.

"Why? What harm is there in it? It's a free country, isn't it? Freedom of religion is our first-amendment right."

"That's OK, Clay. I'm sure the lady would deny all this on the stand. Besides, I'm not the attorney, Ramón is. Just one thing, did it work?"

She stamped out her cigarette, gazed down at the Steuben glass ashtray. When she looked up again her eyes were an iridescent gray, pupils distended, as though a frightful scene of some kind had just played out on her memory's inner screen.

"Very well, I'm afraid. The man who was planning the takeover fell in his bathtub and cracked his skull. We were saved."

"Did Schnitzer pay Ramón for this?"

"I don't know if he ever knew how effective his attentions were. Barry did say he told Valdez to help himself to some bracelets. He gave him a discount card or some such."

I looked at Clay. He averted his eyes. "You've known all along, you son of a bitch."

"I didn't think it was material."

"Not material? That's the motivation for their going to the store. They weren't planning a robbery, they just wanted to get what was theirs back! That's not a special circs case and you know it. No way they could get the death penalty for that."

"That's if you can prove it," countered Clay.

"You unprincipled bastards."

"Why don't you just quit it, Mr. Morell. It doesn't matter what their intentions were, there was a bloodbath and my husband was killed."

"In the eyes of the law there is a difference between something that got out of hand and willful murder."

"You mean to say six people dead were all accidents?"

"It could very well be."

She put in her last bid.

"A quarter million, Mr. Morell. That's how much you will get. Two hundred fifty thousand dollars if you just walk away, right now."

I got up, pushed the table out.

"I am going, but you can keep your money. I have to sleep nights."

She smiled, almost sweetly. "All right, then, but watch the road. I hear there's a lot of bad drivers out there."

Was it she who had ordered the Crips to push me down the ravine? Or was she just waving her contempt before me like the cape before the bull?

"My policy has your name on it, lady. Don't be surprised if the cops come knocking at your door if I buy the farm on the freeway."

I walked away, crossing in front of Chuck, the waiter, who stood before a table, pad in hand. "Did I tell you about today's specials?"

—

If walking through a Hispanic barrio is a visit to an occupied territory, going into the black ghetto of Los Angeles is like stepping into a war zone where hand-to-hand combat has been dragging on for years. There's a stillness of the spirit that rises up to the blue dome of a cloudless sky, the chill that surges when the orange sun sets and the shootings start ringing in the night, homeboy squad cars full of gang members playing hip-hop music as loud as the speaker will blast, slipping in and out of alleys, sewer rats come up to claim the streets. Swarms of petty dealers gather around customers' cars, flashing rocks, pot and guns, while in the homes of the neighborhood, families huddle behind barred windows and try to drown out the curses, cries and shootings with a new prayer, the new ritual of the people, the ceremonial watching of the 27-inch stereophonic hi-fi television set and videocassette recorder showing the icons of sitcom land.

The heart of the ghetto was where Sergeant Porras had sent me, searching for the homeboys who'd tried to bump me down the Benedict Canyon grade.

"Go ahead," he dared, "make this duck walk." He handed me copies of the reports, laboriously extracting them from the pasteboard looseleaf binder. "You're such a hot dick, let's see if you figure out who wanted you dead."

I parked in front of the first location in the report, set in the middle of a long block of storefronts near the Long Beach Freeway. J- PAUL'S, said the sign, YOU BUY, WE FRY. It was the only establishment open at eleven in the morning. The other stores, a sundry collection of used-tire places, liquor stores and appliance shops, were still shuttered tight, as though the owners were expecting Nazi tanks to roll in at any moment and start firing.

The smell of catfish and cod frying in vats of bubbling brown fat laced the air as I pushed open the dusty front screen door. A young black woman with layers of corn rows dangling in front of her pitted face looked up from the chopping board where she was slicing green cabbage.

"Yeah?" she said disdainfully.

"I'm looking for Bernice Adams."

"Who are you?"

It was time to act official. I showed her my card quickly, then pocketed it just as fast.

"Private investigator appointed by the Los Angeles Superior Court."

She stopped chopping long enough to give me the kind of look usually accompanied by a shove and a curse.

"You mean you a detective, like on TV?"

"Something like that. Is Mrs. Adams in?"

"You be with the poh-lice?"

"No. I'm with the courts. Could I speak with Mrs. Adams?"

"Who be looking for me?"

A short, obese black woman with thick eyeglasses and rollers in her hair, wearing a green dress that showed three escalating layers of fat wrapped around her stout middle, came out of the back room. She slipped on a clean cook's apron, bringing the long sashes around the front. A row of gold bracelets jangled as she tied a butterfly knot.

"Girl, you deaf? Somebody asking for me?"

"It's this man, Auntie. He come from the police."

My cue to play smart and courteous. "From the Los Angeles Superior Court. Are you Mrs. Bernice Adams?"

"Yes, I am. Is Gerard in trouble again?"

She moved over to a counter and felt her way around, her fingertips skimming the surface of the salt and pepper shakers, the pot covers, kitchen knives, to find her bearings. Out of a bin she extracted a couple of long yellow rubber gloves, put them on and bumped her way to the sink.

"LaTona, that catfish's ready. You go take it out."

The girl laid down her knife and removed the basket with the frying pieces from the tub of oil, hooking it above the fryer to drip dry. Mrs. Adams dipped her gloved hand in a bucket in the sink and took out a still wriggling catfish. With her other hand she grabbed a cleaver nearby and in one measured thump chopped off its mustachioed head.

"You can come over here if you want, mister. I can't see too well in this light."

She chuckled at her private joke as she took a knife and split open the fish, its bloody black and blue innards spilling out on the chopping board.

I stood next to her, breathing in her dusky, violet-based perfume and the briny fumes of the eviscerated fish. She seemed wrapped in a layer of warmth and life, at ease in her own abundant skin.

"I don't know how many times I'm going to have to bail him out of troubles. I thought after you take him to Y.A. camp that he learn his lesson, but things don't go in that thick head, he don't want to listen none. I'll tell you right now, he ain't been home in two days."

"I'm not here for Gerard."

"You ain't? Then you should be! Somebody got to teach that boy a lesson and it sure ain't me. If only my poor sister was still alive, she'd whip him something good but I can't properly do that. Only thing I catch is catfish and that's because they in the bucket already, heh, heh."

"No, ma'am, I wanted to talk to you about Rusty Thompson."

Mrs. Adams shook her head disapprovingly.

"He don't know when he got it good either. What he do now, go steal some old lady's purse?"

"How well do you know him?"

"Rusty? He was Gerard's best friend for a while. I took him in after his folks got sent away for selling rock. He no longer here, though."

"When did he move out?"

"'Bout six months ago. He be bothering LaTona here and I wasn't gonna have none of that so I showed him the door is what I did."

LaTona tucked her head in between her shoulders and chopped the cabbage into even thinner slices, softly, to catch our conversation.

"What happened to him?" asked Mrs. Adams, rhythmically slicing and filleting.

"He died in a car accident."

"*No!*" I heard behind me.

LaTona put down her knife and ran crying from the room. Mrs. Adams gave a sigh and continued her work.

"I always afraid he come to no good, that boy. I'm sorry to hear that."

"When he died he had some religious objects in the car."

"Religious? What kind you talking about?"

"Voodoo dolls, necklaces, things like that."

"You mean that gris-gris stuff. Yeah, I recollect he be interested in all that, saying that was African gods, a black man's religion. Him and Junior was always talking about that."

"Junior? What's his full name?"

"Eric Howard, I believe. He be always at the Big Hole up on Vermont."

"Thank you very much. I'll be on my way."

"You do that."

I looked back as I walked out. Surrounded by the bloody carcasses of dozens of catfish, Mrs. Adams chopped on, even as tears unwanted rolled down her face.

The Hole was a drive-in coffee stand shaped like a giant doughnut, the apex of its diameter fifty feet above street level, an altogether unappetizing structure of lath and plaster a few blocks from the freeway. Ten miles down Vermont Avenue you could see the fog-wrapped Palos Verdes peninsula, but here the sun was warm and careless. A handful of BMWs, the crack dealer's vehicle of choice, were parked around the building.

I sat at the chipped Formica counter, two dozen brown eyes in black faces fixed on me. There are times in this business when you can't help but sound like a TV detective, asking the right question of the wrong people. I was just hoping that like in the movies the hero would live to see another day.

I asked the counterman if he knew Rusty.

"Sure do. Blood was always messing round here. Ain't seen him lately. You the police?"

"No, I'm from the courts. How well do you know him?"

"The brother, I've known him since he was ten. I tried to make him see the light but I cannot say I succeeded."

"Excuse me?"

"I'm a Jehovah's Witness. I asked Rusty to our meetings but he would rather hang around with them."

He gestured at a table of leather-jacketed observers.

"Drugs are our tribulation, mister, a sign that the end is near and we should prepare."

"Do you know if he believed in *santería*?"

"What's that?"

"An Afro-Cuban religion. It says African gods still visit us."

"And the Lord said, 'Thou Shalt Have No Other God But Me.' No, sir, I can't..."

An elbow nudged my ribs. I turned to face a short, slim black man with freckled complexion and tightly curled nappy red hair, wearing several chains of gold on his all-black outfit. Two massive gentlemen, looking like tryouts for a Raiders linebacker position, flanked him.

"You looking for Rusty," he said.

His two sidekicks smiled a shade less than friendly.

"He's dead."

"I know. So what?"

"He tried to kill me and I want to know why."

Red turned to his guards, flashing a "poor idiot" smile.

"You with that Cuban motherfucker who iced the people at the store?"

"Yes."

"I knew Rusty couldn't do it. I told him, use a Mac 11, chop him up good, but that ofay say no, push you down the cliff. Shit, man, I said, shit man, that's bullsheet but he wanted you dead in an accident. Let me shake your hand, dude." He took my hand in his small, soft paw. "You one lucky motherfucker."

"What did this white guy look like?"

" 'Bout your height, green eyes, sandy hair. Oh, yeah, he had this birthmark, looked like a heart, left side his face."

I felt true terror the moment he said that, a shard of ice ripping my insides, my heart galloping in a red cloud of fear. I thought I would fall off the stool. I gripped the edge of the counter, took a breath.

"What's with you?" said Red.

"Nothing. Here." I took out my wallet, showed him a picture.

"This the man?"

"That be him. Who's the kid?"

In the picture my father grinned at the camera, clutching a very happy ten-year-old.

"That's me."

12

to this day I don't know how I spent that weekend. In fact, I can't even recall how I made it home from Compton. I suppose the fever I'd been struggling with finally broke and that I drenched my bedsheets with the gallons of perspiration that stream out of my body whenever I have a temperature. But on Monday I arose like Lazarus to greet a baby blue sky, jays chirping from the branches of the jacaranda outside our balcony. The ghost of the morning moon lingered over the green hills, casting a sad look at its blinding mate before hurling back into darkness.

How could it be, I asked myself. Can the spirit of my father . . . C'mon, Charlie, knock it off. It's impossible. You're just under stress and Red didn't know what he was saying. The dead don't return. There are no wandering souls. You scattered Papá's ashes over the Atlantic almost twenty years ago. This is Los Angeles and the ghosts of the East don't surface in this desert. It's the stress. Forget it. Forget him. Forget.

For several days Lucinda had been gauging me for signs of the spell she thought I was under. Not that she was less affectionate. If anything, her concern increased over my affliction so that she practically overflowed with tenderness, bringing me *café con leche* in bed, arranging cut flowers throughout the apartment, leaving little notes hidden in the folds of my clothes telling me how much she loved me.

She always took pride in being a cunning lover and at that time she felt compelled to give me greater proof of her virtuosity. She found an inexhaustible supply of things to do with my cock and my mouth so that, after a warm bath and a cold shower, where we would scrub and finger-fuck each other, we'd rush to the bed, teasing and playing with every membrane, every orifice and follicle, joining body parts that no manual I knew had ever conceived of joining, experimenting in ways I had only shamefully fantasized before. I never knew my big toe and second toe would fit so easily into her dripping cunt or that a common everyday vegetable inserted up her ass, while I fucked her from the front, would cause such squeals of joy. I bound her and punished her with my leather belts, whipping her ass until it burned to the touch then sticking my cock in her mouth so that she, tied up to the bedposts and with her eyes covered by a blue silk scarf, would know only pain and penetration as her sensual contact and she would suck my dick like a babe a mother's tit, till I would be on the verge of coming, then I would stick it up her ass until I could delay it no longer then I would whip it out again and explode all over her beautiful blindfolded face, her pink tongue dashing to and fro, trying mightily to catch the white jism that oozed down.

At other times I would be her slave, compelled by strikes of flyswatter or clothes brush to run my tongue up and down every inch of her body, from her black-and-gold-flecked toenails to the roots of her henna-tinted hair; then she would slap me and pummel me till I would cry and then would push me down to the hollow between her legs, holding my head down with both her hands, guiding my tongue, like a darting hummingbird's, to the exact spot in her groove, I spreading open the labia so that her hard little clit would push its way out of the curly bush, demanding to be stroked and pinched and kissed and nibbled. Lucinda would wrap her legs around me, arch her body forward and press even harder, her pelvic bone a fist in my mouth, as she rubbed my lips raw and she would come in torrents of dense, briny juice four, five, six times in quick succession. She then would kick me away, my breath forced out of me and I'd go tumbling to the floor, only to crawl back next to her and ask for her forgiveness as she lay burning, eyes rolled white to all-seeing heaven above.

In essence Lucinda had become a kept woman, my mistress, housekeeper, confidante and counselor, my brown-skinned tropical Albertine. Not that she minded. She positively bloomed under my lustful ministrations. She lost that boniness that made me think of a fashion model or an escaping Central American refugee, rounding out her hips and swelling her bosom so that when she disrobed, her two full tits would stand up unaided by bra or bustier, dark nipples proudly pointing forward. Paradoxically, the few extra pounds made her face even more angular, as the cheekbones fleshed out, making a permanent dimple that carried the eye delightfully down to the full fleshy lips. I opened charge accounts for her at Magnin's and Neiman's, bought her shoes on Melrose and Rodeo, had her hair done by José E. and her nails by Miss Julie, that is, I turned her into my own Galatea, a living *poupée* whose only chore was to take care of my needs. She excelled to such a degree I had the feeling she had been waiting for someone like me to come her way and give her the final sheen she so desirously adopted as her own.

But in spite of our sexual transport, I can't say that I really loved her. Whenever I was away from her, her image would fade from my memory, her face and body not crossing my mind until I would turn the key in the keyhole and she would run to my arms with a kiss and a story, her perfume wrapped around us like a garland. Then I would look at her and I would again be surprised, like the tiger eyeing the ocelot, by her beauty and liveliness, as striking as the first moment I saw her.

Don't misunderstand me, I thought myself very lucky indeed to have her. The few times friends and colleagues saw us together, at an outdoor cafe in Santa Monica or exiting a movie theater in Westwood, I felt exultant at their envy. But whenever we were alone, away from bed, I would invariably, in my mind's eye, pick out the small defects in her beauty, flaws so small they could hardly be called flaws, perhaps just irregularities, like the high curve of her nostrils or the flat, blunt ends of her fingers or her knobby knees, and I would want to be a surgeon or God to wipe away these imperfections and make her the pristine image of my desire. Perhaps it was best that I never succeeded, for who knows what monster might have resulted, what terrifying creature, born out of my efforts, I would have held by my side all my days long. I was searching for someone or something and Lucinda became the handiest expression of that unformed longing, the path out of the thicket of the instant, at the end of which waits the mighty creature who feasts upon the foolish and unwary.

"Daddy," she said to me one afternoon, "daddy, let's go dancing, it's been so long since I went dancing."

Her choice was Alberto's, a converted rice hulling factory on the edge of Chinatown, next to the railroad tracks. From the moment we set foot inside, Lucinda was in a swirl of smiles, kisses and dances, the doorman letting us in ahead of the line, old friends greeting her with *abrazos*, the barman sending a drink to our table, the leader of the band dedicating to her a Latinate "Love Me with All Your Heart."

"I used to come here every weekend before I met you," she whispered as we danced.

"Am I keeping you prisoner?"

"Ah, *papi*, no, no, daddy, of course not. It's just that every so often I wish you wouldn't pay so much attention to that stupid trial. You worry too much. That's why you're sick all the time."

"So you don't think someone put a spell on me anymore?"

"You're so bad. Even if they did, you can always fight back. So when things happen, you can face up to them."

"What things?"

She brushed her lips on my earlobe. "Oh, things like your father coming to life before your eyes or thinking other people have seen him. That's done by someone who wants to destroy your self-esteem, your center. The way you fight back is with a cleansing. If not, then with plenty of entertainment." She laughed. "Yes, I recommend we go out more often, to break that spell."

"I didn't know I was living with a witch."

She pressed her body against mine, her thigh in my crotch.

"I'm not a witch, I'm just magical."

It took a while before her friends and acolytes left us alone at the upholstered booth. She twirled the bamboo umbrella in her drink and gazed wistfully at the couple on the floor.

"I always wish I'd been a dancer. You know, like in the Tropicana? To go out there with all those costumes and just show them on stage. But back in Cuba my dance teacher said I wasn't good enough. You know how it is there, the government tells you what to be. We don't need any more dancers, she said. She said, every *mulatica* like you wants to go on stage. What we need is teachers, more physical education teachers. So that's what they had me doing. Let me tell you, I was so happy when I got off the boat in Key West I almost kissed the ground."

"Didn't you?"

"*Ay, chico,* no, it was too dirty." She snuggled up close. "I'm so glad I found you, daddy. Or that you found me."

"Have you ever thought of studying a career? I'd help you, you know."

She frowned at the prospect of serious work. "I don't know. I don't really know what to do. Sometimes I look at the television, you know, and I wish I were a lawyer or a doctor or any one of these things these American girls are. Even a capitalist! But then I tune in my *novelas* and I know everything is going to turn out all right. That's when I realize a woman's job is to love her man, that her happiness is to have someone by her side through all the tragedies that life inflicts on us."

"What would you do if something happened to me?"

She pulled away slightly, sizing up my question, then snuggled in close again.

"Nothing. I would die, that's all."

I was in the bathroom, a white-tiled cavern with fifteen-foot ceilings and a long troughlike urinal when the drunk stumbled in. He was reeling from the combined effect of who knows how many beers and *aguardientes* and he staggered off to the toilet, where he retched quickly and efficiently then cleared his nose and came to take a leak.

"Bad night?"

"*Coño, chico,* it must have been the *tamal* I had at the Gallego's. That meat was bad, I'm sure."

His dick was dark, long and uncircumcised, like that of many Cubans. He shook it carefully several times, dropped it inside his trousers, zipped up. He splattered water on his face at the washstand, his wiry hair and coarse features glistening in the yellow light.

"So how's Palito doing?" He spoke with a thick pasty voice, the native Cuban intonation modified by another fast-clipped dialect that I failed to identify.

"Excuse me?" I walked to the towel dispenser, pulled one out, dried my hands .

"Palito. Ramón Valdez, *coño*. How is he doing?"

This was new. Palito? Ramón had friends?

"Yeah, he's a buddy of mine," he said." We go back to the Mariel. You hear from him lately?"

"He OK, considering he's facing the gas chamber."

"You're fucking with me. He's in the soup again. That son of a bitch, he never learns."

"You didn't know? It was in all the papers."

"I just got back into town. I've been in South America several years, eh, in the lumber business, you know? We don't get many papers in the jungle."

"Has he always been crazy?"

"Ramón? Like I said, that son of a bitch never learns. I saw him cut open a guy's throat in an argument once. You don't fuck with him, that's for sure. The funny thing is, he always claims he didn't do it, the gods did it, Oggún did it, Oggún this and that. He was always pulling that witchcraft shit on us. We worked together for a while, you understand, back in Miami."

He rolled up the paper towel, threw it in the open oil drum that served as wastebasket. I could hear the band starting to tune up back on stage, the horn riffs, the twanging of electric guitar and bass.

"How did you know that I know him?" I asked as we walked back out together into the pressing crowd.

"*Coño*, man, you're with Lucinda, I saw you."

"So?"

He stopped, grinned. The band broke into a merengue and the dance floor filled with spinning couples.

"They were man and wife, didn't you know? *Muchacho*, she sure is keeping you ignorant. You better ask her a few questions, know what I mean?"

■

We came home at four in the morning, sweaty, tired and with more than just a haze of alcohol. We stopped in the stairwell to kiss, I sucking her tongue, feeling her breasts, she running her hand down my crotch and squeezing my cock, fingernails sinking into the pants fabric. I carried her upstairs, she giggling every step of the way, dropping a shoe in the landing. I struggled with the lock, popped open the door, set her down on the couch and without even closing the door, without more kisses or foreplay or any words of anticipation, I tore her panties off her and stuck my cock inside her. She was ready, her cunt running hot and drippy, a hand that came out from between her legs and held me and squeezed me as the vaginal walls clamped around the shaft of my dick. She writhed the moment I entered her, throwing her arms around me, lifting her legs and wrapping them around my back, her pubic bone rubbing against mine, burying her head in the crook of my neck. She shuddered as she came and I ejaculated. We uncoupled. I fell, thumping on the carpet. She made her first sound then, a low-throated purr of delight. She stretched her arm and ran a hand through my hair. I could hear a bird singing, anticipating the warm dawn.

"You're such a lover, Charlie."

"As good as Ramón?"

She whipped her head around. "Where did that come from?"

I got up, pulled up my pants. She made no effort to cover her nakedness. I sat on a tufted leather footrest she'd picked out at an antique shop.

"Why didn't you tell me you were married to Ramón?"

"Ramón who?"

"Stop fucking around. Ramón Valdez."

She adjusted her dress, sat on the couch. Then she leaned over, kissed me on the cheek.

"You're such a child, really. I'm dripping. Let me go to the bathroom."

I was sitting in the same spot when she returned. I had not had a thought during the interval.

"And?" I asked.

"And what?" she replied, sitting primly, legs closed. "I don't see what the problem is."

"Were you married to him or not?"

"I may have been."

"What cunt-faced answer is that? Were you or were you not—and if so, why didn't you tell me?"

"I told you he stayed with me when he was released from Atlanta."

"But it's different if you're married to someone, don't you think? I mean, at least you'd remember that."

"You're annoying me. What is your problem? I don't see why you should be so concerned about something that may have happened years ago."

I got up, put my face up against hers, inhaling the sweet smell of vodka in her breath, the fragrance of love and French perfume. I fought a maddening desire to kiss her and make love to her again.

"Because you're living with me, that's why. Because I'm working to defend your former husband, if he was married to you. Because you're taking me for an asshole, pretending the sun don't shine. Because, and this is the main reason of all, you didn't tell me the truth. So tell me now, because tomorrow it will be simple enough for me to find out. I want to hear it from you first."

She looked me in the eye, the bits of yellow in her iris shining from the reflection of the hall light. For the first time I detected an emotion I had never noticed in her before, a feeling that became more powerful because she was trying so desperately to conceal it. She was afraid. The possible reasons for that fear rose fully armored from the soil of my imagination.

"*Ay, mi amor*, I'm so sorry. I didn't want to hurt you. There are so many things we do for love, when in love, that later we regret. One remembers then the stupidity of it but not the delirium that pushed you into doing these things. Do you understand me?" I leaned back, saying nothing, keeping my face as blank as I could, while passion and pride did battle inside of me.

"No, you're not a woman, you wouldn't understand. You can't comprehend the things we do for those we love. When Ramón came out of Atlanta, he was different from the man he is now. He was so happy to be free again—the world was full of possibilities for him. He had plans to take up his engineering career, to start a new life. The first thing he did was learn the language. In a matter of months he was fluent in English. I was so amazed. He seemed determined to make his own way. We started going out then, he was so sweet." She stopped, gave me a perfunctory smile. "If it is any consolation, you are a better lover. You're more inventive. He was never that interested in anything other than the standard. But then sex isn't everything, love is."

She took a breath, reliving those moments as though to make sure no important aspect was left out.

"Then something happened. He had a job selling kitchen appliances from door to door, frying pans, pots, things like that. They told him he was being let go because they were cutting down the sales force. But he thought it was because he was black and Central American housewives wouldn't open their doors to him. He tried getting a job with other Cubans, but the Cubans who came right after the revolution, like you, they didn't want him either. He was a Marielito, a common criminal, and black. So then he tried to get work with an American company, run by some negros selling hair products. But they said he was Hispanic and they turned him down too. He began doing drugs. Funny thing was that's when he finally started making some money, with Juan Alfonso, fixing houses for resale. But it was too late by then, it was easier to sell dope.

"After he stole from the lady's house in Pasadena, I was let go so I went to live with him. I don't remember much of that time— it was all a string of parties, nights spent waiting for deals, days lying in worried sleep.

"We got married. We thought it was a fun idea, so we took a plane to Las Vegas. We pretended to be Puerto Ricans and we were married in a chapel up there at two in the morning. That's all I remember of that. I don't know how long we stayed there or anything. When we got back we told everybody so I became his wife. You know that the marriage is not valid if you give false information. We knew it too, but we wanted to believe so we pretended.

"Already he'd gone back to *santería*, thinking it would protect him. But then he got more and more into it, like he was someone else, the gods riding him every day and riding him hard. When Oggún would come down, he'd be abusive and insulting and would fuck all these women right in my face. So one day I just walked out. Juan Alfonso helped me. He's a good man, he's been like a father to me. That's when you came in."

She turned expectantly toward me. I contemplated her fine bones, her tawny skin, her frightened eyes. Was it fear that we would break up, or was the cause something else altogether? She sidled over, laid her head on my lap. I played with her hair.

"When you moved out," I asked her, "had he already gotten the jewels from the store?"

"What jewels?"

"The ones he used on his altar, the bangles, pendants, that sort of thing."

"Oh, those. He said he had gotten them from a friend of his. I don't remember who." She offered her face to me again. "Will you forgive me for not telling you before? I was so afraid."

"Afraid of what?"

"Of losing you."

If it is true that the eyes are the gateway to the soul, Lucinda was expecting a full frontal attack and had barricaded herself for the fight. The fear was gone and those shiny orbs were coolly observing my reactions.

"There's nothing to forgive," I said, planting a kiss on her forehead. "You just forgot to tell me, right?"

For the briefest moment she was startled. "Oh, yes, daddy, yes, that was it. I forgot. I forgot. God, I love you so!"

13

"**a**re you sick?" asked Ramón, looking up from the open murder book. The bright overhead light in the interview room cast away all shadows.

The old feelings of nausea and desperation had swept over me as the sally port clanged open and the deputy showed me into the interview room at County Jail.

Ramón had been waiting, deep into the law books, preparing the motions and legal citations he would press in his defense.

"I've been better," I answered.

"You don't look too good. My mom always used to give me an infusion of chamomile leaves. You should try it."

"Is your mother still alive?"

Ramón's eyes went soft for a moment. "No, she died after she got out of the prison camp," he said without regret, distant.

"Is that why you turned against Fidel?"

"I was never for Fidel, I just liked to fight, that's all. I lost interest in the revolution when I came back from Angola. I was a hero of the revolution, with a degree, and the best thing I could get was a one-room apartment in Old Havana. Then my kid died from typhoid, just like we were in some undeveloped country. That's when I said this is a piece of shit. At that point, I decided all I wanted to do was to leave the country. But, *oye*, enough of this shit, the past never helped anybody. You gotta look ahead, *mano*, look ahead."

Never again did Ramón mention his family. To him, the past was a gallery of rooms, once lived in but now nailed shut and abandoned, the undisturbed dust of memories growing thicker every year. To him, that was the natural order of things.

The thrust of Ramón's reasoned defense was a very simple yet specious proposition. It centered on a version of the diminished-capacity defense called the McNaugton test, which posits the innocence of a defendant when he cannot distinguish the difference between right and wrong during the commission of a crime.

"The legislature changed the McNaugton test after Dan White," I reminded Ramón. "You can't claim that sort of thing 'cause it won't fly."

"You mean diminished capacity, not the sort of cultural argument I'm going for."

"You really think that you will be able to convince an American jury to spring you after you—" I stopped, but he finished my statement.

"After I killed innocent men, women and children and left the store like it was a butcher shop?" I nodded. "Carlitos, why else are we here?"

"I don't see how you can convince them."

"I told you it's a cultural defense. Look, to prove murder you have to prove criminal intent, correct?"

"Yes. But if you think the jurors are going to close their eyes to the deaths and let you walk, you got another guess coming."

"Wait a minute. We also have the special circs, right? Murder in the commission of a robbery. My point is, there was no robbery here."

"I know that's what you claim." I stopped, debated whether to tell him about my conversation with Mrs. Schnitzer but opted against it. I knew she would deny everything if called to testify. Besides, I wanted to see how much he would reveal. In the final analysis, it was his case, his defense, his problem. Not mine. "That's not what Pimienta is going to say."

Ramón winked at me, almost lewdly.

"You let me handle Bobo. After I finish with him, the jury will see he's accusing me to get his ass off and he won't be believed either."

"You mean just because he's getting immunity he's automatically discredited? Don't count on it. When you have something as bloody as this, jurors will go out of their way to give the prosecution every advantage. They'll probably figure that if they can't get both of you, they'll get just you then."

"OK, we'll see who's right when the time comes. Meantime, get in touch with this lady, ask her when she'll be available to testify." He pushed over a paper with the name Graciela de Alba.

"The ethnologist? C'mon, Ramón, she's at least eighty years old and lives in Miami. If she's not dead already."

"She's seventy-seven. She's well, don't worry about that," he said with self-confidence. "Just ask her when is the most convenient time for her, but that we'll probably only be able to give her about forty-eight hours' notice."

"Is Reynolds going to let this through?"

"He has to. He doesn't want to be reversed on appeal. Which is exactly what will happen if I can't bring all the evidence regarding state of mind."

I leaned back in the chair, stared at the stamped tin ceiling. "It might work. You'll probably get murder one and beat the special circs. Shit, you may even get manslaughter and get out in ten or twelve."

I would have thought this possibility would have cheered him but some people are always seeking the absolute.

"No way, José. We're beating this. We're walking here."

"Oh, yeah, sure, and I'm Robert Redford. Wake up, guy, you'll be lucky to get manslaughter. We're talking six dead, including a little girl."

"I'm not responsible for the little girl."

"And the rest, Ramón? How can you ignore those bodies crying out for justice?"

"Maybe so but I didn't do it."

"Right. So it's back to blaming Pimienta, right?"

"No, not at all. I don't know who did it."

"C'mon, we've been through this before. Don't play games. If it wasn't you and it wasn't Pimienta, then who the hell did it?"

I could hear myself screaming, hurling the words like so many bullets at him.

"Oggún did it, I didn't do it. Oggún is the one you want."

The day the courts reopened Los Angeles was socked in by the thick tule fog usually found in the Central Valley, making it impossible to see more than ten feet away from your nose. When I opened the shutters that morning, leaving a mumbling Lucinda under the covers, the dense layer of marine air was cotton candy shredded over the garden. A few red roses stood out spectrally in the mist.

Downtown, near the CCB, some romantic graffiti artist had spray-painted red letters on sidewalks, posts and traffic light boxes—"I loves to fuck womens because their pussy feels so good." Outside the CCB itself, the poet had changed his song to "I loves to fuck policewomens because their pussy feels so good." Wondering what paeans of praise he would write on knowing judges, district attorneys and deputy sheriffs, I surged with the crowd into the building.

Workers on scaffoldings were inserting earthquake-proof rods in the walls, their whining and drilling an aural backdrop throughout the day to the play of the courts.

At Reynolds' court the day's business was in full swing as I entered. I caught the judge in the middle of a lecture to a black prisoner for still selling cocaine at the ripe age of fifty-two.

"Mr. Helms, now, that's a young man's crime. You have too many white hairs on your head to be doing that kind of nonsense."

"Yessir, Judge."

"It's not the magnitude of this crime, sir, it's the ludicrousness of it. Now, what are you going to do if some young one comes along and wants to take over your corner? Why, you probably wouldn't have the strength to fight him off and Lord knows what you might have to resort to."

"Yessir, Judge."

"I'm mighty sore at this, sir, Mr. Helms, I'm mighty sore. I just cannot tell you how disappointed I am that a man with your age and experience is still doing this kind of foolishness."

"Yessir, Judge."

Reynolds saw me enter and waved me over to sidebar.

"Good morning, Mr. Morell."

"Morning, Your Honor."

At sidebar: "Charlie, we won't be starting with your case until eleven this morning. We're hearing a lot of matters from the closed courts. You can go get yourself some coffee. Or maybe you'd want to stay and watch justice being done."

"No offense, Judge, but I'd rather go get some breakfast. The thought of justice is more than I can bear on an empty stomach."

Then I saw him. My father.

"Mr. Morell!" shouted the judge as I stepped out. I heard the stomping of boots running after me.

I trembled from the tom-tom drumming of my own racing heart. He glared at me for a second, then dashed into the hallway leading to the stairs and the men's room. I saw the door to the men's room flash open.

Fighting a current of history and emotion and reality struggling to carry me to the other shore, feeling that my steps were taking hours for each shoe to reach the tiled floor, I ran slowly, almost floating, to the men's room.

We were alone there. I saw his legs inside a stall. Behind me I heard faint steps and a distant voice that carried an urgent message.

"Charlie, Charlie!"

Slowly but ever so strongly I raised my leg and kicked the stall door open. The man inside had his back to me. He turned and again I saw my father's face, black circles under his eyes, the heart-shaped birthmark on his cheek, blue-gray eyes brimming with pain and meaning.

"*Recado para tí*," A message for you, he said, then waved and vanished slowly into a gray mist that left nothing in the stall except a large cordovan-brown roach on the toilet seat, waving its antennae. I stepped on the roach, then saw an explosion of light and a voice cried out, "Charlie, Charlie, what's with you?" and then darkness.

I came to briefly in the ambulance. The paramedic injected something in my arm and I felt myself impelled through the city streets, the siren of the ambulance a comforting harbinger of release. A dense soothing darkness grew rapidly around me so that, ever so briefly, I was cocooned, returned to the primal liquid of warmth, love and security.

The light hurt when I opened my eyes again. A nurse by the bed was taking my pulse. I was the only patient in the room, the other beds empty.

"Am I going to live?"

Nurse Pavlovich, as per her tag, with creamy skin, blue eyes and salt and pepper hair, answered just as facetiously, "Another fifty years or so, if you take care of yourself."

She dropped my hand, wrote on a chart that she placed at the foot of the bed and walked away.

"You had a nervous collapse, sir," said Dr. Patel later. Nut brown, with thick glasses and bad skin, he seemed ready to sell me some concoction at a Bombay bazaar. "You must try to relax, it is no good for the body to be subjected to so much stress. Have you perhaps had auditory illusions?"

"Better than that, Doc. I've seen ghosts. They wanted to know the time of day."

"That is very disturbing. Your physical exhaustion must have depleted your psychic energies as well. You would be well advised to take a vacation, some kind of break from your routine. Who knows what will happen otherwise? I cannot be held responsible for what may occur. No, Mr. Morell, I want no accountability of any sort. You must relax."

"Sure, Doc. All I've got is the biggest murder trial since the Nightstalker case. I suppose I can call in for a replacement and spend a couple of weeks in Acapulco."

"Oh, no, longer. Yes. I would most definitely advise you to take a very long vacation. A sabbatical, perhaps?"

"You sure you don't work for Mrs. Schnitzer?"

"Excuse me?"

"Forget it. I can't do it."

"Then there is only one thing left to do."

"What's that?"

"Face up to your fears and make your work your vacation. Yes.

Not everyone can do so, but if you personally do not succeed, I am afraid it could be drapes for you."

"Curtains, you mean."

"Yes, of course. You have a funny way with words, Mr. Morell." He chuckled.

Clay visited me that afternoon, looking bashful, as though not sure he should be there at all. I was certain he'd come to see if I was out of the game altogether rather than from any goodness of his heart, if he had one, but I was glad to see him all the same—hell, to see anybody besides the comedy team of Pavlovich and Patel.

"There are easier ways to get off the case," he said.

"Believe me, this is not something I thought of."

"You know, Reynolds really thinks you're an integral part of the defense team."

"I'm flattered."

"You should be. He stopped the trial until we get further word on your condition. Ramón put up a fuss but he overruled him."

"What do you mean? I thought it would be Phyllis who'd push me out."

"Not at all. She wants to preserve all semblance of fair-mindedness and is bending over backwards." Pause. Smirk. "Ramón doesn't want that. He wants errors for appeal, in case he bites it."

"So Ramón wants to go on?"

"Yeah, he said you were obviously overworked. I joined, of course. Hey, what can I do, you know where I stand. I can't cut a deal until everybody is there."

"Ramón wanted to proceed without me?"

"Shit, he said maybe you should be taken off the case altogether. The judge nixed that."

"Tell them I'll be back on Monday. Chill out."

I tried reaching Lucinda several times that day without success, but she finally rushed in, breathless and worried, in the late afternoon. My landlord, Enzo, had already dropped by and shared a split of Monte Albano, which I mixed with the Demerol that Patel had prescribed so that by the time she arrived, I was feeling exceedingly fine and proceeded to prove it by pawing her all over. She slapped my hands.

"*Niño malo*, bad boy, you know you're not supposed to do that here, wait till we get home."

"*Mañana, domani,* tomorrow, *volare,* oh, oh."

"You mean they will let you go tomorrow."

"*Cantare,* oh, oh."

"You're very happy for someone in your condition. Here I was, thinking you had a heart attack and you're singing and want to make love."

"I'm a free man, my girl, I'm free, free. *Libre de todo pecado.* Tomorrow I'm out of the Valdez case. Forever."

"How's that?"

"I'm sick, that's what, you know, *enfermo.* I can't go on anymore."

Lucinda looked worried for a minute, tilting her head at me questioningly, as though not certain of what her pretty ears were hearing.

"Are you sure?"

"*Positivo.* Look, there's the story."

The TV set, which just moments before had been showing the travails of love and greed in Santa Barbara, now slid into the even more fascinating real-life stories of corruption, lust and murder in the "Five O'Clock News." I saw myself being taken out of the CCB on a gurney and slid into the ambulance like a loaf of bread into the oven.

"Must have been a slow news day," I said.

The anchor, a pretty redhead with an upturned nose, gave a succinct account of my now world-renowned nervous collapse, which made my heart cheer even more. Then the other shoe finally dropped.

"Our reporter, Jim Ollin, has been following the Valdez and Pimienta case since the beginning. In an exclusive report, he has uncovered that this is not the first time controversy has dogged the steps of investigator Morell. Just a few years ago, when he was an attorney practicing in Florida, a major scandal developed when he also suffered a nervous breakdown during a trial. Jim?"

14

" ■ s this on the record?"

I The question floats disembodied, ethereal, in the sunny confines of Judge Reynolds' chambers, a wisp of smog that filtered through the double-paned windows and left its smelly presence in the room. I look at the grave, somber expressions of people who must perform an unwanted chore, withdrawn, weighing the consequences of their instant actions. Phyllis, in a blue Ungaro suit, sits gathered and erect. Clay, leaning back, in a gray suede chair, unbuttons his custom-made pinstripe jacket. The judge, at a black leather chair behind his teak desk, sips from his mug of decaffeinated Kenya Roasted and stares at me. They all stare at me. The question goes unanswered.

"Judge, are we on the record?"

The source of the question is finally clear. Janine, the reporter, straddling her machine, points her crooked nose at the judge.

"Right," says Reynolds, clearing his throat. "This is the case of the People versus Valdez and Pimienta. We are meeting in chambers, myself, Judge Reynolds, Prosecutor Phyllis Chin, Defense Counsel Clay Smith and court-appointed investigator Charles Morell. Off the record. Janine, this will be sealed after delivery of the transcript. Back on the record. The purpose of this hearing is to determine the competency of investigator Morell following allegations of professional misconduct. In addition, it is to consider the request by Mr. Morell to be discharged from the case because of illness. Mr. Morell, suppose you tell us why you want to be taken off the case."

It is now my turn to cleave an opening of escape. I hesitate. Do I want to expose myself, tell them that I think my father is haunting me, that I'm paying for something they have no inkling of, couldn't possibly conceive? Then the moment is lost.

"Your Honor," interjects Phyllis, "I'd like the record to show that the prosecution is categorically opposed to this hearing. The purported misconduct on the part of Mr. Morell, were it to have happened, which is yet to be proven, lies outside the jurisdiction of this court and is irrelevant to the conduct of the case in chief. We're talking about events that happened in another state years ago that have no bearing on the handling of this trial or on Mr. Morell's performance since his appointment thereto. Moreover, since Mr. Morell is Mr. Valdez's investigator, it is clear that only Mr. Valdez can discharge Mr. Morell, unless there is gross negligence on the part of Mr. Morell, which has not been seen so far. Since the allegation of improprieties have thus far been unproven, and since Mr. Valdez has not demonstrated any actual desire to discharge Mr. Morell, given we have not received any written motion to that effect, the District Attorney's office maintains that this hearing is moot, insofar as the competency issue is concerned. As regards Mr. Morell's request because of a medical condition, that is something only a qualified medical doctor can give an opinion on. I'd point out that we have no testimony before us from any such medical expert, so again we move that this hearing be closed for lack of good cause."

Reynolds suddenly ignites like a haystack when someone drops a hot poker. Clay wants to object but the judge waves him down. I sit and watch in agony.

"Objection, Your Honor, the prosecution—"

"Just a minute, Mr. Smith. Off the record. Phyllis, just what the hell are y'all trying to accomplish here? Do you want us to have a clean slate or not?"

Phyllis, unperturbed: "I'd like to go back on the record, Your Honor."

"No, we are not going back on the record just yet. I want you to tell me why you don't want the light of day to shine on these claims and why you wouldn't let Charlie here bow out for reasons of health."

"Your Honor, I will not answer any questions until we're back on the record."

Reynolds tries to stare her down but Phyllis simply returns his gaze. The judge quits. I think, how will Ramón ever defeat a woman like this?

"Fine, have it your way, then. Back on the record. Now, Ms. Chin, having heard your arguments, I'm still not certain why the District Attorney's office would want even the tiniest scintilla of misconduct to surface at this trial, which will be later grounds for reversal on appeal."

"Your Honor, I'm pleased that the court feels the People will win this case, even if I don't agree this particular issue would cause a reversal. The position of our office is that Mr. Morell has been a competent qualified investigator and that appointment of a new investigator would hamper our efforts to conclude this trial expeditiously. It is now two and a half years since the incident and witnesses may soon start to become a problem. I need not go into how recollection fades with time, I'm referring just to availability. As I said before, none of the interested parties, the prosecution, Mr. Valdez or the court, has officially moved to replace Mr. Morell so we believe this whole hearing is moot."

"Objection renewed, Your Honor."

Reynolds again waves at Clay, as though he'd heard enough of his protests.

"This is not a formal hearing, Mr. Smith. No need to keep pressing your objection. Now then, Ms. Chin, I have heard your arguments and to tell you the God's honest truth, they don't make a lick o' sense. I'm sure you're aware the magistrate, at his discretion, and with sufficient cause, may discharge any of the parties that have been appointed by the court for a particular case. Now, these here are serious allegations which resulted in Mr. Morell's suspension from the Florida bar. In addition, he has personal difficulties that must be addressed."

He turns to me in his most paternalistic plantation-owner pose. "I know how difficult it must be for you, Charlie. We're all here to help."

"Thank you, Judge," I mutter.

"You Honor," adds Clay, "I must put on the record as counsel for Mr. Pimienta that we are opposed to any further continuance of Mr. Morell's services on behalf of the codefendant."

"I heard you."

"We believe that his actions are prejudicial and that the semblance of misconduct on his part cannot but—"

"Off the record. Clay, will you shut up! You are here as a courtesy, you shouldn't give one rat's fuck whether Charlie is in or out. It can only make your boy look better, especially if District Attorney Pellegrini finally gives his OK on that deal you and Phyllis cut. So pipe down now, will you? Back on the record. Objection noted, Mr. Smith."

The judge turns his sorry countenance upon me again. "Well, Charlie, what did happen?"

I swallow hard, feeling the hair on my forearms standing on end.

Her name was Doris Diaz. She was short, fair skinned, with russet-brown hair, hazel eyes and the cutest upturned nose, which made her resemble an Irish lass more than a child of old Spain. Only, she was Cuban and that's where the problem started.

At the time, like so many other husbands, I thought I was happily married, burying myself in work and sports, surfacing only for a quick recharging of sexual batteries, a scan of the emotional horizon. I had a flourishing practice in Dade County, a house in Coral Gables and a cabin in the Keys, a new Porsche, a beautiful, successful wife and a wonderful little boy who was conveniently taken care of by a succession of nannies. I'd managed to put away all memories of my father, to the point that on the occasional Sunday when I would visit my mother at her stifling apartment off Eighth Street, I would be puzzled to see his picture amid the votive candles and religious portraits; his image no longer carried any emotional weight. My sister, Celia, had left on her ongoing South American adventure so I was the only child, the faithful son.

I don't remember exactly which of my acquaintances or satisfied clients recommended me to Doris's brother, Guillermo, who hired me after her arraignment. What I do remember is our first visit and the haunting impression she made on me.

Before going on, I must confess that after I grew up, I never cared much for Cuban girls again. I thought they came mostly in two types. The most common was the dark-haired, bountifully endowed fair-skinned woman, the Latin bombshell of hourglass figure and sparkling eyes. Then there was the alternative, the thin, animated type, with small breasts and wide hips, shrewish and commanding where the other was sweet and complaisant.

Doris did not fit into either of these forms. She did have a slight problem, though—she had killed her boss with an old Roman dagger.

That Doris had handled the knife, that the body was dead and lying on the floor like some tropical Scarpia when the police arrived at the high-rise office overlooking mauve Biscayne Bay, of that there was no doubt. In fact, she had called the police herself. At one point during pretrial discovery I listened to the tape of her call to emergency assistance.

"Hello, police? I would like to report a killing. The victim is Bob Lazo, the architect. At our office, 2648 Brickell. No, I'm afraid he's dead, I checked for vital signs. Yes, I was there. I am she. I killed him. My name is Doris Diaz, his assistant. Yes, I'll be right here, waiting. Thank you very much."

In the normal course of events she would have been at liberty during the duration of the trial on her own recognizance or, at worst, on, say, fifty thousand dollars bail, since she had no record of any kind, had a large and concerned family and a spotless work history. A model citizen. But then politics stirred the pot.

At that time Dade County had one of its recurrent racial flare-ups, one of those occasions when a Cuban officer, more prejudiced than any Mississippi redneck, bashed in a black student from the Overtown ghetto. The black section exploded in fiery rage for four days and nights, leaving in its wake ashes, six dead and dozens wounded in confrontations with the police and the National Guard. The few local black politicians argued that the root cause of the conflict was the unequal system of justice in Dade County, that one set of law books applied to blacks and another to Anglos and Cubans.

Doris appeared in court for her arraignment the day after the riots finally sputtered to a close. The prosecution, feeling the pressure from every local politico wanting to cleanse his hands, declined to take into consideration Doris's background or the uniqueness of her crime and asked for no bail. Failing that, the District Attorney's office asked for a million dollars bail.

The magistrate, who truly believed all men are equal before the law (and whose son had been left at the altar by a Cuban girl) granted the million-dollar-bail motion without hesitation. No sooner had he banged his gavel than the bailiffs were bodily removing Doris from the courtroom, to the loud anger of her many friends and relatives.

Her public attorney, Chuck Windham, was more than happy to pass on her case.

"She's cuckoo, Charlie, if you ask me," said Chuck, his ferretlike face expressing unaccustomed dismay. "She won't take the deal they're offering and she won't give me any defense. She refuses to talk about what happened. I don't know what anyone's supposed to do in a situation like that."

"I guess she thinks you're Saint Jude."

"I'm Jewish, what do I know from saints?"

"He's the patron saint of lost causes, Chuck. Really, you should be a little more ecumenical, you know."

"I got all the ecumenical I need at home already, thank you very much."

When the matron at the jail brought Doris out in her shabby, worn shift, without makeup or jewelry, she looked like a small and tired schoolgirl. She barely acknowledged me when she sat down at the metal table. I started introducing myself in Spanish, as most Cubans do in South Florida. She cut me off right away in a lockjaw New England accent, saying she preferred English, an unusual request among Cubans, who pride themselves on preserving the language and customs of the homeland.

"Did my brother William hire you?"

"You mean Guillermo? Yes, he did."

"That's so pretentious. I don't know why he feels he has to impress people with his Cuban-ness. He was named William, he was christened William, we've always called him William. I don't know what his problem is."

Had I been listening, truly listening, that short statement right there would have told me all I needed to know about the case, would even perhaps have advised me to disqualify myself. But my ears were plugged and I was thinking with only one organ, the one rising to attention between my legs. My spontaneous erection was the second warning sign, the major bell to the minor ringer, alerting me to the perils ahead.

"I've filed motions for a new bail hearing in your case. No matter what happened, I think a million dollars is excessive. It's not like you're a drug dealer ready to take the next flight out to Colombia. Or are you?"

She smiled, shook her head. Her eyes showed some life, a little color appeared timidly on her cheeks.

"Good, I didn't think so. I've received all the papers from Mr. Windham, your previous attorney. He said you weren't willing to take the offer they made you, second-degree homicide, fifteen to twenty-five. Is that still the case?"

She nodded.

"All right, then we'll go to trial. But, as you know, I have to find out what happened. I have to mount our defense. Mr. Windham said you wouldn't tell him anything about the incident or why it happened. I'm sure you understand we can't very well prepare a case like that."

"I suppose you're right, but there isn't much that I can tell you."

"Why don't we start with your relationship with Lazo. Was he something else besides your employer?"

"You mean were we lovers?"

"That's one possibility."

She looked sideways, eyeing the frumpy matron sitting in a corner of the room, eyelids dropping in sleep.

"Can I tell you a story?"

"Only if it's true."

"You decide after I tell you."

"Fine. Go ahead."

■■

She told, I realize now, a common enough story among Cubans, similar in ways to mine—a girl divorced from her family by character and circumstance, vowing to become an architect no matter what. But Doris's way had been blocked by an apparently unsurmountable obstacle, her sex. After graduating from a northern school of design, she was employed by a firm where the lead architect had stolen her work on a major project, then blackmailed her into having an affair, supposedly to help her get credit for her own work. In the end the architect claimed the plans as his own anyway, then dismissed her for incompetence. After a nervous breakdown she moved south, thinking her own people would be kinder. But her last employer, the victim in the case, the dearly departed Bob Lazo, had started intimations of the same game—no sex, no credit—and was trying to seduce her one night when she grabbed the poniard from the display case and sank it in four inches above the meeting place of his shoulder blades.

"It's a fascinating story," I said. "But I'm afraid it doesn't get you off the hook."

"Why is that?"

"Because the circumstances of the two incidents are not connected casually and there is no corroboration of the state of mind at the time of the murder. There is no proof that the first architect stole the plans, only your word. But let's assume the jury were to believe it happened, it still wouldn't condone the actual killing, since it was another man who was murdered. And the deceased did not steal any plans. The prosecutor and the judge will keep out all reference to the prior incident as irrelevant. You lose all justification for the killing."

"Lousy system of justice."

"It's the only one we have. Unfortunately, it doesn't take too kindly to related circumstances. Have you been examined by a shrink?"

She recoiled, as though I'd slapped her. "Why?"

"Because right now that's probably your best bet to get off, to claim temporary insanity."

Doris was about to lash out but then she crumbled. All of a sudden I wanted to hug her and tell her everything would work out fine, that I would find a way for her to come out clean. I noticed that my erection had dropped and that all the feelings had gone to my heart instead, which now watched in sorrow.

"Whatever you say," she replied. "I don't know what to do anymore."

"Fine, that's what we'll do. Let's see what the shrink says and take it from there. He's a good friend of mine, Dr. Malcolm Richards. He'll be contacting you in the next few days to talk things over. How are they treating you in here?"

She glanced up and her eyes welled with tears for the first time. She tried to smile, but the grin became a grimace.

"It's so bad in here . . ." Her voice trailed off.

"I know. I'm sorry. I'll try to get you out as soon as I can. Is there a message you'd like me to give someone, your boyfriend maybe?"

She smiled wanly, feeling sorry for herself. "I don't have a boyfriend. Sometimes I think I've forgotten how to love, all I know is hate."

"Don't say things like that—things will work out."

"Yes, of course."

At first I didn't notice my constant distraction with Doris. I would just find my mind wondering back to my talk with her at the most unlikely places—watching the Dolphins, arguing before a judge, even playing ball with my son. Every time I'd think of her I would experience the same stirring in the groin, a desire to run my lips all over her, and I would wonder what she was doing at that very moment, whether she was watching the same rainstorm or being bitten by mosquitoes just as much.

Even after I failed to get excited over making love with my wife, I didn't think I was in trouble. But Olivia easily noticed something was amiss.

She grabbed her pack of Kent Lites from the nightstand, lit a cigarette and exhaled, studiously examining the smoke blowing out of her nostrils.

"What's wrong with you?" she finally asked.

"What do you mean? I'm sorry, honey, I'm just worried about work, I guess."

"Is there another woman?"

I turned to her, dramatically grabbing her hand.

"You know I've never cheated on you. Why are you saying this?" She jerked her hand free. "You know we hadn't made love in three weeks?"

"I'm sorry."

"No, you're not. You're hiding something. I don't know what it is, but you're not paying attention to anything but that."

"I'm just busy, that's all."

"That's no reason to neglect your family. Or your wife."

What does she know, I thought, taking refuge in my hurt feelings and indecision. She's probably worried about the ratings at the station. If we're talking neglect, let's not forget who's gone Saturdays and Sundays, who doesn't have time to play with the kid because she's too busy with her career, who's the one who thinks marriage is just a part-time obligation. Not me, that's for sure!

But I didn't say any of those things, I just let their poison seep slowly through me to the bitter end.

Frieda Kohler, my investigator, came in to see me with her report a few days later.

"You got yourself a pretty one, Charlie." She slapped the report on my desk.

"She's just a client," I replied guiltily.

"I meant a pretty good case, son. If you can get her out, I'll have to hand it to you."

"No one said it would be easy. Does her story check out?"

"By and large. Did you know Doris was a party to a divorce? Name of Gottschalk. He was her first employer."

"No, I didn't know that."

"Mrs. G said Doris had been carrying on for years with him. It sure wasn't very secret. She claimed they owned a condo down in San Andres Island. Couldn't confirm that."

"And for the rest?"

"Checks out mostly. Oh, maybe she was bending the truth a little here and there. Like her boyfriend. It's true she doesn't have one now but she was going out with this Carlos Montalvez Correa here in Miami for a while. You know the Montalvez?"

"You mean *the* Montalvez of Cali?"

"A distant relation, apparently. This one is a cattle rancher and his son was here studying animal husbandry. The boy's gone back since."

"Thanks. Where's the bill?"

"Right there. But Charlie, watch your step. She's a slip of a girl but she has something. She knows how to play hearts. Rare gift nowadays but she's got it."

"Thanks, Frieda. And don't forget to call Ann Landers, she needs a hand this week."

I finally had to go see Doris again, I couldn't put it off any longer if I wanted to keep representing her. She was thinner than before and there was a black and blue shiner on her right eye. She broke down in tears when she saw me.

"It's so awful here," she said.

"What are they doing to you? I'll get a court order and stop it from happening."

"It's not the guards, it's the other prisoners. They pick on me, they call me names, they make me, oh my God, I can't tell you what they make me do."

I should have asked her about the boyfriend, I should have grilled her about Gottschalk, the divorce and the condo but the sight of her in tears rent my heart. She wouldn't tell me who had been forcing her to do the things she dreaded or what they were exactly, just that they had to do with sex and servitude. Instead she rushed away from the room, crying, asking to be put in solitary.

I was moved in ways I thought I would never be by such simple devices as a nameless accusation and a handful of tears. But you see, I wanted to believe. That is the only reason I've been able to adduce in all this, that I craved faith and absolution and I found them by taking up her cause. I went all over Dade County, from chamber to chamber, trying to get just one judge to remove the million-dollar bail but none would. The threat of political defeat at the polls come the next election stayed every learned hand, no matter how much they privately sympathized with Doris's plight.

All I obtained was a court order placing her in a private cell.

"That will be fine," she said, "but you know, it's the trusties, they won't leave me alone."

"Yes, they will, you'll be all by yourself."

"There's no escape, Charlie. No escape."

Just hours after my last visit, I was at home preparing the trial brief when the prison called—Doris had tried to hang herself. A matron had found her in time and cut down the bed sheet that she had looped through the overhead window bars.

I rushed to the prison hospital. She lay handcuffed to her bed, surrounded by five black women inmates. I touched her face; she rewarded me with a wan smile.

"Hi, Charlie. I'm sorry, I failed."

"No, you haven't failed anyone. I'm the one who's failed you, I should have been able to get you out."

"Charlie," she whispered.

"Yes?"

"There is a way to end this. I need something."

"What are you talking about?"

"I'll whisper it in your ear."

I drew my ear to her mouth, as my heart raced with excitement. *"Yeyo,"* she whispered, and kissed my ear. It burned from her kiss.

"Para quién?" For whom?

"Para la guardia. Please. I can't take this anymore." I stood up, nodded.

"OK." That was all she needed, that was all she had to say. She smiled again, closed her eyes and fell asleep.

Dr. Richards' report came in as I was busy trying to fulfill Doris's request. Upon examination he concluded that Doris was greatly delusional and harbored unresolved conflicts arising from her cultural ideation and that these conflicts could have resulted in uncontrollable acts of aggression when pressed by events. Although she was sane and stable most of the time, at moments of crisis she could snap and in effect lose control of her faculties. This was the best news I could have had, for now there was no way the prosecutor could stop me from bringing in the previous incident to explain her state of mind at the moment of the murder.

I told Doris the good news in the attorney interview room.

"We've also gotten an early trial date—we start picking the jury next week."

"That's wonderful, Charlie. What about what we discussed?"

The walls echoed the throbbing in my eardrums. As nonchalantly as possible, I slid out a trial brief and waved it in the air so the matron in the corner could see it was paper I was handing Doris. The matron nodded. I passed it across the table.

"Here's the trial brief and depositions of Mrs. Gottschalk. I think you'll like the fourth page."

"Thank you. I won't forget all you're doing."

"So we have a date when you get out?"

"I'm all yours."

I was in heaven.

We didn't see each other again until the day before jury selection was to start. I went by the jail to review the statements and documents. That's when she said, "I need more, Charlie."

"All gone?"

"It's not for me, you understand."

"I can't. It's too risky."

The next day at the trial, when she was brought into the courtroom, her forehead was slashed and a big bruise had swollen the side of her head. I took a look at her and nodded. She put her hand over mine and squeezed it ever so lightly as the TV crews pointed their cameras at us and the show began.

By the end of the day we had selected the twelve jurors and had only to pick the four alternates. But instead of preparing my papers I drove down to the bar in Miami Beach where I had gone once before for Doris. Armando recognized me from the news.

"You sure go through the stuff, Counselor."

"Comes with the territory."

"You should know. That will be a hundred dollars."

Once in my car I opened up the paper bindle and spread its white powdery contents on a flat sheet of paper. I took a bottle of white correction fluid, spread a thin line around the edge, then carefully lowered the third page of a brief down onto the second paper. I restapled the brief and headed down to the jail.

I was waiting in the attorney room for Doris, nervously going over our papers, when a deputy tapped me on the shoulder. I jumped up, startled.

"Easy, Counselor," said the matron, "don't get so rattled. Just wanted to tell you Miss Diaz will be down in five minutes, her bus just pulled in."

I took out a yellow notepad and started writing my opening argument, which I intended to give the following day if all went well. I opened with a literary quote by Eudora Welty, a touch of theatrics that always goes down well in the South.

"Mr. Morell?"

I glanced up unworriedly. "Yes?"

Two male sheriff's deputies stood before me.

"We're conducting a search of materials for possible contraband. Could you please hand over your briefcase."

I put down my pen almost at the same time that the second deputy seized my attaché case.

"You have no right to do that!"

"Just a routine search, sir. We've received reports cocaine has been smuggled into the facility and we're searching everyone." The younger deputy flipped over and emptied my briefcase on the table, then felt every one of my papers, running his fingers expertly along the edge of each sheet.

Doris was walking into the room when the deputy felt the double page and turned excitedly to his superior.

"We got something here, Sarge."

The young man ripped open the page and at once all the white powder poured out. The sergeant shook his head regretfully.

"Better come with us, Counselor."

Doris watched in silence as the two deputies lifted me from my chair and hauled me away.

"I'll see you tomorrow!" I shouted at her. She waved Italian style, one hand opening and closing, then turned and walked out of the room.

———

Ultimately I was proven right. The deputies did not have a right to search my briefcase since by doing so they violated the confidentiality of my papers, and therefore no formal charges were filed. My license was not revoked and I was merely suspended by the bar. But the media had a field day with the incident, which led to a mistrial. A new judge took the case and this time granted fifty thousand dollars bail, which Doris promptly made and promptly skipped out on, fleeing to Colombia. The papers found out what Frieda and I had not known, that Lazo, Doris's lover, was laundering money for the Cali cartel and that his projects were just a facade for his more profitable business arrangements down south.

There was speculation Doris had actually killed Lazo as a contract killer for half a million dollars, since he had stolen capital from the cartel to subsidize his life-style. There was also talk that Doris took the fall thinking that with her background she would be able to get out on bail. When the terrain shifted and her sterling character was of no use to her, they looked for a chump and found the biggest one in all Dade County, a lawyer who let his heart and his dick tell him how to defend a case.

Olivia and I divorced after that. Eventually, I chased my last dreams down to California, where I remain, doing penance. My father, my sister, my mother, my wife, my son, I have failed them all.

■

"Well, Charlie, what did happen to you in Florida?"

Judge Reynolds barrels his bushy eyebrows at me again, expecting his answer. I finally give it to him.

"Nothing happened, sir. Nothing at all. It was all lies and speculation."

He holds my gaze for a moment, then looks away, satisfied.

"Well, there you have it. No point in continuing with this hearing. Nothing happened at all."

15

after that hearing, everyone sort of lost interest in my background. I realized nobody was really interested in me or in
getting me off the case except for Clay and Mrs. Schnitzer. I was
just another tool in their legal strategy, a cog to be tended to but
certainly not fussed over. Surveying the emptiness of my life, I
declared myself fit for duty again and once more into the wind we
sailed.

For some unexplainable reason, the number of alternate jurors
had dwindled to nothing while I was gone, as though some celestial
landscaper were weeding out the laggards, leaving us only the
blessed, the devoted and the loyal.

We had selected the usual twelve regulars, along with twelve
alternates, making sure in our minds that there would be enough
to go around in case something unexpected occurred, as it always
does in a trial. But first, six of the alternates were laid off when
their employer, a huge aerospace concern with wide latitude in jury
service payment, closed its doors and moved to Nevada. The alternates, without a source of income to guarantee their attendance
at the trial, were released for financial hardship. Then came the
odd illnesses.

One alternate came down with appendicitis, another with
Epstein-Barr, a third with, of all things, gout, and a fourth had
major dental surgery that wired her jaw shut for months. Then,
of the last two, one had a car accident that landed him in traction

and the other developed liver cancer, so that, at the end, we had no alternates left.

The prospect of having to declare a mistrial should any of the jurors take ill did not bother Phyllis, however. She felt confident the judge would allow the case to proceed with fewer than twelve jurors.

"There's ample precedent," she said in the Criminal Courts Building cafeteria, when the first six had bowed out. "It's all at the discretion of the magistrate."

I took a sip of my milk. At a nearby table an unkempt, emaciated woman with no teeth smoked a cigarette as her three children played with their fried chicken to the woman's total indifference.

"Not with this judge. Reynolds wants to make sure there are no reversible errors."

"If he thinks that's possible, he's even more of a fool than I thought," she replied, studiously biting into a small piece of prime rib. "Unless there is a wanton disregard for procedure, more errors are made from excessive caution than not. Anyhow, he knows which side his bread is buttered on. He's up for reelection next year and I'm sure he doesn't want the D.A.'s office to go against him."

"Just because of our case?"

"This is a major case. We don't intend to let it slip away. I don't intend to let it."

"That's nice."

She gave a small cry of laughter.

"That's right, I keep forgetting who you work for."

"The courts, the courts."

"Of course. But I don't see you as—"

"What? The type that associates with known criminals?"

"Oh, I know it's silly of me, but I've never understood how anyone can defend those people."

"Here we go. A, I'm not defending him. B, what do you propose, we line them up and shoot them all at the crack of dawn?"

"Something like that."

My look must have stunned her for she quickly corrected herself.

"Just kidding. Anyway, that's what they did in China, I remember that. I wouldn't want that to happen here."

The gravity of what she remembered fell on her features like a dark veil; at that moment she was no longer the giver of a justice impartial and stern but a still frightened woman looking over her shoulder at a gory past.

"You know I'm Cuban, don't you?"

She took measure of me. "No, I wouldn't have thought it."

"We went through a revolution too. How bad was it for you? When I was a kid the militia came looking for my dad. He hid behind the pots and pans in the kitchen cupboard, but this young kid with a submachine found him."

"How did you, did he . . . ?"

"He paid off a local *comandante*. We all left safely within a week."

"I'm afraid mine was worse than that. We lived in Canton and my father had been with the Kuomintang. When the Communists took over they came and killed him in the front yard of our home. They beat him with sticks till he died."

"I'm sorry. That must have been awful."

"Must have been. I don't recall. I was only three years old. My mother says I wasn't crying but I was so frightened I was singing and wetting my pants. I still have no memory of it."

"How did you get out?"

"After they killed my dad, the troops left saying they'd be back the next day for us. An uncle of mine had a Buick and he came by and took us to the Yacht Club. Somehow we managed to get a boat ride to Hong Kong, my mother, my sister and myself. I stayed there until I married Paul, my former husband. Then we came to America." She turned to me, her oval black eyes gathering inward storms. "You see, we all have our losses, our dead to bury. You know what happened to me before I came down here."

"Yes. I'm sorry about that."

"Thank you. But that's why I don't put up with people like Valdez, that's why I asked to be given the case. I know what Pellegrini thinks, that he'll stick me with the dead if I lose. Well, I don't think I will but even if I do, I don't care. You know why? I have a big burial yard and I've buried a lot of people in it already. I don't live for politics or money, I care about principles. That's why I won't put up with the kind of argument Valdez is going to make. Oh, I know what he's going to say, society made him what he is.

Well, I don't buy that. We all have a choice. We can be diamonds or we can be dust. The end is up to us."

She wiped her mouth with a paper napkin and stood up.

"We can't all be diamonds, Phyllis."

"No, but we sure can try. Trial resumes at two. See you there."

———

I find it difficult to describe the tumult caused in me by the detached and precise words of Phyllis's first trial witness that afternoon—the county medical examiner.

"Doctor, how do you pronounce your name?"

"With pleasure. My name is Lakshmanan Sathyavagiawaran Tagore. That's spelled L-A-K-S-H-M-A-N-A-N-S-A-T-H-Y-A-V-A-G-I-A-W-A-R-A-N-T-A-G-O-R-E. But you can call me Lou."

The jurors and the audience burst into laughter, even Ramón looked up from his pad and smiled. Only dour, dedicated, steadfast Phyllis remained serious, her tight little body in a black and white silk suit fully erect by the podium. Death is no joking matter.

She waited until the laughter died down, then looked sharply at the jurors. Her frown cut them short.

"Could you tell us what is your employment, Doctor?"

"Most certainly. I am a forensic pathologist employed by the Los Angeles County Coroner's office."

"Will you tell us about your training and experience in the field of forensic pathology."

"Gladly. I was educated at the University of Bombay..."

Ramón looked up at the judge, rattled his ankle chain. "Stipulate to the doctor's expertise."

Clay looked at him, then shrugged. "Stipulate."

Judge Reynolds cleared his throat and addressed the jury.

"Ladies and gentlemen, what you have heard is a stipulation of fact. That means the attorneys for both sides, Mr. Smith for Mr. Pimienta and Mr. Valdez in propria persona, have agreed to accept a particular piece of information. In this case it's the qualifications and expertise of Dr. .... of the doctor. You are to regard that fact, the doctor's expertise, as having been conclusively proven even though no evidence was presented."

Phyllis moved to the side of the room and brought out a large piece of cardboard, wrapped in brown paper, which she placed on an easel by the witness stand and uncovered. There, in large blown-up color pictures, were the likenesses of the victims, before and after their deaths. Smiling faces on one side, the happiness of snapshots at the beach and business occasions next to photos of lifeless bodies, bullet riddled, gore tracing lacy rivulets of blood on their complexions.

"Doctor, did you perform autopsies on these bodies?" said Phyllis.

The doctor removed thick bifocal glasses from his coat pocket, placed them on the tip of his nose. "Yes, with regret."

"Objection!" boomed Clay. "Irrelevant!"

"Sustained."

"Your Honor," contended Phyllis, "I believe the doctor's state of mind—"

"The doctor's state of mind is not at issue here, Ms. Chin. Please proceed to your next question."

Blocked in her attempt to milk the impact of the pictures, Phyllis offered herself as the subject of emotion and turned to the doctor with tear-brimmed eyes.

"Doctor, what did you think when these bodies were brought to you?"

"Think? This was work to be done, deplorable work, to be sure, but work. It is sad to be the undertaker of society, cataloguing the results of its ills, but it's the job I have chosen. Rama—"

"Objection, Your Honor," countered Clay again. "I don't see what role the doctor's opinions or religious beliefs play in all this. Irrelevant!"

"Sustained."

"But I want to hear it!"

All our heads turned to the speaker, Mrs. Gardner in the jury box, who looked with defiance at the judge.

"You are . . ." Judge Reynolds looked down at his notes. "Mrs. Chauncer."

"Mrs. Gardner."

"That's right, Mrs. Chauncer was disqualified. Well, Mrs. Gardner, we ask the questions and determine what you should hear to decide upon."

"Why is that? Why can't we ask questions?"

"Because then you'd ask stupid questions like the one you just asked."

Gardner looked shocked. "Excuse me," the judge hastily corrected himself, "I didn't mean to say stupid, just unimportant, er, irrelevant. The judge is the trier of law, not you. You are the triers of fact. You decide, based on what we present to you. Now, remember, you swore an oath to follow my instructions."

"All right, but I hear in other states juries are allowed to question witnesses. I want to know why we can't."

"Because you can't!" bellowed Reynolds. "The law in this state does not allow it. Any other questions?"

"No. I just don't think it's fair."

"Then write to your legislator and tell him you want the law changed. Proceed with your questioning, Ms. Chin."

"May we approach?"

"Yes, of course. Counsel?"

Clay moved to the bench. I looked at Ramón, who nodded at me to go on over. When I reached the group, the judge was trying his best to lower his voice and not quite succeeding.

"I just can't believe all these things in one cotton pickin' trial. First an uppity defendant, now an uppity juror. You folks want to kick her?"

"Judge, we can't," said Phyllis. "We have no alternates. Maybe we should call a break for people to cool off."

"People?" The judge smiled at her indirection. "You're probably right." He looked up and announced, "This court is taking a ten-minute recess."

The jurors filed out.

"Well, folks, you better take a break too 'cause I'm afraid this ain't gonna get any easier."

As I walked out into the hall, heading for the snack bar, I overheard Mrs. Gardner tell Mrs. Vaught as they entered the ladies' room, "All them southerner's prejudiced, anyhow. I'll be damned if I'm gonna do what he says."

I told this to Ramón when I visited him in the lockup, moments before the trial resumed.

"*Chico*, that cracker's putting it on a fucking silver platter for us, God bless his heart."

"Which god, Ramón?"

"Any god, all the gods!" He looked in a small hand mirror, adjusted his tie—my tie, my suit—and grinned. "Like Mrs. Gardner said, 'Showtime!'"

The show was long, difficult and at times hard to follow, but never tedious, as the doctor explained, in his best layman's terms, the mayhem wreaked in the jewelry store. For two days he spoke at length of bullet trajectories, pierced aortas, shattered femurs, splintered cervical spines, crumbled larynxes, burst eyeballs and blood. Blood types, blood prints, blood marks, blood everywhere.

Phyllis showed us more pictures of the destruction—the owner of the store and the manager lying side by side behind the cases, gray matter oozing from gaping wounds in their foreheads; the security guard folded in on himself, his gun still in his hand in his futile attempt to halt the tragedy; the Vietnamese grandmother, her face contorted in fear. Death throughout, death at its most brutish, its most insolent, its most incomprehensible.

When the litany of gore ended, Reynolds turned to Ramón and, with what little sangfroid he had, attempted—and failed—to ask him neutrally, "Cross, Mr. Valdez?"

Ramón took off his glasses and rubbed his temples, as though still reeling from all the unaccustomed blood, saying, by his actions, that he too was in shock, that he could not believe the abomination that had just been shown.

"No questions," he replied, and shook his head.

Reynolds gave a snort of contempt. "Mr. Smith?"

Clay looked up, tapped his finger on his notepad.

"Just a couple of questions. Doctor, you say that victim number two, the security guard, died when the bullet entered the left side of the chest and came out through the back, piercing the sac of the heart and clipping the aorta. Is that correct?"

"That is correct, yes."

"Why was that?"

"It is very simple. The bullet first caused an internal hemorrhage, since the blood is no longer being carried through the aorta. Then, of course, the heart itself is wounded, so it rapidly ceased to function."

"You say just one bullet did this, even though he received two other bullets?"

"Yes. It was bullet number three, the last one, that did the deadly deed."

"I see. You say he also had a gun in his hand when he died?"

"That was the information I received from the police report and from my observation of the pictures taken at the scene by our people, yes."

"Did you conduct a gunshot residue test on the guard's fingers to determine whether he had fired the gun?"

The doctor shifted uncomfortably in his seat, adjusting the microphone so that now the sound came out squeaking through the speakers with a ghostly feedback: "We did the best we could."

The feedback rose to an unbearable screech. The bailiff stood up and readjusted the mike. Clay pressed on.

"What do you mean when you say 'We did the best we could'?"

"You see, under ordinary circumstances a gunshot residue test is ordered by the investigator at the scene. It is one of the many routine items that are carried out. For some unfathomable—"

"Excuse me, what was that?" asked the court reporter.

"Unfathomable, as in unexplainable, unaccountable, beyond understanding."

"Why is that, doctor?" Clay said.

"The investigator on the scene did not ask for such a test. It wasn't until the bodies were taken to the morgue, as I reviewed the paperwork, that I determined the test had not been conducted out in the field. I hurriedly ordered my assistant to sever the hands of the victim and carry out the test. I'm afraid it was too late."

"Meaning?"

"The results were inconclusive. We cannot tell if he actually fired the gun or not."

The investigator, Detective Samuels, engaged in a heated whispered exchange with Phyllis, who then shook her head in desperation and looked away from him at the judge. Even then Samuels continued pouring out his story until she finally put up her hand to stop him.

"No more questions," said Clay.

"Redirect?" asked Reynolds, looking at Chin.

"No questions."

"Thank you, Doctor. You are excused."

I turned to Ramón, who checked off an item on his list. True, it was a minor victory. Going through the reports we had noticed that the guard's gun had been inadvertently destroyed by the police before tests were conducted, which meant that no one would ever know if he fired at Ramón first. That could serve as a half-measured argument for self-defense, since Ramón could conceivably claim he had no intention of shooting to kill. The remarkable aspect of it was that Ramón had not even had to raise the issue, that Clay had done it for him, almost as though they were coordinating their defense strategies. But there were two other bullets fired at the man and in any case, the guard was only one victim. Ramón was a long ways from gaining any solid advantage.

———

The buzzing was incessant, like the sound a cheap radio alarm makes after you muffle it with your pillow. Then it died. Through the walls fragments of conversations seeped from the courtroom next door. The murmur of downtown traffic, the occasional toot of a pesky car horn, punctuated the uneasy calm of the empty jury room.

I took out a copy of *La Opinión*, the Spanish-language newspaper founded in 1926 by a Mexican immigrant which today boasts the largest circulation of its kind in the U.S. Ads for lawyers and legal assistance of every kind crowded the meager columns of print in the paper. The attorneys promised all kinds of satisfaction for job-related grievances, whether from accidents, nervous exhaustion, insults, aggravation or overwork, from whatever ailment the readers might suffer. In all colors and sizes the attorneys sprayed their pictures throughout the paper, changing their first names into the Spanish equivalent, hoping to reap more clients from the poor and dispossessed—at the rate of seventy to two hundred dollars an hour, *naturalmente*.

"There is no justice," I said as Clay and Phyllis entered the jury room.

"What's that, Charlie?" said Clay. "Of course there is. If you pay for it."

He plopped down on a swivel chair and rolled up the sleeves of his custom made jacket.

"Hello, Charles," said Phyllis, laying her leather portfolio on the table. I pulled out a chair for her, but she refused.

"I should tell you this is not my idea. I'm opposed to any deal whatsoever."

"Don't tell me," I said, pointing at Clay. "I thought you two had already come to terms. I'm just here for discovery and compliance."

"Well, Charles, if you don't mind, I'd like to wrap this up first. You ought to know the terms as well."

"Now that you mention it, I would. Some people are not very reliable sources."

Clay reeled back in mock surprise.

"Well, Mr. Pellegrini has made his decision. Clay, he's offering your client second-degree homicide if he agrees to testify against Valdez."

"What?" Clay was genuinely surprised. "Hold on a minute. Our deal was second-degree manslaughter, that's six to eight, not homicide. That's twenty. Something got lost in this translation."

"No, I'm sorry, that's not what I said."

"Yes, it is, Phyllis. Don't play this game with me. Look, I'll put it to you straight. Connors, Pellegrini's man, he told me himself you have the authority to pull this off. My client wants to do it. We had a deal. You can't back out of it like this."

"Clay, the crime is heinous."

"So's any murder! All killings are heinous. The point is, without my guy there's no frigging way you can make this case airtight and you know it. The LAPD did not take any fingerprints off the weapons and you know they botched up the investigation. Their usual shit job. No one was there to actually see the murders. There's always a chance some crazy juror will say she can't believe anyone, and then where are you? Look, make it second-degree manslaughter and we'll pin the tail on that Cuban ass."

Phyllis turned around, walked to the window and looked through the grimy glass at the gargoyles of the old Hall of Justice. Clay nervously lit a cigarette, then glanced at me with an apologetic shrug.

Phyllis turned around. "OK, you've got a deal. Charlie is the witness."

"Great! Let me go tell my guy. I'll call you this afternoon to set up a preliminary meeting."

Clay stood, shook her hand. "You won't regret this." He rushed out, leaving behind him a trail of Calvin Klein's Infinity.

"If you don't mind, Charlie, let's go over the discovery this afternoon. I should tell Pellegrini the deal is done."

——

"*Chico*, it's the best thing that could have happened to us. Who's gonna believe him?" said Ramón, ecstatic.

"About twelve jurors."

"You mean you don't think I'm credible?"

"I'm saying you haven't done anything to make them take our side. I'm saying, unless you get up there and testify, I'll be visiting you at the big Q. And if you do testify, I'll still be seeing you there. I mean, you don't look like the repenting kind of guy. You look calm and in control and he looks stupid and subservient. It's easy to believe that you were calling the shots. That you were firing the shots."

"Well, that's the way it is."

"It may well be the way it is but that's not going to help you any when he makes you."

"You know, you should have been a padre. Everything is black and white for you. Everything is always gloomy and doomed. I'll bet you're the kind who hates a sunny day because it might rain in the afternoon."

"Look, if my negativity is getting to you, I'll sign off, OK?"

Ramón shook his head in bemusement. At times like that, he pulled some kind of inner chain and the light of kindness shone through his features; he became less monstrous, less like a haunting nightmare of duty and death and more like the loudmouth who lives for rum, women and gambling. A regular kind of Cuban.

"That's just the way I am," I said. "What do you want? You

want to hear something? When I turned eight years old our *criada*, our servant, made a big whoop-de-do and carried me on her shoulders and kissed me and hugged me because I was eight. Then she looked at me and said, 'What's the matter with you, you look so sad.' You want to know what I was thinking? I was thinking, Great, I'm eight years closer to death. What do you think of that?"

Ramón leaned in close to me, his face practically touching mine over the low glass divider. "Let me tell you something. Don't be afraid of death. It's the most beautiful thing on earth. Nothing can compare."

16

the jurors filed into the jury box with their usual sleepy-eyed morning looks. But they began to whisper when they saw Ramón and myself sitting alone at the counsel table.

Judge Reynolds dashed into the courtroom. "Good morning, ladies and gentlemen," he said, buttoning his robe.

"Good morning," roared back the jury like a well-behaved class of fourth graders.

"Hope y'all had a nice weekend. Now, some of you may have looked over there at counsel table and noticed one of our defendants is missing. That would be Mr. . . . ." Here the judge made a brief show of looking up the name in his papers, as though it could conceivably have slipped his mind. "Mr. Pimienta. Well, what we can say is that his case has been handled without your assistance. You are not to consider that in your determination of Mr. Valdez' innocence or guilt as regards the charges."

"Your Honor, may we approach?" asked Phyllis. "Without the reporter."

I glanced at Ramón and he nodded. I crossed the well in front of the judge's bench and joined the huddle by the clerk. The crowd of spectators had thinned out, with only half the seats taken. But the rows reserved for the media were still full.

"Judge, we will be calling Mr. Pimienta as a witness for the People so perhaps the court could consider some kind of statement to that effect."

"Mr. Morell?" asked Reynolds.

"Your Honor, I'm just here as a mouthpiece. However, were I representing someone, I would say it probably would be best to wait until the prosecution actually called that witness and then let the jury draw whatever conclusions it chooses. After all, a lot of things could happen between now and then."

"Well, Charlie," snorted Reynolds, "short of another quake, I just don't see what else could occur but your point is well taken. Sorry, Phyllis, I'm not going to tout your coming attractions. You can do that yourself pretty well, I know."

Phyllis muttered the time-honored reply of counsel, no matter what the instant decision. "Thank you, Your Honor."

Back at the counsel table Ramón leaned over.

"I hear the judge is banging one of the clerks."

"That's not going help you any."

"It might put him in a better mood. Looks like you could use some too, *mano*. When was the last time you got laid?"

"I get fucked every day."

"The People call Remigio Flores."

Detective Samuels shot a glance at his two cohorts in the back. They nodded, stepped out of the courtroom and returned with the parking attendant.

Remigio had put on a lot of weight since our interview at the park, when he had attempted to run away from Detective Moat. The LAPD had probably canceled his soccer playing, thinking the next time he ran for it they might not catch him. Moat now had a partner, another imposing blond specimen of surferhood, so that little Remigio seemed like a paunchy, undergrown little devil being brought to the altar of justice in some faded nineteenth-century print.

Remigio's eyes darted nervously around the courtroom, taking in the expectant curious faces of the jurors, the judge, the audience and gave an audible "ah" when he saw me and Ramón. His right hand shook as he took the oath.

"You were right," said Ramón. "I can see the tattoo."

"Yeah, it looks like he tried to rub it out," I said. "Look at the discoloring in the skin around it."

"Please state your name, spelling the last name for the record," said Curtis.

Remigio eventually informed the court that he was twenty-three years old, a native of Guatemala and a resident of Los Angeles for the last three years. Yes, he had been the parking attendant the morning that Mr. Valdez, the defendant in the gray suit and red tie, had driven in with another man, both dressed all in white and smelling of 4711 cologne.

"Did you see the defendants enter the store?" asked Phyllis.

"Yes, I did."

"Could you see inside the store while they were in there?"

"Yes. One of the walls has a large picture window facing the parking lot. It was real clear."

Phyllis stepped to the back of the room and came forward with a diagram of the location that she set up on an easel. For the next hour she filled in all the blanks that a juror might possibly have wanted filled—the lighting, the distance, the perspective and orientation, the numbers of cars and people, the sight line from the attendant's booth, the number of times he walked away to move other cars. All the variables that might have helped the defense were wiped out one by one.

Now for the final rivets in the edifice: "Did you see the defendant, Mr. Valdez, shoot any of the people in the store?"

Remigio paused. His testimony up to that point had been faceless, exact. Now he had to start paying his debt to society and the D.A.'s office and name names, point fingers. He glanced straight ahead, looking neither right nor left but focusing on the back wall of the courtroom forty feet away.

"*Sí.*"

"Yes," replied the interpreter with an inappropriate grin.

"Who did he shoot?"

"I saw him shoot the manager."

"With what?"

"With a short rifle, like the ones they use on TV. An Uzi, I think."

The questions came in rapid-fire succession, like the hail of bullets that raked the store that winter morning.

"What position was the manager in when you saw him shot?"

"On the ground."

"Did you hear the shot?"

"Yes, I did."

"How many shots were there?"

"Many. A blanket of shots. About twenty, I think."

"Who was firing?"

"The defendant."

"Did anybody else fire?"

"No."

"What about the store guard? Did you see him?"

"Yes."

"Did the guard have a gun?"

"Yes."

"Did he have it in his hands?"

"Yes."

"Did he fire it?"

"He never had a chance. That defendant there struggled with him and shot him. Then everybody started screaming."

"What did you do?"

"I got scared so I ran back to the booth to call the police."

"Did you hear any more shots?"

"Oh, yes. But I didn't hang around. I was afraid of stray bullets. I almost got killed like that once in Guatemala."

"Did you ever go near the store again?"

"No. No. I quit after that."

"No further questions."

Judge Reynolds turned to Ramón. Phyllis had shown that Ramón had killed during the commission of a robbery, which fulfilled the requirement of special circumstances for a capital case. Now Ramón truly had to prove what kind of pro per attorney he could be.

"Cross," said the judge.

"Thank you, Your Honor. Mr. Flores, where in Guatemala are you from?"

"Objection, irrelevant," piped in Phyllis.

"Overruled," said the judge, no doubt thinking the best way to hang Ramón was to give him plenty of rope.

"Guatemala City."

"I see. What *zona* in Guatemala City are you from?"

"Excuse me, I don't understand," Remigio said.

"*Zona*. Area, zone, *zona*. Guatemala City is divided into *zonas*, neighborhoods. Which one are you from?"

Remigio snapped back, "Seven."

"I see. That's near the Reformer's Tower, right?"

"A few blocks away."

"Very good. Now, how long did you say you've been in this country? Three years?"

"Objection, irrelevant."

"Overruled."

"Three years, yes."

"So, are you here legally?"

"Objection, Your Honor. It's immaterial what his legal status here is."

"Overruled. That might affect his testimony."

"Thank you, Your Honor. Exactly what I think."

"Uh, I'm indocumented."

"Indocumented. That's a beautiful word, Mr. Flores. It just means illegal, doesn't it? You're an illegal alien, aren't you?"

Remigio looked at Moat, a glint of desperation in his eyes.

"I have to answer that?" he pleaded in anguished English. "You say I no have answer that."

"Mr. Flores, please answer the question," ordered the judge.

"Well, are you illegal, yes or no?" repeated Ramón.

"Yes, I am," snapped Remigio in Spanish, "but I at least do not go around killing people!"

His accent finally gave him away. I knew we were right.

"Motion to strike everything after 'Yes, I am,' Your Honor. Not an answer."

"Granted."

"I would like the jury to be admonished too."

Reynolds smiled wryly at Ramón's request.

"Ladies and gentlemen of the jury, please disregard the accusations of Mr. Flores against Mr. Valdez. After all, it has yet to be proven that Mr. Valdez goes around killing people, no matter what others may say. Proceed."

"Thank you. So then, Mr. Flores, now that we know where

you're from let's talk a little about you. You ever use the name Francisco Miranda?"

"I don't remember."

"Or Carlos Céspedes?"

"I don't know."

"Or how about Manuel Ochoa?"

"I don't know why you ask that. I always use my own name."

Ramón pulled a computer printout sheet from the file, unfolded so that its full three-page length was visible to the jury.

"Mr. Flores, I have here before me your rap sheet. It says you are thirty years old, that you have been convicted of burglary, auto tampering and sale of a controlled substance, cocaine, and that you have been in this country for seven years, two of which you spent at Chino Penitentiary. Are you going to deny that?"

Flores looked down. "No." Then he glanced up. "But I still know what I saw."

There's life in the boy yet, I thought. I wonder for how long.

"Yes, so you say, a convicted felon."

"Irrelevant, Your Honor," countered Phyllis.

"Overruled, Counsel." Reynolds was emphatic. "Your witness has just admitted his record."

"Thank you, Your Honor," Ramón said. "Now, Mr. Flores, what is your religion?"

"Objection, Your Honor. Totally irrelevant."

"There I agree with you, Ms. Chin. Coun—" The judge corrected himself in time. "Mr. Valdez, unless you show cause—"

"I have an offer of proof, Your Honor. I will show it to you outside the presence of the jury *and* the witness."

The judge glanced up at the clock. "Well, I think it's almost time for a break. Why not?"

Moat and his surfer buddy escorted Flores out.

When the last juror had exited, Reynolds turned to Ramón with as little condescension as he could bring himself to show.

"Mr. Valdez."

"Your Honor, I have reason to believe that Mr. Flores belongs to a different religion from mine, one which in fact is an enemy of mine. I think that makes prejudice on his part and bias which can color his perceptions."

"You mean like he's a Muslim and you're a Christian or something like that, right?"

"Yes."

"Motion denied. Just because somebody's of a different religion doesn't mean he's going to want to send you to the gas chamber or tell a lie, which here amounts to the same thing."

"But Your Honor!"

"No buts, mister! I call the shots. Get back to your cell."

Phyllis waited for me when I went out into the hallway.

"How could you?"

"How could *you*? You're supposed to give me all the information you have on our witnesses. I had to go out and get it myself."

"I didn't know. Samuels just told me. He found out last night. How did you find out?"

"His landlady had his Social Security number. What am I supposed to do, close my eyes and not do my job?"

"You could have warned me."

"What are you talking about?" I moved down the hall to the snack bar, Phyllis on my heels, nipping.

"You know he did it, you know he killed those people. It's unconscionable."

I whipped around, full of self-hate but still not ready to be called a monster.

"We went through this already, Phyllis. Everybody has a right to a defense. Even Hitler, even the devil has a right to the best defense, including an investigator. That's our system, that's the law, that's the way we want it to be. That's the way we have to be."

"You could have warned me," she hammered.

"And lose my license and my self-respect to make your job easier? It's your fault if those idiotic cops don't know how to conduct an investigation. You're supposed to ride them, you're supposed to keep tabs on them, not me."

"You listen to me. We're trying to put scum like him away. For once you should try to be on the side of the righteous and not of the dirt. If you had any dignity left you wouldn't be doing what you're doing."

"I suppose I should join the D.A.'s office to get my soul in working order because you folks are obviously God's hand-picked weapon. Forget it, lady. You want to convict him, prove it in court. With evidence that's valid. Don't preach. And don't expect me to do your job for you."

A handful of jurors stared as I stole away down the staircase. I couldn't care less if I prejudiced them or not with my outburst— that was her problem. What was I supposed to do? But I had to stop at the landing and catch my breath. I felt my heart spinning and the building twirling. All my defenses could not stop this gnawing feeling in the pit of my stomach, this infusion of dread running through my veins. I was adrift in a sea of loathing with only the feeble raft of duty to brave the waves of guilt that threatened to drown me.

Remigio had regained his composure when we returned after the break. He sat self-confidently, adjusted his microphone, then inhaled, clearing his nose into his throat.

"Colombian courage," I said to Ramón.

"Really? I just thought he had a bad cold, *pobrecito*." Then, raising his voice, "Mr. Flores, before the break you told us you are a convicted felon. Your last conviction was for drugs. Are you on drugs now?"

Everyone turned to examine Remigio at that moment. His veneer of self-confidence became transparent and the fear in his eyes returned.

"Objection."

"Overruled."

"No," muttered Remigio.

"You didn't go to the bathroom during the break to snort cocaine to give you the valor to come back?"

"No! I am a man. I don't need that to do what I have to do."

Again the interpreter gave his most benign smile, as if by reflex or total cynicism.

"Good. So then you can tell us why you claim to be Guatemalan when your arrest papers show you are a Cuban refugee."

"Objection, Your Honor," clamored Phyllis. "Assumes facts

not in evidence. Is Mr. Valdez going to testify of his own knowledge?"

Ramón held up the papers for the bailiff to take to the judge. Reynolds glanced quickly at the document.

"May I see that?" asked Phyllis.

"Of course." The bailiff took it to the D.A.'s side of the table.

"I'd like that to be marked defendant's Exhibit A, Your Honor," said Ramón, "the certified copy of the arrest report."

"So be it marked."

Ramón held up another paper.

"Your Honor, this is a Rand McNally map of the city of Guatemala City. Please have it marked Exhibit B."

"It's so marked."

The bailiff came back again and took this document with a not too happy expression.

"I would like the court to take judicial notice that the Reformer's Tower is not in Zone Seven but in Zone Nine, which is all the way on the other side of town."

Ramón turned his chair and smiled broadly at Remigio. "Well, then, Mr. Flores, are you or are you not Cuban? That's what you told the officer who arrested you. Of course, that was back in 1984, when they weren't putting Cubans up in Atlanta awaiting deportation. Because you see, if you're Guatemalan, you can't tell me you lived where you lived. Zone Seven is nowhere near the Reformer's Tower. Why are you lying to us?"

"I am not lying."

"Then what is it? Were you lying then to the officer because you were afraid of being deported back to Guatemala?"

Remigio looked around desperately, searching for a way out.

"Yes," he answered, almost inaudibly.

"So you were lying to the officer then."

"Yes."

"But you're not lying now."

"No. I know what I saw."

"OK, let's talk about that. How long have you been working at the parking lot, six months?"

"Yes."

Ramón turned to me, motioned at the leather briefcase. I handed it to him.

He took out another document, a pink sheet with a stamp certifying it to be a true copy. He glanced at it, set it down on the table for a moment.

"So during this time you noticed delivery trucks coming into the parking lot, is that not right?"

"Yes."

Ramón pointed at the diagram of the parking lot next to the Jewelry Mart still on the easel where Phyllis had set it up.

"For obvious reasons I cannot get up from the table, so Mr. Flores, *por favor*, could you please get close to the drawing?"

Flores approached the easel. For a second time we went over the distances, places to park, entries into the building. Remigio reluctantly told the jury how deliveries were made through the double steel-plated doors on the south side, facing the booth, at a particular spot marked just for that purpose.

"Such a truck would have blocked your view, no?"

"Maybe. I saw what I saw."

"But on the day of the incident, you say you had a clear view of the inside. Is that not true?"

"Yes."

"Now, the incident happened at 11:07 A.M. You told us you knew the time exactly because you looked at the clock when our parking ticket was obtained, right?"

"Yes."

"Are you telling us the truth? Is there something you forgot?"

Remigio again looked at Moat and Phyllis for support, but found none. "No."

"No, you're not telling us the truth or no, you have not forgotten something?"

"No, I haven't forgotten anything."

Ramón sighed, then lifted up the pink paper.

"Your Honor, I have here a certified copy of a bill of lading from Abelson Express, certifying that a delivery was made to the mart at exactly 10:59 A.M. Their drivers have to punch in their loading documents when they arrive at the mart for security purposes."

Reynolds snatched the paper out of the bailiff's hands and examined it.

"Your Honor, I don't think I have been shown that."

Reynolds gave it to the bailiff, who passed it to Phyllis.

"As you can see," said Ramón, "this shows departure time of 3:16 P.M., after the entire incident was over. That means the truck was parked in the delivery spot blocking your view, isn't it true, Mr. Flores?"

"That's not true, I saw you!"

"Oh, yes, you saw me. You saw me walking in. But you never saw anything else, Mr. Flores. You invented everything because you are being supported by the Police Department while you testify, isn't that so?"

"Objection, irrelevant, Your Honor," said Phyllis.

But Ramón wasn't going to let up.

"Is it not true that the LAPD is paying for your apartment, your living expenses, even promised you a green card if you testify?"

"Yes, but . . ."

Then it all followed in rapid-fire succession: "So it's a yes, then. So you have been lying, no? After all, you're a follower of Shangó, no? You want the servants of Oggún to die, no?"

"Your Honor, objection, irrelevant, this has nothing to do with these proceedings!"

"Mr. Valdez, I urge you—"

"Listen, Flores, I know you're Cuban and *santero* so let me tell you this, *Oggún areré, alawó, kokóro yigüé yigüé.*"

"Your Honor!"

"Bailiff, remove Mr. Valdez . . ."

But before the bailiff could react, Remigio pushed the interpreter aside and jumped out of the witness stand, bolting over the barrier into the audience and out the door. Ramón grinned at me as Moat took off after Remigio.

"Thanks for the tip."

"Don't mention it. I'm only doing my job."

■

Lucinda was waiting for me when I got home. As a special treat she had fixed me paella, redolent of saffron and iodine.

"No, no, I don't want any, it's all for you," she said when I noticed there was only one place setting on the table. She set the clay vessel on the tile trivet and scooped the mounds of glistening rice and shellfish onto one of the white Villeroy and Boch plates she'd bought at Bullock's—"on special and they're so pretty with the flower border and all," she'd said when turning in the bill for fifteen hundred dollars for six place settings.

"How's the trial going?" she asked.

I finished chewing, took a swig of my Watney's.

"You are a great cook."

"*Gracias.*"

"The trial is going fine so far, but the heavy guns haven't been wheeled out yet. There was nothing we could do about the coroner but Ramón really gave it to the parking lot guy. Had him so scared the guy took off running. He's still missing."

"I know. I saw it on TV."

She poured the rest of the beer, stroked my forearm.

"So you think Ramón will win."

I looked up at her and scanned her features looking for, what? Surprise? Desire? Expectation?

"Why? You want him out?"

She played with her hair, shrugged.

"I don't know. I mean, he deserves everything he gets but still, I keep thinking it wasn't him, you understand? I guess I'm just looking for an excuse."

"Too bad you're not on the jury. He'd love to have you there."

"Yes, I know. Isn't it too bad."

We made perfunctory love that night, a quick in and out more out of duty than lust. Afterward she ran to the bathroom and came out wearing a red flannel nightgown and daubing cleansing lotion on her neck.

"Enzo came to see you this afternoon," she said, tossing the used cotton balls in the toilet bowl. I grabbed a copy of a travel magazine, seeking an escape, a dream of canopied beds and sugarcane plantations by a crystal shore where tree frogs sing.

"What did he want?"

She climbed in next to me in bed, smelling of disinfectant and toothpaste, the death of bacteria and love.

"He said he was wondering if you knew someone who could be his maître d'. He had to fire the last one, he was stealing from him."

"He told me he was having problems. Too bad. No, I don't know anyone."

"Yes, you do." She snuggled close for a moment.

"Who?"

"Me. I told him I was out of a job and I didn't have anything else to do and that I'd done it before. Of course I lied. But he said he'd try me out. I'm supposed to start tomorrow night, the night shift, six to midnight. You don't mind, *corazón*, now do you?"

Of course I minded, of course I didn't want her out of my sight, of course I wanted to control her completely.

"No, of course I don't mind. I'm happy for you."

She kissed me on the cheek. "I knew I could count on you, my life. Thank you. Good night."

"Good night."

She turned over, put out the light and went to sleep. I felt all the anchors of reality in my life drifting away in a current of orange blossom darkness.

▬

"The People call Vlad Lobera to the stand."

Enters a short, heavy man on the borderline of obesity, with a ghastly white complexion, full lips and a beard so dark it becomes a veil over his features, the kind of beard no Schick can eradicate, only a straight razor wielded carefully by a barber. He wears a thick wool pinstripe suit, a white shirt and no tie, a figure out of an Eastern European social realist canvas.

Vlad, his expression suggesting his Impaler namesake, strides purposely to the witness stand, spells his name, sits, looks forlornly at Phyllis.

"I happen to know that Fatso there deals in excess of ten million dollars in jewels every month," whispers Ramón.

"How do you know?"

"Sources, Charlie. I may be in jail but I have ears everywhere."

"Could you tell us your occupation?" asks Phyllis.

"I'm a jewelry salesman. High volume. Best aquas in town."

Chuckles from the courtroom at the brazen pitch.

"Thank you for the information, Mr. Lobera," says Reynolds, "but please answer only the question asked."

"Why? You no like aquas? They're the mirror of the sky. I have good emeralds, too. Wholesale."

"Please, Mr. Lobera. Counsel."

"Mr. Lobera, were you supplying Barry Schnitzer with jewels?"

"Who?"

"One of the victims in this case, the owner of Schnitzer Jewelers."

"Oh, you mean Levi. Poor schmuck. Yeah, sure. I was there when he got it. Almost got wiped myself."

More chuckles in the room. Vlad looks around, surprised anyone would find mirth in his sayings.

Phyllis stands up, walks behind Ramón.

"Do you see somebody in this courtroom who was there at that day and time?"

"Yeah, sure. The black fellow there in front of you, he was there with another Neg—What do you call them now, Afro-American? Him I see, I don't see the other guy. Big guy, you know. Kind always makes me nervous on account the jewels I carry."

"For the record, he has identified the defendant, Mr. Valdez."

"Yes. Proceed."

"Where did you see them?" asks Phyllis.

"They are standing by the jewelry case, looking at it. I noticed because they were dressed all in white and smelled kind of funny."

"What do you mean, funny?"

"Like cheap cologne and ether, you know? Very strange smell."

Phyllis is about to ask another question but instead wheels around and sits in her chair. She riffles through her papers. Seconds pass in expectant silence.

"Counsel?" asks Reynolds.

Phyllis plays the distracted fool. "Yes?"

"Anything else, Counsel?"

"Oh, no. No further questions."

I turn urgently to Ramón, a strange reversal, Faust advising Mephistopheles.

"Don't ask any questions! It's a trap. He hasn't said anything that could incriminate you. She's waiting for you to trip. Just say, No questions."

Ramón brushes me away. "I know what I'm doing."

"Mr. Valdez?"

"Thank you, Your Honor. Mr. Lobera, you said you saw me and someone else at the store. Tell me, did it look as though we were carrying weapons?"

"Who knows? I didn't see any."

"How close did you get to us?"

"Close enough to smell you."

Laughter again. Even Ramón cracks a smile.

"So that would be, what? Five, six feet?"

"Yeah, more or less."

"Did we say something? What were we doing?"

"You didn't say nothing while I was there. You were just staring at the jewelry case, like you was looking for something, that's all."

Phyllis smiles to herself. Ramón has fallen into the trap. Or has he?

"You say you were in the store during the incident. Where were you exactly?"

Vlad shifts in his seat, the weight of revelation now uncomfortable.

"Well, to tell you the truth, I was in the crapper."

This time everyone laughs. Vlad shrugs.

"What can I tell you? Had a heavy breakfast. I shouldn't, I have a nervous stomach." He pats his overhanging belly. Ramón waits for the laughter to die down.

"So if you were busy like you say, how do you know something happened?"

"I heard it. I mean, it was just right outside. I heard all this shouting, then Levi, I was showing him my aquas, he says, 'You wait here a minute, Vlad.' So then he goes outside. I'm wrapping up the stones when I hear the sound of glass breaking and then, *pow, pow*! Two bullets and then all kinds of shouting. Then all hell broke loose."

"So in other words, you never saw what happened, you just heard it."

"That's right. Those damn walls are paper thin, I could hear everything. I was shitting in my pants, pardon my French, thinking you guys were going to hear me and come in."

"Now just a minute. You don't know that we were there after you went into Schnitzer's office, no? You never saw anything."

"Yeah, that's right."

"Thank you. No more questions."

The judge enters his notes on a laptop computer, then gestures at Phyllis.

"Redirect?"

"Yes, Your Honor. Mr. Lobera, you just heard the defendant, Mr. Valdez, speaking. Wasn't his one of the voices that you heard that day inside the store?"

"Oh, without a doubt. It's him. I recognize it for sure."

"Thank you. No further questions."

Reynolds gestures at Ramón but he's already asked Lobera, "But, Lobera, were you able to understand what was being said?"

"Oh no, not that. I mean, I don't speak Spanish or whatever you fellows were speaking. Couldn't understand a word."

"So for all you know, I may have been telling someone to put down his gun and surrender, isn't that correct?"

"Objection, calls for speculation."

"Sustained."

"Thank you, Mr. Lobera. No more questions," says Ramón.

As Lobera leaves, Ramón adds, "Fast out. That's how you win the game, Charlie."

"Wrong. You just stole a base. That's a far cry from stealing home."

"Just gimme time, Carlitos. Gimme some time."

17

oes time flatten when you look back upon it? Is our perception
of our own history like that of the stars Sirius or Alpha Cen-
tauri, whose light is dappled red when they're close and blue
when they are far, so that the nearer our memories the more they
are colored by our emotions, and the farther they are the more they
assume the sad azure of neglect?

I ask this because there are certain things about the trial that I
have forgotten and I don't know why. The days rolled on in a
repetitious accumulation of horror that after a while became senseless, detached, incomprehensible. If the jurors felt as I did, there
was no longer any emotional impact to the detailing of the murders
as narrated by the investigating officer, Detective Samuels. With
the slow methodical tone of the man for whom murder is a living,
he droned on about the technical findings in his investigation—the
bullet holes, the layout of the location, the amount of debris found
scattered on the floor, the thinking behind the decision to surround
the store and not to rush in, the exact deployment of the attending
officers.

Then there was the criminologist, a totally bald, gaunt man in
a polyester leisure suit who had not experienced a new thought or
emotion since 1975. He too dragged on about bullet calibers, angles
of penetration, stippling and barrel marks and shots fired in the
laboratory to identify the weapon, so much detail that the denseness
of the testimony seemed too hard to bear. Phyllis was following
the prosecutor's manual—pile on the evidence until it becomes such

an overwhelming mound that it passes understanding and all that is left in the minds of the jurors is that this mountain of facts can only mean the defendant is guilty as charged.

The normal defense posture in the face of this attack is to fight fire with fire, to undermine the experts, to find the famous fly in the ointment by pointing out the hidden inconsistencies and logical deficiencies. The defense will run its own tests on the murder weapon and call in its own experts on what it all means, so that it becomes a question of whom do you believe and why should you care at all. The principle of reasonable doubt sits in the courtroom like a specter everyone alludes to but no one actually calls by name.

But Ramón wasn't doing any of that; he was letting Phyllis spend herself in the barrage of minutiae, trying so hard to prove every point, to cover every angle, that by the end even Judge Reynolds was barely restraining himself from yawning. Ramón merely sat back and watched her spin her wheels, following a strategy that was becoming clearer by the day. Let the evidence accumulate pointing to a killer, but shift the blame onto someone else. I tried to convince him to poke holes in the technical testimony but he only asked a handful of questions of Detective Samuels:

"Detective, did you take fingerprints of the weapons that were fired that day?"

The lieutenant consulted his report, then glanced up, mildly annoyed. "No, we did not."

"Is that not standard procedure?"

"Not really. It depends on the situation. When we feel we have enough evidence to support the charges, we do not necessarily lift prints off the weapons."

"Could that be done now, taking the prints?"

"No. We tried a few months ago but we found the weapons had been contaminated, that is, too many people had handled them so it was not possible to lift any prints."

"So, in other words, you really don't know who fired those weapons."

Samuels smiled for the first and last time during his testimony. "Well, that was quite simple. It was either you or Mr. Pimienta or both of you."

"But still, you don't know that for a fact, do you?"

"You were the only ones left alive."

"But you don't know who did it, is that not true?"

"Well, I don't know if the sun will rise tomorrow but I believe it will. That's the degree of certainty I have."

"Please answer the question, sir. Do you know specifically if I fired those weapons?"

"No, I don't."

"Thank you. That is all."

The sun was an orange ball dipping into the ocean when I pulled up in front of the house. A postmodernist villa of limestone, white stucco and glass-block walls, it had two conical-topped towers sheathed in copper so new it was still a shiny red. A few square windows opened the walls like the eyes of a robot, seeing everything and understanding nothing. A motor court trimmed in stone in front of the building was already jammed with the limos and the preferred power vehicles of the elite of Los Angeles—Jaguars, Porsches, Ferraris and Range Rovers. I knew it was going to be an all-out Halloween party when I spotted the parking valet handing tickets to the vehicle owners at the door. I made a U-turn and drove a block down the hill, parking underneath a still blooming bottle-brush tree.

Mae West answered the door when I rang the bell. That is, Suzan Nash, deputy D.A. in Van Nuys Superior Court, dressed like she'd done someone wrong.

"Is that a gun in your pocket, big boy?" she asked, batting eye-lashes that seemed ready to stick together and never open again from the globs of mascara.

"No, sugar, it's a subpoena duces tecum. Show me the goods."

"Anytime, fellow." She kissed me on the cheek and hailed me inside. "Help yourself, the party's just starting."

"Where's our wonderful host?"

"Clay is probably in the kitchen, checking out the tamales," she said, taking me by the arm and leading me into a living room with a view of the coastline from Palos Verdes to Point Hueneme.

"So you two are still an item?" I asked Suzan as we walked down the steps to the second level of the living room by the curving balcony.

Frank Sinatra's "Witchcraft" drifted at that point out of the high-power stereo speakers painted the color of the fuchsia walls.

"When he wants to," said Suzan.

"Excuse me?"

"You know Clay can't commit to anything but his practice. Tell you the truth, I'm not so sure I'd like to be married to someone like that."

"And miss out on all this?"

I gestured at the large buffet table, catered by two former movie industry executives who called their outfit Catering Girl even though the only female was the Salvadoran woman who did the dishes. Starlets, movie directors and studio executives dressed like cats, lions, ghouls and Richard Nixon—that is, like their true inner selves—mingled with corporate lawyers, judges and real estate developers, in the interlocking community of concerns that runs the state.

"It's only money," said Suzan. "There are greater things in life."

We stopped next to a Hockney print of the San Fernando Valley under a sculpture of neon-colored fiberglass that looked like the four-level interchange of the 101 Freeway downtown.

"Anyways, I heard you have a girlfriend. Where is she?"

"Working. She's a hostess at Baldocchi's. Halloween's a big night for Italian restaurants, didn't you know?"

"You mean like the Mexicans? I didn't know that. He should be in there," she said, pointing at two swinging etched glass doors.

In the kitchen Clay, dressed as Zorro, down to the whip gathered by his side, was sampling the cone-shaped tamales a tall brown-skinned woman in a red dress was presenting on a platter.

"No, no!" he was telling her, "too salty, no mas salt, oh shit."

"*Dice el señor que están muy salados los tamales*," I said. The woman, very indignant, replied all her customers liked them that way.

"Boy, am I glad to see you. What's she saying?"

"That you're going to have to pay her for all those tamales because that's what you ordered, otherwise she'll sue you."

"OK, OK, *está bien. Ándale, ándale.*" The woman picked up her tamales and very calmly strode into the living room.

"What the fuck, everybody will get so smashed they'll probably love the extra salt. Hey, where's your costume?"

"I'm not staying long."

Clay turned, admiring himself in an imaginary mirror.

"Always wanted to be Zorro when I was a kid. So, what's up? Wanna drink? *María, cerveza para Charlie!*"

"I wanted to talk to you about Pimienta and his testimony."

"Guy, what are you, all work, no play? It's Halloween, kick back, have a drink, do some toot, get laid. It's fantasy time!"

"Clay, it's always fantasy time in L.A. I want to know what Pimienta is going to say."

One of the maids brought me a Corona with half a lime.

Clay tried some of the tamale, digging his finger in the masa and extracting a chunk of fried pork.

"Cholesterol city. Shit, I was dead drunk when I told her to cater this. You know she works at El Coyote? Serves me right."

"Pimienta."

"All right! Look, what can I say? The guy's going to finger Ramón, it's that simple. He'll give Phyllis book, chapter and verse on their whereabouts, actions and intentions."

"Such as?"

"Such as Ramón had planned to kill the manager and the owner to begin with and maybe the guard too. The rest just got caught up in the flow of things. It's like that old Dr. John song, 'I was in the wrong place but it must have been the right time.'" He looked for a towel to wipe his finger but finding none on the marble-topped island, he turned on the gold-plated bar faucet and rinsed it off.

"You think he's telling the truth?"

"The truth?" He laughed. "These guys wouldn't know what the truth is if it bit them in the ass. They're full of this macho shithead posturing, they think Cubans are the best and everyone else is jealous of them and that's why everything happened. They say Mexicans are resentful of them."

"I don't get it."

"The manager of the store was Mexican. They feel he was responsible for the store repossessing the jewels even though Barry had given them the jewels. Pimienta claims they tried to cut a deal but the manager told them, Fucking Cubans, you think you're so smart all the time, let's see you get these back, or something like that."

Clay lifted his finger at one of the maids, who brought another beer without delay. He gulped down half the bottle, belched.

"Now I feel like a real Mexican. I'm not sure but I think Pimienta is going to say he was under the influence of Ramón and couldn't help himself, you know, the Jim Jones devil made me do it bullshit. He's going to claim that now he's been in jail all this time he's been able to cut the umbilical cord, so to speak. Like a newborn babe in the land of the free, which is what he's going to be in approximately three months, if not earlier, with time served. Let's go in, I'm tired of hanging out with the help. Hey, no offense intended."

"None taken," I said, as we swung open the double doors and stepped back into the party. "Assholes will be assholes and always full of shit."

His reaction was totally unexpected. Either the beer had paralyzed his flapping tongue or the costume was making him act different. Clay pushed me against the wall, toppling a cadmium blue vase from a corbel. He leaned on my throat with his forearm, pressing it tight.

"Where do you get off calling me an asshole, Carlos?" His breath reeked of garlic and beer. "You fucking Cubans are all the same."

I closed my fist and hit him in the groin with a hammer blow then lifted the elbow to connect with his chin as he tilted down. He flew backward and I gave him an uppercut in his solar plexus, throwing him to the ground, face up.

"Who the fuck do *you* think you are, Clay?"

Heads turned in our direction, silence fell in the room, broken only by Tony Bennett's "I Wanna Be Around" in the background. Clay turned his head and puked on the bleached white oak floor.

"You make me sick," I added.

I knew Clay was back to normal when he turned and wiped the vomit from his chin with a grin. "Feeling's mutual."

"I'm outta here."

All turned as I walked out. No one—no banker or developer, no D.A., no PD, counsel, cop or judge, not even the mayor or his ever present bodyguard—said a word or stopped me from going. It was very simple, as simple as a Jew in a room full of Nazis, the yellow star on my clothes shouting out, Scum, subhuman dreg, stinking spoor of defiling animal, Hispanic shit, leave the room.

Out in the motor court I was stopped by an arriving Bentley. As the valet swung open the door, long legs in sequined hose connected to an Irma La Douce costume stepped out—Mrs. Schnitzer.

"Leaving already, Mr. Morell?"

"I knew you were coming so I came out to say goodbye. Clay's inside. A little the worse for wear but I'm sure he'll be glad to see your checkbook again."

She smiled, threw her purple boa over her shoulder. "I'm so glad I never paid you off. Even though I would have enjoyed the satisfaction of owning you, it's always terrible to pay thousands for what's only worth a nickel."

"I know. Look at what your husband got. He died so you can play patsy with fruitcakes."

"Nice meeting you again, Mr. Morell."

"Yes, have a nice day."

Down Hollywood Boulevard, on my way home, I saw the usual gallery of runaways, druggies, Hell's Angels and whores joined by impromptu Halloween revelers in Vampirella wigs, Freddie Krueger costumes and Ronald Reagan masks, all traipsing up and down the blockaded street, as overweight traffic cops with flashlights attempted to stop the nocturnal procession from degenerating into a riot.

It wasn't the spirit of revelry that envelops New Orleans in Mardi Gras or San Francisco on Halloween itself, what I saw on that boulevard but a burgeoning cry for release, a shifting onto a public sphere of all the fears, desires and malfunctions of private life so that the street became an arena, a competition between contesting forces, not a means of expression but a way to power, to accumulation of display. Who would sport the sharpest getup, who's got the cherriest low rider, the most outlandish lingo, the most drugged-out state. Halloween in Los Angeles became yet another ring where the ambitions that rule the city presented themselves, only in their rawest form because so close to the source, so close to that throbbing desire to possess, to use, to accumulate, to despoil and abuse, the frenzied feeding of the material world by a society acting as though MENE MENE TEKEL were written on the wall instead of LST 19 or ROLLING BREAKS CONQUER or JESUS HATES SEX.

I could smell traces of Lucinda's Giorgio perfume in the air when I came home. As usual, she had left the bathwater in the tub. I drained it, opened the windows.

In her rush she'd left the bed undone and her discarded clothes in a mound on the floor—the aubergine skirt that was the wrong color, the chartreuse blouse that didn't feel right, the black stockings with a previously unnoticed run. I am living alone already, I told myself, what is the use in all of this?

I left the house again and got in my car, driving aimlessly around, not knowing why or where, just pointing the wheels in whatever direction felt right until, by chance or inner compass, I found myself traveling down the easy slopes of Silver Lake. The air was warmer and grittier, the accumulated exhaust of cars and buses from Sunset and downtown gathering in grimy clouds around the reservoir.

Some kind of perverted desire must have brought me to Juan Alfonso's house, perverse in that I was not even aware of what I was doing but was acting as though my life and sanity depended upon it. I noticed the lights were on in his house and parked some ways down the street. The moon was laced with clouds, with a few stars peeking through the smog. I pushed open the fence gate and climbed up to the porch, a sweet fragrance of freesias welcoming me into the house. I knocked on the door.

"Anybody home?"

No answer. I pushed the door open. The large TV set was gone, as were the couch, the chairs, the table, the leaded glass buffet with miniatures of tropical fruit, all gone except for a handful of folding chairs and a card table under a lonely light bulb dangling from the end of a wire.

"Juan Alfonso? Are you home?"

On the kitchen counter sat a box of takeout from Pollo Loco, the barbecued chicken breast half eaten, the containers of beans and yellow rice opened, a plastic fork stuck in each. I heard a thumping downstairs in the basement.

"Juan Alfonso, stop playing!" I said in Spanish.

No reply, or rather no voice answered, instead a quick rapping like that of a bongo drum broke the stillness in the house. The riff lasted a few seconds then halted abruptly and the house seemed to wait for my next move.

My heart announced its presence; a faint trickle of perspiration ran down my shirt. At that moment I wished I was carrying my gun, not to kill anyone but just for the sheer feeling of security it afforded me.

"*Carlos, ven acá,*" said a voice from down below.

Suddenly my fear turned into rage. You want me to come, do you? You want me to come to you? I grabbed an empty beer bottle from the trash. I'll show you, I'll beat your fucking brains out!

I rushed down the shaky steps but with every step I felt as though I were entering a universe of viscosity, where every step was like a plunger through water, only this time I was rushing into the flow.

A red light flooded the basement, the kind that photographers use to develop their film, and an almost overwhelming smell of jasmine hung in the room. As I stepped off the stairs, bottle in hand, I felt a cold wave hitting me in the chest and a cloud of yellow butterflies flew out of nowhere, breaking around me as I touched the ground. This is not happening, I thought, this is not life. I'm either hallucinating again or I'm finally dead, and if so, why is there no relief?

I saw a semicircle of wooden chairs set where the altar had been during my last visit and seven different people sitting in these chairs. At first I saw only their feet, all black, all shoeless, and for a moment I couldn't figure out why I could not lift my eyes, and why my neck was bent forward as though in obeisance. With great effort, making an ultimate act of concentration, I lifted my face and saw that each of the people wore masks fashioned out of straw, cowrie shells and mud, African masks with tribal markings on their cheeks and fleshy African lips. The red light emanated from behind them, a red sun shining at their backs. They all spoke in one voice.

"Carlos leave alone, Carlos leave alone!"

I tried to speak but couldn't, my tongue was pressed to my palate, and the chanting became louder and louder, burying me in the folds of its persistence until I finally unstuck my tongue and shouted, "Leave who?"

And at that moment the figure in white in the middle chair removed its mask and I saw my father and I saw myself and I saw Ramón, all of them all of us, smiling at him, smiling at me. I lifted my arm slowly and threw the bottle at the figure which smiled as the bottle struck it in the jaw. A loud great noise rent the room and a cloud of yellow smoke burst from the forehead of the figure as the bottle burst the face into shards of dried mud which clattered to the ground and I fell backward on the floor from the impact of the blow and everything turned a deep blue which eased into soothing black, into quiet, peaceful nothingness.

A bright light was shining somewhere, a light that filled the world while a husky, sibilant language was spoken. Then the pain came in waves, a stinging sensation all over my body. I opened my eyes and found myself in Juan Alfonso's basement still, staring into the liquid brown eyes of a scrawny man in a grimy undershirt.

"Wake up, mister, wake up or we call police!"

I lifted myself up on my elbows, shook my head. Another man, chubby, unshaven and olive skinned, stood behind the first one, hands on knees, peering intently at me.

"You OK?" said the second man.

I got up. "Yeah, I . . . I guess so. Who are you?"

"I'm Greg," said the fatter of the two, "this is Vartek. We own this house."

"You all right?" Vartek asked. "We found you here this morning. Somebody mug you?"

"No, I guess I slipped and fell. Where is Juan Alfonso?"

"He sold us the house two months ago. We fix for resale."

I staggered to the wall, leaned on it, catching my breath.

"I see. Well, thank you." I took a deep breath then slowly moved away. I wobbled to the stairs, held on to the railing. The two Armenians conferred in rapid-fire conversation.

"Hey, you, you no sue, no?" asked Vartek worriedly as I trudged up the stairs.

"Don't worry, I no sue, no."

The sun was shining bright when I walked out into the street. I looked at my watch. Nine-fifteen. I'd spent the entire night in that basement. Miraculously no one had busted the window of my 944 or even run a key along its side. But someone had left a message, a card stuck under the windshield wiper.

"*If you think I have forgotten you . . . I haven't.*"
Signed, "*God.*"

18

as Clay had so aptly predicted, Pimienta's story was a straight-line narrative with one purpose—to put Ramón in the chair when the cyanide tablet drops into the acid and the People's will billows out in a choking gas. The testimony lasted three days, covering their upbringing in Cuba, their meeting at the Peruvian Embassy, their voyage to our promised land, and their subsequent life of violence and crime.

Pimienta's sincerity and contrition, his humbleness as he responded to Phyllis's incessant prodding, eyes fixed on the ground, thick lips barely muttering the answers that the interpreter would blare to the courtroom, all this added far more weight to the appearance of culpability than the actual substance of his confessions. In spite of his sorry-sinner pose, Pimienta claimed he did not know Ramón would kill anyone at the store. This presented a major legal obstacle since it deprived the prosecution of the usual element of malice aforethought necessary for the death penalty. Fearing that some softhearted juror would find Ramón not guilty in the first degree because he had no intentions of killing anyone beforehand, Phyllis handled Pimienta with the delicacy of a butcher hacking a rack of lamb.

Dressed in flaming red—shoes, belt, Escada dress—she approached the stand with vivid determination.

"Isn't it true, Mr. Pimienta, that on the morning in question, you and Mr. Valdez discussed the possibility that someone might be killed during your robbery of Schnitzer Jewelers?"

"No, I didn't imagine that. We thought we might have to disarm the guard and maybe wound him, but we didn't have any intentions of killing anyone. We were just there to grab the jewels of the saint and go, teach them a lesson."

"Oh, so you did contemplate the possibility someone might be hurt?"

"Well, yes."

"And you're absolutely certain that lesson you mentioned did not include taking the life of the manager for the humiliation he'd made you go through?"

Pimienta finally looked up, catching the drift that if he didn't cooperate, his deal would be history.

"I didn't imagine that's what Ramón meant."

"What did you imagine?"

"Well, he said he was going to teach them a lesson they'd never forget, that they'd never do this to a Cuban, to a Latin again. But I just thought he was talking about taking the jewels back, that's all."

Clay sat in the audience, watching his client put on the performance. He seemed satisfied with the show.

"Why a Latin? Do you have any idea what he meant?"

Here Pimienta actually brightened, his face becoming animated with the interior light of a child who remembers his lessons well.

"That, yes, of course. We talked about that a lot. All the time. It was his, his . . ." Here the interpreter faltered. She glanced up at the grid ceiling, as though expecting a cribbed answer from above. "His bête noire," she finally said, not quite certain if she'd found the right word. I was impressed by her vocabulary. Pimienta had actually said weak point, but bête noire was much closer to what I knew would be coming.

"Please explain."

Pimienta gestured broadly for the first time in three days.

"Sure, it's easy. All you have to do is look around you. Hispanics in this town are treated very bad. You have practically everybody Latin and there's no Latin mayor, all the political power belongs to the Anglos. The Orientals and the Jews all own the banks and the movies and even the blacks, they have a mayor, but nothing ever gets done for them. They're still oppressed."

"Tell the truth, brother," muttered Mrs. Gardner in the jury box.

"Objection, Your Honor," said Phyllis, as a murmur of disapproval went through the courtroom.

"You're objecting to your own witness, Counsel?" asked the judge.

The interpreter did not tell Pimienta an objection meant he should stop so he continued his peroration and the interpreter continued translating as a clamor of protest rose from the audience.

"He always said California is a conquered land and the Chicanos here have never learned how to stand up for themselves, they're always getting it up the ass, that's what he said."

"The court will sustain its own objection and will admonish everyone in the room to be quiet or the room will be cleared," warned the judge.

"What we need here is a revolution, he always said, somebody has to teach these guys you can't mess with Latins, that sooner or later they're going to have to pay the price and that they can't keep fucking us like this," continued the interpreter, who still hadn't told Pimienta to be still. Reynolds finally turned, his face the same shade of red as Phyllis's dress.

"Mr. Pimienta, shut up!"

Pimienta finally grew still.

"I will not put up with any racist statements in my courtroom, no matter what the justification. Racism is not germane in this matter and will not be accepted."

Ever smiling, Ramón raised his hand. "Objection, Your Honor. I believe his statement is necessary to explain the state of mind."

"Mr. Valdez, I think we already have a pretty good idea of what your state of mind was. Overruled. The testimony will be stricken. The jury is admonished to disregard the witness's last statements from"—looking at his notepad—"'his bête noire' to 'fucking us like this.'" He looked up. "Proceed, Counsel."

Phyllis bit her lip, then hurried back to her side of the counsel table. She glanced at some papers, asked the investigating officer a whispered question, then sat down, folding her hands on the murder book.

"No further questions."

Reynolds wrote in his notepad and muttered, "Mr. Valdez."

"Thank you, Your Honor."

Ramón adjusted his glasses, consulted his notes, then ostentatiously set them aside.

"José, did I ever tell you I wanted to kill someone?"

Pimienta glanced down at the carpet again. "No, you just said there might be some trouble."

"What did I tell you I wanted to do when we went to the Schnitzer store?"

"You wanted to take back the jewels of the saint because they had been given to him."

"What did I want to do with them?"

"Put them back on the altar."

"What altar?"

"The altar of the saint, Oggún, our father and protector."

"Do we both belong to the same religion?"

"Yes, we do."

"What is that?"

"*Santería*. We are children of Oggún."

Now I understood why Ramón had never mentioned that the jewels were a present from Schnitzer. How they were obtained was not material, the only thing that mattered was how José and Ramón viewed the jewels and that they intended to get them back. In one swift stroke Ramón had now eliminated the dangerous need to call Mrs. Schnitzer. Her testimony would only have put Ramón in even hotter water. Once on the witness stand, everything could have come out, including his lethal prayers on behalf of her husband.

Phyllis sat up, as though ejected by a spring from her seat. "Objection, Your Honor, irrelevant. There was a ruling—"

"I know what my ruling was but since your witness spontaneously brought up the question of religion, Mr. Valdez has a right to question him about this," said Reynolds.

"I don't recall."

"Counsel, you should pay closer attention." Reynolds read off the rectangular screen of his computer. "Mr. Pimienta said they were going to get the jewels of the saint during direct, said it again during cross. Objection overruled. Proceed, Mr. Valdez."

"Thank you, Your Honor." The judge sighed and sank back into his leather chair.

"Why did we have to get the jewels back, José?"

Pimienta was forthright, looking straight at Valdez. "You know, because if we don't, the saint will be angry and who knows what the saint will do. Well, you know."

"Yes, I know. But the good people of the jury don't. Why don't you tell them."

Pimienta fingered his gold ring. "Oggún is a mighty god but he doesn't like people who laugh at him. If anybody take anything from his altar he gets upset and then, watch out, because it's death on wheels."

"Excuse me, Madam Interpreter?" asked Reynolds.

"Your Honor, that is what the witness said. Actually, he said it would be death on a bicycle but on wheels is the closest English equivalent."

"I see," replied the judge. "Proceed."

"José, of your own eyes and experience, what have you seen the saint do?"

"Of my own?" He paused, slightly nervous, scratching his forearm, where he'd tattooed an arrowhead cross, the Cuban prison symbol of the enforcer.

"Yes, with your own eyes."

"Well, I have seen him come in the meetings, take over a woman and make her eat dog excrement for having laughed at him. I have seen him make someone jump from a four-story window to the street, becoming paralytic for the rest of his life. I even saw him kill people in revenge. You don't mess around with Oggún."

"I think I've heard enough of this. We are getting further and further away from the subject," said Reynolds. "I've allowed you to delve into this area, Mr. Valdez, but that's no excuse to present a defense by indirection through the mouth of the witness. Please move on to another area."

"Just one last question in this area, Your Honor."

Reynolds hesitated. "All right, but just one."

"José, have you ever known anyone to take jewels from Oggún and live?"

"Never."

Reynolds, obviously fed up with the questioning, glanced at the clock. "I see it's time for our noon break. We'll reconvene at two o'clock."

Reynolds walked down the bench and called me over. He whispered with more than a hint of anger, "You tell your boy to stop trying to bring in irrelevant matters or I'll reverse myself and order him a lawyer, you understand? If he doesn't know how to question, then he shouldn't be doing it."

"I'll tell him, Judge."

"You do that," he said, his robe flying after him. I caught a glimpse of Linda Powell's red hair and bright smile in the Judge's chambers moments before he slammed his door shut. I had a feeling that, even though she was the clerk at Master Calendar Court, they had business other than judicial to transact.

"Judge," hollered Burr, "we have to get back to Department 100 on the Ramsey matter! Shit." He turned to me, frustration digging holes in his skin, "Can't get him to do anything anymore when she's around."

"It'll pass. Courthouse flings don't last."

"Let's hope. He moved in with her, you know."

"That is serious."

As I turned, I saw Pimienta getting off the stand and looking at Ramón with questioning, sad eyes. Ramón smiled before the bailiff led him back into the lockup, ankle chains rattling on the blue carpeting.

The bailiff let me in once he put Ramón away, forcing him to surrender his tie and his shoelaces and his belt, so as to protect him from the singular temptation of suicide. Ramón was smoking a cigarette, sitting alone on the built-in concrete bench lining the wall. An art gallery of graffiti covered the walls, from the simple HELP ME to CUCA TE QUIERO to the stylized curlicues of the Rolling Thunders 269. The largest message read, in Spanish, *I was found guilty but I swear to God I am innocent. I am Pancho.*

Ramón seemed downcast. "*Chico*, I don't like what I have to do," he said in Spanish, stretching the sounds like a child in a playground after he's hit his playmate.

"You have to impeach him, isn't that the strategy?"

"Yeah, but after all we've been through, you know, to put him down like that. I mean, I haven't even started."

"If you don't do it, you might as well start selling tickets to the execution right now."

He grinned, put out his cigarette. "No, that won't do."

He ripped open the plastic wrap of the sandwich the county gave him for lunch—three slices of bologna, with mayo, on white bread.

"What did the judge say?" he asked through a mouthful of food.

"He warned you that if you don't ask better questions, he's going to withdraw the pro per and name you an attorney."

"Bullshit," he said in English, then he reverted to the mother tongue. "That's a bluff. I haven't done anything a lawyer wouldn't. That's just his excuse for whipping me in line. Reversible error and he knows it."

He shrugged, crumpled the plastic wrapping into a ball and tossed it overhead into the sink at the far end of the room.

"Would you believe they never taught me basketball in Cuba? They tried to put me on the boxing team, they said I could be another Stevenson. It's a good sport, basketball. Anyhow, you tell Mr. Georgia Cracker that he'll like what I'm gonna do this afternoon. I mean, I feel sorry for José but, that's how life is."

He grabbed his luncheon apple, weighed it in his hand. "You know you could kill someone with this?"

"How?"

In a quicksilver motion, without a rest or break, he threw the apple like a pitcher does a baseball, so fast it became a red blur in the cell before slamming against the wall and splattering into thousands of tiny pieces.

"That's how. When that strikes you, it's as hard as a bullet."

"I'll remember that the next time they overcharge at the market."

"Oh, no, don't do that, *chico*, you might wind up here and then, who would defend you?"

I went down to the mall under City Hall, a sorry-looking basement cast in shadows, where grime-encrusted homeless sit on benches drinking syrupy sweet coffee and studying the crowd of clerks, office workers and attorneys passing by. I walked through the center courtyard, where a few plastic tables and chairs had been set on a cobblestoned ring looking out on the smoggy sky above. Raggedy palms and spilling trash cans surrounded the tables. I crossed through the gallery, exited on Main street and made my way down to Japantown. At the Kyoto Cafe I called home, trying to reach Lucinda. On the fourth ring, the answering machine picked up and I heard my voice asking for the message. After the beep, I asked her if she was in to pick up the phone but there was no reply. I hung up and sat at the counter sipping the miso soup.

"Don't look so sad, my friend, it will only give you a head of gray hairs like me." I looked up at Marty Green, the only FBI agent I knew who willingly became a court-appointed investigator upon retirement. His white frizzy hair was a halo around his black face, shiny from perspiration. His thick gold neck medallion glistened in the sun.

"That's OK, it'll just make me more distinguished. Like you. Still investigating?"

"You know, Charlie, people like us never stop," he said, in his native Barbados lilt. "What are we going to do? It's a compulsion, looking into other people's affairs. I've done it now for thirty years and I don't think I'll stop till the Good Lord take me away. Besides, my wife wants to buy a new house so I have to work for the money. You all right?"

"I've been better."

He turned to another man at the door, blue suited, impatient.

"Just a minute. Listen, I hear you have been working for that Valdez character. Let me give you some advice. Drop the case. Drop the case and run like crazy."

"C'mon, Marty, you know I can't do that. Anyhow, it's almost over."

"No, it is not. You know he tried to hire me before you? He originally was asking for a P.I. from the islands. He wanted a white man from Cuba or Puerto Rico. He said only a white man would understand. When you came on the case he asked me about you and wanted me to investigate you. Wanted to know all about you."

"That's normal."

"Not when he wants to know about your family and everything.

I understand he got Kelly to check you out. Beware, my friend, he is no good."

"Marty, I've never seen an angel accused of murder."

"Listen to me, he wants to control you, Charlie. He wants to own you. Give it up, go back to being a lawyer. I got to go now. Call me for lunch sometime, OK?"

▬

Pimienta did not relish the question. He shook his head sideways, like a toy winding down on its battery.

"What do you mean?" he asked, casting an anguished look at Phyllis.

"I mean just what I said," said Ramón. "What is our relationship?"

Pimienta silently queried the interpreter, who shrugged her shoulders. "You know very well. We're friends. I mean we were friends."

Ramón took off his glasses and rubbed the bridge of his nose. I could see the lenses were clear glass, another trick for effect.

"Could you be more specific. Where did we meet?"

"*Chico*, you know where we met, at the Peruvian Embassy. We were there with thousands of people, camping out."

That was an out-and-out lie. José had told me they met at a *santería* initiation rite. Or had they? When were they lying and when were they telling the truth? Did they know the difference? I said nothing.

"OK, who introduced us?"

Phyllis finally spoke up. "Objection, irrelevant."

Reynolds looked at Ramón. "It certainly appears that way. Is there an offer of proof?"

"Your Honor," said Ramón, "if the court please, the aim of my questioning will become apparent very soon. I am trying to delve into our relationship."

"Mr. Valdez, I gathered that much. No matter how much contempt you may have for this court, I am not stupid."

"Your Honor, it is not my intention to insult the court."

"All right, all right, just proceed. Let's get this moving."

"Yes, Your Honor."

Ramón put on his glasses again, then, as though it pained him, asked, "Who introduced us?"

Pimienta hesitated. "Pepita Ramírez."

"Pepita Ramírez. Is that a man or a woman?"

"A man."

"A man," repeated Ramón. But before he could go on, the interpreter interrupted again. "Excuse me, Your Honor. I would like to correct myself. The name is Pepito with an O."

But Ramón interjected. "Objection, Your Honor. The interpreter had it right the first time."

"Oh, who cares, Mr. Valdez? Whether it's with an O or an A. Just go on."

Ramón raised his hands as though to press the point but waved it away. "OK. Was Pepito a former prisoner?"

"Pepita. Yes, she was."

"José, why do you call her 'she' if Pepita was a man?"

Pimienta whispered something that I could not hear but that made the interpreter turn with a quizzical expression and ask, in rapid-fire Spanish, "What was that?" Pimienta repeated his answer and then the interpreter said, "Because she was a bird."

Chuckles in the courtroom. Ramón smiled. "Yes, a bird. Does that mean she could fly, she had wings and a tail and claws and flew, like a falcon or like a hawk?"

"No, I mean that he was a *maricón*."

"Maricon? How do you spell that?" asked the reporter, turning away from her machine.

"Standard spelling is M-A-R-I-C-O-N," said the interpreter.

"What does that mean, *maricón*?" pressed Ramón.

"He was, he liked men, he was a pervert."

"I see. That's very interesting. Is that why Pepita had been in jail?"

"Yes."

"Anything else?"

"Well, for prostitution."

"I see. Well, how did you know that?"

I would have sworn that Pimienta was about to cry. "Because I knew her."

"How well did you know her?"

Pimienta put his head down and covered his face in shame. "I loved her, all right. She was my girl."

"Hold it, hold it. But you said she was a he. Does that mean you're homosexual, José?"

Phyllis again stood up. "Your Honor, this is totally irrelevant. What the witness's sexual inclinations have to do with the crime for which the defendant is charged is beyond my understanding."

"Your Honor, this goes to show his bias and how that affects his testimony."

"Mr. Valdez, unless you can show me in two more questions how this relates to bias, I will prevent you from conducting your own defense on the grounds of incompetency."

"Thank you, Your Honor," said Ramón.

"Do you like men, José? Are you homosexual?"

"I don't like to but I can't help it."

"Weren't you jealous of my relationships with women?"

"I don't know."

"Isn't it a fact that you have been tested HIV positive, that you have AIDS and that you blame me for giving it to you?"

"Objection, lack of foundation, Mr. Valdez is testifying!"

"Sustained," said the judge. "The jury will disregard that last question, which will be stricken from the record."

"OK, OK," clamored Ramón. "José, were we lovers, yes or no, just answer that, yes or no?"

Pimienta turned and his red eyes were a supplication for pity, for compassion, for consideration, for all the things that Ramón had long forgotten.

"Yes, we were."

"When did we stop?"

"When you married that girl, Lucy. You said I was ugly."

"So are you testifying here today because you hate me for leaving you?"

Pimienta gave a sigh, shook his head, and for once there was a certain kind of sad, haunted beauty to him, the beauty of dignity and hurt feelings.

"No, Ramón. You know I could never hate you. I am just here to tell the truth, that's all."

"And you say the truth is that I killed all those people?"

"Oh, yes, but you didn't mean it. I know that."

"Stop." Pimienta was about to continue talking but at seeing Ramón's hand go up, he halted in midbreath. That should have told me something, but at that moment, the significance of such obedience escaped me. "So why are you testifying here?"

Pimienta paused, looked at Phyllis dubiously. She gave a barely noticeable nod.

"Because I was promised a deal."

"A deal, you say. What kind of deal?"

"That I'll get six years if I talk about what happened."

"Six years. But you say you were involved in everything we did, right?"

"Yes, I said that."

"You were there when we made the plans, right?"

"Yes."

"You helped load the guns, carry them in the car, you drove, you went into the store with me. Correct?"

"Yes, that's true."

"But you're getting six years. Do you know what I'm facing?"

Pimienta shifted his eyes, like a puppy caught nibbling at the family roast.

"Yes, you told me."

"You know the law says you're as responsible as I am?"

"I don't know, I don't know what to do!" He put his head down briefly, then he glanced up. "You want me to take it back, you want me to say it isn't so?"

"No, José. I want you to tell me the truth. That's all. Did I do it? Did I, Ramón Valdez, shoot those people?"

"Yes, but it wasn't you."

"I don't understand. Was it me or wasn't it me?"

"Yes it was you but it was Oggún, you couldn't help it!"

Ramón took a deep breath, set down his pen. "No more questions."

Phyllis stood up, then walked over to Pimienta. She stood in front of him, her body almost trembling from her concentration.

"Tell me, Mr. Pimienta, did I ever tell you to say anything that wasn't the truth?"

"No, you didn't."

"Is everything that you've told us here today and for the last three days the truth?"

"I swear, the truth."

"You wouldn't be lying just because Ramón is not your lover anymore?"

Pimienta touched his heart and turned to face Ramón. "I still love him but I have to tell the truth, I can't live with myself otherwise."

"Thank you."

Phyllis walked back to her chair, sat down, then leaned over to the investigating officer. They exchanged a few words, then she glanced back at the judge.

"Your Honor, the prosecution rests."

Reynolds, who had been watching the entire questioning with his head in his hands, sat up with a jolt. I glanced at the jury and saw that at least half of them had also been leaning over, but now, caught by surprise, returned to their distanced posture.

"Well!" said the judge, and everyone laughed, out of embarrassment in being caught up in this strange melodrama. Reynolds looked at the clock.

"It's three o'clock. Mr. Valdez, are you ready to proceed?"

"Your Honor, I would request a recess until Monday. I am expecting a witness to contact me shortly."

"I'll do better than that. I'm going to give you a week, how's that? Ladies and gentlemen of the jury, because of scheduling problems (I looked at Ramón with surprise, he shrugged) this court will be dark for the next week. So this being Thursday, and since we don't hold trials on Fridays, I will see y'all a week from Monday. Have a good week!"

With that he dashed off the bench to his chambers. I walked over to Phyllis.

"What was that all about?"

"I thought he'd told you guys," said Phyllis. "His wife got put into the hospital, she OD'd on Seconal. He's going to stay with her and try to work things out."

"I'm sorry to hear that."

"You shouldn't be. That will give Valdez a little more time to prepare. He's going to need it."

"Who are you saving for rebuttal?"

"C'mon, Charlie, you know I can't tell you that," said Phyllis, stuffing her papers in her black Mark Cross briefcase. "No, excuse me, I misspoke, I still haven't decided. I'll give you a list when I do."

"When, the day we start?"

She smiled maliciously. "I still haven't decided."

She picked up her case and walked out, the IO opening the doors for her.

In the audience, Pimienta was sitting next to Clay, blowing his nose with Clay's embroidered handkerchief. Clay nodded at me. I came up, offered my hand.

"Sorry about the other night."

He looked at my hand, then at me, smiling. "I'm not. You're still hired help. Cheap, too."

"That's a relative term, Clay. Every whore's got her price."

"I suppose that's right. You won't be needing my client anymore, will you?"

I looked at Ramón, being conducted into the lockup at that moment.

"I'll check but I don't think so. Just tell me one thing, is he really HIV positive?"

Clay gave me the poor-schmuck look. "You believe that? Good thing he's pro per. He's a better lawyer than you." He stood up, tapped Pimienta on one of his massive arms. "Let's go, Joe."

Pimienta got up, then asked me in Spanish, "You tell him I'm sorry, OK? That I didn't have any bad intentions but that's the way he wanted it."

"I'll tell him that."

"And if you can, give him this."

Pimienta took off a massive gold and iron key dangling from his neck on a leather strap. I raised my hands, stepped back.

"No, I'm sorry. You go through the channels. I don't do that kind of stuff."

"But it's the key to Oggún, so he won't be harmed!"

"Don't worry about him, I'm sure he'll be fine."

◼

Ramón was insufferably happy when I visited him at County Jail, slapping five with other inmates, whistling, smiling, in all, looking like a man who saw things coming his way.

"His testimony just convicted you. You couldn't shake him. He says you were the one who did it. Why are you so happy?"

"Don't you see? He said I didn't mean it!"

"Yeah, but that you still did it anyhow. Phyllis is going to argue that you were perfectly aware of what the consequences would be if you went to the store armed like you did. She'll say that you had every intention of stealing those jewels, because since you can't prove otherwise, that's exactly what you were doing according to the law, no matter what you may have thought you were doing, whether claiming it for Oggún, Mohammed or Jesus Christ, that's still robbery. And you killed those people. You're a goner, Ramón. Listen, you can still cut a deal."

"A deal?" Ramón leaned back, as surprised as if I'd slapped him hard across the face. "A deal? Are you crazy? What are you talking about?"

"I'm talking about living, man, that's what I'm talking about. You will face life without parole or the gas chamber and by the looks of it, you're going to be saying hello to your god sooner than you expected. Phyllis is offering straight life. You'll be eligible for parole in twenty."

"Twenty years in prison for something I didn't do?"

"Everybody says you did it and all the evidence is there that you did it. Even your cohort has accused you. What else do you want?"

"No deals, Nitty."

"What?"

"Elliot Ness. What kind of Cuban are you, you don't know Elliot Ness. No deals, Frank Nitty."

"Ness was the cop, Ramón. *You* are Nitty."

"Really? Well, still, forget it. No deal. I didn't do it."

"Right. My mother did it."

"No. Your father."

Chills coursed up and down my spine, goose bumps like someone had scratched a nail on glass. The lights seemed to waver and the walls undulated for just a moment.

"What did you say?"

"Just kidding. Oggún, he's our father."

"Not mine."

He grinned wolfishly. "What makes you so sure?"

I hesitated for an instant, then I asked him, point-blank, "Did you ever have me investigated?"

"Me? Why would I want to do that?"

"The guy who you tried to hire told me. He also said Kelly may have done it but since Kelly's retired by now, I don't know. I do know he was sleazy enough to have done it. So why did you do it? What did you hope to gain?"

Ramón shook his head reprovingly. "Your problem, Charlie—"

"Stop telling me my problems! I am fucking well aware of them. I want to know why the hell you're sending an investigator to look into my fucking life when I'm the only man who's trying to make sure you get a decent shake out of this fucking system. Just who the hell do you think you are?" I rose to my feet, screaming. Ramón didn't budge. He just stared into my eyes and said softly, "I never did such a thing."

Two deputies rushed over to our booth, blackjacks in hand.

"Any problems, Charlie?"

I shook my head. "Just the usual. Ungrateful scumbag."

"OK, Valdez, let's go. Interview's over."

A deputy unshackled Ramón from the chair. Ramón stood up, in his most dignified manner, then looked me coldly in the eye. "I wanted to but I didn't. The county wouldn't approve it."

19

"**Y**'all must be kidding me!"

Judge Reynolds looked up from the motions at us, as bewildered as a hound fooled by a possum playing dead. He grabbed the long yellow notepad pages printed neatly by Ramón and shook them in the air, as though wanting to get rid of some noxious roach. He had chosen his chambers to go over the motions informally before making his ruling in public with Ramón present in court. But right now, sitting on his hunter green leather couch, staring at the commendations from the U.S. Attorney's office, the Sheriff's Department and the Tuscaloosa Volunteer Fire Department Association, it did not seem as though Ramón was going to get his request.

"You are asking this court to pay for the transportation expenses and lodging of an expert all the way from Florida?"

"Judge, she's the most prominent figure in the field in the entire country."

"Why the hell can't you call someone a little closer, like San Francisco or Sacramento?"

"That's where most Cubans live, Judge, and that's where those studies are conducted. Ethnological surveys of the type de Alba conducts are not even done on the West Coast. Besides, she literally wrote the book on the comparative study of Santería to other religions. She's a crucial witness to the case."

Something I said must have struck home for the judge's angry astonishment now turned to an attitude approaching perplexity, a strange emotion for someone paid to have an opinion about every-thing. Reynolds picked up his pipe, his latest attempt at controlling the temper that so often threatened to run off with him. He lit the pipe, puffed out signals of vanilla-scented smoke.

"What do you think, Phyllis?"

Dressed in white and beige, Phyllis slid her silver bracelets down her wrist.

"It's a judgment call, Judge. No pun intended. As you know the prosecution cannot get involved in matters like this. But, in general, I tend to agree with you. We don't see the need to bring in someone from three thousand miles away. I'm sure there are perfectly good ethnologists at USC and UCLA."

"They're not the same," I said. "They're not Cuban, they don't have fifty years of research behind them."

"I hope you are not saying that only people of the Hispanic race—"

"Hispanic is not a race, it's an ethnic group."

"Whatever. That only those people can study it."

"That's not at all what I'm saying. What I'm saying is that we're entitled to the best."

"At county expense?"

"You pay your consultants two hundred fifty dollars an hour for drunk driving cases. Why are you worrying about this?"

Reynolds put down his pipe. "I think I've heard enough."

"Before you reach your decision, Judge, I want to remind you again that the prosecution is inalterably opposed to this kind of evidence. We feel Santería and religion have no bearing on this matter and we are opposed to the introduction of such as a defense."

I couldn't let that pass—even though I fleetingly saw images of gods vanishing in and out of the white walls.

"Judge, that's the heart of the defense. Valdez' position, as he has explained it to me, is that the events can only be understood if viewed within the religious context. Valdez is an active member of the cult, a priest, in fact, and the jewels that were taken were presents to the god."

Reynolds reached for his pipe again. "That raises a very inter-esting proposition, Charlie. Does that mean he's suggesting that anyone whose sacred objects are taken from him—whether justly or unjustly—has the right to murder the person who took them?"

I paused, thought quickly on how to respond. The cross of the Jesus Saves church glistened in the distance.

"Judge, that's implying that these deaths were a deliberate act of punishment against the perpetrators of that hypothetical crime, which is not the case at hand. However, on a historical note, I should point out that in fact millions of people have done just that and with the sanction of the highest religious figure in Christendom. It was called the Crusades and we had four of them."

Phyllis sneered. "You're not going to compare some voodoo-hoodoo mumbo jumbo with the faith that is the ideological under-pinning of our society."

This was easy to counter, though not necessarily to be believed.

"True, but that was a mere accident of history. Christianity was only one of several cults prominent in the Roman Empire around the time of the Caesars. If not for Nero and Tiberius, who united the Christians because of their persecution, we might be on our knees before the sun symbol of Zoroaster or the bull of the Mithraic cult."

"Charlie, your knowledge is impressive but like my momma used to say, it ain't worth spit here."

"I'd say it's worth more than that, Judge. This cult, religion, whatever it is you choose to call it, is at the same stage as Christianity was at the time of the Emperor Valerian."

"Who?" asked Reynolds.

"A hundred years before Constantine made it official. Its follow-ers are strong-minded zealots, not unlike Saint Paul."

"I never read in the Bible that Saint Paul killed innocent women and children," countered Phyllis.

"Maybe not, but old Jehovah did a thing or two to Sodom and Gomorrah as I recall—not to mention Pharaoh and the Egyptians."

Phyllis was going to argue some more but Reynolds cut her off.

"Charlie, I'm impressed. I'm going to add another credit to your list, theological prevaricator. I will let the evidence in. This is the kind of thing a jury should decide."

"Excuse me, but I thought that already had been settled. What about the fee?"

Reynolds sucked on his pipe. "Unfortunately that I cannot au-thorize. She's not on our list of approved experts. I'll tell you what, get yourself a local expert. Or better yet, maybe your boy can tell us all about it when he takes the stand. Though maybe you should, you probably know more about it than he does."

———

The address was on Bonnie Brae, a few blocks away from MacArthur Park, in the kind of neighborhood that has to be barricaded and turned into a prison camp patrolled by the men in blue before neighbors can walk outside. A row of banged-up aluminum garbage cans overbrimming with refuse was lined up in front of the building. From an open window came the brassy sounds of salsa music, the aural counterpart to the smell of decay and cat piss. A handful of jivey *vatos* drinking beer on a stoop eyed me briefly as I stepped into the vaulted entryway leading to the inner courtyard. A crisscross of balconies rose before my eyes for eight stories. This looks familiar, I thought, as I climbed the stairs to the fifth floor, the steps and landings covered with tiny black and white tiles. The moment I knocked at the door I remembered. This was where Lucinda and Ramón had moved after Pasadena, this was where I had slipped my card under Lucinda's door, looking for her so long ago.

It was the last door at the end of a darkened hallway. From inside the apartment I could hear a guitar and a violin playing a sad Mexican tune. A small woman with a three-colored rebozo opened the door. Brown, round faced, with buck teeth, she seemed an exotic but friendly type of rodent.

"Who is this who knocks at the house of Ramo in this hour of happiness?" she queried in the musical Spanish of southern Mexicans. I could smell the pulque on her breath.

"*Buenas tardes.* I am looking for the family of Pedro Ramo."

"Please step forward, sir. You have found the house you were looking for. May the great happiness descend on you on this great day."

She stepped aside and ushered me inside. About fourteen people were crammed into a small room no bigger than twenty by twenty, drinking beer, tequila and spiked hibiscus flower punch. A gigantic pyramid-shaped altar took up the far wall of the room. Decorated with brightly colored foil and divided into shelves, the altar was set with offerings—faded photographs in tin frames, beeswax candles, fruits, flowers, cones of brown sugar and chocolate, sweet Mexican breads, cigarettes and liquor.

In the middle of the room, the guitar player and violinist played their tune to the object of the ceremony, the aim of the spectacle—a dead boy in a pine coffin. About four years old, the child was dressed in a little brown suit, his bulging eyes closed, a cowlick of jet black hair still standing from the crown of his head. The guitar player sang:

"Goodbye, my loved ones
I go to sad oblivion
Goodbye, my dear home,
where I was laid to rest.

Goodbye, my dear house
where once I roomed
I beg of all my loved ones
Not to forget I once was.

From this world all you will gather
No matter how much gold you have
Is a poor man's death box
In which you will depart."

A short dark-skinned man, his eyes rimmed red from tears, came up to me. "Whoever you are, stranger, welcome to this day of great happiness to us."

I didn't know what to say—what kind of unorthodox custom had I chanced upon that would celebrate death with joy?

"You are Pedro Ramo?"

"Yes, but on this day I am the proud father too of Leonardo, who has gone over the mountains to join the chorus of little children in the valley of the moon. Drink to our happiness, *por favor*, join us!" He pressed a can of Tecate on me.

"I am sorry."

"No need for that. We tried to keep him with us but the music over there was too sweet."

"I am here because I am the court-appointed investigator on the case of Ramón Valdez."

"Who?" His face creased into puzzlement.

"Ramón Valdez, a black Cuban. He said you know him."

"Allow me to question my wife. I do not remember him."

Juan walked a few feet away to where his wife, the teary-eyed cook, was patting down a tortilla. I looked around the room and smelled sweet freesias, incense and beer, tequila and sadness.

"I am sorry I had forgotten. My wife, she tells me you must mean the *brujo*, Don Ramón."

"Yes, I suppose so."

He stood firmly on both legs, thumped his chest.

"I will be happy to lay down my life for Don Ramón. He came here and convinced my boy to stay with us on this earth last year, when he was so desirous of going over to the other side. Just tell me what I can do."

"If you can come and testify for him in court that he's a man of good character."

"Good? He's the best. No one here owes him a greater debt than I and I will always stand ready to pay it back. Here, take this, help us celebrate my son's departure." I lifted the shot glass and gulped down the fiery mescal.

Juan's eyes filled with tears. "Tell Don Ramón we love him and that we will be there when he wants us."

"Good. I will come for you then." I put the shot glass down on the table by the dead boy. "Tell me, did he charge you anything for your son?"

"No," he said proudly, "he did it all, he said, for the love of God."

■

My apartment was empty when I returned. Not empty in the physical sense, for all my furniture was there, the Tabriz rug on the hardwood floor, the Frank Romero painting of the freeways on the wall, the TV and the stereo and the answering machine, the leather couch and the cocktail table with a half-drunk bottle of wine, all those things were there. In the bedroom, too, the down cover on the bed, the old Philippine *santo* on the oak dresser, all the other details that spell domesticity were still there—all except for Lucinda and her things.

Her closet was cleaned out, her suitcase gone, her cosmetics swept up or tossed into the garbage. Only a solitary hair barrette had been forgotten, hidden at the back of a bathroom shelf. In the entire apartment, the only other trace left of her was a picture of the two of us taken in front of Sleeping Beauty's Castle in Disneyland.

Five o'clock. At first, when she had just moved in, at this time she would have been waiting for me, glass of Cabernet in hand, Vivaldi on the stereo, the garlicky, oniony smell of Cuban cooking greeting me from the kitchen. She would kiss me, dressed in a silk palazzo outfit that would feel cool against my fingers and I would slip the top off and we would fall into bed, while the overhead fan stirred the orange blossom air. But first the cooking stopped, then she would no longer run to me when I came home, then even the music ended. Lately all I had were her notes, in her childish scrawl, telling me she'd be working late at Enzo's again. Then, in the middle of the night, she would arrive reeking of garlic and wine, more than a little tipsy, waking me up with her laughter and her sudden desire for sex, which would find her passing out in the middle of the act, face turned to the wall. In the mornings I would leave her still sleeping, white sheets draped around her tawny skin, gathered and enfolded like a babe in swaddling, tendrils of coppery hair falling off her brow like a madonna's.

I searched the apartment for a letter or a note but found none. The green light of the answering machine blinked on and off. I played back the message. Lucinda's sparkling voice came through, against a background of rattling dishes.

"*Hola*, Carlitos, how are you?" she said in Spanish. "You must have seen by now that my things are gone. Nothing has happened to me, I just moved. I am sorry but for a long time I have had the feeling that our relations were drawing to a close. I'm calling because I didn't know how to tell you all this in writing and I don't think I have the courage to tell you face to face. I don't know what happened. These things happen but I never thought it would happen to us too. I know it's not your fault but I don't think—" A buzz as the time allotted for an answer on my machine ran out. Another beep and the following: "*Hola*, it's me again. I guess I have to make this short. I'll be all right. I moved to an apartment around here that Enzo helped me find. He says he'll also increase my hours and my salary so I don't have to rely on your support. Well, I don't know, I guess that's it. God bless you for all you have done. We had some wonderful times together, Charlie, and you'll always be in my heart. I love—" The beep went off in the middle of the phrase and darkness fell over the fields like a hood over the head of the victim.

Four hours and two bottles of wine later I finally weave my way down Vermont to Enzo's. A din of voices, music, clatter of dishes. All the booths are taken, all the tables full, people lined up against the wall waiting for a place. A seafood pizza, carried on high by a tiny Mexican waiter, passes right under my nose to a table nearby. Enzo sees me from the side of the bar and comes up.

"*Ciao, Carlo.*"

"*Ciao, stronzo,*" I tell him. Hi, shithead.

I see Lucinda coming out from the back, still laughing at a lewd comment by a waiter. Her silk dress reminds me vaguely of a leopard skin. She notices me, her smile drops. She stops for a moment, then walks directly up to me. We stare at each other in silence, Enzo by our side, whispering, in Italian, "Don't do anything stupid, Charlie!"

Lucinda keeps her eyes level with mine, she doesn't run, she doesn't bend.

"I'm sorry," she says at last. "It had to be."

I stick my hand in my jacket, feel the butt of the gun. I grab the gun, slide it out of the holster, bring it out into the open.

Enzo steps in between us but I push him away. Gasps among the diners when they see the gun. The hubbub dies down. We are observed in frightful silence. Lucinda does not flinch.

I snap the safety catch, cock the hammer, then twirl the gun and present it to her, butt first. She looks down at it.

"Take it," I say, "go on. Finish the job."

I grab her hand, put it on the gun, forcing her fingers around the handle until I know she's holding it.

Her hand shakes. Her eyes stay down.

"OK, then," I say. "Keep it. Anytime you want to, I'm ready."

I walk out, expecting the kiss between my shoulder blades. It doesn't come. Instead the crowd of diners opens silently before me. I walk up the crowded street.

Hours later, up on high, at the observatory, I see the city lying before me, lights twinkling. I stand on the edge of the platform around the building and look at the red tile roofs a thousand feet below. A shooting star blazes across the night sky.

"I wish for hell!" I scream into the darkness.

A vague echo floats back up. Another shooting star.

I know my wish has been granted.

20

udge Reynolds turned to Ramón. "Do you have an opening statement, Mr. Valdez?"

"I do, Your Honor."

And with that Ramón rose for the first time. Reynolds eyed him askance. He leaned back in his chair, every gesture saying Here's the rope, there's the gallows, let me help you.

The chain twinkled as the chair eased back. Leaning forward, his hands on the table, Ramón looked straight at the jury through the horn-rimmed glasses that made him look like a somber court clerk or a divinity student.

"Ladies and gentlemen of the jury, you will forgive me if I don't approach you, but as perhaps you know I have been in chains all the time I am in this trial. It would be most uncomfortable, in fact it would be embarrassing for me to show my chains. You see, I feel I don't deserve to be in them. But then, that's natural, is it not?"

The jurors smiled sympathetically. Ramón's accent draped itself over the words softly, like down. Never had I seen someone use his foreignness to such an advantage, to be able to enjoy the benefit of both worlds, the alien and the native, the Hispanic and the Anglo.

"Perhaps it would have been easier for all of you to understand me if I had an attorney. The accent and all that. But as you can see"—he waved magnanimously at me—"all I have is an investigator. I am my own attorney. I am sure you are asking why is that.

"Well, I will tell you. I believe that when the facts of the case are so different, so exceptional, and the truth of the matter depends on one's personal interpretation, in that case, I believe it is better to be without an attorney. It is better in that case to be without legal shields, without weapons, and to appeal directly to you, the jury, to understand what happened.

"I don't believe there is a single attorney who would do justice to my case the way I can. You have to see me, you have to hear me, then you can decide if you believe me. You have to see me through the trial, too, not simply when at the end I get on that witness stand and testify. No, because truth is something that flows completely out of your body—out of every pore of your being the smell of truth must come or else no one will believe what actually happened. Every action of mine must have the smell of truth be-cause otherwise, it is all no good."

Ramón coughed, took out a handkerchief. The eyes of the jurors were riveted on him. Mrs. Gardner coughed sympathetically, too. From my chair I could see the notes Ramón had written in his handkerchief, so that no one would know how thoroughly he'd prepared for this statement, how hard he'd worked to make it look natural and spontaneous, the unplanned reaction of an unjustly accused man.

"Now all of you have been seeing me since the trial began, especially since I had my little . . . problem at the beginning." Here he glanced at the judge, referring to the opening salvo of their warfare. The jurors chuckled.

"I think at that time you saw that I am a man of principle. I was shackled and put in solitary because I refused to follow an archaic concept of undue respect."

"Objection, Your Honor," said Phyllis.

"Mr. Valdez, unless you . . ." All the jurors turned to the judge.

"Yes, Your Honor?"

"Please refrain from making comments not directly related to the case. Proceed."

Ramón looked at him for a moment, sincerely hesitating, con-templating in a whir all of the possibilities that would present themselves should he defy the judge at that point. Then he looked away and shook his head at the jury.

"I cannot tell you any more about my principles. As you see, the judge says that has nothing to do with the case." Here he turned to gaze fixedly at Reynolds. "I disagree. Everything in this case has to do with me personally, with my character, with my personality, with the kind of man I am and the kind of man everyone else says I am. Because you see, in the end, there is only belief—belief in one person, belief in one another, belief in the gods."

Ramón smiled at the jurors. In the corner, the eye of the camera zoomed in on his every move.

"Now, prosecutors sometimes use an analogy of the opening statement being like a road map. It shows you the highlights of the trip, where you're going, what you should watch out for. Miss Chin here did not do that in this case, wisely I think, for a reason—no road maps can apply to this case. There are no roads going in and out. The reason is very simple—because no one knows."

He paused, a momentous pause, eyes fixed on his audience. "No one knows because it is all a mystery. *Terra incognita*, in Latin. I am sure you are asking yourself, what the devil does he mean? This is no mystery, everybody says he did it. The prosecution says I did it, the police say I did it, my friend, my former lover, the former defendant in this case, he says I did it too.

"But I am going to tell you a secret. I didn't do it. I, Ramón Valdez, as I stand here, facing you, before this court, before the flag of this great country, I tell you I didn't do it."

Another pause, perspiration pearling his brow. He made no effort to wipe it off.

"I know it sounds ridiculous but it's true. I didn't do it. Something bigger than us, something beyond our everyday existence, a cosmic force came and used one of us for the greater meaning and design He had in mind.

"Ridiculous, you say? God is not cruel, God is kindness, God is love. But is He really?

"In an old novel by a Russian author—the Russians, they know much about the soul, you know—Jesus Christ has come back to earth. He is brought before the Grand Inquisitor in Spain. The Grand Inquisitor is incredibly agitated for he can't believe Jesus has returned and that he has Him before him. And the main question the Inquisitor asks Jesus is, how can you allow the bad to exist in this world? How can we believe in You, in Christ, in God, when innocent children suffer for no reason at all?

"Just the other day I too ran into something like this. In jail, a man I knew was crying. I asked him why he cried. He said his little girl, four years old, that he had left with his brother for safekeeping while he served his sentence, that little girl had been sexually abused. A broomstick had been stuck inside of her until she died from the bleeding and then her body was put in a bag and burned in a park. All this by the very same brother who was supposed to be taking care of the little niece.

"That is the soul of the question I would have asked Christ if He were here and if I were the Grand Inquisitor. Today, after Auschwitz, after Treblinka, the labor camps of Stalin, the killing fields of Cambodia, the famine of Ethiopia, how can we believe in Christ?

"Do you know what the answer was, ladies and gentlemen, the answer Christ gave the Inquisitor in that novel? No answer. No answer at all. Do you know why? Because God goes beyond human understanding, God goes beyond good and evil, God is—"

"Objection, Your Honor," interrupted Phyllis. "Mr. Valdez is giving us a Sunday school lesson that has no relevance."

The cold stares the jurors directed at Phyllis should have warned her not to insist but she pressed on. I noticed that Ramón's face seemed devoid of color, a film of sweat running down to his shirt collar.

"I think Your Honor should remove Mr. Valdez from his pro per status and appoint an attorney who can conduct a competent defense for him."

Reynolds held his ground. "Counsel, opening statements are allowed a wide latitude in their subjects," he countered, but emphasized, "as long as they ultimately show the connection to the case. Proceed, Mr. Valdez, but remember, I'm waiting to see where all these theological musings are leading. Objection overruled."

Ramón looked wide eyed at the judge, threw an arm into the air, then jerked spasmodically. He spoke in a rush, breathlessly, almost as though the weight of his words was unbearable and he had to unburden himself of them as soon as he could.

"Where will it lead us, Your Honor, where will it lead us? I will tell you where it will lead us, to the gates of Hell, Your Honor, to the gates of the *infierno*, that *abre sus puertas y nos espera allí* in the darkness amid the gnashing of teeth *y el concierto de las almas malditas*, *allá* in the heights, where the empyrean *coro de angelitos danza en torno* the clouds *mientras que un* God choleric wreaks his wrath . . ."

I was stunned, I couldn't believe what I was hearing. The non sequiturs in Spanish and English rolled in and out of Ramón's mouth, which now drooled and slavered, as though some perverse spirit were seizing control of him. Jurors looked at each other with amazement, not knowing whether the seizure was real or feigned.

Reynolds looked at Ramón like a lepidopterist examining a still fluttering specimen. Phyllis sprang up, raised her hand accusatorily. The bailiff also jumped out of his chair, arm muscles rippling from contained fear.

"You Honor, Mr. Valdez is demonstrating his incompetence. He has lapsed into gibberish and we request that he be taken off the case!"

Ramón paid no attention, his mouth now drooling freely, eyes moving rapidly left to right, as if scanning the vision of the Christian heaven that now appeared to him, a heathen, and was denied to us believers.

". . . *y las plagas del Santísimo* will spread triumphant throughout the land as *el Señor dice* I will not spare your firstborn this time, no, *no lo haré, porque ni* the prayers *de un justo habrán de apartarme de mi* divine wrath for you have sinned, people of Israel, you have worshiped false gods and *el Dios de la Dulzura y el amor ya* doesn't exist and I will come *para abrir los caminos—*"

"Mr. Valdez, get ahold of yourself! Mr. Morell, please speak to your client!"

"He is not my client, Your Honor!" I said as I got up and shook Ramón, trying to get him to stop.

"Well, he's going to be unless you put an end to this!"

"*Ramón, cállate, cállate, la boca!*" I said, but he hurled me into my chair with just one arm and sent me sliding ten feet across the room.

". . . *y la cólera de Dios no ha de parar* and I will visit your houses, O Israel, *y la sangre de la oveja* will spill—"

"Bailiff, remove this man from the court!" shouted Reynolds.

The deputy, who had already rung for help and was only waiting for the order, leaped on Ramón, wrestling him down to the ground. Now three other bailiffs entered from three different doors, jumped over me and seized Ramón, one of them unlocking the chains that tied him to the table.

"*Palabra de Dios*, the word of God, the word of God!" was the last thing Ramón said as the door into the lockup banged closed.

I got up, straightened my chair.

"This court is in recess! Mr. Morell and Ms. Chin, please follow me into chambers!"

—

I go down to the lockup. Ramón sits alone in his cell, his back straight against the wall. Above him, some hapless soul has scratched on the wall, *Play the white man's game—computer crime!* Ramón turns his head slowly, sees me and smiles. It's 12:35.

"That was a great show but I don't think the jury bought it," I said. "Do you really think anyone understood what you were saying? The reporter didn't write it down, the jurors that speak Spanish don't know it that well. It was gibberish. But you knew what you were doing, didn't you? You can't give me that possessed shit. I know that this is all a game—make believe to get your ass out of here."

Ramón doesn't answer, just smiles knowingly, blankly. I sit in the chair by the sally port, and for a moment I wonder which one of us is really behind bars.

"Why can't you take your punishment like everybody else? Why can't you plead guilty and take the deal they're offering? It would be so easy for all of us. I know you did it, you know you did it. There's no way to avoid that. One must always live with the consequences. Or die from them, as the case might be. But not you. You will not even recognize the evil you've caused. You want to do what you want and never ever have to pay for it. You want the moon to come down and fit in your pocket. You want everyone to say there's never been anyone like you and the rules don't and can't apply. I wish you would vanish. I wish you would die. But mostly, I wish I had the courage to kill you myself."

Ramón is still staring, his smile still fixed on his lips. I shake my head, weary.

"The judge wants me to act as your attorney. He says you're incompetent and he's removing your pro per privileges. You had it coming, but then I suppose you knew that all along. So what do you want to do?"

Ramón lifts a hand, asking a question with his fingers, demanding something.

"Didn't you hear me? I said . . ." I glance at my watch for some unexplained reason. It still reads 12:35, the second hand still sweeping slowly across the roman numerals. I realize he hasn't heard a word because I haven't opened my mouth yet and all those words are still unspoken. I have imagined my speech, I have talked to myself in silence in the cell.

Ramón groans, then whispers hoarsely, "I lost my voice!"

■

"Ladies and gentlemen of the jury," intones Reynolds, "we all knew this was an unusual case when we started. I think the events of this morning have given us ample proof of that."

I glance at the expectant faces of the jurors, who can't quite figure out what the judge is going to say next. Neither can I, as I wait for my turn to defend the darkness.

"Normally in a situation like we had this morning, when a pro per acts the way Mr. Valdez did, there is more than just the usual delay while the person recovers." Reynolds looks quickly at Ramón, at me, then glances back at the jury. "Like my momma used to say, it's more trouble than two hounds fighting over a hambone." Smiles and chuckles, a brief welcome break.

"Since it has become exceedingly clear to me that Mr. Valdez was unable to conduct his own defense in the correct fashion at the time this, this . . . here thing happened, a whole passel of problems just popped out. A new lawyer has to be named, he has to familiarize himself with the case, perhaps file new motions, all the long and tedious work that judges and attorneys carry on while you folks are drinking coffee, smoking cigarettes and reading out in the hall-way, waiting for us." More chuckles.

That's good, Judge, keep them happy, warm them up for me because I haven't the faintest idea what to do.

"But before I proceed," continues Reynolds, "there's just one little thing I got to ask y'all. You're not going to hold it against Mr. Valdez here that he couldn't hold his end of the bargain and conduct his own defense, now are you?"

The jurors shake their heads. Phyllis examines their faces carefully for signs of dissembling. I look at Ramón, who smiles unworriedly. God knows what forlorn expression I have on.

"If anybody here is going to, please raise your hand, I'd like to know right now. I see no hands are raised. Fine, so I can proceed. I knew you were open-minded folks. Now, as I was saying, this kind of . . . change sometimes creates undue delays because of the difficulties in getting a lawyer in at this late stage of the game. So we've come up with a solution I think you will like. You see that good-looking gentleman there in the black suit, next to Mr. Valdez?"

All the faces turn to me. The news camera focuses in on me mercilessly. I smile.

"That's Mr. Morell, Mr. Charles Morell. So far he's been Mr. Valdez' investigator but actually, you see, he's also a lawyer. And a fine one too, I might add. Please stand, Mr. Morell."

I get to my feet reluctantly, feeling the sweat streaming out of my underarms, wondering if it will soak through the jacket.

"Mr. Morell obviously is very familiar with the case. He's helped fashion Mr. Valdez' defense, even. Seeing as to how we find ourselves in this hour of need, he's graciously agreed to take on the case for the duration of the trial. So, Mr. Morell, have a go at it."

I nod, pick up my yellow legal tablets on which I've scribbled the half-dozen defense arguments I think should be made to the jury. I move to the lectern. Slowly I turn it around so I can observe the faces of the jurors.

I hear a strange loud noise in the background. I realize it's the sound of my own heart. I remember the old rules and tricks. Take a deep breath and smile. Look at small groups of twos and threes in turn. Make everyone feel recognized and appreciated. Smile as hard as you can, then smile some more.

I stop. The moments pass. Everyone stares.

I realize all the arguments I have collected have no purpose. There is nothing I can say that hasn't been stated or implied. I have no defense. I have no arguments. Everything is lead and dross.

Reynolds clears his throat. "Mr. Morell?" he prompts.

"Yes, Your Honor," I reply, the good doggie at the show, ready to trot for his master.

"Ladies and gentlemen," I start, "as you may surmise"—*stop the fancy words, get plain and simple!*—"it's not easy coming into the middle of a case like this so I must ask for your indulgence if I seem somewhat less than at ease. While it's true that I helped Mr. Valdez with his defense, it certainly never occurred to me that one day I'd be here standing before you, facing you, entrusted with the case. I hope you'll bear with me." *That's good, keep it straight, make them feel important.*

"When Mr. Valdez was interrupted by his . . . condition, he was in the middle of answering a question from the judge, a question that I think sheds light on the way that we view this case.

"Now, everything here has already been said, that is, the factual arguments to counter the proposition of the prosecution that Mr. Valdez is the man who murdered those six people at the Jewelry Mart. The question, as you will recall, was what did Mr. Valdez intend with all those arguments about God and man and evil and sin and all of the terrible things that we see in our world every day. I believe that if Mr. Valdez could talk—and by the way, he can't, he has lost his faculty of speech—"

"Objection, Your Honor," interposes Phyllis. "Irrelevant."

"Overruled. Proceed, Mr. Morell."

"Thank you, Your Honor. As I said, could Mr. Valdez finish what he had intended to say, I believe he would have told you this. Men are sometimes picked by God to be the instruments of His will, without their being aware if they are chosen to be the sword that cuts or the hand that heals. That, ladies and gentlemen, is what happened here."

The rolling rush of fear and excitement courses through me, as the strategy unfolds like a white ribbon in a blood red field.

"One of the two occurred. Either Mr. Valdez or Mr. Pimienta—who has obtained a deal from the prosecution for his testimony, as you saw—one of them was visited by their gods during this incident at Schnitzer Jewelers. In plain English, one of them was possessed. Yes, possessed, like the people in the Bible possessed by devils, who Jesus cast into swine, possessed like the saints who levitate and work miracles, possessed like the girl in *The Exorcist*—possessed, in other words, by a force that recognizes neither right nor wrong, that laughs at our Christian morality and seeks only its immediate gratification."

I pause, let the words sink in. "Whether it be sex, food, love, hate or death, only the immediate exists for that force. It's beyond our good and evil, beyond what we believe is due and proper. It comes from a world that none of us really knows, from that African world of pagan deities—from there came these gods."

Now the last words, the sobering brooch to the fulsome story.

"We intend to prove that both Mr. Valdez and Mr. Pimienta were followers of an Afro-Cuban religious cult known as Santería and that these deaths occurred while they were in a trancelike state, when the gods descend and possess the bodies of their followers, and that therefore Mr. Valdez cannot be found guilty of the crime because he had no consciousness of his actions while under the spell of these dark and ancient gods. Thank you very much."

I sit down, empty and exhilarated. I hear Reynolds tell the jury that because of witness problems, the defense will not resume for three days. The jurors are still filing out when I finally turn and look at Ramón, who's now being tapped on the shoulder by the bailiff to return to his cell. He makes an O with thumb and index finger and mouths a silent OK. I watch him rattle into the lockup, my heartbeat slows down.

God help me, I think. God help me.

21

graciela de Alba did not look at all as though she'd just left her deathbed. Short, stocky, leaning on a Nigerian ceremonial tribal cane, with a head of bushy red and gray hair and deep green eyes, she was a baobab, a tree of life in the plains of LAX, surrounded by hordes of passengers around the Pan Am counter. She raised the silver-handled cane when she saw me approaching, wagging it in the air.

"You must be Charlie," she said.

"Yes, I am, Señora de Alba. Sorry I was delayed, a truck jack-knifed on the Santa Monica Freeway."

"I know, I know. Four cars smashed, two dead. Terrible."

"How did you know?" I was ready for revelations from afar. She pointed at the speakers in the newsstand nearby.

"Radio. Ready?"

Her luggage consisted of a large black steamer trunk that weighed at least two hundred pounds. The porter who carted it to the 944 shook his head wearily when he dropped it in the back.

"What you got in there, lady? A body?"

"Four. For good luck."

"Four?" The man looked at her surprised, then burst out laughing. He wheeled his cart away. "You crack me up."

De Alba waddled around to the front of my Porsche, bent over the front fender.

"They didn't do a very good job fixing this," she said.

"What do you mean?

"See these waves in the body?" She pointed out some barely discernible ripples along the side of the right front fender. "The man at the shop didn't smooth that out correctly. If I were you I'd ask for my money back. I mean, this is a nice car and all." She extended her hand. "Mind if I drive?"

I couldn't help a smile—the little old lady from Miami with a four on the floor—five, actually.

"Sure." I tossed her the keys. She grabbed them with her free hand and, opening the driver's door, slid behind the wheel. Her wide girth forced her to slide the seat all the way back, so that by the time her belly fit inside, the tips of her shoes barely touched the pedals.

"You sure you want to do this?" I asked.

"Positive." She gunned the engine. "Love sports cars. I got a Lotus back home."

She drove fiendishly around the traffic circle in front of the terminal, cutting off a Cadillac to make a light and exit on Century Boulevard out of the airport. She didn't slow down below sixty until we reached the 405 on-ramp, where she decelerated briefly to fifty, then revved all the way up to ninety, weaving in and out of the chugging lanes of traffic with the assurance of an Emerson Fittipaldi.

"But my car back home doesn't handle like this. Nice set of wheels."

"Thank you. You said you were sick. What happened, too much car exhaust?"

She glanced around, her eyes gleefully taking in the dull green hills leading to the Mulholland Pass. "If that made you sick, I think all of L.A. would be one giant rolling hospital. No, cancer of the colon."

"How did you beat it, with chemotherapy?"

She looked at me puzzled. "What chemotherapy? Didn't Ramón tell you?"

I should have known I'd be set up for the sucker punch. "No, he hasn't been quite himself lately. He can't speak."

"Really? How did that happen?"

"He had a seizure of sorts last week. Right in the middle of opening arguments. Sort of like he swallowed his tongue."

"The orisha must be very angry at him. That must be his punishment." She eyed me quizzically. "Perhaps it's something else. Maybe they wanted you to handle the case."

"I'm sure. Watch out for the truck!" De Alba glanced forward again. The car was about to plow into a smoking cart of roofer's pitch towed by an aging Ford barely making forty up the grade. She braked, but just at that moment traffic opened up two lanes away so de Alba shot straight for the opening. By the time I regained my breath, she was tooling along at a normal seventy-five per hour.

"Sorry about that," she said. "Your freeways are really busy."

"Now you notice."

She drove on in silence for a while, observing the green and gray masses of pampa grass growing along the sides of the road, the strands of oak, the compact shadowy chaparral.

"These hills have much *nganga*," she said.

"What's that?"

"Spiritual power. I can feel it in spite of this traffic. This place is truly like a magnet, isn't it? Oh, my God!"

We'd come over the pass, leaving Mulholland behind us. The entire San Fernando Valley opened before us, the tall shoulders of the San Gabriel range looming portentously over the paved-over orange groves, the car dealerships, California ranch homes and shimmering swimming pools.

"This is truly a magic town," she muttered, almost in disbelief. "It's an oasis, just like everybody says."

I had nothing to say to that. If this was the watering hole, then what was the desert like?

"How did you meet Ramón?" I asked.

"Look at the houses!" she said, pointing out the tile-roofed homes of the Hollywood hills as we descended through the Cahuenga Pass. "Just like Italy. Bell tower and everything. How quaint! How did we meet? Well, you know, we never have."

"You haven't?"

"No. I know of him. He is a very high-ranking *babalawo*, you know, a high priest of Santería. I have been told he's an *omokoloba*, a high initiate into the mysteries of the religion. We have mutual acquaintances in Miami."

"But isn't a priest supposed to lead an exemplary life?"

"Yes. That's his problem. He's been ignoring the dictates of his god. Besides, I hear he's gotten into *palo mayombé* as well."

"You mean the black witchcraft, raising the dead and all that?"

"Yes. Maybe because his saint left him and he turned to the dead, maybe he's power hungry, I don't know. What do I do now?"

She pointed her chin at a fork in the road, one to Pasadena, the other to downtown and Santa Ana.

"Take the Harbor and off on Sixth Street. So you think that's what happened to him in the Jewelry Mart?"

She drove swiftly through the joining lanes, skirting traffic at the interchange. "I don't know what happened there but I'm sorry I wasn't here when it did happen. It was a divine retaliation of some sort. You know that in Santería, prisons and jails are two of the five manifestations of evil in the world, especially for Oggún, Ramón's saint. He must have sinned enormously to be locked up on charges like this."

We exited on Sixth and slipped down to the old, gilt Biltmore Hotel at Pershing Square. She screeched the Porsche to a halt, grinned. "Great car. Have to let me drive it again some time."

She picked up her cane, waddled out into the street and waved at a bellboy to pick up her trunk.

"Listen," I said, "you never told me. What happened to your colon cancer?"

The bellboy huffed, lowering the trunk to the dolly. "Careful, there!" she warned. Then, "I had a dream that Oggún came with a potion. When I drank it he told me I'd been cured so I could come help his son, who sinned but is still loved. The next day the cancer was in remission."

"How did you know it was Ramón?"

"Oggún held up a figurine of Ramón. He spoke to me and told me where to come. He was holding another one. I didn't know who it was then. But now I do."

"Who was it?"

She smiled at me and the chill of realization tore down my back. "See you tomorrow in court," she said.

It was about eleven-thirty, just a half hour before our lunch break, when I finally called in our first witness. Pedro Ramo took the stand with the practical ease of someone who's had to justify his existence countless times, not certain of what story he would tell but knowing that once again his thoughts and actions would be displayed in the bright light for all to see. I'd already reviewed out in the hall the questions that I'd be asking him, so now, having sworn to tell the truth, he looked directly at me, calmly waiting for the testimony to begin. The interpreter, an old bull of a man with a gray mustache and a hearing aid, translated in the singsong rhythm of East Los Angeles.

"I don't know how to write," said Pedro, when asked by the clerk to spell his name. Reynolds rolled his eyes in exasperation and instructed the interpreter to give the standard spelling.

My turn. I rose, walked to the lectern, put down my notepad, made believe there was no one else in the courtroom, that Pedro and I were there only for a few friendly questions.

"Mr. Ramo, do you know the defendant, Mr. Valdez?"

"Oh yes, I do. He has been very good to us, me and my family," he said. "He has been our protector."

"How long have you known him?"

"Ooh, a long time, almost five years now. May I say something?" He looked imploringly at the judge, but Reynolds cut him off before he could go on.

"Wait until the lawyer asks you the question."

Ramo's features tightened from repressed storytelling.

"In what capacity do you know Mr. Valdez?"

"He's our priest, our savior. Without him we would have known great calamities."

"What do you mean?"

"When we first came to Los Angeles he helped us find a place to stay, then he told us where work could be had. He has been a very helpful man."

"Has he ever been cruel or acted badly toward you?"

"Oh no, never."

"And your family? Do you know how he has acted toward them?"

"A very good man he has been. May I say something?"

Reynolds again cut him off peremptorily with a wave of the hand. "Wait until the question is asked."

I looked to my side and instead of seeing Phyllis scribbling notes or preparing for objections, she was very calmly filing her nails with an emery board no bigger than her little finger. Ramón grinned at me, approving my sorry performance so far.

"Do you have any children, Mr. Ramo?"

"Oh, yes. Five. Tomasito, Gabriel, Lupe, José and Panchito, he's on leave."

"Excuse me?" I said. Ramo had used the word "*feriado*," which the interpreter had mistranslated. But the old man now engaged in a soft-spoken, rapid-fire exchange with the Indian, which ended with the interpreter nodding, turning toward me and saying, with dubious conviction, "He's on holiday."

"A holiday. How old is he?"

"He's five, yes."

"Isn't he a little too young to be on a holiday?"

"Oh no, the holiday can come and strike you at any time, you know."

"I see. Is this a permanent holiday?"

"Yes, unfortunately."

"Is this what we call dead?"

The word *muerto* resounded almost like a child's song in the courtroom.

"*No, no está muerto con tal de que yo lo recuerde,*" he declared. No, he's not dead as long as I remember him. Now everyone in the courtroom stopped what they were doing—Phyllis her nails, Reynolds the crossword puzzle on his legal pad, the bailiff leafing through his *Guns and Ammo*, the audience reading the *Reader's Digest* and the *Times*, to gaze briefly at a father who would not let his child go.

"I understand," I said, "and please forgive me, for I know in your heart Panchito still lives. But his body, it is in the cemetery?"

Ramo, crestfallen. "Yes, it is."

"Did Mr. Valdez know Panchito?"

"Yes. He was the one who convinced him to stay with us once before."

"How was that?"

"He had the fever for going, he was wasting away, but don Ramón gave him a bath and he got much better and decided to stay with us for a while."

"You had taken him to a doctor?"

"It was no use, they said, he had the malady deep inside him. It was in his bones."

"And you are sure that Mr. Valdez, don Ramón, like you call him, helped your son get better?"

"I know so. He lived for another two years. What wouldn't I give to have him back with us. He was the light of our house."

"Did Mr. Valdez charge you something for this?"

"Oh, no. He's our priest. A good priest. He doesn't charge."

"What religion is this?"

"It's the religion of the saints, he says. Saints."

"You mean Santería."

"Yes, that."

"Were you the only one who belonged to this religion?"

"No, there are many of us. We were a flock but now our shepherd, he's here in jail and all the sheep have strayed. May I say something?"

Reynolds is again going to stop him but I speak up first. "What would you like to say?"

"I'd like to say that the man who cured my boy is not the man you have here, that was a different man, if it's true what they say that don Ramón did at that store. But I also want to say this, don Ramón, we love you and miss you and we are waiting for your touch and for your help. Thank you very much."

I stood there, gripping the lectern, waves of restlessness pounding at my forehead, the room spinning, until I heard myself ask, "Mr. Ramo, do you believe in Christ?"

"Christ? Yes, he's a saint, isn't he?"

I took a deep breath, picked up my notepad, returned to my chair. "No more questions."

"Ms. Chin?" asked Reynolds.

Phyllis bent to whisper something to Samuels, who shook his

head no. I knew Ramo had no record, there was nothing they could hang on him.

Wearily, almost reluctantly, Phyllis answered. "No questions."

Reynolds turned to Ramo. "I have a question. When did your son go on holiday, like you say?"

"Last week, señor."

"And you feel if Mr. Valdez had been there your son would not have left you?"

"I am sure of it."

"You think Mr. Valdez is a good man?"

"He is the best man I have ever known, Mr. Judge. The very best."

Reynolds turned his head, skeptical. "He didn't pay you to come here, did he?"

"No, señor. My testimony is free and voluntary. I'm here because I love him."

A moment of silence. "You are excused," said the judge.

Ramo got up, gazed at Ramón with compassion, then walked out in silence. Ramón grinned ferociously, a mask of teeth around his feelings.

I walked around downtown for the two hours we had for lunch that day. Restless, half-formed feelings and vague memories assaulted me in the brassy light that winter afternoon. A block west, on Broadway, a river of Hispanics surged and flowed on the sidewalks, from First to Olympic, past the grandiose movie theaters built like Aztec temples and the concrete and masonry buildings with money-changing offices and *farmacias* and Spanish-language newsstands and discount electronic stores on the first floor, past Pershing Square and the Japanese-owned Biltmore Hotel and the bloodied Jewelry Mart where this tragedy had struck on a winter's morning almost three years before.

I had been told the Schnitzer site was to be turned into a fast-food place, but in reality it had been converted into yet another jeweler's, Arossian Brothers. I peered inside but did not dare enter in spite of the entreaties of the long-nosed clerks, who pleaded for the pleasure of my business. I was about to leave when my eye was drawn to a sparkling diamond and sapphire pin shaped like a dove in flight. My eyes flickered and for a moment I thought I recognized my father's reflection in the glass, but when I turned there was just an empty sidewalk and a crack dealer peddling his dream wares at the corner.

At one point I found myself chewing on something and discovered I had a blood sausage taco in my hands. I stood in front of a food stand at the Central Market. Old housewives, potbellied Mexican cowboys and five-dollars-a-blow hustlers taking a break from the life surrounded me. The girl behind the counter proffered a cup full of a pink liquid.

"Your sorrel drink, señor."

I shook my head, tossed my taco in the garbage can and walked away. I looked back and saw an ocher-skinned old man in stained white shirt retrieving my taco from the can and taking a bite from it, before grabbing my drink from the counter as well and rushing to hide in a corner behind the fruit stand. I had no words, I had no feelings. A lamb's head in the butcher's meat case, skin pulled off, pink gristle over white bone, fixed its gaping blue eyes on me. I hurried out. Give me strength, Lord, guide me through this valley.

White puffy clouds rose like castles in the background as I ascended the hill on Olive Street. They were unlike any I had ever seen, tall, glimmering statues of vapor that rose thousands of feet into the air, crenellated towers of gossamer that pushed in from the San Gabriel Mountains. There was a host of them, white structures looming against the sky, surrounding the Criminal Courts Building like so many giant sentries, waiting for an order to strike. For the first time I was frightened by what these creatures of nature, wild, unthinking, inhuman, could do.

"Santa Ana wind is blowing them in from the desert," said Camille Clark, a former public defender who'd shucked the poor for a job in Century City defending insurance companies against medical malpractice claims. "Always happens this time of year, surprised you never noticed before. Things should start popping pretty soon."

"What do you mean by that?"

We rode up in the packed elevator, the reek of alcohol from a potbellied biker almost palpable to the touch.

"The static, when the clouds come in like that and run into the tropical front we've been having lately, all kinds of things happen. It's actually tornado weather, just like in the Midwest. You know, Charlie, you don't look too good. You should take better care of yourself."

I stepped out on my floor, the elevator doors snapping shut like a guillotine.

"Call me!" were Camille's last words.

Pimienta was waiting out in the hallway, his bulky figure slouched on the brown concrete bench by the courtroom. I'd subpoenaed him to be my witness the following day, since I wasn't expecting de Alba's testimony to take up more than an afternoon, so for a brief moment I thought he'd simply gotten the date wrong. He glanced up, stopped me. One of the jurors went around us, dashed into court.

"Morell, we have to talk, *coño*," he said.

"We will, tomorrow, don't worry."

"No, I got to talk to you before."

"I don't know if I can. Where's your attorney?"

"Señor Smith? He's not handling my case anymore. He got married and went to Paris on his honeymoon."

"So you have no attorney?"

"That doesn't matter. Listen to me, we have to talk."

"What about? I got to go into court now."

"I've been having dreams, Morell, bad dreams. I see the faces of the dead, their fingers are choking me, their shouts and cries, and I find myself in the store again but this time it's all on fire and I can't get out. Every night I have these dreams."

"Well, we all have nightmares, José. I really can't talk to you right now. Look, why don't you—"

The bailiff came out. "Better get your ass in here, Charlie. The old man's fuming."

I turned to Pimienta. "Look, José, sit right here and wait for me. I'll get back to you in a little while."

I walked briskly into the court.

De Alba had somehow entered the court during the lunch break and set up an entire Santería altar at a far wall, next to the jury box. Split in several levels, with offerings of flowers and live pigeons in baskets and sweets, the entire thing was surmounted by a picture of Saint Peter holding the keys to heaven.

A dozen men and women dressed in white sat in in the front row while de Alba, all in black, braced herself on the bar speaking to the oldest member in the group, a thin black man with tribal markings on his cheeks and forehead.

The jury was already in the box, distracted by the altar and all the strange objects. Reynolds was in his chair, Phyllis and Ramón in theirs. As always, I was the last one to the party. Reynolds gestured at me and Phyllis to approach.

"Don't we want the reporter in here?" were Phyllis's first words.

"No, no, that can wait, this is strictly between us. Listen, Charlie, I told you I was going to give you a wide latitude in your defense, but this is making a circus out of the whole thing. I mean, this is a damn altar this here woman has set up. Now, this is no church and I sure ain't no preacher, so what is it that you two are doing?"

What are you doing, Charlie? booms the echo in my mind. How can you show like at a carnival, the wounds that suppurate, the joining at the hip, the grinning bearded creature?

"Judge, this is just for demonstration purposes," I improvised. "There will be testimony about the religion, so I felt it would be good for the jurors to get a good look at what it's all about."

"She's not going to be casting any spells, is she?" asked Phyllis. "She looks like a witch to me."

"I don't think so. But maybe I'll ask her to cast a hex so I can win this."

"Fat chance."

"And who are the folks in white on the front row? Just look at them, it's like a convention of souls of the departed."

"I'll ask."

I walked up to de Alba and leaned over the bar.

"Mrs. de Alba, who are these people?"

"These are some of the main *babalawos* of Los Angeles. I told them I was going to be testifying so they wanted to see what was going to happen. They won't bother anyone."

"I see. Are you a priest too, by the way?"

"Oh heavens, no. I'm just an anthropologist. I don't even belong to the religion."

I walked back to the judge. "They're spectators."

"I can see that for myself. What else are they?"

"Members of the religion. They are interested in the case."

The judge sighed. "Well, hell, it's still a free country, they have a right to be here too. Let's proceed."

After Curtis swore in de Alba, she bowed to the altar before sitting down. The bailiff tried to bring the microphone closer to her but she pushed it away.

"I don't need this. My voice carries. I hate mechanical things."

I took my post at the lectern, yellow pad at the ready. On it I had written down a single question—why?

"Mrs. de Alba, could you tell us your occupation?"

She adjusted her seat. "Certainly. I'm an anthropologist." Her Cuban accent, which had been very faint, became more pronounced under the stress.

"Could you tell us your qualifications and experience?"

"Of course. I'm a graduate of the University of Havana, 1932, in anthropology. I studied with Dr. Franz Boas, one of the founders of modern anthropology, at Columbia University in 1933, then obtained my doctorate in Harvard in 1935, also in anthropology. I have diplomas from the Sorbonne, Cambridge University, the universities of Berlin, Heidelberg, Vienna. I have published, what, sixteen books and over a thousand articles for publication. I have also conducted field studies among the Indians and blacks of Brazil with Dr. Claude Lévi-Strauss and, when she was with us, with Dr. Margaret Mead. In addition—"

"That's enough. I think we can all agree you had a solid education."

Laughter in the courtroom. I panic. I'm not supposed to be funny, I'm supposed to bear down on this case, to remind everyone of the forces behind us.

"Yes, you might say so," said de Alba.

"What is your field of specialization, if you have one?"

"My particular field is the study of Santería, an Afro-Cuban religion with about five million followers in this hemisphere."

"I see. Do you know Mr. Valdez, the defendant in this case?"

"Not personally. But I've heard of him."

"What have you heard?"

Phyllis rises, red silk dress rustling. "Objection, Your Honor, hearsay evidence."

"Sustained."

How can I get around this, to bring out her knowledge of who Ramón is? And do I really want that?

"What do you know about Mr. Valdez?"

She stared unblinkingly at Ramón. "I know he once was a very prominent priest of Santería. His reputation was that of a miracle worker, years ago."

Should I follow this line of questioning? No, let it lay, the words miracle worker are suggestive enough in themselves. Move on, Charlie, you have a big job to do. He is waiting for you.

"You mentioned your special field of study is Santería. Could you tell us what kind of religion that is and how it is different from other organized religions, like Christianity or Buddhism?"

"Certainly. Santería is a syncretic religion. By that I mean it has fused together two separate strands to form a new one. It is a combination of West African religion and Catholicism, wherein the old Nigerian Yoruba pantheon of gods is identified with the saints of the Catholic church. It was born during times of slavery, when African slaves had to hide their religion from their white Spanish masters."

"Excuse me for interrupting your questioning, Counsel," said Reynolds with the look of someone sitting on boil, "but Mrs. de Alba, are you saying that this voodoo stuff is actually a religion? I mean dolls with pins and all that?"

I could have objected, argued that this was tantamount to judicial meddling and deserved a mistrial but I let it go. I figured most people in the jury were thinking exactly like Reynolds.

De Alba turned to the judge and spoke in the enlightened tone of a teacher with a benighted student. "Actually, Your Honor, believing that dolls with pins are effective is not so different from thinking that the waters of Lourdes can cure the sick or that the liquefaction of the blood of the patron saint of Naples foretells disaster for that city. It's a question of selective belief. After all, if you think that praying to a man on a cross can bring you what you desire, there's not such a great leap to thinking getting a lock of someone's hair will give you the power to affect that person. Do you follow me?"

"Like a hound after a hare, ma'am. But what you're describing sounds to me like witchcraft."

De Alba harrumphed. "Well, Your Honor, witchcraft is a pejorative term used by members of one religion against practitioners of another. It's a mind-set, you see. Santería is a religion in that it holds a set of beliefs and theological principles that guide the behavior of its followers. It believes in an immanent, transcendental supreme being and advocates the very same principles of goodness and brotherhood that Western followers of the Judeo-Christian tradition hold dear."

Reynolds hesitated. "Proceed."

"Thank you, Your Honor," I said. "Now, Mrs. de Alba, you bowed before this altar, I suppose you call it, which is next to you, before sitting down. Could you explain to us what this is?"

"Certainly." She wiggled out of her seat, leaning on her cane, took the two steps down to the altar.

"As I said, Santería uses Catholic images to represent the gods in its pantheon. There are seven main gods worshiped in Santería. They are all representations of several aspects of the main god, Olorun, the immanent supreme power. Saint Peter here is one of them, he is the symbol of Oggún, the god of war and warriors. Now this here," she said, pointing at the altar, "is called a *plaza*, an offering to the god whose picture appears here."

"Excuse me again, Counsel, but ma'am, I just have to ask, do you really believe in these gods? I mean that they actually exist?" asked Reynolds.

"Your Honor, I myself am not a member of the religion; that would affect my standing as an anthropologist. But there are many millions of people who do believe."

"That wasn't my question. What I want to know is if you really believe in the actual, corporeal existence of these gods?"

"Well, Judge, I tend to think of them like the Swiss psychoanalyst Carl Jung did, that they are representatives of the collective unconscious, which is present in each of us simply because we're humans. Each god represents a certain aspect of our personality so that, when in the hold of the god, when possessed by Shangó, Obatalá or Oggún, the attributes particular to that god are the personality traits that we are bringing forth through the power of the unconscious mind. That is why in Santería two people in the same room can be possessed by the same god because, in essence, we carry the god within us."

"So they don't really exist."

"Oh yes they do, they exist in our mind, in an ontological sense, just like the entire universe exists strictly speaking in an ontological way."

Reynolds looked peeved. "Serves me right. Ask a simple question and you get ontology in return. Whatever that is. Proceed."

Laughter this time, but nervous, a little release but no escape.

"Mrs. de Alba, you said this is an altar to Saint Peter here, also known as the African deity Oggún. Now, he is the god of war, is he not?"

"Oh yes, a very difficult god he is too. Let me show you." De Alba picked up a toy gun on the altar and pointed it at me. There were cries in the courtroom.

"No, no," said de Alba, "it's just a toy! See!" She pulled the trigger and a click was heard. "You don't need the real thing, just a facsimile."

"Just like if you were entering a contest?"

"Exactly. This gun and this knife here"—she picked up a steak knife from a woven basket—"these are the symbols of Oggún's warrior status. He is also the master of everything that is made of iron, because he is the blacksmith of the Yoruba gods. Besides, he is also the god of anger and revenge."

"So these are sacred offerings, are they not?"

"Now they are, certainly. They are filled with the *aché*, the power of the god."

"What would a follower of a god have to do if the offerings he'd made were taken away from the altar?"

De Alba paled. "Oh dear, that is a most terrible sacrilege. The first thing is, the person who desecrated that altar and those responsible for it would suffer the wrath of that god. Which can be terrible, ranging from financial loss to disease to death itself, if the losses are severe enough and the god is a fierce one."

"Would you say Oggún is a fierce god?"

"Most definitely. In the pantheon of Santería he is known as the Warrior. He's a very vengeful god indeed."

"So then, what would the follower of the god have to do?"

"He, or she, would be duty bound to recover these offerings, otherwise the wrath of the god would be visited on his or her head too. It's a sacred duty."

Good. The duty has been shown. Proceed with the rest of the gory list of excuses.

"I see. But I suppose there are nicer gods than Oggún, softer gods, like the god of love, for instance?"

"The goddess. That's Ochún, represented by the Virgin of El Cobre, the patron saint of Cuba."

"Can't a follower of Santería choose one god over another, say, pay homage to Ochún instead of Oggún?"

"You can ask each god to grant you the blessings that are in its power—but you cannot choose your saint."

Yes. Open the door and let us in.

"What do you mean by that?"

"Well, you see, in Santería it is believed that your destiny is known from the day you are born and that you have a saint, a god, that rules your personality, your life, from the moment of conception. In Mr. Valdez's case it is the god Oggún, the one shown here."

"Wait a minute. You mean to say Mr. Valdez had no choice regarding his god?"

"No, because when the saint descends, when he takes over his follower, you're in a trance, you're supposed to be the god's horse, his *caballo*, because he's mounting you. Well, at that point, you have no control, no choice."

"What do you mean? Can't you say, no, I won't let that happen to me?"

De Alba laughed. "You can no more stop the god from coming than you can stop the sun from shining."

"It is a force of nature, then?"

"Yes. What's more, when that happens, and I have seen it myself many times, when that happens you are not yourself. You do things that you would never suspect or imagine and when you come to, you do not remember a thing. Because you see, it wasn't you who was doing all these things, it was the god through you."

Now ram it open, tear it down!

"Does that mean the person possessed does not know what is happening, that he is not in possession of his faculties like a reasonable human being?"

"That's correct, you are not yourself, it's the god who is in you. You are not there. It's like you were dead or asleep, your own personality is not there. You have no conscience, no awareness of anything that has happened."

Done. The breach is wide enough to march an army through. If they believe her.

"So do you believe Mr. Valdez was in possession of a god while these murders were committed?"

Phyllis rose, a red beacon of righteousness.

"Objection, Your Honor, assumes facts not in evidence, goes beyond the expertise of this particular witness."

Reynolds scratched his ear, seemed to chew on an imaginary bone in his mouth. "Well, Counsel, I think the facts are evident enough. Mr. Valdez is here on trial for murder. As regards the testimony, well, Mrs. de Alba is here as an expert witness and I certainly feel she is entitled to give her opinion as to what happened. The jury should remember that it is an expert opinion, subject to the limitations that appertain, and that they should give that opinion the weight that it deserves. Objection overruled. Proceed."

"Your answer, Mrs. de Alba?"

"Yes. In my opinion, he acted as a man in a trance following the actions that a vengeful god would take."

I was about to ask the follow-up question when a loud crack was heard in the room.

"What was that?" Reynolds asked.

"It's the wind, Your Honor," said the bailiff. "It's blowing very hard outside the building."

"It must be blowing mighty hard when we can hear it all the

way in here. Well, proceed, Mr. Morell. But no, wait a minute, you don't mind if I interrupt?"

"Not at all, Your Honor."

"Mrs. de Alba, I have a question. You have this altar here and you talk about honoring the gods and all that. Now, I wonder, just how is this worship conducted?"

De Alba turned to the judge and offered him her warmest smile. "If Your Honor wishes, I could give you a demonstration. I have several priests in the audience who would gladly do it."

"Objection, Your Honor," cried Phyllis, but Reynolds shook his hand impatiently at her.

"Overruled, Ms. Chin. I believe it's proper in this case. Why, sure, why don't you call your friends up here if you want. Been meaning to see one of these for some time now. Always heard about them."

"My pleasure."

Reynolds glanced at me benignly. So this was his secret weapon, his gift to the prosecution. This was the reason why Phyllis had made no effort to get her own expert witness on religious cults. All the trial long Reynolds had been leaning toward the prosecution, making rulings that could never be appealed but that ever so subtly swayed the case Phyllis's way. Now we faced the final, brilliant stroke. He had maneuvered us into staging a ceremony that would reveal Santería to be a noisy farce, a sham, a sorry substitute for a real religion, a mask of hollow gods.

It doesn't matter, I hear, amidst the pounding of drums. We are ready. Let us in.

De Alba stepped down from the stand and then quickly spun around.

"Just one thing, Judge. Is it OK if they smoke?"

"As long as it ain't pot, it's all right by me."

Everyone laughed. I whispered to de Alba as she walked past, "Is this all right? Here?"

"*No te preocupes, chico,*" she said in Spanish. "Don't worry, this has all been foretold."

The seven white-clad santeros in the front row, five men and two women, listened eagerly as de Alba explained what the judge desired. Then, all seven nodded their heads yes and stood up.

"May we begin, Judge?" asked one of the men, tall, black, with a pockmarked face.

"Go right ahead. Just make believe we're not here, folks. Make yourselves at home."

The man opened a duffel bag at his feet and took out a long *batá* drum, adorned with white and purple beads, while another man took out a gourd, also covered with beads. The tall man tapped his fingers lightly on the drumhead and received a rhythmic reply from the gourd. A third man, short and compact, took out another drum and also played a short riff, which the two others answered.

"This is called a *güiro*, Your Honor," said de Alba, pointing at the gourd. "It's a hollowed-out gourd used to invoke the presence of the gods, in this case, the patron saint of Mr. Valdez, Oggún."

"Maybe we shouldn't be doing this, Judge," said Phyllis, but the rat-tat-tat of the drum drowned her out. The man with the güiro let out a cry in Yoruba:

> *"Oggún niye o Oggún aribó*
> *Oggún niye o Iya ki modé*
> *Oilé abé re Oggún de Oggundé ban bá*
> *Owa ni yere ko ma se O Iyaó*
> *Awa ni ye Oggún arere ko ma se Iyá."*

One of the women went before the altar and prostrated herself on the floor. The drums picked up a roll and lifted it to a swelling crescendo of percussion, as the man continued:

> *"Oggún ma kué akué kué kué*
> *Oggún ku ere o*
> *Oggún orilé fe re gun*
> *Kon ko su o aná ló."*

De Alba shouted over the pounding of the drums. "She is now paying obeisance to the god, honoring him. There is no guarantee he will visit us, of course."

"Of course" I could read on Reynolds' disdainful lips, but his words were drowned out by the singing.

The drums rattled on, the güiro shaking in contrapuntal fashion. One of the men handed out a bottle of rum, out of which all seven drank.

"That is rum, Your Honor!" screamed de Alba. "It's to honor the god! Like wine in Mass. Now comes the invocation!"

The blare of the drum and the chanting and shaking of the gourd was a wall of sound, a ladder of notes being raised to a higher unknown plane. I glanced at Ramón, who sat calmly in his chair, only his hands tapping along to the rhythmic beat of the drum.

> "*Oggún areré alawó*
> *Oggún areré alawó*
> *Oddé mao kókoro*
> *Yigüé yigüé*
> *Oggún areré alawó*
> *Oggún areré alawó.*"

In a few moments the drumming picked up in intensity as the santeros began to stir according to the way their particular god moves. One of the women was the first to be entranced. She gave a great cry and fell down to the ground, then swept herself off and swayed back and forth like the goddess Yemayá, her long hair slashing the air like the waves of the ocean, then the other woman also fell into a trance and moved around the court thrusting her pelvis forward like the virile god Shangó, then the men too started showing the symptoms of possession, one of them hobbling about like the ephemeral Babalú Ayé, as though he were lacking a leg and were chased by hounds, and all the while the music kept pounding, the drums tap-tapping a pattern of unconscious thought as some people in the audience, not knowing how the miracle of mass psychosis manifests itself, also rose and started dancing, shimmying and shaking as though they were being ridden by gods or devils who wanted their presence felt by even the most hidebound unbeliever and some in the jury box began pounding the bar to the beat and then the movements of the dancers became even more agitated as the group fell into the true iron grip of the saints and Shangó mounted his horse with full spurs and the woman saluted and pranced around the room and greeted everyone with wide open eyes and beat her chest with her fists and then one of the lights in the courtroom went out then another then another until all of the available light emanated from the candles but the electricity wasn't all gone it kept on going but in ways no one imagined as the reporter turned on her computer and the cursor dashed across the field of green making concentric and curlicued patterns and she looked up and asked, "What's going on?"

A sound like a thunderbolt was heard in the court, like the tearing of a veil. The walls seemed to shake, the seal of the state of California flapped back and forth on the planked redwood walls, the glass of the window in the jury room shattered. A howl of wind came into the room and a light like Saint Elmo's fire danced over our heads. The doors of the courtroom were flung open as Pimienta burst in, jumped the bar and leaped on the counsel table, shouting louder than any human being possibly could, louder than the roar of the wind, louder than the roll of the drums that now heralded his undeniable arrival:

OGGÚN, OGGÚN
ERERE NA NA NILE
OGGÚN, OGGÚN

He somersaulted across the room and landed by the bailiff, slamming him against the wall and knocking him out, while the other saints, Ochún, Yemaya, Babalú Ayé, greeted each other by slamming right shoulder into left. Mrs. Gardner rose from her seat, her eyes rolled up blank. At first she spoke gibberish, but then she cried, with a man's deep anguished voice, "What is this tragedy you visit upon my children in the halls of injustice?"

She passed out and fell down as a howling rain-driven wind lashed the room as though we were in the dipping prow of a vessel sailing stormy seas. Phyllis, recalling the last natural disaster, took refuge under the table while Judge Reynolds hid behind Curtis's desk. The gales buffeted the courtroom, tumbling pictures, overturning files, sending upward, spiraling in a flurry of paper, probation reports, police reports, case files and prison records then suddenly Pimienta howled and ran out of the courtroom and he was never seen again and the dancing ball of fire dwindled into nothingness and the lights came back on again and all the santeros dropped to the ground and the wind died out and a great quiet descended on the court, the quiet of exhaustion, the quiet of peace, the quiet of death.

22

he jury filed in quietly, almost religiously, as though in a procession carrying invisible tapers, silently taking their places in the box. It had been several weeks since the storm of possessions. Everyone's first thought had been to declare a mistrial, but then the reality of gathering the witnesses for a second trial sank in. Remigio, the parking lot attendant, was gone, as was Vlad, the jewelry salesman, and Bongos, the radio DJ, all out of town or out of reach; even Pimienta seemed to have vanished and investigators had no idea where any of them could be found. There had been no prints lifted off the weapons and there were no survivors, so what else could Phyllis do except keep the jury? A second trial would have been impossible for the prosecution.

I argued for a mistrial. I figured that notwithstanding the pyrotechnics, the jury would vote to convict, if for nothing else out of a sense of shame and ridicule, in a process of denial whereby our own dark drives would be hidden and the episode in court forgotten.

Reynolds refused to grant the mistrial and ordered that all records of the demonstration be wiped out, as if they had never existed. He cited a number of legal reasons—lack of foundation, no question pending, beyond the scope of examination—but they all amounted to the same thing—fear. Fear of the unknown, fear of the dark, fear of something alien that had ripped the books of justice and scattered its pages. Since all the TV cameras had stopped working the moment the lights went out, there was nothing left but our memory of the event, an impression of a moment that all wanted to forget.

Even the reporters who witnessed firsthand what had happened refused to believe, refused to admit that their senses had been right and the impossible had indeed transpired. So when the papers said that a local atmospheric disturbance had created an unusual tornado which had swept down the Civic Center and broken windows at the Criminal Courts Building and the Hall of Justice jail, creating panic and confusion ineffable and unexplainable, we all believed it. And when the judge said that the events of that demonstration had been nothing but mass psychosis, a case of suggestibility and hysteria, that those few people who thought they were possessed were santeros and therefore professional fakers, we nodded and assented, not wanting to admit that our reality was only a fragile scrim over a storm-filled void.

"It's just like in the jewelry store, *chico*," croaked Ramón at the jail, his voice barely above a whisper. "We were all there and we all saw it and now everybody is saying it didn't happen. Nobody ever wants to know the truth."

But would the jurors also feel the same way? I had called no further witnesses and neither had Phyllis. We went straight to our arguments, Phyllis mentioning time and again the deliberation of Ramón's actions, the guns he had taken with him, the oath of vengeance he had sworn when the bangles were taken. In all her arguments she avoided the words altar and religion and gods, but the words and the facts were a gaudy backdrop that hung, visible but unmentioned, behind her words.

My own argument had been brief. I had pledged myself to defend him and I proceeded to do so in the best way I knew how—by stating that no one knew what had happened inside that store. All the witnesses were either dead or tainted, and there was no objective account of the tragedy. The tree had fallen and no one had heard it fall. I toyed briefly with the idea of arguing that even if Ramón had committed the murders—and he had, God forgive me, he had—Ramón himself was not to blame for he had been in the grip of a force far, far greater than any of us. But I didn't say it. The unsaid was more convincing than any argument, than any flight of oratory

I could have concocted. Instead I had simply read them one of the very first sections of the California Penal Code.

"It reads as follows, ladies and gentlemen. 'Title One. All persons are capable of committing crimes except those belonging to the following cases. . . . ' It lists some exceptions, then comes to the one that concerns us, the fifth exception, quote: 'Persons who committed the fact charged without being conscious thereof.' End of quote. Conscious thereof, ladies and gentlemen. That is the key and it cannot be denied. That is the law. If you have no awareness, no consciousness of your actions, no matter how heinous the crime, how repugnant or unconscionable, you are as innocent as a child, as pure as a spring lamb. Without knowledge there is no crime—or sin."

For two weeks the jurors deliberated, trudging in and out of the jury room during their appointed breaks like Benedictines off to take their meals before recommencing prayers. Now their answer was about to be revealed.

Reynolds turned to the jurors. I looked at Ramón, staring at the judge, and at Phyllis, and the bailiff, everyone in the court avoiding the eyes of the triers of fact whose terrible verdict would soon be rendered. A row of santeros with the white and purple beads of Oggún sat in the back. I heard the humming of the TV cameras.

"Ladies and gentlemen of the jury, I understand you have reached a verdict in this case. Will the jury foreman please rise."

Mrs. Gardner stood, one hand gripping the bar, another firmly grasping the verdict forms.

"Have you reached a verdict?"

"Yes, we have."

"Please turn it over to the bailiff."

Gardner handed the sheaf of papers to the deputy, who brought the forms to Reynolds. He glanced at them, going through the sheets rapidly, then looked up and stared fixedly at the jurors. Mrs. Gardner glared back. Reynolds took a breath, waved the papers.

"Bailiff, please give these to the clerk to read."

The bailiff carried the fateful papers to Burr.

"In the City and County of Los Angeles, Superior Court District, State of California . . ."

I looked at Ramón—tightly reined concern, eyebrows gathered together, lips pouting in defiance.

"Case number A875–4316, the People of the State of California versus Ramón Valdez, defendant—"

Burr must have read ahead for he stopped, blinked, cleared his throat and proceeded in a higher, nervous pitch.

"We, the jury in the above titled action, find the defendant, Ramón Valdez, not guilty of violation of Section 187a of the California Penal Code, murder in the first degree, as alleged in count one of the complaint."

Not guilty! rang in my head. NOT GUILTY! NOT GUILTY! NOT GUILTY!

With the first verdict, the court broke into a maelstrom of cries and curses, while in the back the santeros stood and cheered. Reynolds looked for his gavel to bang but not finding it, he banged his coffee mug on the desk and ordered the restless crowd to keep quiet, but with each succeeding verdict—NOT GUILTY! NOT GUILTY! NOT GUILTY!—the clamor rose higher and higher until at the end the tumult was practically uncontrollable. Burr read all the thirty-two counts against Ramón with the answer invariably the same in every instance—NOT GUILTY! NOT GUILTY! NOT GUILTY!

I sat fixed to my seat, chilled by the success of my efforts, feeling I personally had fired the shots that killed each and every victim.

"Is this your verdict, ladies and gentlemen of the jury, so say you one, so say you all?"

The jurors answered firmly. "Yes, YES, YES!!!"

Then came the real clamor as the audience, certain now that the last act had closed, rose as one and clapped and cheered and whistled and booed and fights broke out among the spectators and sheriff's deputies arrived from other courts to break up the factions as Phyllis and Samuels escaped out the side door with the jury while Reynolds ordered the bailiff to set Ramón free so the tumult would end. The moment his chains were off Ramón gave a great cry, "*Victoria!*" then jumped into the crowd, his followers carrying him aloft out of the courtroom. I sat in my chair, ignored by all, as the commotion swerved around me, feeling the weight of my acts press down upon me. *You were too good, Charlie, too good the wrong way.*

I stayed seated until the contingent of bailiffs cleared the court and only Burr and I were left behind. He pulled out a couple of files, dusted them off.

"Got to start getting ready for tomorrow's cases. Justice never sleeps."

I nodded, then walked out the side door, down the judge's corridor, to the small service elevator, leaving my briefcase and notes and files on the table. It doesn't matter, I thought, this too will pass.

I exited through the downstairs garage onto Main Street, jaywalking in front of an RTD bus which announced its destination in big yellow letters, Paradise Cove. I entered the parking lot and left in my car, avoiding the swarm of TV reporters doing their stand-ups by the curb against the letters that read Criminal Courts Building. As I drove off, I read on a traffic-light box the latest message from the anonymous porno graffiti artist—"I loves to fuck pregnant women because they carry God inside and I come in Him."

I drove home up Sunset, past Ana's Quinceañera and Bridal Shop, past the Club Tropical with its cumbia and salsa and Nico and the Cohetes playing this weekend, past the brown brick Paradise Motel on a hill overlooking downtown, up the grade into Echo Park and Lupe's Famous Burritos and El Asturiano Restaurant with the best paella in town and El Carmelo with its glazed guava pastries and the hundreds of stores of all kinds where the Hispanic population tries to duplicate the little neighborhood stores of San Salvador, San Pedro Sula, Granada and Sancti Spiritu they had come from, an alien sibilant presence with brown eyes and faces and callused hands and bandannas wearing polyester suits and chino pants with Hush Puppies and white T-shirts and rebozos and serapes and flouncy lacy dresses eating watermelon with paprika on top and paletas of a thousand fruit flavors, a quiet cooker building steam that one day will erupt just as Ramón had done, and I pondered all this and dreaded the day and feared for my soul as I drove up Hillhurst and into a thin pink fog that fell over the white-walled mansions of Los Feliz, Hollywood, Beverly Hills, Brentwood and Rancho Park, from the ocean to the mountains, a cool, clean pink fog draping itself with good intentions and total misunderstanding over my home, the Town of Our Lady the Queen of the Angels of Porciuncula, Los Angeles, my one and only love.

23

but that was not the end. The conclusion to the story came after a telephone call from the LAPD, which directed me again to the green halls of County Jail. There, behind the glass partition dividing prisoners from visitors in the attorney's interview room, his left hand shackled to a bar beneath the seat, sat a gaunt man in his late sixties with sad blue eyes and a tuft of white hair standing on the crown of his otherwise bald pate. Although his blue jail jumpsuit hung loosely on him, he was paunchy, the weight having all gone to his stomach.

He recognized me right away and waved at me with fingers gnarled from arthritis. I sat across from him, stunned, drawn by filial desire. The resemblance was uncanny. We stared at each other for a full minute, my heart racing.

The man smiled, revealing stained yellow teeth sprouting from pale pink gums. His breath bore the stench of cigarettes and stale food, his arms were scabbed and, in general, he smelled as if he hadn't seen a shower for longer than it had been since I'd had a good night's sleep. But at that moment all that mattered little. His blue eyes watered in a sad smile identical to my father's.

"You must be Tom Elliot," I said. There was no one else he could be except for another man who had died with countless tubes sprouting from his body in a Miami hospital.

"That's me, Charlie. You don't mind if I call you Charlie? After all, I know all about you."

"No, I don't mind."

"Funny, ain't it?" he said. "To see somebody like me. I figure you must be all spooked by now."

"Not at all. I've been looking forward to this."

"Tell you the truth, so have I. That's why I told the detectives to call you." He patted his bulging stomach. "This is getting pretty big and the doctors say it will be any day now. Shit, I feel like a fucking pregnant woman when I know that I'm going to—"

He stopped, his face contorted into a sudden spasm of fear and pain.

"How bad is it?"

"Doctor can't stop it worth shit. Been giving me radiation treatment but it's too advanced." He stopped, drew a breath. "Three months, tops."

"Sorry to hear that."

"What the hell, we all got to go sometime, don't we?"

"Dust to dust."

"And ashes to ashes. You Catholic too? Of course, I should have known, your being Cuban and all. Yeah. Well, like I said, I got a couple of things I wanted to get off my chest before I check out."

"Should I guess or are you going to tell me?"

"No, I'll tell you. I mean, I don't know if there's somebody up there after all, like they say, but I've never been much of a gambling man. So I suppose I should do all this now, before it gets too late."

"Too late for whom?"

"What? I don't understand."

"Nothing. So where did you meet him?"

His expression switched from apology to injury and he reared in his seat.

"Don't you rush me now! I'm in no hurry to get anywhere."

"Fine. You go ahead at your own speed." I sat back. The old man licked his lips, dry and blistered. "Well, we was sharing a cell together. He'd been brought in for that stuff, oh, about three or four months before and they was housing us here on the Two Block. I was on my way out after doing a year for selling a little dope so they figured—hell, I don't know what they figured, never been able to figure out these fucking sheriffs. So's, when he comes in, after dinner, he starts looking at me funny, real funny. So I grabbed my shank, nice and sharp, and I flashed it, let him know I wasn't gonna get butt-fucked by anybody. So he looks and he smiles and says in that funny accent of his, 'You wanna make some money?'"

"So you said yes."

"First I asked him what I had to do to earn it. Wasn't going to suck his dick for it either, if you know what I mean. So he pulls out this folder from his file, the case file he always carried with him. He starts going through all the papers and then he pulls out this picture, a real old photograph, I don't know where he got it from. It's in black and white and shows a little kid on horseback with a man and he looks at the picture and I look at the picture and I say 'I'll be damned' and he says, 'That's right.' I mean, it was really weird how this fellow looked like me, I mean, with a little change here and there. Had to paint this birthmark here on the cheek but that was about all."

"He told you to follow me."

He looked down, then up, then sideways and spoke without looking at me.

"I really shouldn't have done it. Never done anything like that. I tell you, I didn't know he wanted to really do it. He told me it was your pa and that he just wanted to scare you. He thought you'd be easier to control that way. So I went along. I mean, you were easy enough to find. Tailing you was pretty easy. The hard part was running away in time. Most of the time, that was hard. I'm proud of that. Bet you never thought it was somebody for real."

"No, I didn't."

He took a deep breath, stared at his grimy fingernails.

"Then he put the squeeze on me."

"What do you mean?"

"He sent some of his voodoo people over to my place, those guys dress in white and stuff."

"Yeah."

"They came with a message he'd written, instructions, money. When I read it, I tried to back out but these guys, you should have seen them, six four, six six, all muscle, like some heavy hitters. A fuckin' nightmare. Well, these guys said he'd told them if I didn't follow the instructions, they'd be back, cut my dick off, stick it down my throat and then cut me up into little pieces and leave me to bleed."

He glanced up. "You believe me, don't you."

"Sounds believable so far. What was the message?"

Tom made eye contact with the deputy and signaled at him that the interview was over. As the deputy climbed off his platform and walked over to us, Tom blurted out, "That I should go hire those black boys to ram your car down\the gully."

The deputy bent down, inserted the key in the hole, released the cuff.

"I'm sorry, Charlie. Didn't wanna do it, it was circumstances, you understand."

He stood, hunched over, belly like a basketball, trembling, the weight of guilty conscience relieved. I wanted to get on my knees and ask him to forgive me, that I knew not what I had done. Instead: "I understand."

I also stood, picked up my briefcase. "Sleep in peace."

"Thank you."

"Let's go, Elliot. Back to your cell," said the deputy, hustling the image of my father away.

Looking back, I can't recall if the events that followed happened all on the same day. Even if they didn't it amounts to the same thing, for the evidence of my manipulation by Ramón and Lucinda's betrayal was a pall that bridged both instances, foreshortening time, rendering the end of this affair a darkened prism shot through with loss and regret.

The photograph Elliot had mentioned was the last one taken of us in Cuba. I kept it in the leather-bound photo album in my office. I found it, but looking at the back of the picture I saw it had been unglued, then hastily stuck again with cheap tape. It was all of a piece, including Lucinda's quitting her job at Enzo's the same day that Ramón was acquitted.

The sad-faced Ligurian had knocked on my door that day, gesturing with open hands.

"*Dov'è la bella?*" he asked. "All my people they ask, where is she, where is she? I call up her place and there's no answer, I go there and nobody knows where she went."

"I don't know, Enzo. I haven't seen her in weeks. You remember the night."

"Oh, I thought, well, you know, you two were so close, maybe..."

"Enzo, let me tell you something about Cubans. We believe in final acts, in keeping our word if it kills us. I'd never go back to her."

"*Scusa*, you know, I...You take life too hard. Well, OK, I'll find somebody else. Eh, it's only a girl. Life goes on." He walked away from the door, then turned and looked at me as though for the first time.

"I didn't know you were Cuban. You don't look it."

"What do Cubans look like?"

"Ah, I don't know. Like Castro or Desi Arnaz or, you know, *negri*, black."

"I'm not black, a revolutionary or a band leader. I'm a white lawyer without a beard, that's all."

He shrugged, the eternal Italian acceptance of life as given.

"Eh, OK. You're a good man, I don't care. You call me if you see her, *va bene*?"

"*Va bene*."

I was sitting in the living room, watching the searchlight at the Griffith Park Observatory scan the night sky.

I glanced around, taking in the stubs of the cigarettes I'd started smoking again, the carpet askew, the tossed pillow, the dusty windowsills, the discarded empty beer bottles, the unopened L.A. *Times* still in its plastic rain bag, the half-empty bottle of pepper vodka and I started laughing. You're turning into a cliché, I told myself. The heartbroken sap weeps for his lost love. I thought that was the funniest thing I'd thought of in weeks, the laughs issuing from me in a long-denied eruption, a belch or a vomit. I fell out of the couch, knowing all the while how pathetic anyone watching would have thought me, how out of control and helpless, as I choked in my own glee, tears coming out unheeded, laughing at the observatory, the bottles, the room, the city, my family, my child, my loves and my life, everything that flashed before me was covered with laughter and derision, it was all laughable, it was all contemptible, it was all a joke. Then I heard the loud report of a hand gun being fired.

I stopped laughing, sat on the floor, my heart racing. I wanted to think it was a car backfiring, but I knew the sound of a gun, that peculiar loud snap of cordite thrusting brutal steel through the air. There came a second shot, but this one was muffled, as though through a clumsy silencer, a pillow or blanket.

I glanced at the clock on the mantel. Ten to five in the morning. Outside my window, banners of fog melted under the streetlights. No cars or pedestrians on the street, just a stray possum slithering into some bushes across the way. Then I heard a third shot, and a noise like a jar or a vase crashing violently. I got up and went to look for my gun. I couldn't find it. I grabbed the only weapon I had in the house, an old machete from a trip to Yucatan and headed toward the source of the noise—Enzo's apartment downstairs.

I tried Enzo's front door but it was bolted. Sticking my ear to the door, I detected faint voices of people inside, in the rapid-fire delivery of fear of discovery. I went to jump the side fence but someone had already gone through it. The padlock was snapped open, probably by the bolt cutter now lying under the camellias. I pushed open the gate and dashed to the backyard, to the French doors facing Enzo's precious rose and herb garden. Those doors were open too, although the curtains were closed and I couldn't see inside. I raised my machete, ready to strike, and glided silently through the drapes.

My eyes fell on Enzo's body, fallen by the side of the oblong rosewood dining table. Strewn awkwardly, he was facedown, his right hand pushed over and out, palm down, as though in death he had incongruously wanted to give a parting Fascist salute. His white T-shirt was soaked with blood on one side, the crimson liquid forming a glistening puddle around the waistband of his flower-printed boxer shorts. On the far side of the dining room I saw a splattering of gristle and brain, which followed the trajectory of the bullet when it embedded itself in the wall. The table had been set for two; calamari had slopped over onto the lace placemat, while an open bottle of Montefalcone sloshed onto the basket of bread.

To my right I saw Lucinda going through the drawers in the

ornate side buffet, tossing papers hurriedly to the ground, a mad desperate dash as she trampled on photographs, recipes, clippings, bills. She was wearing a black teddy, the same one I'd bought her at Magnin's our first week together.

"Lost something?"

She turned with a gasp, her face livid with fatigue, surprise and degradation, wide black rings spreading under her eyes. She was thinner, more awkward and jittery than I had ever seen her. She found the presence of mind to calm herself down. "Oh, Charlie!" she said, rushing toward me. I put my machete forward. She stopped.

"I was looking for the number to call the police. You wouldn't believe what happened."

"Tell me anyway."

She breathed fitfully through her mouth. "We were having dinner, Enzo and I."

"When did this happen? Just the other day he had given you up for lost."

"What? Oh, that, you mean, because I took some days off, the poor man, he didn't know but now—"

She broke into tears, head down, sobbing.

"Skip it. What the fuck happened here?"

She looked up, her face contorted into the same rictus of agony I'd seen under another guise, when once she writhed in my arms.

"We were eating and this burglar shows up. I guess he came in through the window. He asked Enzo for money and when he wouldn't give it to him, he shot him. Enzo fought but he shot him again."

I moved around, looked again at the table, then at Lucinda.

"You were sitting right here, to his left?" I pointed at the up-turned seat.

"Yes, I was."

"That's funny. How come you didn't get any blood on you, baby?"

"I don't know. I stood up, I guess."

"And why did he let you live? You're a witness. Why kill Enzo and not you?"

"I don't know, I guess because . . ."

I felt a gun stuck into my side and a familiar fetid breath, the dank putrescence of the dark.

"Put down your machete, Carlitos," said Ramón, standing behind me. I dropped the weapon on the floor. It landed next to Enzo. Ramón pushed me to the side, against the buffet.

"So that's what this was," I said. "A fucking holdup. For that you got to kill him."

"Shut up, you don't know what you're talking about. You find it?"

Lucinda produced a key to a bank safety box.

"What are you going to say now, Ramón? Which god made you do it?"

Ramón took the key, put it in his pocket.

"No god. This is something for us humans. You"—he waved the gun at Lucinda. "Go put on some clothes. We're going right now."

Lucinda moved to the bedroom down the hall. I saw the gun Ramón was holding was my own, the same .38 I'd been searching for before coming down.

"He took Oggún's jewelry too?"

Ramón looked startled for a moment, then laughed.

"I told you, this has nothing to do with the saints. This key is very special, because I know in that box he's holding fifty thousand dollars—and two keys of cocaine."

"Enzo a drug dealer?"

"Not really but it was like money, you know? I guess he thought it was as good as gold."

We stared at each other. The sun began to break through, the drapes becoming progressively whiter with the light.

He sighed. "Guess I'm going to have to kill you. I don't particularly like to, *chico*, but you know, business is business."

I put my hands behind my back and began feeling for something on the buffet I could grab hold of.

"Why didn't you have your Crips really do the job? Why do it now?"

"So you found out about that? These American niggers, they

don't know shit. All I told them was to get you into an accident, not to get you killed. You know, in case something went wrong and I lost, I had something I could appeal on, you know, delay in the case and all that. Goes to show you, you want something right, you have to do it yourself."

"So now you're going to kill me, after all I did for you?"

"You didn't do it just for me. You had your own agenda. I was your tool, just like you were mine. We wanted two different things. I wanted freedom, you wanted absolution. We both got it."

My fingers wrapped themselves around a bottle neck. "How did you find out about my dad?"

"I had you checked out. I have friends who can hire detectives too, you know. Real P.I.'s, not make believe like you."

A beam of light shot into the dining room, the golden ray falling on Enzo's bloodied head.

"Lucinda!" shouted Ramón. She came running back, buttoning her dress.

"Am I OK like this?"

Ramón diverted his eyes for a moment and I threw the bottle at him. He fired but I threw myself to the floor, picked up the machete and slashed at his hand. I hit with the flat of the blade, not cutting him but knocking the gun out of his hand. I jumped on him when he leapt for the gun and covered him the moment his fingers closed around the revolver. I kneed him in the kidneys, but he wouldn't release the gun so we both rolled on the ground, bumping against the legs of the table, against the wall, against Enzo's body.

"Hit him! hit him!" he ordered Lucinda, who grabbed the bottle and hovered close, waiting to strike. She came down and struck me on my back so I twisted Ramón around, pinning him against Enzo, rolling in the sloshing blood, feeling surges of strength I never imagined I had. The gun went off.

"Hit him again!" he ordered. The blow landed on Ramón's shoulder, causing the gun to fire again. The bullet entered her neck. She gasped, then vomited blood, falling. I finally rammed Ramón against the window casement, forcing him to surrender the gun. I got to my feet and kicked him in the groin. He doubled over.

"Don't you fucking move!" I screamed as I went to look at Lucinda. She lay flat on her back, eyes open in shock, blood surging out of the hole where her larynx had been. Ramón sat, panting, leaning against the wall.

"Forget her, she's dead," he said, almost out of breath. "It's just you and me, like it always was."

"I don't know what the fuck you're talking about. Don't move!"

"Sure you do. It was always you and me, that's what it always was. She was just a bridge, like the trial, like everything else." He stopped, took a deep breath. "Think about it. You could be my lawyer again. You can defend me. You can say this was just a crime of passion, she was fucking Enzo so I lost it and shot them both. You can get me off, I know you can. You'll be the most famous lawyer in the whole country—you'll save the same man twice from the gas chamber. You can do it."

I held the gun on my left, still pointing at Ramón. With my right I grabbed the machete and opened Lucinda's throat, so she wouldn't choke on her own blood.

"Forget her, Charlie, forget her!"

"Don't you fucking move!"

I bent over Lucinda and at that moment Ramón surged forward, plunging through the window in a shower of glass and wood splinters. I fired but missed. The gun was empty. I tossed it away and tried to revive Lucinda but it was too late—her eyes clouded over, her heart stopped. I stood up and roared like a wounded beast and also raced out the window.

I could see Ramón running up the street, up the hill toward the observatory. In the distance I heard the wailing of a siren and saw the three-color light bars of the patrol cars careening up to the house.

I took off, running after him, up the steep incline, past the red tiled houses and the vast estates, into the steps leading up the hill. I could see him at the top, making his way into the park. I bounded up the steps, three, four at a time, the hunter after the quarry, the spirit after the flesh.

When I reached the top of the steps my lungs were on fire and my legs about to break into jagged pieces. Then I saw Ramón scurrying into the bushes, up the trail to the top of Mount Hollywood. I took off after him, jumping over the barbed wire fence, tearing my pants, feeling the barbs sinking into my flesh but shutting out the pain, determined never to lose him again, never to fail again. The trail ended in a clump of thorn bushes. I saw Ramón up ahead, on all fours, clambering up the hill under the branches. I threw myself down and ran on all fours up the storm channel by the bushes, the thorns ripping my shirt off my back, rocks and broken bottles in the channel gashing my hands and knees.

I saw him again once I reached the top, veering to the left, toward the clearing. I knew I had him—there was no way out of the spot except down the path I was on. When I reached the clearing he was staring at the city below, teetering on the rim, a thousand-foot drop to the houses below. He turned to me, his face a mask of primal anger, the mask of the ancient god. He held a broken bottle in his hand.

"I am Oggún niká!," he said, slashing the bottle in front of him. "I am Oggún, the master of war! *Come meet your fate!*"

He rushed me, the bottle headed straight for my face. I waited until the last possible moment then stepped to the side, grabbing his lead arm between my two forearms, snapping the bone in two. But he seemed not to feel the pain and grabbed me with his left hand and somehow whipped himself around and lifted me off the ground with just one hand, taking me to the edge of the clearing. He cast me down, but I grabbed hold of a chaparral bush and pulled myself up. He jumped on my hands, then kicked me in the face. I swung around, threw a kick. But he took the blow to his body as though it were just a child's touch. I pounced on him and pummeled him time and again, but it was like the nightmare where you strike your enemy with all your might and the blows land as though deadened by a pillow. He butted me in the stomach with his head, throwing me to the ground, then grabbed my arm and was about to toss me down the gully, down the thousand-foot drop to my death, when something or someone pushed him instead.

He fell on the ground then trembled with fear at whatever was behind me. I kicked him in the chest and saw him fly down, down, down, down to the rocks below, where he struck and opened up like a doll.

Panting, I got up, then felt a chill course down my back, the chill of love and recognition. Standing there, smiling, was the image of my father. Not Tom Elliot's impersonation but my real father, just as I knew him when I was a boy, young, strong and full of hope, wearing a white linen suit.

"*Bien hecho, mi hijo*," he said. Well done. As I approached him he walked backward to the edge of the clearing, then past it so that he stood floating in the air, his body becoming transparent. The sun came out and dawn vanished and so did he.

"*Estás perdonado*," he said. You are forgiven. Then he was gone and the sun surged up in a blazing ball of light and the City of Our Lady, the Queen of the Angels, shifted under her covers and sat up to greet the new day.

On my way home, before the police, before the media, before the questions and the answers, I stopped at a phone booth and placed a call to Miami.

"Hello, Julian? Hi, it's your dad. I'm coming home. I love you, son."